BILLY'S

George Donald

For Anne, My Very Own Mrs Happy

Also by George Donald

Charlie's Promise

A Question of Balance

Natural Justice

Logan

A Ripple of Murder

The Seed of Fear

A Forgotten Murder

The Knicker-knocker

The Cornishman

Chapter 1

October rain drizzled onto the windscreen as Willie McKay slowly turned the key in the ignition. Once again the engine turned, but didn't catch. He sighed and sat back into the seat, irritably pressing his spine into the soft fabric material and anxious that too many turns of the key would flood the carburettor. The old Ford Mondeo had given Willie many years valuable service, but now apparently decided to protest too little inadequate care and attention. His eyes took in the layer of fine dust that had settled on the dashboard, the sweet wrappers that lay in the open ashtray, evidence that his normally fastidious wife hadn't travelled in the car for some time. The Boomtown Rats belting out *'I don't like Monday's'* on the car radio seemed somehow appropriate to the start of his week. Willie counted to ten and gently turned the key, silently begging the old girl not to let him down. The whirring noise grated on his already taut nerves, but still the engine didn't catch. Slowly, his eyes shut tight against the drum that now begun pounding in his skull, he let his head sink forward onto the steering wheel. Dampness Willie decided, regretting not having the car serviced at the last MoT. Sitting upright, he looked at his watch and realised that he'd never get to police headquarters on time for the start of his 8.30am shift. A knock at the driver's window startled him. Adele Cairns, his elderly upstairs neighbour, was standing by the car, five foot tall and with floral umbrella ineffectively held in her right hand against the drizzling rain. Willie forced a smile and opened the driver's door.
"Morning, Adele, you'll catch your death, standing in

this weather with just your dressing gown on."
"I heard you trying to start the car Willie and I thought I might give you a shove?"
He smiled at the image of his 72 year old upstairs neighbour, resplendent in pink dressing gown, one hand on her brolly and the other pushing Willie's Mondeo down Kings Park Avenue with him at the wheel. Even the most cynical Glaswegian would have been hee-hawing with laughter at that sight, he thought. Decision made, he shook his head.
"Thanks, Adele, but you and I won't get this bugger going. I'm off to the station for the train. You'd better get yourself inside."
"Will Margaret not help, then?"
Willie sighed, knowing that Mrs Cairns was fully aware that nothing would get his wife out of her bed at this time of the morning, particularly anything that involved helping Willie. He pushed his six-foot frame from the car and stood, towering above the slightly built woman.
"Right, my old darling, let me see you inside so that I can get off to work. Now away you go."
"Oh, Willie, you're an awful man," tittered Mrs Cairns behind her raised hand as he ushered her to her doorway. "Bye, Willie".
Willie strode down the path then, pulling up the collar of his dark blue coat, turned to close the garden gate and saw a slight movement of the curtain at his front window. Seems like Margaret is up, then, he inwardly sighed.

The brisk five-minute walk to the railway station did nothing to improve his mood. Arriving at the crowded platform, Willie discovered the trains running their usual winter month's schedule of ten to fifteen minutes late. The elderly, bored attendant at the ticket kiosk was scanning the sports page of Glasgow's favourite tabloid, The Glasgow News, and ignoring the hostile stares of the passengers filtering through the waiting room to the windswept platform. Drumming his fingers on the counter, Willie waited patiently while the attendant, with obvious reluctance, put his newspaper down. "Help you, pal?" he inquired in a tone that suggested he was doing Willie a favour and then in response to Willie's question, "No idea, pal. Just got a message saying the trains are late. And I can't change a tenner, you'll need to get a ticket on the train from the conductor."

Willie was about to retort that maybe the bastard should improve his customer relation skills, but realised the poor sod had obviously experienced a personality by-pass and instead, made his way onto the now crowded and silent platform. This is great start to the day, thought Willie, knowing that any excuse he offered would be treated with derision by Detective Sergeant Ian Reid, Willie's supervisor at Criminal Intelligence. Bugger him, decided Willie, cheered by the arrival of the city centre bound train and squared his shoulders to get ready for the rugby scrum that would squeeze him into the already packed carriages.

The Criminal Intelligence office at Police Headquarters is similar to most other city centre offices, the difference being that this one, with desks cramped together and more filing cabinets than comfort allowed for, had walls festooned with information boards, themselves decorated with photographs of local and well-documented criminals. Swing a cat, it was wryly remarked, and you risked giving it concussion. The dozen or so male and female detectives working in this cloistered environment had little time for décor, other than the obligatory notice above the tea trolley direly threatening expulsion to those unfortunate enough to be caught skipping their weekly dues. Willie liked most of his colleagues. Though generally he didn't socialise with them, he thought them an amenable crowd, for the most hardworking and experienced detectives. With a nod to those who acknowledged his arrival, Willie hung his sodden coat on the crowded hooks behind the door and run his fingers through his damp hair. Flecks of grey pushed through the heavy dark brown mop and shone like silver streaks. Shrugging his suit jacket off, he hung it on the backrest of his swivel seat and sat down, pushing the buttons that activated his desktop computer. While the machine warmed up, he idly flicked through the paperwork that awaited him in his in-tray and glanced about him, aware that Ian Reid wouldn't have missed his late arrival. A shadow loomed over his shoulder. "You're late", snarled Reid, "so what's the excuse this time DC McKay?" Willie, aware that the rest of the team were intently studying weekend intelligence reports, but all ears just the same, smiled and in an even voice replied, "Car problem, Sarge."

"Aye," hissed Reid, "well remember you've an annual appraisal due shortly, so you might want to consider your position here." The veiled threat left hanging, Reid moved to stand over the desk occupied by Jackie Fulton, the young and pretty civilian clerk, blonde and buxom and the fantasy of many of Willie's male colleagues and also, he suspected one female colleague. It was unkindly said that if you wanted anything circulated throughout the office, you merely told Jackie and asked her to keep it a secret.

Willie watched Reid lounge against Jackie's desk, likely regaling her with stories of his wild weekend. Known throughout the department as 'Pampas', it was a nickname conferred on Reid when his colleagues came to realise he was the biggest grass in the world. Not just unpopular amongst the officers he supervised it was widely known in the ranks of the CID that he was a pompous little shit and certainly worth the watching. But right now, as far as Willie was concerned, Reid was the least of his current worries.

"You want to watch him." Willie turned. His friend, DC Archie MacDonald stood holding two stained and chipped enamel mugs of tea in his hands. "Get that down you, Willie boy." Archie, his lanky fair hair curling unfashionably over his ears, shirtsleeves rolled up and tie undone, pulled a chair over and sat beside Willie. "That Reid has got it in for you and you give him every opportunity to knock you down. How many times have I told you, smarten up and get real. You should be doing his job, but you consistently let him needle you."

"Great brew, first of the day," replied Willie, sipping from his mug and ignoring the rebuke. "And how was your weekend?"

Archie sighed. "One of these days, Willie boy, you'll listen to me and my weekend, if you're really interested, was shite." He placed his mug down heavily on Willie's desk, slopping the tea onto a file that lay open.

Willie used a tissue to mop up the spilled tea. "Why, what happened?"

Archie tugged up his trouser leg and sat his ample

backside on the corner of Willie's desk. "Jean's pregnant again."

Willie, his eyebrows raised but unsure how to respond, hesitantly asked, "Are you not pleased, then?"

"Willie, I know that you've not got kids and maybe that's through choice. I love my three, but just when I thought we were starting to get back on our feet, this happens. Things are tight enough, at the minute, what with the one wage and the mortgage rates going up. Jean and I thought that if my mother could maybe watch the kids a couple of days a week, Jean might have got back to part time nursing, or even perhaps a couple of nights doing agency work. But that's been hit on the head." Archie, with a sigh, rubbed his face then grinned. "Ach, well, back to the grindstone."

Willie smiled. He knew his friends' sombre mood wouldn't last long. "Look, Archie, you and Jean have got a lot more going for you than most people. At least you like each other."

Archie paused, slightly embarrassed and acutely aware that Willie's relationship with Margaret was going downhill, fast. From what he had seen and the little he knew of Margaret, Archie thought that Willie must look forward to coming to work, rather than endure the cold and brittle atmosphere of the McKay house.

Willie smiled, again, "And for what it's worth," he raised his mug, "Congratulations."

Archie lifted his mug to acknowledge Willie's toast, when a voice behind him snapped,

"Don't you two love birds have work or are you looking for something to do?" Ian Reid, stood behind Willie and Archie, his hands on hips and playing to the audience of detectives in the room, aware all eyes were upon him.

"Is that crepe soles you have on your shoes then, Sergeant?" asked Archie, his voice oozing innocence.
"What?" demanded a bemused Reid.
The room burst into laughter, then to more laughter, a soft lilting Aberdonian voice from the background called out, "I think he's suggesting your shoes are indicative of someone who is commonly referred to as a brothel creeper, Ian."
A puzzled Reid looked at his feet, and then turned to Archie, his mouth suddenly dry, the insult choked off by Detective Chief Inspector Roddy Munroe, Departmental Head who stood at the door and beckoned him.
"Can we have a wee word, Ian?'
Munroe, stout build and wearing his customary tweed jacket, black handlebar moustache, thinning salt and pepper hair and unlit pipe clenched in his farmer like hand, looked every inch the northern gentleman he was. He waved his pipe at the room. "Wee bit less noise and more productive work please, ladies and gentlemen." The laughter died away. The detectives turned to their desks, grinning into their paperwork and computer screens as the door closed behind Munroe and Reid.
Willie smiled, grateful for Munroe's' timely intervention, then turned to his in-tray. The criminal intelligence reports, scraps of paper and telephone messages made quite a pile. His morning had begun. Looking at the paperwork, he murmured to himself he ought to have brought a can of petrol, then, drawing his computer keyboard to him, typed in his password.

"Close the door, Ian."
Reid, his face still flushed with embarrassment and tense with anger, sat in the chair facing Roddy Munroe, his clenched fists resting on his thighs, the knuckles white as he strained to suppress the urge to reach over and take this old fool by the throat.

For his part, Munroe knew that the younger officer was outraged and desperate for his support but how could he, in all consciousness, lend his approval to this insufferable prick. Munroe had thirty years of policing in the tough streets of Glasgow and knew that Willie McKay, who himself had almost twenty-five years service under his belt, could lose Reid when it came to criminal intelligence. Hell, he could lose most, if not all the team in any police related work, but Reid was the sergeant, duly appointed by the Chief Constable and fully aware that Munroe was obliged to support him in any dispute with a junior rank. Using a well-worn silver pocketknife knife to tamp down the blended tobacco into his pipe afforded Munroe some seconds to contemplate his discussion with his sergeant. He realised Reid was furious at the laughter, would consider it a personal slight and believed it was time to apply some salve to his wounded ego.

"Ian, son," he began in what he hoped sounded like a concerned and salutary manner, "do you not think that maybe you should ease up a bit on McKay? I'm not saying that you're not running a tight ship or anything, but sometimes easing back on the reins can be more productive, in terms of work output, than picking fault all the time." Munroe continued to fumble with his pipe. He rightly suspected that this was going to go badly. Nothing that he said to Reid was ever taken as constructive advice, viewed rather as criticism by the younger man. As did most other officers who worked in the CID, Munroe knew that Reid believed himself secure in his career in the knowledge that his father, a retired Assistant Chief Constable, still retained a certain influence within the Force hierarchy. Or as was more likely, Munroe mused, Reid's father was privy to some senior rank indiscretions that granted him some privileges for keeping his mouth shut. Though Munroe knew that Reid had no managerial skills, little CID service and still had to grasp the concept of achieving some kind of rapport with his colleagues, none of this would interfere with his steady and assured rise in rank. Or, put bluntly, his ultimate promotion to a level of incompetence.

Reid, for his part, could scarcely contain himself. His dislike and contempt for this doddering old fool was so strong he could barely suppress his anger. With a will, he gathered himself together and spoke through gritted teeth.

"With respect, sir, I believe that DC McKay is swinging the lead. His timekeeping is outrageously poor and I'm sick and tired of giving him verbal warnings. With your approval it is my intention to issue him with a written warning that any further lapses be recorded and the matter passed to the Complaints and Discipline Department, for their perusal and attention."

Sitting bolt upright in the chair, Reid refrained from sneering, from shouting with delight that at last, he had cornered Munroe into a position from which the old bastard had no option but to support his detective sergeant.

Munroe stared at his sergeant and considered this statement. Slowly shaking his head, he leaned forward and looked Reid in the eye, his face dead-pan but thinking, two can play this game, sonny.

"Now, I think that's a bit extreme, Ian. Have you truly considered how such a report will be received? Can you not see that any such report might be viewed as a failure on your part?" he raised his hands, palms outward in a supplicate manner. "I mean, a disciplinary hearing against McKay might presume that you are passing your problem on, that you are unable to exercise any control of McKay or deal with the problem at your supervisory level. It might even bring into question your suitability as a supervisor, if you find difficulty in motivating one man. You wouldn't want that now, would you, Ian?" Munroe eased slowly back in his chair, his pipe, which remained unlit, clamped between his teeth. Checkmate, he thought, refraining from a smile and working to keep his face calm.

Reid was visibly paled. He knew Munroe had stymied him. Any report of complaint he produced against McKay might reflect badly on him.

"Perhaps," continued Munroe, knowing he was giving the little shit an easy alternative, "if I was to have McKay in here and give him a verbal reprimand, would that do the trick do you think?"

Let him down gently, thought Munroe. Let him believe the decision is his.

Reid, university educated with an honours degree in Physics and a retired senior ranking father, knew he was nigh on certainly guaranteed a successful career with the police. Having completed nine years service, albeit mostly in administrative roles, he was self-assured and confident in his own ability, but suddenly realised that the machinations of a wily old bastard like Munroe could still catch him wrong-footed. Almost choking with rage, he forced a reply. "Yes sir, I believe that would be the best course of action."

"Right then Ian," replied Munroe, smiling he rose to his feet and indicated the discussion was over, "leave it with me and I'll roast McKay's arse for him. Send him in, if you please."

Munroe sat down and awaited Willie McKay, the unlit pipe now firmly clenched between his teeth, a silent but visible protest against the strict no smoking ban forcibly imposed throughout the building. He knew from office gossip and a quiet word with Archie MacDonald that in the recent past, Willie was having problems at home. According to Archie, and he had no reason to doubt the young man, Willie's wife Margaret was very possessive, even jealous of her husband leaving her to attend his work. An out and out snob was Margaret McKay, according to Archie, house proud and overbearing. In a rare fit of confidence, Archie had revealed his wife Jean would no longer visit Willie and Margaret, so afraid was she her three boisterous children might damage or mark the 'Margaret MacKay Mausoleum', as Jean insisted calling the MacKay house. However, an old school type of policeman like Munroe would never bring Willie's home-life into the conversation, not unless Willie himself broached the subject. Odd, though, he thought to himself. No children.

"Willie, Willie, Willie. What am I going to do with you?" Munroe shook his head and indicated with his pipe for Willie to sit and then himself remained standing with his back to the window. In his soft, lilting voice he continued, "You are, without doubt one of the hardest working detective's I've ever worked with, yet you continuously manage to piss off every supervisor you've ever had. Is it a socialist thing? Are you on some sort of 'piss the boss off' crusade?" Reaching over, he placed his pipe down on his desk and grasped the back of his chair with both hands. "You've been divisional CID, Serious Crime, Drug Squad Intelligence and even had a crack at Special Branch work. Now you've landed here when we both know you could be... should be..." he emphasised with some energy, "sitting at my desk."

With a frustrated shake of his head, he slammed his hands down on the back of the chair and stared at DC McKay. "Christ almighty, Willie, can you explain to an old fart like me what's going through your head?"

"Look boss," began Willie "I know that DS Reid is unhappy with my timekeeping, but there has never been any complaint about my work...."

"Willie," interrupted Munroe forcibly. "Your work is at least on a par, if not exceeding that of your colleagues, but you must realise that your timekeeping or whatever is only a part of your function in this department. I don't have to remind you we are, after all, a disciplined service. Now," sitting back in his chair, "I accept that Reid can't be the easiest of sergeants to get along with and if the truth be known, he's probably a little intimidated, what with being the youngest and most junior serving officer in the department. But the fact remains he is your supervisor and I am asking, no... I'm *ordering* you to get along with him. Willie, for my sake please make the bloody effort, okay?"

Willie nodded, realising at the same time that the likeable but still sharp old bugger was, rather than handing out the expected reprimand, instead offering fatherly advice. He also suspected that Munroe was more aware of the office politics than even Willie realised and probably knew more about Willie than he let on. Office gossips, Willie thought, you can never be up to them. Standing, he turned to leave the office as Munroe added, "Oh, and one more thing, DC McKay. When you leave my office, please have the good grace to look as though you've had your arse kicked."

Chapter 2

Billy Thomson didn't have a great start to life. Raised by Ina, his grandmother, Billy thought that his mother probably lived somewhere in Glasgow, but he'd never bothered taking the time to try to find her as she hadn't bothered to contact him. As far as he was concerned, his Gran was all he needed. She'd raised him as her son and Billy was the first to admit she'd done not too bad a job and any bother he'd got into, particularly involving the law, was his own fault. Now he was really in the shit and Billy didn't have a clue how to deal with it. Govan, as far as Billy was concerned, was the best place in Glasgow, the place he knew like the back of his hand and where he most felt safe. He'd had always prided himself in his local knowledge and anything he ever needed or wanted could be had in Govan; he knew who was who, the wheelers and dealers, who could be trusted or who would grass you up to the cops for the price of a pint or a one-time hit. No, not trusted, probably rather than trusted, relied upon, but only for some pay back at a later time. Painful experience had taught Billy that where junkies were concerned, nobody had any friends, nobody could be trusted. Well, none that couldn't be grassed up for a ten quid bag, a 'tenner hit'. And right now, Billy knew that he had no friends in Govan, or anywhere, for that matter, except maybe Angie and his Gran. At least they'd look out for him. But no one else, none that would stick their neck out, none that would dare now that Billy had incurred the wrath of that vicious and well-known psychopath, Maxie McLean.

Standing in the tenement entrance on the Govan Road, looking out towards the bustling shopping area of Govan Cross, Billy knew Maxie would have his cronies and anyone else interested in making a few quid, out looking for him with the instruction to fetch him for a wee chat. A chat that was Maxie's idea of at best a severe hiding or worst, something Billy would rather not imagine. As well as the fear of capture by Maxie's team, Billy was hurting and knew the last hit he had, several long hours previously, was wearing off. His skin was beginning to crawl and the sweats had begun. A fine sheen of perspiration clung to his forehead and the hairs spouting on his upper lip. His mouth and throat felt as though the skin had been scraped off with a blunt knife and his stomach was constantly churning. Adding to his discomfort, his bowels were reminding him of their need for a sudden release. If he didn't get to his stash soon, he'd be in a real state. Only thing worse than feeling like this, he thought to himself, is being a fucking Celtic supporter. He recalled the last time he'd been with Angie and inwardly prayed she'd not do anything stupid. This

wasn't the time for nerves. Keep the head, he had told her and all our troubles are behind us. Remembering their last conversation, before he left to do the business, Billy had promised her "Just a little while longer, sweetheart. Not too long to wait and we'll be alright."
But that hadn't been the whole truth. That wouldn't have been fair to her, just in case something went wrong. Afraid to admit to himself that even Angie, whom he loved and who said loved him, could be hurting too and might reveal his plan for a tenner bag. But nothing would, he took breath and corrected himself, nothing could go wrong. After all, who could ever have guessed what he'd planned. Who would have credited him with having the bottle to go through with something like this? Wee Billy Thomson, he grinned to himself, The Man. A sudden memory then the harsh reality of his situation set in. With a sigh, he remembered his first problem was this morning learning from his lawyer that the police had been issued with a warrant for his arrest, the matter of a 200 pound fine that he had neglected to pay. Neglected to pay? Where the fuck was I going to get two hundred quid, he'd angrily screamed at the useless twat. Not what he needed to hear right now. Of all the stinking luck! His chest thumping, his mouth dry and palms sweaty, Billy knew he'd have to make a move soon, but to where? Gran would, of course, defend him with her dying breath. She had dealt with the coppers before and he sighed. Nothing new there. All those bastards would do was lift him and throw him into jail. But even there he wouldn't be safe. Not from Maxie. He involuntarily shuddered at the thought. In jail he would be defenceless with no place to hide, no place to run. And if Maxie's team came calling to his Gran's house, what use would she be

against the like of Franny McEwan or Davie One-ball Smith? Maxie chose his team with care, knowing that if it came to defending him, bampots like those two would take it in the chest like they mad Secret Service guys the US President has about him. If brains were dynamite, Billy inwardly grinned, Franny and One-ball wouldn't have enough between them to blow the sweat from their low brows. The real problem was evading them long enough to get Angie and his Gran together. Then they'd be away and nothing would stop them. He sniggered to himself. Maybe even pay off my fine.   Billy's difficulty, he knew, would be in persuading his Gran to come with him, leave her beloved Govan. But right now his first priority was a hiding place, somewhere to hole up, for now. He screwed his eyes up against the bright winter sunlight and saw a police car, with two officers inside cruising along Govan Road towards him. Instinctively, he backed his thin body into the shadow of the 'close' and up against the closed security door, pulling the zipper of his cheap, black windcheater up tight against his throat. Nervously, he licked his lips as he watched the car pass by, the driver apparently laughing at some remark made by his colleague. Billy edged out, bracing his shoulder against the cornerstone of the entrance, watching the car disappear and blissfully unaware of the two plain-clothes officers across the street, whose curiosity was aroused by the sight of wee Billy Thomson, a known junkie, hiding in broad daylight.

"Only one reason for his actions", whispered Constable Gerry Higgins to his young partner, "he's dirty. Carrying something and my guess is it will be more than for just personal use, Annie. I know that guy. He's been done in the past for dealing."

PC Annie Burns, Higgins's partner, or neighbour in police parlance, was miffed at the older cops explanation. She wasn't some dumb probationary cop, she sighed with annoyance, just out of training school. By now she could recognise the body language signs as well as this old fart. She took a step to cross the road towards Billy, but was seized by the elbow and forcefully tugged back by Higgins.

"Hang on, Annie," he advised her, his grip like a vice on her elbow. "Let's just check first and see if our Billy's wanted on warrant or something."

Higgins, the older and more experienced copper, now in the twilight of his service, stared across the road to where Thomson stood and instinctively knew that something was definitely wrong. Carrying too much weight and silently regretting the two rolls and bacon he'd breakfasted on ten minutes earlier, Higgins knew that if he spotted the officers and took off, they'd have little chance of catching Thomson, whose adrenalin would be pumping and spurring him on faster than shite off a hot shovel. Admittedly, Annie might be in with a shout of staying up with or even catching Billy, but Higgins's old-fashioned chivalry was, as he was constantly ribbed by his younger colleagues, outdated in today's police service. A dinosaur was how he laughingly described himself to his wife. The young cops teased and chided him about his lack of faith in his female colleague's physical abilities, particularly when the women were called upon to wrestle with some of the drunken and violent customers that frequently came their way. Higgins knew that Annie Burns was fit, keen and fleet footed, but he didn't want her chasing after the Govan junkie. Junkies, Higgins knew from painful experience, could be very, very unpredictable and his main fear was that Annie would catch young Thomson.

"G344 to Control," radioed Higgins, using his divisional call sign.

"Go ahead, Gerry."

"Can you check the local warrants for Billy Thomson, aged about 22 or 23 years of," he hesitated, wracking his memory for Billy's address, "I think its number 16 Elder Street, Govan."

"Standby."

Billy, anxious, frightened and looking all about him, had by now spotted the two plain clothes officers, particularly that Fenian bastard Higgins. He remembered an incident when, some years previously, Higgins had been one of a number of uniformed police officers accompanying the local Loyalist flute band through Govan, at the time when the teenage Billy had belonged as a flutist. Higgins had been one of the uniformed officers detailed to accompany Billy's band and followers, most of who had been drinking heavily since early morning. Halfway along Langlands Road, an elderly drunk had staggered from a nearby pub and broke through the ranks of the parade, infuriating the parade stewards who carried the ceremonial wooden batons. So intoxicated he could barely walk, the drunk was set upon by the stewards, who in turn found themselves under attack by an enraged baton wielding Higgins. Following the melee, the drunk and three of the stewards needed hospital treatment for various wounds, while still others had sported black eyes and burst mouths, most courtesy of constable Higgins whose batting average exceeded anything ever reached at the Lords Cricket ground. No charges, however, had been made against any of those concerned, the police content to let the matter drop rather than provoke further sectarian problems in the volatile and religiously divided Govan. Billy knew Higgins by reputation as a hard man and didn't relish the thought of being captured by the big bastard. Pretending he hadn't seen them, he took a deep breath and with a shaking hand, reached behind him and frantically tried to turn the handle of the close entrance door, only to discover it locked. Reaching up, he hastily began pressing all ten house buttons in the hope of finding someone at home, someone prepared to allow him entry to the close and then to the rear courtyard, where safety lay in his ability to climb the courtyard wall and run like fuck.

"Control to G344, over", the radio cackled.
"Go ahead, Jim," responded Higgins, his eyes never leaving the darkened close mouth from where he knew young Thomson must by now have eyeballed him.
"Gerry, that check you asked for about Billy Thomson. I've spoken with the warrants officer and she tells me that one just arrived today, non-payment of a two hundred pound fine, imposed for the Misuse of Drugs

offences. Do you have him, over?"

"Jim, he's in a close at 612 Govan Road, about 60 metres from us. I think he's seen us, but he's giving us a dizzy. He's about five foot seven, skinny build, spotty complexion, dark hair and he's wearing a black coloured short jacket, blue jeans and the usual run faster training shoes. As I recall, he can move like a whippet. Can you get a panda to go round to Vicarfield Street? If Annie and I approach, I think he'll be off through the close and over the wall. A panda crew at the other side should be able to cut him off."

Higgins, now confident that more resources were being deployed to assist him, relented to Annie Burns pleading eyes and urged her to cross the road between the traffic. To her annoyance, he barked a warning at her. "Don't forget, treat all junkies like potential fighters and watch out for their spikes," he added. "And remember. Don't use your fists till your feet are bleeding from kicking him," he grinned at her.

Burns nodded her understanding, angry that Higgins ignored the fact she was no longer a probationer and was well aware that dealing with junkies, to exercise caution and the danger of syringes.

Higgins wished she didn't keep shooting glances towards Thomson, accepting now that Thomson would have spotted the officers and be preparing himself to run. Without a backward glance, Burns was off and across the road, intent on watching her prey and oblivious to the taxi driver who screamed a warning as he fought to keep his vehicle from colliding with a bus. Higgins turned his eyes to heaven and shook his head.

"Who is it?" inquired the disembodied, elderly female voice on the intercom.
"Eh, I'm trying to get in, love. I'm visiting my uncle, but he's not answered. Can you press the door buzzer for me, please?" Come on, you old bag, thought Billy.
"Visiting who?" wheezed the elderly voice, breath rattling in her chest.

Burns sought refuge in a close two down from where Thomson hid, as her radio crackled into life. "Annie, I think he's clocked us and he's trying for the door. Start walking towards the adjacent close and I'll walk along this side. If he gets in the close, he'll do a runner through the back. Make your way in a parallel up Shaw Street and try to cut him off."

Think, Billy think! Any name! "McCoist... Ally McCoist," he almost screamed at the intercom, a sudden panic overtaking him. Jesus, thought Billy, I hope she's not a Rangers fan.
"Oh, aye right'. Security satisfied, Billy's elderly and unwitting accomplice agreed to admit him.
The buzzer sounded and Billy burst through the door. Feet pounding on the stone floor, he sped through the dark, fetid reeking close and snatching open the unlocked back door, burst into the bright, blinding sunlight that for an instant caused him to screw his eyes shut. Heart pounding, breath laboured, Billy took a lungful of air and ran towards the eight foot, brick perimeter wall, a legacy of the days when tenement buildings in the Parish of

Govan each had their own back-courtyard separating them from the other tenement buildings, a parochial area that served the families residing in the close as a clothes drying area, children's playground and meeting place for housewives to complain about their men folk. But in recent times, the courtyard had become the refuge of drug abusers and wino's, whose debris lay scattered about the ground, which was about to prove very unfortunate for Billy Thomson.

"Control to G344, Gerry that's Golf Panda Charlie now into Vicarfield Street. Do you have the suspect?"
Lungs bursting, Higgins raced as fast as his now aching legs could carry him towards the doorway, recently quit by Billy. "He....he's into the close," gasped Higgins. "I'm following."   Higgins arrived in time to prevent the lock on the heavy wooden front door clicking shut and then stopped to listen. Forcing his breathing to be still, he heard no sound from inside the darkened close. Too long in the tooth to follow a suspect into a dark and confined space, Higgins knew the folly of dashing after a desperate junkie, particularly one that might possibly be armed with a syringe. The threat of contamination with the AIDS virus is every officer's worst nightmare. With bated breath, Higgins forced himself to stand still a further few seconds then heard the rear door slam shut. Clicking his radio send button, he gasped "Suspect possibly through the back into the rear court. Am pursuing!"
"Control to Gerry," his receiver barked, "I'm putting you on radio talk through. Go ahead Annie."

Good man, thought Higgins, a fine controller can make all the difference and be of enormous assistance to the officer on the ground. His mouth dry and his tongue rattling against his teeth, he stumbled towards the rear door.

"Annie to Gerry," her voice screamed at him

"Go ahead, Annie," Jesus, he reflected, his chest burning, "I'll need to give up the spicy food."

"Gerry, the panda crew and I are in Vicarfield Street. Any update?"

Billy, powering across the courtyard and reaching with both hands as he ran, knew from previous experience of running from the cops that his speed and a jump, combined with the adrenalin, would carry him more than halfway up the wall, enough for him to reach up and grab the top and enable him to pull his thin and wiry frame over. But that's when the discarded, cheap wine bottle came into play, least when Billy expected to meet something underfoot that gave way when he stood on it, causing him to slip and slide, then tumble head first into the brick wall in an inevitable and bone crushing collision. "Oh, shite," was Billy's last, panic-stricken thought.

"Wait, one. I think he's run through into the back courtyard," panted Higgins. Pulling open the door, he tentatively stepped out into the morning glare from the shadow of the close and recoiled slightly, anticipating his suspect might be hiding behind the wall at the doorframe.

At first, his eyes narrowing against the bright glare, he didn't see Billy lying at the base of the wall, amongst the years of garbage and long grass. Cautiously, as he ventured further into the courtyard, Higgins saw the huddled heap and approached with some apprehension. Immediately sensing something was wrong, yet with his first concern for his own safety, he used his foot to nudge Billy. Getting no reaction, he again used his foot a little more forcefully to turn Billy over and instantly saw the bloodied head and lifeless eyes staring at him. Higgins staggered back, a sudden dryness in his throat.
"Annie, to Gerry, any update? Annie to Gerry, come in Gerry. Gerry?" There was a slight pause, then her voice betraying her anxiety, she said, "Constable Burns to all stations, no response from Constable Higgins."

Chapter 3

Maxie McLean stared out of the panoramic lounge window, through the metal railing fence and at the gas van, parked across the road, its driver's cabin unoccupied. Funny how all these police vans, no matter how they're done up, they all have clean, shiny windows, thought Maxie. All the better for taking photographs, he presumed. He continued staring at the van, but directed his question to the man who stood nervously behind him. "What do you mean, you can't find him?" he asked, his voice soft but clear, his arms by his side, clenching and unclenching his fists in a visible state of tension.
Franny McEwan couldn't take his eyes off Maxie's hands and wasn't fooled. Maxie might talk soft, but failing to recognise the edge to his voice could land you in a heap of shite. It paid to be careful and pay attention

when Maxie asked something.

"We tried his granny's house," replied Franny. "She says she hasn't seen him. That junkie bird he knocks about with, Angie Bennett from Rathlin Street, says that he knows we're looking for him and she'll give us a bell when he shows at her place."

"She's the junkie that's the love of young Billy's life, isn't she," Maxie answered his own question, his attention still occupied by the gas van. Turning, he ran his hand through his wiry grey hair. Thin, almost gaunt, the uninformed could be forgiven for mistaking Maxie as a patient suffering some debilitating disease, his body marked forever with the signs of the alcohol he'd consumed from an early age, despite the fact he'd been sober now for almost ten years. The years of abuse, though, reflected in his face. Combined with the odd razor and knife scars he'd received from past fistfights, his face resembled the harsher side of the moon, all craters and holes. Every time Maxie looked in a mirror he was reminded of the time when some anonymous smart-arse at the Drug Squad, sent him a Christmas card containing a small bag of poly-filler. It rankled then and still did.

Franny, built like a sumo wrestler, the light reflecting off the sheen of sweat on his hairless head, shuffled uneasily as most people did when Maxie was in a foul mood. Watching his discomfort, Franny's sidekick, 'One-ball' Smith, thin as a rake with greasy, shoulder length dark hair, resplendent in an ill-fitting off the peg three piece suit and sporting gold studs in both ears, was a complete contrast to Franny, yet both worked well together at Maxie's bidding, with Franny habitually taking the lead in any matter that required a decision. Local punters quipped that One-balls IQ was halved when, many years previously, the police Alsatian removed his left testicle on that memorable night he didn't quite make a clean getaway from the warehouse break-in.

"So tell me again, Franny boy, what word have you put out on wee Billy then?" purred Maxie.

'I passed it about there's a 'monkey' in it for whoever spots him, Maxie. Plus whoever does the business knows that you'll be grateful."

"You half-wit!" roared Maxie, his echoing throughout the massive area of the lounge. His thick cigar nestling between the fingers in his right hand, he rubbed his forehead with the heel of his left hand. Taking a deep breath, he turned to Franny and growled, "I don't want my name bandied about in any connection with Billy Thomson. Don't you realise what's at stake here?"

"Sorry, Maxie," pleaded Franny, his hands in front of him in supplication, "I didn't think," he whined in a half whisper.

One-ball shifted nervously, aware that with Maxie riled, all were viable targets in the fallout area.

"What's wrong with you, One-ball?" asked Maxie, looking at the lit end of the cigar in his hand.

"Nothing Maxie, it's just that I think that Angie Bennett might know more than she told us. I scudded her jaw for her, but she's a game wee lassie and took a swing at me. I don't think she'll grass Billy up though, Maxie. Do you want us to go back and see her again?"

Maxie walked slowly back to the window. The van was still there and his wife's discreet gossiping with his timid neighbours hadn't disclosed any of them having problems with their gas.

"No. Billy and the bags will turn up. He knows what

would happen if he stiffed us. After all, how much value would you place on your grannies life? Aye," he slowly nodded his head, "he'll turn up. I'd just rather it was sooner than later. We're on a tight schedule here and I don't want to be left hanging by my short and curlies."

DC Andy Dawson was regretting the previous evenings' piss-up. If he'd known then he was drawing an eight hour shift in the surveillance van, he might have re-considered the usual end of night curry and stuck with something lighter. Three hours, two litre bottles of flavoured water and four headache tablets into the shift and the confines of the van smelled something awful. His neighbour, DC Mary Murdoch was still gagging and threatening all sorts of damage to Andy, most of which ended with the promise of a cork stuffed up his arse. Ever the pessimist, he thought it now unlikely that she'd take him up on that offer of a night out. Andy, to his never-ending surprise, was always getting knock-backs from birds. Truth be known, he reluctantly had to admit, where women were concerned he couldn't catch his fingers in a door. Standing at five foot ten, broad shouldered with wiry black hair and a permanent seven o'clock shadow that gave him an almost Mediterranean look, he wasn't an unattractive man. Yet none of the women that he'd previously dated seemed inclined to hang around more than a few weeks. Not that he was a heavy drinker, but his fondness for the rugby, real ale and male dominated pubs did, he realised, put the ladies off. Particularly if they were looking for the romantic type, of which Andy

definitely wasn't. His digestive system didn't lend itself to his efforts, either. His radio headset stuttered into life.
"Base to Alpha three, is there anything doing, over."
"Alpha three, they're still in there boss, McEwan and Smith. I can see McLean's wheels, but no sign of him so far. Over." He glanced towards Mary, her nose pressed against the one air vent that permitted a slight draught of fresh air.
"Right Andy, if there's no movement from McLean within the next hour, we'll pull out and call it a day, over."
"Roger, alpha three out."

Maxie sat down. It didn't occur to him to invite Franny and 'One-ball' to do likewise. He thought about the van outside and the trouble the police went to record and catalogue his movements. Maxie's immense fortune had been acquired through the years by an ascending ladder of criminality, his formative years spent dodging school and stealing scrap from the derelict tenements during the Glasgow slum clearances, progressing through money-lending, post office and bank robberies, graduating to the crime with the least risk yet greatest financial reward, the procurement and distribution of illegal drugs.
"The beauty of the drug-trade," Maxie was fond of explaining to his cohorts, "is it's the little man who takes the fall." But Maxie couldn't deny, even to himself, the one thing that really excited him, the buzz. The knowledge that he was putting one over on the cops, that he continually proved that he was smarter than them. For all their resources and technology at their disposal, they

never had nor ever would pin the big one on Maxie and as for their informants? Well, as Maxie was fond of saying, he could still sniff a grass at a hundred yards. Many a man, and some women, carried the razor slash wound inflicted by Maxie, a visible sign to the world he lived in to be aware that Maxie McLean was a man to fear. Some had paid the ultimate price for their treachery. Those, Maxie was confident, would never be found.
"Let them watch," he sneered, turning to stare again at the van, "the big one is yet to come, boys."
Maxie's two custodial convictions, amounting to a mere eighteen months, had taught him a valuable lesson. Never get caught, let some other bastard take the fall and face prison. With the minimum formal education, he had in later life invested in an evening tutorial course, learning the rudiments of accountancy and bookkeeping, both skills he considered useful and crucial in his quest for further profit. A quick learner, he had found something during the course even more valuable than education. He had found Lena.
For the day-to-day operational running of his organisation, he employed intermediaries. When people needed to be hurt or intimidated or a succession of faceless couriers found to run the trade, he used muscle like Franny and 'One-ball', but Maxie maintained his solid grip on the helm. He was the spider at the centre of his massive web and had only one true and tried rule that he never deviated from. Keep things simple and trust nobody. That's why he would never be caught. With a finger in more than one pie, his turnover was staggering, with profits from all his enterprises winding their way to his middleman, Harry Cavanagh, who purchased and invested in property on his behalf, throughout the city

and abroad. But never in Maxie's name, for that would attract the curiosity of the Inland Revenue. No, Maxie had Lena for that. Good quality buildings, Maxie had instructed Cavanagh.

The property market boom of the nineties resulted in a massive profit on his investments. According to the police Fraud Squad, who consistently tried and failed to monitor his accounts, these investments now reputedly run to double figure millions, all appreciating in value through the passage of time. As for Maxie's criminal profits, that was anybody's guess. Aye, Maxie was doing well for a boy from a council estate in Glasgow's south side. A knock on the door interrupted his thoughts.

"Come in."

Lena, Maxie's much younger wife, hair tied back in a ponytail, black sweater tight against her breasts and black ski pants, came timidly through the door. A natural beauty, the slight dab of make-up under her left eye failed to completely hide the fading bruise. She cleared her throat and asked, "Will you be wanting your lunch now, Maxie?"

"No, the boys are just leaving. Get their coats, will you hen?" said Maxie, smiling.

Franny wasn't fooled. The open show of affection by Maxie playing the loving husband was as much a front as was the palatial Newton Mearns house, fancy cars and membership of the golf club. To Franny's recollection, the only time he had seen Maxie using a golf club was when he'd swung it above his head to clobber some opposition during a gang fight in their teens. He didn't love Lena, Franny rightly guessed. She was a possession, like everything else in Maxie's life. And that was a pity.

Because in Franny's opinion, Lena, with fulsome figure and her long shiny black hair, was a right darling, but he knew that she was as shit scared of Maxie, as were the rest of them and anyone stupid enough to make a play for her risked having his balls posted to his next of kin.

Andy Dawson saw McEwan and Smith leave through the front door and being waved off by McLean's wife. "And a proper little darling she is too," reflected a wistful Andy.
"Put it back into your trousers, Andy," snapped Mary, her face dourly registering her disgust at this ape of a neighbour the boss had inflicted upon her. 'You don't know where she's been. And *PLEASE*! Stop farting, will you?"
The radio crackled into life. "Alpha three from base, stand down."

Chapter 4

Ina Thomson, Billy's widowed grandmother was best described as a matronly woman, her grey hair tied in a neat bun, her ruddy complexion reflecting years of struggle and deprivation, a constant and worried frown her defence against emotion. No stranger to visits from the police, Ina had come to expect two when they called banging on the door, with a third officer usually stood in the rear courtyard, at the kitchen window round the back of the ground floor flat, to prevent Billy jumping out and escaping. When the knock came that day, Ina instinctively knew that it was trouble. Though just turned sixty, like most Glasgow working class people of her generation, she still harboured a respect for authority and an almost servile attitude to the police. With a sigh, one hand patting a loose hair into place and the other smoothing down her wrap-around apron, she opened the door to be confronted by two solemn faced uniformed officers, an Inspector and a sergeant, neither of whom she knew. Being used to finding either constables or plain clothes officers on her doorstep, she was uncertain and taken aback, her standard response of "Billy's not in," died on her lips. A chill run through her body and her hands fell to her sides, her chest suddenly tight as the energy drained from her.

"Can we come in Mrs Thomson," the sergeant softly said, while removing his hat, "I'm afraid it's bad news." The next ten minutes seemed to go by in a blur. Ina was aware of her neighbour from upstairs, a woman she normally wouldn't pass the time of day with, handing her a cup of tea. I haven't cleaned the kitchen, thought the normally fastidious Ina, what will she think? But none of that seemed important. Billy was dead. Killed, said the Inspector in an unfortunate accident. A head injury, he added, them my regrets. Running away, she heard. Then there was something said about a back courtyard off Govan Road. All the information seemed to run together. Ina couldn't take it all in.

"Do you have Billy's birth certificate, Mrs Thomson?" inquired the Inspector.

"What?"

"There will be an inquiry by the CID, just to determine the exact circumstances, you understand." The Inspector wasn't comfortable, trying to explain someone else's fuck-up and the woman clearly wasn't taking all this in. Added to that he thought, the nosey bugger from upstairs is all ears and no doubt by the time she adds her tuppence worth to local gossip, the police will have battered the wee shite to death.

"What circumstances?"

"Well, in these circumstances we have to investigate all the details and ensure that Billy's death isn't attributed to anyone and also determine if his death might have been prevented." This isn't going well, at all, he thought. And with that fire burning away, it's as hot as hell, in here. Not a native of inner city Glasgow, the Inspector had grown up in a suburban, detached house and family money had eased his way through University. How these people managed to live crammed into these tenements, he would never know. Still, as he looked about him, nice tidy wee house. The old woman intruded in his thoughts.

"Why do you need his birth certificate?"

"Eh, there will need to be a report to the Procurator Fiscal, who has primacy in all sudden deaths and the certificate will provide details which we need to complete the report."

"So who investigates my Billy's....death?" asked Ina, lip now trembling, her composure slipping away from her.

"The investigation will be conducted by the police, acting on the PF's instruction. On his behalf you understand." The sergeant, a former detective officer with vast experience in the city's sprawling housing estates, knew fine well the wee woman didn't understand what was being told to her and sat stony-faced, wondering when this bumptious clown of an Inspector would start speaking English to her. Christ, he bristled, can he not see she's hardly taking in a word he's saying? Exasperated, he couldn't stand this any longer and interrupted. "Mrs Thomson," he softly addressed her, "we know from previous dealings with Billy that you're his granny, his next of kin so to speak. But are his parents still alive or has he brothers and sisters we can contact for you?"

Hands outstretched, palms upwards the sergeant continued, attempting to break through the 'them and us' barrier. "Honest, hen, we're trying to help in any way we can." Aye right, he inwardly seethed. Let's start by getting us - the police - off the hook first, though.

Ina rose from her seat and walked heavily to the old, solid but chipped sideboard unit, a legacy of her wedding day, presented to her and Bert by his parents. Pulling open the bottom drawer, she retrieved a small, battered brown suitcase, the lid held closed by an old drawstring from a dressing gown. In obvious discomfort from arthritic knuckle joints, she began to pull at the knot holding the drawstring tight.

"Can I help?" asked the sergeant, reaching out his hands. Ina handed the case over. The sergeant rested the case on his knees and undid the knot, then handed the case back. Ina fetched a brown envelope from inside the case that she handed to the Inspector.

"Billy's mother left him with me, just after he was born. The father was a Catholic and my Bert, God forgive him, wouldn't have her lad in this house. Bert was so ashamed that his lassie bore a Fenian's child, and him a member of the Orange Lodge. She was all we had, Bert and me, and it fair broke his heart. She didn't take anything with her and at first we thought she was missing, that she'd maybe hurt herself, if you know what I mean." Head bowed, her eyes misted. The inferred suggestion her daughter had killed herself. Memories from another time still capable of inflicting their painful wounds. "We reported her missing to the police and they came round, searched her room and took some things away. Told us if she was found," her voice faltered, hesitant at using the word, "you know.... dead, they'd be able to.... identify her because they had taken her fingerprints from.... some of her things." Ina paused, wringing and twisting at the handkerchief that appeared in her hand from her apron pocket. Taking a deep breath she continued. "I don't think that the lad knew she was pregnant because they broke up not long after she found out she was expecting. Anyway, she didn't put his name on the birth certificate."

Gently, the sergeant sat beside Ina. He recognised the poor woman was embarrassed, ashamed at having to discuss her family secrets. "Do you know where she is, Billy's mother? Or how we can contact her?"

She sat upright, her voice growing firm, the sorrow now being borne with an acceptance. "I haven't seen my Rita since the night she left Billy here, that's nearly twenty-three years now. I have no idea where she might be."

The sergeant knew it had to be asked and the Inspector was leaving it to him, arse that he was. Shit! He'd forgotten that neighbour was hovering about. Turning, he spoke to her and ushered her towards the door. "Thanks for your help, Mrs, eh, yes. Well, I'm sure we'll manage from here, thank you." The sergeant waited.

With an ill disguised look of annoyance, the neighbour stormed out of the room, slamming the front door in her frustration.

The sergeant again turned to face Ina. "Sorry hen. I'd forgotten she was there."

Ina shook her head. She was past caring what folk thought of her. Billy's death overcame what little pride

that she had left.
"Mrs Thomson. I know this is really difficult and I am sorry to be asking you, but we both know Billy had his difficulties with us. Would you mind if I took a wee look in his room? Just to eh, remove anything there that you might not want to have in the house, if you know what I mean." Don't make me spell it out, he silently begged her.
But Ina knew exactly what the sergeant meant. She hated Billy taking drugs, hated the thought that he might bring such things into her home. But he was....had been her only living relative. Rita didn't count. Rita had left her and Bert had died because, Ina firmly believed, Rita had abandoned Ina, Bert and wee Billy. Wearily, she nodded her consent. "Go ahead, but I want you to make me a promise, sergeant. Promise me that you will come and visit me and tell me what's happening about your inquiry. Promise me that you'll tell me the truth, please." The sergeant swallowed. 'Of course, Mrs Thomson, if that's what you want."
"Promise me, then."
"I promise." The Judas promise, he inwardly thought, feeling a bad taste in his mouth. Agree to anything, just as long as it doesn't reflect badly on the police.
"It's the second door on the right, the one with the padlock."
Mrs Thomson didn't have the key. The sergeant thought it was probably with Billy's possessions at the city mortuary, but the flimsy padlock seemed more a privacy marker than a serious attempt to keep out intruders and it gave way at the second blow of the sergeants' side handled baton.
The Inspector pushed open the door to Billy's bedroom

and moved into the room, ahead of the sergeant. It was obvious from the smell of dirty socks and discarded, sweat soaked training shoes that Mrs Thomson seldom, if ever, ventured into Billy's room. However, both the officers were surprised at the neatly made bed and folded clothes that hung over the single wooden chair.
The window, the Inspector saw, must have been painted when it was closed tight and had likely never been opened since that time. He assumed that would account for the lack of fresh air. "Potpourri wouldn't stand a chance in this place," he wryly remarked. Posters on the peeling wallpaper declared Billy's allegiance to the American rap king Eminem, Glasgow Rangers Football Club and a pouting, scantily clad Kylie Minogue. "Looks like my youngest daughter's room," the Inspector smiled. The sergeant replied with a humourless smile, certain this toffee nosed plonker would have a hairy fit if his daughter ever had to live in the general squalor of a room like this. Both officers donned polythene gloves and began a systematic examination of the small, square shaped room. A brief cursory search in a set of DIY drawers, with handles missing and paint peeling from the top, soon turned up an old King Edward cigar box, the lid bound by a strong rubber band. The contents proved to be Billy's works. Knife, bent spoon, strip of elastic, cheap plastic coated cigarette lighter and syringe with several Health Board needles, still in their protective wrapping. All these items lay on top of a cheap blue notebook, which bore the Glasgow Rangers' football club logo. The sergeant puzzled over the handwritten entries, but decided CID or the investigating team could deal with the notebook. 'Don't think Mrs Thomson will miss this', opined the sergeant, holding up the notebook for

inspection. The Inspector absently nodded his consent, his interest taken up by Miss Minogue. But no drugs were found. On this occasion, his last police bust, Billy Thomson was clean.

Chapter 5

At home now, Gerry Higgins sat on the closed lid of the WC behind the locked door in his downstairs toilet, his head in his hands. He couldn't believe what had happened. One minute he'd spotted a known junkie and pursued him, the next the junkie is lying dead and those callous bastards in CID are giving him knowing winks.
"Well done, my son."
"Mountie Higgins, always gets his man."
"Did he squeal?"
Even Higgins's neighbour, Annie Burns couldn't look him in the eye. She thinks I did for him, as well, thought Higgins. He knew that the general consensus of unspoken opinion was that he'd grabbed Billy Thomson and run him head first into the wall. Shaking his head, his eyes moist, he whispered to himself, Jesus, they think I killed wee Billy!
"Gerry?" The insistent knocking at the door was followed by a plaintive call. "Gerry, are you alright in there?"
Alison Higgins knew there was something badly wrong. Twenty years of marriage to Gerry had, if nothing else, taught her that when he locked himself in the loo, he needed time on his own and not just to let nature take its course. She knew it must be bad. Gerry hadn't even taken the morning paper in with him.

Superintendent Iain 'Father' Ross was of the old school. Thirty-five years policing Glasgow and her citizens had taught him a thing or two about human nature. And right now Ross knew that one of his boys, Gerry Higgins, would be feeling like the world had come collapsing down on top of him. Ross had attended the locus of the sudden death, the filthy, rain-soaked back courtyard where the poor wee laddie Billy Thomson came to grief. The attending Scenes of Crime personnel and local divisional detectives had joked and wisecracked. To the uninitiated, their conversations would have seemed macabre and ghoulish. To those who attended scenes such as this in the course of their professional life, coffin humour was a means of emotional release, a way to avoid dealing with the harsh reality of coping with a fellow human being lying dead amongst filth and garbage. Ross had remained tight-lipped, acutely aware that with his presence, the conversation had died into a whisper, a gradual realisation that 'Father' Ross wasn't happy. He'd guessed the whispered innuendos that alleged Gerry Higgins had somehow contrived or caused Thomson's death. Rubbish, of that Ross was certain. He knew Gerry Higgins and believed him to be incapable of such a deed. But then his thoughts turned to the Complaints and Discipline crowd. Those boys were another story. Ross had stood alone, silent and composed. A staunch and regular attendant at his Baptist church, none could know that he was inwardly praying, praying for the repose of the soul of Billy Thomson. Junkie or not, thought Ross, he was somebody's son. Or grandson as it happened, in this particular case.

Driving back to his office at Govan police station, Ross reflected on the circumstances that were known and what course the inquiry in young Thomson's death would take. A grandfather himself, he knew that some of the younger officers under his command thought of him as a grizzled old timer, well past his 'sell by date'. He'd peaked early in his career, remaining in uniform and attained Superintendent rank fairly quickly, but remained at that level while younger and less experienced officers had passed him by on the way to command police Divisions and, in some cases, ultimately command their own Force. It had been unkindly rumoured that Ross' reluctance to retire was his response to the system that he believed thwarted his promotion prospects. In truth, he paid no heed to what people thought of him, believing that enough of those he commanded respected and liked him. Those who knew him well believed Iain Ross was far too honest to be a policeman. In common with most of his colleagues, Ross had a life outside the police and that life was his family. He carried his commitment to Christian values forward from his personal life into his professional life. His life was his wife, children and grandchildren and in that life he included most, but not all, of the men and women under his command that he considered to be his extended family. And right now Ross' number one priority was Gerry Higgins, a good man and a good copper who, if the Thomson inquiry wasn't handled properly, could find himself charged with the capital crime of murder.

Constable Annie Burns sat in her car in the police yard and rolled a cigarette, an unusual habit for a female, she was the first to admit then lit her umpteenth cigarette of the day, picking the loose tobacco strands from her mouth. That done she fetched the folded sheets of paper from her anorak pocket and was surprised to find her hands shook slightly as she re-read her copy statement, but nothing had changed. No, she couldn't definitely say she saw Higgins go into the close. No, she hadn't heard anything from her side of the wall. And no, she hadn't heard Higgins threaten to 'get' Billy Thomson. The questioning had been relentless. The two rubber heels from the Complaints and Discipline Department had worked the good guy, bad guy routine and the ninety minutes had seemed like several hours. She'd told the truth, but even to her it had sounded contrived in the re-telling. No doubt, with the benefit of hindsight, she should have had a police federation member there as a independent witness to her treatment, just as any criminal suspect was entitled to a lawyer. But demanding anything like that might have hinted that she wasn't telling the whole truth. She slammed her free hand down hard on the steering wheel. Shit! How the fuck could it have gone so wrong! She sat back in the seat and, turning her head slightly, blew smoke through the partially opened drivers window, then angrily threw the lit, half finished fag out into the tarmac car park. A determined and motivated young officer, Annie understood her appointment to the shift plain clothes was the first step in achieving her ambition to join the CID. At first, working with Gerry Higgins had been educational, his tutoring based on lengthy service and experience, though she soon decided his experience was outdated in the modern police service.

Keen to progress in the police, Annie believed Higgins, in the twilight of his career, wasn't as motivated as she and anyway, he'd had his time, hadn't he? It was the age of the young team, officers like her who were better educated and more attuned to the needs of modern society, more adept at dealing with the diversity of the racially integrated community than Higgins and his 'heed the one warning or else, then lock them up' brigade. Twisting the key in the ignition, she fiercely revved the engine and thrust the stick into first gear. Her nostrils flared and she gritted her teeth at the memory of the younger of the rubber heels comedy duo suggesting she might be protecting Higgins, because she fancied him! Aye, right! She steered the car towards the exit gate. No way was she going to let this incident interfere with her ambition to join CID. As far as Annie was concerned, her career came first and Gerry Higgins? Well, it was his fuck-up so he was on his own.

Iain Ross checked his watch. 5.40pm, time he was heading home. He began packing away his files and then he remembered. One last thing to do before I go, he muttered to himself. The flight of stairs leading down from the divisional command suite led him straight into the CID general office. The duty late shift detectives both respectfully got to their feet, as Ross entered. He motioned for them to sit down. "Evening lads, how goes it?"
Detective constable Tam Black, the senior of the only two detectives on duty, liked 'Father' Ross. Unlike some of his more junior colleagues, Black knew that Ross

didn't shirk when a man was down and needed help, not like some of the gaffers that bailed out at the first sign of trouble. Black recalled an incident, two years previously, when he had himself been caught with the booze on his breath. Ross had been called for by the duty Inspector, a career flyer that saw Black's scalp as a trophy to brandish in his quest for promotion. Black had sweated in the Inspectors' room, while Ross was briefed by the Inspector about Blacks' consumption of alcohol whilst on duty, a flagrant breach of the police discipline code. He never discovered what happened in that room, what was said. The first he knew was a grim faced Ross ordering an unmarked car to take him home. The following day, as instructed, Black reported to the Superintendents' room where Ross gave him the verbal version of a right good kick in the balls. And not once, Black remembered, did Ross raise his voice. He didn't drink on duty, after that episode, nor would he again. He knew that Ross had saved not only his job, but his pension as well. Aye, he knew, a good man is 'Father' Ross. Curiously, the Inspector was promoted out of the division, shortly after that.

"Tam, my boy, can you show me what was found within Billy Thomson's house?"

Black fetched the evidence box, the contents delivered earlier by the sergeant who had turned over young Billy's house. "Watch your fingers, boss. There's a syringe and needles in there. You never know what you might catch." Gingerly, Ross used his biro to prod amongst the cigar box. "What's this wee book?"

Black shook his head. His curiosity hadn't extended to looking through the box's contents. "Don't know boss. We've been told to keep everything here at CID in case the rubber heels from Discipline want a shufti. I'd imagine it's Billy's tick book, customers, you know, contacts and that. Probably be of interest to the divisional drug squad. Do you want me to send them it?"

Ross flipped through a few pages. A city centre shop till receipt, slipped in between two pages, seemed a natural place to open through the book. Ross spread the pages and read names, mostly nicknames, mobile phone numbers, some house numbers and dates, most of which seemed to coincide with the Rangers playing home at Ibrox stadium. Some notations that seemed to be football scores were scribbled alongside the dates. Then one name he recognised that stood out from the others. Ross blinked twice and stared at the scribble. A memory and a sudden flashback to many, many years before, a large, bald man, half drunk, bloodied and going wild and wielding an axe in his huge fist in Donnelly's pub at the bottom of Golspie Street in Govan. The baton charge that was led by Ross who, with other uniformed officers, finally subdued the enraged madman called Franny McEwan.

Chapter 6

Willie McKay turned his collar up against the rain and breathed in the cold, damp air. It would have been refreshing, he was sure, but for the diesel and petrol fumes of the vehicles whose engines ticked over as they sat nose to tail in the grid locked Hope Street. Another day over and one nearer to my pension, he mused. Hell of a way to live life, wishing it away like this. His head down, he strode to the Glasgow Central railway station through fine, drizzling rain that never quite seemed to require the need for an umbrella, but soaked you anyway. Willie would never use a brolly believing, as he ducked and weaved through the pedestrian traffic on the wide city pavement, there was a real danger the way women handled they things and grimaced as he turned his head yet again to avoid a poke in the eye. The city office workers continued to scurry past Willie; each lost in their own thoughts as the daily communal race for the bus and the train continued. Only a mug tries to park in the city he thought, but still wishing he'd managed to get the car started. As he walked, he chewed over his interview with Munroe. The old man was a cracking boss, but he'd his hands full acting as a buffer between the intelligence staff and that clown Reid. Pragmatic by nature, Willie knew he'd have to make a determined effort to get along with Reid. This appointment was important to Willie, the best job he'd had in a long time. His last post, working with the Branch, had been a disaster. He'd not cottoned on to the politics of the department and made the mistake of speaking up, openly decrying the nonsense that open sectarian warfare in the streets of Glasgow between the Irish republican and Loyalist supporters, was imminent. Total shite, said Willie, that by and large, they were football hooligans, pure and simple. A few nutcases who needed introducing to Mr Hickory, the policeman's friend, down some back alley. That would have settled the issue. But those days were gone. Mores the pity, reflected Willie, smiling at forgotten memories of his uniformed probationary years and the gang fights he'd attended in the tough, sprawling housing estates, where fists and boots were more often supplemented by swords, knives and anything that might inflict damage. And that, he'd often heard joked, was only what the police carried.

Standing at the pedestrian crossing and waiting for a break in the heavy traffic, he again thought of his time with the Special Branch. It had been Willie's belief the Branch encouraged reports of public dissension, the worse the report, the better to justify the large complement of personnel it carried. Willie instinctively knew he wouldn't fit in. It didn't take the Branch bosses any time to realise that fact, also. Not so much pushed, he had been counselled and advised to continue his career elsewhere. But he was good at his job. Of that Willie had little doubt. His ability lay in assessing and identifying information that might have seemed to others as trivia, but what he could recognise as intelligence, worthy of being disseminated and acted upon, as many a smart-arse now languishing in prison had discovered. He often volubly argued that career criminals didn't have tenure of service and firmly believed that intelligence officers should be groomed, not appointed because of convenience or due to promotion. Or nepotism, he sighed and thought of Ian Reid, a prime example. Dismissing Reid from his mind, he believed intelligence, as Willie understood it, was like a jigsaw. If a piece didn't fit, it likely wasn't part of the picture and should be discounted, but not thrown away. Some day, it might fit elsewhere. Willie couldn't reconcile himself to making intelligence fit and that's when he and the Branch decided to part company or more accurately, they had him moved. Not all the Branch guys were happy toeing the party line, as Willie knew, but when a man is reminded it is in his career interest to play the game, it's sometimes difficult to argue. Or to keep my mouth shut, he grinned to himself and that, Willie decided, was why he was and would continue to remain a Detective constable... if he was lucky.

The lights changed and with courtesy, he stood aside to allow two teenage girls to move in front of him, but caught up in gossip, neither gave the tall, bedraggled man a second glance. Willie dodged their brightly coloured and sharply pointed brollies and hurried past them to the side entrance of the station and buying an evening paper, made his way to the platform. As he scrambled in the inside pocket of his jacket for his return ticket, he thought about Roddy Munroe and again gave thanks that Munroe had been on hand to bail him out and offer him a job with Criminal Intelligence. Willie had a keen, orderly and analytic mind. A requisite, he had once been told, for a good Intelligence officer. He enjoyed the challenge of collating and assessing the scraps of information that landed on his desk, sorting out the wheat from the chaff, researching historical associations and presenting the Intelligence targeting package, with target names, addresses, accomplice details and probable criminal intention to the various police squads, the Drugs, the Serious Crime, the Fraud and sometime, he inwardly grinned, even the Branch.

Granted, he was gracious enough to admit, the different squads did most if not all the legwork, but the targeting packages provided by Willie and his colleagues were primarily the first step in the Intelligence led operations, which often culminated in the arrest of the target. Admittedly, while he enjoyed the sedentary side of the work, Willie still missed the thrill of the chase and often as possible signed out an unmarked vehicle to personally validate and substantiate particulars he would later submit as Intelligence.

Detective constable Willie McKay was, if nothing else, a

meticulous and methodical man, but not he reflected, when it came to regularly servicing his Mondeo, as he peered with sinking heart at the already crowded platform. Descending the stairs into the heaving mass of commuters awaiting the southbound train, his thoughts turned to Margaret. Things had been bad the last few years and nothing Willie did or said seemed to make the slightest difference. Through the years, the arguments had become increasingly frequent to the point when now there was little from her but sullen response. He'd long ago accepted that Margaret didn't want children. If the subject had been politely referred to by curious friends or workmates, he'd pretend it was a joint decision. Sometimes he almost convinced himself. In truth, he confessed to himself, he was worn-out by Margaret. She suffocated him. Their physical relationship ended the night Margaret moved her things to the spare room. Now she could barely speak to him, let alone allow him to touch her. Their few conversations were terse and brittle. Willie just couldn't cope, that's all there was to it. He'd tried to talk to Margaret, some months previously. In his ignorance, he presumed the menopause was setting in, for after all she was in her early forties now and Willie, with nothing other than sneaking a peek at her women's magazines as reference points, knew no other explanation for her behaviour and once innocently but naively suggested maybe she needed to see a doctor. That was probably the worst thing he could have suggested. She flew at him in a rage, her fists beating him about the face and head. She'd scored his cheek, her nail tearing a one-inch gash which bled profusely. It was a small wound, but one that caused some comment in the office. He had passed the laceration off as a shaving cut, but guessed nobody really believed that. Gratefully, his colleagues dropped the issue and the matter, as far as he was concerned, faded as quickly did the slight wound on his face. What Willie didn't realise was, with the exception of Reid, his colleagues in the office liked him and while undecided about his domestic circumstances, assumed there were troubled times at home. In common with most close-knit working communities, word soon got round and no one gossiped quite like the police.

The crowds massed about him, positioned themselves like scrum forwards and awaited the approaching train. As the local southbound train ground to a halt, the doors hissed open and the alighting passengers hardly had time to exit before the masses surged towards the doors, eagerly searching out the few remaining seats. Willie contented himself with a standing position adjacent to the doors. At least here he could brace himself into the corner, the easier to counter the swaying train and open his evening edition of the *'Glasgow News'*. A cursory glance at the headlines indicated more international tension, but Willie concerned himself with the local reports, recognising the odd name here and there, some he was pleased to see being handed down sentences at the local courts. Unconsciously, his professional training took over and he scoured the newspaper for items interest. A report on page nine attracted his attention. Willie read that police had discovered the body of twenty-three year William Thomson of Elder Street, Govan. The three-inch column that was attributed to a *'local crime reporter'*, alleged unnamed eyewitnesses saw Thomson, reportedly a convicted drug abuser, being pursued by police. The article continued that a police source *'declined to comment'*, which he knew was jargon for the reporter being told to get on his or her bike. The item ended with the obligatory phrase *'police inquires are continuing'*. Willie folded the newspaper and shoved it into his jacket pocket, unconsciously smiling that the evening newspaper was known for never allowing the truth to interfere with a good story. Still, he had to admit that he'd picked up more than a few scraps of information by reading the local rags. Turning towards the door, he prepared himself for the crush that threatened to engulf him as his fellow passengers vied for pole position, making ready to exit at Kings Park station.

Shortly after receiving the phone call from Higgins's distraught wife Alison, DC Andy Dawson drove almost immediately towards the Higgins house. On the phone, he didn't get much sense out of her, just that Gerry had been suspended pending some sort of investigation. As he drove, Andy thought about the last time he had socialised with Gerry and Alison Higgins which, he guiltily recalled, was several months previously. Since being transferred from the Govan divisional CID to the headquarters surveillance team, Andy's shift pattern hadn't always coincided with his old friend's. But he knew that was just an excuse. If he had made the effort, he could have seen more of Gerry and his family. He chided himself for being a lazy bastard and receiving the phone call from Alison, felt guilt ridden that he didn't have a clue as to why or what had happened. But he would be there, at their home, soon enough. His thoughts turned to Gerry's current tutoring job, introducing the younger and less experienced cops to plain-clothes work.

It wasn't really Starsky and Hutch stuff. More dealing with complaints that uniformed cops couldn't get close to; nightly group disorder by youths, the occasional housebreaking, complaints that the public made frequently that when a uniform showed up, the bad guys scarpered. Plain-clothes had a better chance of getting closer to deal with the problem or for the capture. Andy had been through the pecking order himself, had been taught by Higgins and graduated through the uniform departments to CID. One of Gerry's success stories, Andy would laugh. But now this, his brow wrinkled. Andy couldn't understand why Higgins, the most honest cop he'd ever had the misfortune to work with, could be suspended. Not that Andy was dishonest, just that he believed if the villains or neds were prepared to tell lies to evade prison, then equally Andy was prepared to bend the odd rule to ensure their conviction. But Gerry Higgins, no way, Gerry was different. As he drove, Andy recalled an incident early in his uniform career when he'd turned up at a children's clothes shop at 3am, shortly after it had been broken into and looted through a hole in the rear wall. Higgins, the local uniformed beat man had happened across the break-in and found two of their colleagues piling clothing into the rear of a panda car, their reasoning being that the insurance would cover the loss. Andy knew they hadn't screwed the shop, as did Higgins, but in the aftermath of the theft were simply helping themselves. When Andy turned up, Higgins had drawn his baton and was squaring up to the two dickheads, both of whom were throwing the stuff back in through the hole and giving Higgins a verbal seeing to. Admittedly, the wages were bad in those days, but even Andy could never condone theft.

Alison was standing by the open front door as Andy drew up in his battered Escort. He guessed she'd been watching for him arriving from behind the curtain.
"Alright, love?" asked Andy, giving her a quick peck on the cheek. Andy was fond of Alison and if he was honest to himself, a little jealous of Gerry's seemingly idyllic life with a good-looking wife, a happy marriage and two smashing teenage kids. He could see she'd been crying.
"Thanks for coming. He's in a right state and he won't talk to me. He just tells me it's something at work. You know what he's like Andy; he never hides things, not things that are important. All he'll tell me is that he's suspended, meantime. What does meantime mean, Andy?"
"Let me talk to Gerry, love. Whatever it is, it can't be too bad. You know him. He takes work too seriously. I keep telling him, he should be more like me, lazy and incompetent." Alison laughed, then began to softly cry, leaning her head on Andy's bulky chest.
Andy, surprised and uncertain, didn't know how to handle this kind of grief and gently prised Alison off him. "Let me talk to him, eh?" he repeated and then added, "let me see if I can get this sorted out", smiling and pulling her upright. "Couldn't half murder a cup of tea." Alison laughed. "That's your answer, Andy Dawson? A cup of tea?"
"Not unless you have some Smirnoff, then."

Gerry Higgins sat on the edge of the bed. Again and again he had run the whole incident through in his mind. No matter how many times he thought it through, the end

result had culminated in the death of wee Billy Thomson. The creak on the landing stair and knock on the door announced the arrival of Andy Dawson. The door opened to admit the big detective; hair tousled as usual, his clothes crumpled after his shift in the surveillance van, a cheerful grin on his face.
"Alright, big man?"
"Hello, Andy. Alison call you?"
"Didn't know you were a detective, Gerry," quipped Andy in response. "And I have to say I'm a wee bit annoyed with you, Higgins."
"You're annoyed? Why's that then?"
"Listen Higgins, am I not your best pal? You get yourself suspended and you don't call me? You know she's down there, worrying her heart out about you. So, is it another woman?"
Gerry snorted and almost with derision, replied, "Don't be ridiculous!"
"Gerry Higgins, there's nothing that I can think of that would cause you to get yourself suspended, not unless you've lost the plot and hooked a gaffer on the chin. Is that what happened? You've lost it and punched out the divisional commander?"
Gerry knew the light-hearted banter was designed to relax him, get him to open up. Hadn't he employed the same tactics for years himself? Shit. Hadn't he taught Andy the routine? He run his hands through his hair and exhaled noisily.
Andy could see his old friend was troubled and it puzzled him. Gerry Higgins was one of the most self-assured individuals Andy knew, a model husband and father. He knew fine well that Gerry would never look at, let alone consider another woman and was even-tempered about

most things; the exception being, Andy knew, assaults made against women or children or anyone unable to fight back. Then Gerry needed to be watched. Gerry didn't like bullies and an opponent's size didn't matter to the big guy.

"I'm suspended because the CID believes that I might have killed a guy, a wee junkie."

Andy was stunned, the simple statement taking the breath from him. That couldn't be right. How could Gerry be accused of something like that?

The door pushed open and Alison entered the room, bearing a tray with teapot and cups, milk and sugar. It was obvious she had heard Gerry's remark, her lower lip trembling and the tears flowing unchecked down her cheeks. She sniffed as she tried to keep her voice even.

"I'll just set this down here and let you boys get on with your wee chat."

"What, no Smirnoff?" said Andy, a forced smile on his face, but the humour was lost on her.

"Gerry, what happened," Alison cried out, finally losing her composure.

Gerry Higgins, husband and father, commended police officer and all round good guy, sat on the edge of his bed and recounted to his bewildered wife and friend, the circumstances of wee Billy Thomson's death that concluded with the suspension of Constable Higgins.

Later that same evening, as the fiery October sun tried to break free and desert the sky through the rain filled clouds, Andy Dawson parked his car in a visitor's bay at Govan police office and made his way up the stairs to the public entrance. Since being transferred to the headquarters criminal surveillance squad, he'd been away from the division for almost three years and didn't wish to irritate anybody by rolling through the staff entrance and giving the impression the big boys were in town. He knew how agitated divisional CID could get, their feathers ruffled when one of the specialist squads from headquarters CID rolled in. Andy, ever the diplomat, used the proven and practised procedure that when calling at any divisional office, good manners and courtesy obliged he announce himself through the uniform bar first. Breeze in without warning and you were likely as not to encounter coolness, suspicion and risk being ignored and that was why Andy had taken the precaution of purchasing a packet of chocolate biscuits, in anticipation of his being made welcome of course, because this wasn't strictly an official visit. In fact, Higgins's suspension was nothing whatsoever to do with Andy Dawson, however, a friend in need can often be an annoying bastard, but not when it concerned Gerry Higgins.

The young and pretty, female civilian support officer behind the public counter, her blonde hair tied in a French plait and prominent breasts threatening to burst out of her tight fitting, uniform white blouse, wasn't known to Andy, but his police warrant card and huge grin convinced her he wasn't any threat to the security of her building. With a smile, she buzzed him through the security door. He briefly hesitated, wondering whether to chance his luck with a bit of patter, but the gold band on her left hand cancelled out that thought. Yes, the young woman replied to his enquiry, the CID is in, and yes, she'd phone and let DC Black know that Andy was coming upstairs. "Anything else?" she coyly asked. Andy was about to reply with a smart arse proposal, but his courage failed him and he could only shake his head, blushing at the thought that suddenly entered his head. As he made his way through the familiar corridors, the administration offices ghostly quiet at this time of the evening, Andy was pleased that it was Tam Black on duty. They had worked together as divisional detectives and Andy believed that, in his opinion, Tam was a right decent guy. Through the grapevine, he had heard that Tam had some sort of problem with the drink, but that was old news now. Andy considered him to be a hard working detective, dogmatic and tenacious in his enquiries. One of the old school, as Gerry Higgins was fond of saying.

"There's a bad penny, if ever I saw one," boomed a familiar voice.

Andy turned to be greeted by his former Superintendent, Iain Ross, wearing a civilian jacket over his uniform shirt and tie and presumably on his way home. Hand extended, Ross smiled, approaching and addressing Andy like an old pal.

"How are you, son? I'm hearing good things about you at the surveillance squad."

Genuinely delighted to meet his old boss, Andy vigorously shook Ross' hand, pleased to see a trusted and friendly face. "Fine, sir, just popped in to have a word with Tam Black in the CID."

Ross wasn't fooled. He knew enough about his lads comings and goings and was well aware of the strong bond that existed between young Andy Dawson and Gerry Higgins.

"Bad business about your pal Higgins," he began. "I know he's suspended, but it's my intention to pay him a wee visit, maybe in a few days, let him know he's not forgotten, know what I mean?"

"I've just been to see him, boss," Andy admitted. "He's having a hard time of it. There can't be any truth to this allegation, surely?"

Ross ran his hand through his thinning grey hair, slicked back and Brylcreemed in the style of his youth. Slowly, he let out a deep sigh. "Don't put me over a barrel, young Andy, but as far as I'm concerned, the whole thing is an unfortunate accident. The scenes of crime boys, well you'll know how busy they are. They've taken most of the contents of the courtyard away for forensic analysis and I'm confident they will find some sort of explanation for that wee lads death. I've known Gerry Higgins even longer that you have and the man hasn't got it in him to commit ....to do that sort of thing." Ross flinched as he corrected himself, reluctant to use the word murder.

"Were there any witnesses, boss, or did Higgins's neighbour, this lassie Annie Burns see anything?"

"Regretfully no, to both your questions, son and Constable Burns has provided a negative statement to Complaints and Discipline in which she places herself at the opposite side of the wall from where the incident took place. There's nothing further at this time and our hope rests with the forensic boys. The suspension is, I'm sure you'll be aware, obligatory in this kind of investigation, so let's not read anything into it, alright?" Ross didn't think it appropriate to add his thoughts regarding Constable Burns and her statement. Not that he would condone one of his officers telling lies, but he hadn't been happy with the lassie's offhand attitude, her determination to distance herself from her colleague. Not normally by nature a vindictive man, he knew in his heart that he'd not forget that, though hesitated, even in his own mind, to use the word betrayal. Loyalty to ones colleagues was a virtuous quality in which Iain Ross firmly believed. Provided of course, he privately conceded, such loyalty did not interfere with the truth. Andy stood silent, knowing that Ross was struggling with some inner problem, yet not wishing to interrupt the older man's thoughts. Like most of the division, he was aware of Ross' firm Christian beliefs and knew the Superintendent could neither deviate from the truth nor would he offer any hint that might raise false hope. Not even, if it meant lying to save a good man like Gerry Higgins. The best Iain Ross could do was to be as neutral as possible. Andy realised that though Ross wanted to believe in Higgins's innocence, in the absence of anything to contradict the allegation against Higgins, the Superintendent had to abide by the official course of action. Agreeing with it, of course, was something else. Ross, patting Andy's arm, turned to depart, but stopped. "One more thing, young Andy, when you speak with Tam Black, ask him to show you the dead boy's wee notebook. There's a name in it I haven't heard for a while. I'm just a bit curious as to how a wee laddie like Billy Thomson would have a gangster like Franny McEwan's name, in his book. Be seeing you, son," and with a wave of his hand, walked down the stairs.

Andy knocked on the half open door that led into the CID general office. Tam Black, hair centre parted and flicked back, his jacket off and exposing broad, Homer Simpson braces over a crisp white shirt and loud tie, was at the kettle pouring milk into three stained and chipped mugs. His neighbour, a young detective not known to Andy, sat at a desk in the far corner, speaking on the phone. The younger detective seemed to be engaged in a heated discussion.

"Hello, Dawson," greeted Tam, "come to see how real detectives operate or are you working? Still milk only, if my memory serves me?"

Andy, smiling, shook hands with Tam and handed him the packet of biscuits.

Tam grinned and hefting the packet in his broad hand, said "Bribery with digestives. I remember it used to be a half bottle that was the going price, but times have changed, eh?"

Andy wasn't sure if that remark was in reference to Tam's alleged new found sobriety so decided to pass on a response. "Nice to see you, Tam. I'm sorry, I don't know your neighbour?" while indicating the detective on the phone.

Black put his finger to his pursed lips and hushed Andy. "John Deans. He's speaking to a complainer. The guy reported his house got screwed and his television and DVD player stolen. John asked him for serial number details of the property. The guy was that pleased he'd remembered to write them down. Problem is, to ensure that he wouldn't lose them he sellotaped them both to the underside of the television."

Andy, unable to contain himself, laughed out loud, which in turn set off Black. Deans, covering the mouthpiece of the telephone, glared at them both.

"I suppose you'll have heard about Gerry Higgins?"

whispered Black.
Andy nodded, licking his lips dry from the scalding liquid. "To be honest, that's why I'm here. Nothing official, you understand, but Gerry is a pal of mine and with him being suspended, he can't attend at or communicate with anyone from the division." Andy decided it prudent not to mention Ross' intended visit to Gerry Higgins. "Listen, Tam. I don't want you to put you in a spot, or anything. I'm just poking around, trying to pick up anything that I can tell him. Anything that'll make him feel that wee bit better. He's in a bit of a state. I'm sure you can imagine."
Tam Black nodded. Indeed, he not only could imagine, did he not have his own personal experience of something like this? He remembered the night those years back when sent home in disgrace and trying to explain to his wife that a couple of halves of whisky might mean the loss of his job. No income, no mortgage, no house and his pension blown. He still shuddered at how close he'd come to losing it all. Yes, Tam Black knew exactly how Gerry Higgins must be feeling, right now. "You understand it's the rubber heel brigade from headquarters that are dealing with this, don't you?"
Andy nodded, only to aware that any dealings with the Complaints and Discipline crowd tended to leave a stigma, regardless of how insignificant the role an officer was involved in one of their inquiries. The problem was that when an officer was interviewed by the rubber heels, they tended to start on the premise the officer was lying and work their way forward from that point.
Black shrugged his shoulders and continued, "There's not really that much I can tell you, Andy. What we've heard on the jungle drums," as he nodded towards Deans,

"is only what the attending casualty surgeon let slip. It seems apparent that Thomson's head wound is consistent with striking the brick wall. You know what these old back courts are like. It's an old wall, crumbling and in disrepair so the likelihood is that there will be some brick dust in the wound. Door to door enquiries turned up nothing, other than a wee woman that lived on the third floor recalling a youngish male voice on the intercom who asked to be let in the close to visit his uncle, Ally McCoist." Black smirked. "Sounds like wee Billy was a bit of a joker, either that or he's panicked and that's the first name that came to mind. Anyway, the witness buzzed the door open, but that's all that she can really tell us. Needless to say Ally McCoist has a more salubrious place out in millionaire's row in Kilbarchan somewhere, so it seems fair to presume that, given the time frame, it can only have been Thomson she spoke with. The only other thing, that might or might not be evidential, is one of the scenes of crime guys that I know told me there is some interest in an old bottle they found near the body.' Andy's brow furrowed. "What, do they think it was used to club Thomson?"

"I don't know, Andy, I really don't. But I can't see Higgins using anything like that, can you? He's a strong boy is Gerry Higgins. I knew wee Billy Thomson and like most of the yobs round here, he'll take off if there's a warrant out for him. But he couldn't fight a cold. He just didn't have it in him. He certainly wouldn't have tried anything on with Higgins. I mean," Black smiled, "would you?"   Both men laughed. Gerry Higgins reputation as a strong man was local legend. A keen footballer in his playing days, Higgins in defence had been an awesome foe to the opposing centre forwards, but he always played fair, something they both agreed on. The only thing that Tam could add to his knowledge of Billy Thomson was that he'd recently turned up during a search of Angie Bennett's house, a young junkie who lived in Rathlin Street. No, Tam admitted, he didn't know if they'd been an item.

"What about Higgins's neighbour, Annie Burns?" Andy asked.

"Not much I can tell you there. I only know the lassie to see around the office, not to speak with. She was interviewed by the rubber heels and likely had to provide a statement. A word of caution, though Andy. I don't think it would be a good idea to speak to her. I've heard she's very ambitious, hoping to join us in the 'cloth' it's said."

Andy nodded, understanding completely. Any contact he was intending making to Annie Burns would undoubtedly be reported by her to, if not to the rubber heels, then certainly to her sergeant and frankly, Andy had no business anyway, involving himself in what was in reality an ongoing suspicious death inquiry. As did Tam Black, Andy knew that many young, aspiring police officers pursued the dream of the CID, or the 'cloth' as it was known in the job. Involvement in an internal investigation could hamper such ambition. Cards would be marked, was the popular phrase, indicating that an officer's career might unduly suffer, if that officer didn't or wouldn't toe the party line. He realised that Constable Burns would likely tell the truth and nothing but the truth. Which is probably where both he and she would differ, he inwardly sighed.

Andy knew and trusted Gerry Higgins and firmly believed his account of the story. And that, according to

Andy's rules, would have determined what kind of statement Andy would have provided, had he been asked. Not that he considered himself deceitful, more that simply put, he was a man of strong opinion and had his own belief in right and wrong. Andy finished his tea, setting the mug down on Tam's desk. "Tam, I'm very grateful for what you've told me. It's going to be a long wait for the big guy, but hopefully scenes of crime and forensic between them will turn something up. Oh, by the way, I spoke with Mr Ross, just before I came in. He mentioned something about a notebook that was found?" Black turned to a cardboard box and gingerly fetched out a small, blue notebook. "This wee diary along with Thomson's works lying there in the cigar box was found by the guys that broke the news to his granny." Handing the book to Andy, Black indicated the page denoted by the till receipt. "The boss seemed to recognise a name scribbled on that page. Franny McEwan. Mean anything to you, Andy?"

Andy knew exactly who Franny McEwan was. Hadn't he been watching him at Maxie McLean's house, earlier this morning? But rules were rules and one of the strictest rules in surveillance is confidentiality. And that had to be strictly adhered to - always. Andy was a vetted officer, background checked and trusted. More than most, he knew that the police network leaked like a sieve and curiously, detectives were the worst. Andy had known CID colleagues who, when in receipt of information, had boasted to suspects during interview to impress upon them just how much the police knew about the suspect. During one such interview, the suspect realised the information being disclosed by the interviewing officer could have come from one source only. The police later discovered the source floating face down in the River Clyde, her hands tied behind her back and her once pretty face beaten to a pulp. Andy, a young cop at the time, had been part of the peripheral cordon securing the locus for the scenes of crime boys. He'd had the misfortune to be present when the lassie was lifted from the water, a memory that stuck with him for a long time after. He'd learned a harsh lesson, that day. When in doubt, eyes and ears open and mouth firmly shut. Just the same, he felt bad about lying to Tam, particularly after Tam had been so helpful.

"Deansie," he indicated with a thumb over his shoulder to his neighbour, "and I have to deliver this box later tonight, to the rubber heels department, at headquarters. All they'll do with it is use it to prove Thomson was a junkie. Anything in the book any use to a big squad guy like you?" Black joked, his eyebrows raised in question, but nevertheless, his curiosity aroused.

Andy didn't want to seem too eager, but asked if he might copy the page?

"If Father Ross thinks it's important, I might as well check the name in our files, eh?"

Tam Black, a half smile playing about his lips, stared at Andy. Twelve years in the CID had taught him well and he wasn't convinced with Andy's explanation. Black was about to tell him so, when the phone on his desk rang. Turning, his attention now diverted by the insistent ringing, he lifted the receiver.

Andy felt a slight relief at being reprieved and grateful the awkward situation had passed.

"Good evening, Govan CID, DC Black. Can I help you?"

Andy mouthed 'photocopier?' and was rewarded by a

hand pointing to the hallway and to the left, down the corridor.

The civilian support officer, who'd admitted Andy into the station, was copying files when he arrived at the machine. Andy smiled and patiently stood waiting his turn.
"I'll be here a while. Is it just one copy you're after?" she inquired, the faint scent of her perfume floating over him.
"Yes, just the one, but I'm not sure I'd know how to work this thing." His eyes widened as she bent over the machine and saw her skirt tighten across her neat little buttocks. Andy swallowed hard, his breath quickened and felt himself drooling.
"Here, let me do that for you," the woman purred. "What is it you want copied?"
"Just the pages from this part of the book," Andy coughed slightly, his throat suddenly dry as he handed her the notebook, held open at the page indicated by the till receipt. While he watched, the woman took the book, placed it face down and pressed the button. Notebook and copy in hand, he thanked her and walked back to the CID office.
The station officer smiled, aware that she'd teased the big guy. Pity he hadn't chatted longer, she thought. It might have been worth his while.

Andy found Tam still on the phone and gruffly suggesting the caller, if he thought he was hard enough, call in to the office and repeat whatever insult was being bellowed into Black's ear.
Another satisfied customer, Andy grinned. Returning the notebook to the box, he mouthed his farewells to Tam

and Deans. Then, almost as an afterthought, he waited until Black had replaced the receiver in its cradle and asked, "You wouldn't happen to know anything about that wee blonde civvie that works at the front bar, downstairs?"

As Andy drove out from Govan police station, across the city Willie McKay was closing the garden gate behind him and saw that the curtains on the front window were pulled closed. He hesitated briefly, took a deep breath and firmly inserted his key in the door. Home sweet home, He thought.

Chapter 7

Govan, until its merger with Glasgow City in 1912, had been an independent Burgh and rightly proud of its workforce whose shipbuilding skills had dominated the known world. The sandstone Victorian tenements had housed many of the families of the labour force during those hey days, but as the work had declined, so had those illustrious buildings. The demise of the local heavy industries saw the skilled tradesmen and artificers called abroad or drifting to seek work in other industries, to Tyne and Weir where the ships continued to be built, to Australia, the promised land where the 'Ten Pound Passage' emigration scheme would guarantee work, to the construction of the oil pipelines in the Middle East and to the North Sea oilrigs. Redundancy and his partner poverty, creeping in to the community like a thief in the night, had taken their toll of this once proud and industrious Burgh and left it decimated. The new era introduced unemployment, apathy and indifference and the heart of the people had been torn asunder. But always the pubs flourished. Even though the children on occasion went to bed hungry, the man of the house was guaranteed his whisky and his half pint, as was his perceived right. Those left behind, facing mass unemployment and declining economy, had little interest in community spirit, choosing instead to party into oblivion and barricade themselves behind closed doors with their drink and in the passage of time, the introduction of the new sense-debilitating craze, their drugs.

Rathlin Street was like many streets in old Govan. Graffiti on the walls declared loyalty for one or other of Glasgow's two predominant football teams, while further paint spray artwork boasted the name of the local youth gang whose parochial allegiance declared they ruled their two or three street territory. The artwork sometimes included and named some of the more unpopular members of the local constabulary, often hinting at their sexual preferences and doubtful parentage. For the officers so named, it was seen as a back-handed compliment, an indication of their effective policing skills. The discarded rubbish and detritus that lay about the pavements and streets seemed indicative of the local council's lack of commitment to the area and highlighted the corrugated tin sheets that dotted the buildings, covering windows where the occupants had moved or fled the debt collectors. That people strived to continue their lives in such conditions was testament to the resilience of their shipbuilding forefathers or perhaps simply that they had nowhere else to go.

Sitting in 'One-ball' Smith's Audi saloon car, both he and Franny McEwan munched at their chip suppers spread out across their laps, while the radio cassette player belted out a counterfeit copy of Dolly Parton's greatest hits. Franny was bored and had been for most of the two hours they had been there. Conversation had exhausted him, privately comparing two hours cooped up in a car with One-ball as the equivalent to two days solitary at Peterhead.

"Do you think he'll show up, back here Franny?" asked One-ball, mouth full and spraying bits of fish and chips across his steering wheel.

Franny belched and shook his head. "If he does, he's a mug then, because he must know by now that the word is out on him. But Maxie says Thomson's to be captured so that's that, me and you, One-ball. Not to question why and that, know what I mean?"

"No."

"You know, the 'Not to question why, just to do and die.' Get it?"

"Oh, aye," One-ball replied, but was confused and didn't have a clue what Franny was talking about, but he didn't want to seem dense, so decided to keep his curiosity at a minimum and concentrate on the remains of his supper. Besides, he thought, this is easy, sitting here eating chips. Better this than listening to Maxie rambling on all day about Thomson and the bags, whatever that was supposed to mean. One-ball accepted that Franny was more of a confidante to Maxie than he would ever be, so he took the view that what he didn't know, wouldn't hurt him.

"How long have I known you, now One-ball?"

"Eh, let me think. Oh aye, since school I think."

"That can't be right. I'm forty-two and your, what, thirty?"
'"Thirty-one," One-ball corrected him.
"Right, so you're thirty-one then. So we couldn't have been to school, together, could we?" Christ, Franny wondered for the umpteenth time, is he thick or what?
"No, Franny, you're right."
"Was it not at Maxie's fortieth birthday party I met you, at the Pebbles Hydro Hotel?"
"Aye, that sounds about right."
"So we're talking what, eight years?"
A sudden rap on the window startled them both. A boy about ten years old, mop of unruly fair hair blinding him, left eye once blackened whose colour was now fading to a dull yellow, a skin coloured plaster across the bridge of his nose and wearing what appeared to be his older brother's Celtic football top, stood at the cars drivers' window.
One-ball rolled the window down.
The boy jutted out his chin and asked "Can I watch your car for you, mister for a pound?"
Puzzled at the cheek of this wee shite, One-ball looked at Franny then turned to face the boy. "I'm sitting in the car, sonny, so I don't need it looked after, okay?"
"But when happens when you leave your car, mister. It might get scratched, right along this side here. Know what I mean?" the implied threat made, the boy stood warily just out of One-ball's grasp.
Franny burst out laughing. "Here, One-ball, you're being threatened by a midget. And with that mug of his, it looks as though he's already taken a couple of second prizes. Better pay up or the wee bastard will set about you."
One-ball grinned. Give him his due, the wee lad had

some nerve. "Here, take your pound, you wee monkey."
"Hang on, son," Franny leaned across One-ball and indicated for the lad to return. "Do you know Angie Bennett that lives up that close over there?" he asked, pointing to the tenement across the road.
The boy looked to where Franny pointed and nodded his head. "Who, Angie the junkie, aye, I know her, mister."
"Do you know her boyfriend, Billy Thomson?"
"Aye, he's a junkie to. But he's dead."
Franny stiffened and felt a chill run through him.
"Dead? No, that can't be the same Billy Thomson, son. I'm talking about Angie's boyfriend."
The boy's eyes lit up and he smiled, excited now and sensing he knew something these two men didn't, something important, something that might be worth a few bob. "Aye mister, wee Billy. He got killed running away from the coppers this morning. Somewhere up in Govan Road, I heard. Angie's guy, it's in the evening paper. Did you not buy a paper, mister?"
One-ball sat quiet. This was way over his head and instinctively knew it was real bad news, bad news that he'd rather let Franny deal with. Rightly, One-ball guessed that Maxie would not be pleased with this news. Not pleased at all.
Franny gave the boy another pound coin and instructed him to fetch an evening paper, with the promise of a further pound when he returned.
"What will we do, Franny? What will we tell Maxie?" wheezed One-ball.
"Let me think," snapped Franny, swallowing hard. "First thing's first. We'll check the paper and see if it's true. Then we'd better have a word with Angie Bennett."

Angie Bennett hated her life. Wringing her hands, she paced the floor across the faded and stained carpet. She hated being constantly afraid, alarmed at every step on the landing outside and terrified at every knock upon her door. Right now, alone in the darkened flat, her nostrils filled with the musty smell of dampness that pervaded the unheated rooms, she anxiously prayed that the flimsy door with both locks on and an inadequately light sofa couch jammed against it, would hold against yet another forced entry. As she marched back and forwards, she gave some thought to her previous life, the life before her descent into this hellhole. Her family, parents who loved her, her younger sister who argued with her constantly, but so wanted to be like Angie. The once driven ambition and talent that was good enough to win her a scholarship at the prestigious Glasgow School of Art, but now all gone and wasted. Parent's who had encouraged, helped, sympathised, wept for her and forgiven her, time after time, then finally disowned her; the final straw being the theft of her grandmother's wedding ring. A cheap piece, not even enough gold in it to buy Angie one hit. Her sister, upset and deceived by Angie, whom she loved. The money and bankcards didn't matter, her sister had screamed at her, but the laptop computer contained all her sister's course work, everything she'd done and worked for to gain the Higher grades she needed for university. All the work stored in the laptop hard drive and now all gone for a lousy fifty quid. She shuddered, shamed and sickened by the memory, but it wasn't just the betrayal of her family that was her main worry now. It was the two men in the red car, sitting watching her window and speaking to that wee laddie who lived further down the street. She watched them from behind the torn and dirty curtain, her body convulsing and hurting, desperately needing a fix. Her whole life now revolved about her heroin habit. Smack was her best friend, her only friend. Smack and her Billy that loved her and who was late, so very late in bringing her the promised fix. Angie shivered and whispered to herself "Where are you, Billy?" Her arms wrapped round her skinny frame, she silently pleaded, where the fuck are you!

The boy returned and passed Franny the *'Glasgow News'*, though ensuring his reward was handed to him before he released the paper. Idly, Franny saw it had already been read and guessed the kid's father would be short of his paper that night. Smart kid Franny mused, probably grow up to be a lawyer. Quickly he scanned the newspaper, finally finding the report on William Thomson's death on page nine. One-ball watched Franny's face slowly turn chalk white. Engrossed, neither man noticed the figure at the driver's door. At the tap on the window, One-ball was about to shout at the boy to fuck off, when he realised the boy was now wearing black serge trousers over which hung a heavy stomach with a thick leather belt about the waist, adorned with a metal handled baton, handcuffs and a radio set. Constable Dougie Simpson, neatly trimmed moustache and bleary eyed, the result of too many late nights propping up the bar at the bowling club, squatted down and indicated for One-ball to roll the window down. Hat tipped back and hands on the doorsill, Dougie smiled at the two men. "Hello there, gentlemen. Strangers to the area are we?"

Caught off balance, One-ball was about to tell this fat, nosey bastard it was none of his business, when he felt an almost indiscernible nudge on his left leg.

Franny leaned over, a warning hand gripping at One-ball's leg and replied, "We were just about to drive off, officer. No trouble, is there?'

"Oh, no," Dougie shook his head, "though I'm just a bit curious, sir. You've been sitting here for quite a while now. Do either of you gentlemen have business here?"

One-ball was about to protest he wouldn't normally be seen dead in this shite-hole, but Franny beat him to the response. "We were looking for a pal of ours and thought he lived in this street. A wee re-union." He added and thought Christ! Where did I pull that one from?

"Perhaps if you tell me your friends name, I might be able to assist you', Dougie offered.

Now Franny McEwan had been caught like that once before, when he'd had a pull from the cops. He remembered how difficult it had been to pull a name out of the air. But this time he was practised and prepared for just this scenario and had chosen the name of a former footballer and inwardly pleased he was ready for just such an occasion. "Joe McBride."

"Like the footballer?"

Smart-arse, thought Franny,

"Aye, like the footballer."

"Can't say I know the name. But while I'm here, routine you understand. It is your car, sir?" Dougie inclined his head to stare at One-ball.

Up to this point, One-ball was content as usual to let Franny do the talking and was rudely taken aback by the shift in conversation. He stammered a reply, "Aye, aye it is." Then more aggressively, "what's it got to fucking do with you?"

Franny realised this was getting out of hand and discreetly placed his right hand over One-ball's left hand, praying his partner would understand and keep calm. Added to that, Franny had also spotted the movement at the back of the car and realised the nosey cop wasn't alone, as a second uniformed figure loomed out of the now fading light. Constable Bill Nixon hadn't been in the police as long as Dougie, but that hadn't stopped the big guy from running up an impressive list of assault complaints against him, usually attributed to the shovels at the end of his arms, where normal people had hands. Mild mannered by nature, his physical strength overshadowed his intellect.

Dougie was swiftly aware of Bill's presence as an arm reached past his head and seized the unfortunate One-ball by the hair. "You'll mind and keep a civil tongue in your head," growled Bill, followed by a polite "Sir," just like he'd been trained to say and pleased he'd remembered. Franny was shocked, but not as shocked as One-ball who squirmed in the big cop's grasp.

"Now let the man go, Bill," chided Dougie, "there's a good lad," while inwardly shaking his head at the calibre of officer being recruited these days. Worse still, Dougie reflected, Bill was sober.

With an obvious reluctance, Bill released his grip then slowly wiped his hand on his trouser leg, round about the lower calf and without bending, Dougie noticed with a sigh. Turning once again to the open window, he smiled softly.

"As I was saying gentlemen and just for the record. Would you oblige me with your names, please? Oh, and," he added, almost as an afterthought, "maybe some identification, like bank cards, just so that we get the spelling right, eh?"

Franny, eyes wide and mouth ajar, quickly appreciated this scruffy bugger was no fool. No chance of using a bum name. Better to give him what he wants and get to fuck out of town, as big John Wayne would say.

One-ball vigorously rubbing his head, cleared the loose hair from his hand and handed Dougie both his and Franny's bankcards.

'Mr Smith. According to my check on our computer, this car is registered to a Mrs Mary Smith. Now that wouldn't be you hiding under all that hair, would it?'

"No," One-ball admitted through gritted teeth, "that's my auntie. It's a disability car. I take her for her shopping."

Dougie patiently filled in his notebook. "And yourself, Mr McEwan, how would you describe your current occupation, sir?"

"Entrepreneur."

"And would that be spelled T - H - U - G, sir?"

Franny shook with rage. Time to hit back, he decided. "You think you're funny, pal. I intend to make a complaint about you!"

"Shall I accompany you to the office and perhaps we can speak with the Inspector there, sir?" asked Dougie politely, accepting the challenge with his customary smile.

Franny knew when to accept defeat. This was getting them nowhere. He sighed with frustration. "Look officer we're just wanting to get away home. We've not done anything wrong. Can we leave now? Please?"

Dougie stared at both men then, as if making a momentous decision, snapped closed his notebook and handed back the bank cards. "By all means, sir,

mind how you go."   Dougie
and Bill watched the car drive off. It wasn't much of a result, admitted Dougie to himself, but those two jokers were without doubt here to give someone grief. "Ah, well," he thought, "deterrent is as valuable as detection." Turning, his peripheral vision caught movement at a first floor window, where that young lassie Angela Bennett stayed. His brow furrowed, his thoughts concentrating on a recent divisional intelligence bulletin he'd read.
No fool, Dougie Simpson recalled the report referred to a drugs raid at the house occupied by Bennett. There had, he was sure, been mention of a boyfriend. Of course, he remembered now, the boy that died today, the lad who'd been chased by Gerry Higgins. Now, what was his name, again? He was certain by the time he got back to the office, the name would come back to him. Maybe not connected with the two jokers in the car but instinct, the coppers constant and unseen companion, was tapping on his shoulder.

Later back at the office, Dougie Simpson procured two cups of tea and, with infinite patience, took time to instruct Bill Nixon in the completion of a intelligence form. He watched as the big man laboriously filled in the numbered boxes with information, the pen lost in the folds of his huge hand. As he stared at the strands of greasy hair caught between the fingers of the big man's right hand, he idly thought about the encounter with the two lowlifes in the car. He guessed that Franny McEwan had mistaken Simpson's laid back manner as relaxed and casual, but when it came to noting details, old habits die-hard. He chuckled to himself. Life in the old dog yet. Carefully, he read over and checked Bill's work and nodded his approval, pleased the big man was picking up the paperwork side of the job, albeit slowly. Trick now was to get him to work his brain and body in unison. He turned his wrist and looked at his watch. With a sigh he realised that at the rate Bill was scribing, it was unlikely Dougie would make the last round at the bowling club.

Through the night, the civilian employee tasked to deal with the divisional internal mail ensured the short, but concise report was dispatched and sent winging its way to the Criminal Intelligence department at police headquarters.

Chapter 8

Willie MacKay removed his damp overcoat and absentmindedly hung it over the radiator in the hallway behind the front door. Taking off his shoes he opened the closet door and placed them beside the neatly racked footwear, both his and Margaret's side by side on the shelf, the laces meticulously placed inside each shoe. Shaking his head and in a childish act of defiance, he smiled to himself as he placed his shoes upside down and with the laces trailing on the shelf. He could hear his wife in the kitchen banging pots, obviously aware he was now home and making an audible warning to him that she was busy and didn't wish to be interrupted. Willie strode into the front room. The newly buffed varnished floorboards sparkled and the rug lay centrally placed in front of the gleaming fireplace, its hearth lying cold and vacant and adding a visible reminder to the coldness of the room. Cushions on the settee, puffed up like bladder fish, dared him to sit down on the pristine covers. He glanced round at the familiar objects. Not an ornament or detail was out of place. Loosening his tie, he undid the top button of his shirt and threw the evening newspaper onto the settee. Scratching his head, he moved to the kitchen door and attempted a smile. "Hello, there, something smells good," he greeted her, his voice full of forced cheerfulness. Margaret stood at the sink with her back to him, her dressing robe wrapped about her thin body. She didn't turn around, but snapped, "I'm busy."

Willie closed his eyes and swayed slightly, overcome by an inexplicable sense of rage. I won't be provoked, he vowed. Not tonight. "How was your day?" he softly inquired as he tried to keep his voice even.

Margaret laid her hands on the kitchen worktop. Under the loose fitting robe, he saw her body tense. She jerked her head up and stared through the window into the darkness. Still she did not turn to face him, but snarled over her shoulder, her voice tinny and whining. "The same as every bloody day, the same as yesterday, the same as the day before that and the day before that."

Willie drew breath, cupped his chin in his right hand and leaned his left shoulder against the doorframe. "This can't go on. I'd like us to sit down tonight, Margaret, and maybe have a wee chat?" he softly urged.

"We've had chats or don't you remember? According to you, I'm going through the menopause. It's my fault." Her body shook and she began wailing.

He moved closer, his hands reaching towards her. A vain attempt to soothe and protect her from the temper that threatened to engulfed them both.

She pushed him away. "Don't touch me!" she screamed at him, her fists raised protectively as though expecting him to strike her.

A floorboard from above squeaked. Mrs Cairns, he rightly presumed, hearing every damned word. He knew his presence would only provoke Margaret more and turned to leave. She spun to face him, a sneer upon her tear-stained face.

"That's right. Walk away. Always the big man, Willie MacKay! Can't face up to life. Stuck in your dead end job. Blaming me for not having kids! Blaming me for not having a life! Blaming me for your failure!"

He faced her, his hands outstretched, palms upwards, beseeching her forgiveness for wrongs of which he had no knowledge. "Margaret, that's not true! We've been...."

Screeching now, she was crying and spitting mad, her eyes wide with loathing and scorn.

"...happy for nearly fifteen years. It's just a phase..."

She was coming for him, her fists raised and clenched

"....we're going through, like other couples," he pleaded, backing into the front room, hands rising to protect his face from the expected onslaught.

Then, as though a switch had been thrown, she stopped, stood still, mouth open and stared at him. The seconds slowly passed. Margaret blinked her eyes in surprise.

"You're frightened of me?" she whispered, her voice now barely audible.

Willie stared at his wife, numbed by her sudden change in tactic. Her clothing a complete contradiction to the neat and tidy home she kept. He was shocked at her appearance. Margaret Devlin. Once a happy and pretty blonde, her hair now lank and unkempt, the dark, untreated roots revealing her natural auburn locks, her face pale and pinched, her lips thin and trembling with hate.... for him. The dressing robe had fallen open. He saw her stained nightdress underneath, encompassing her once firm body, the body Willie had once and still longed to hold, to comfort her and tell her that it was alright. That thing's would get better. He made to reach for her and tried to speak, to tell her he loved her, but his throat was tight, his eyes moist. No sound came.

Margaret relaxed as a smile edged its way round her mouth. "Big hard man, going to cry?" she sniggered.

He clenched his fists. The taunt seemed to jerk Willie MacKay into reality. This wasn't his fault. He'd done nothing wrong! The rage returned, but Willie backed off, afraid of himself, what he might become, that he'd lose it. Afraid he'd hit her, his wife. Still she goaded him, her language vile and offensive. In the midst of the tirade and unable to take his eyes from her, Willie MacKay knew her screams and shouts would be heard by their neighbours, above and through the wall, knew that if he didn't end it now, the police, his colleagues, would be summoned. Questions would be asked, reports filed. At last, he found his voice, but was unable to stop it quivering with emotion. "I'm leaving, I've had enough," he finally announced.

Margaret stopped, gawked at him and laughed, a raucous laugh without humour. "You're leaving me? Running away? Go, you pathetic excuse for a man. Get out! Get out!" she screamed and advanced towards him, her clenched fists now by her side.

He turned and walked away, ignoring her taunts and jibes. But Willie had already retrieved his coat from the hallway, shoes slipped on, the laces undone, and was now at the front door.

"And don't ever come back!" she screamed at the top of her voice, "Do you hear me, Willie McKay! Don't ever come back!"

The abuse followed Willie through the open door, but he didn't look back. Hastily, his head bent low, he stumbled down the path, past his immobile car, ignoring the curious faces at the lit windows and into the rain filled night.

Maxie McLean, his brow furrowed and eyes narrowed, stared malevolently at Franny McEwan.
One-ball stood at the open lounge door, hands tightly clasped in front of him, the knuckles showing white. "I do not like the way this is going," he nervously thought to himself.
"He's dead?" Maxie growled, his beady eyes set upon Franny McEwan's now profusely sweating face. "How the fuck can he be dead?" he asked, with a voice full of venom.
"According to the newspaper, Maxie..."
"Fuck the newspaper!" he screamed, then slowly, releasing his breath, continued, "Do realise what this means? Do you know what you've done?"
Franny put his hands up, as if in a vain attempt to deflect Maxie's anger. "Wait a minute, Maxie, all I did was....."
"You found him," Maxie pointedly reminded him, "he was your responsibility. You told me, no, you *PROMISED* me on your life, remember? Your fucking life Franny! You promised that Billy Thomson could be trusted and now he's fucking *DEAD*!' Maxie screeched. The emphasis on his life was not lost on the now wilting Franny. He could feel a thin rivulet of sweat trickle down his spine. Crazily, his mind wandered. Maybe it was about time he admitted to a size twenty collar and

chucked out all those size eighteen's?

Maxie sat down, the soft black leather of the armchair sighing as it enveloped him in its folds. He shook his head and ignored his two lieutenants. With his right forefinger, he drummed on the arm of the chair. "Right, let me think. What do we know? Did you speak to Thomson's bird, eh, what's her name again?"

Franny swallowed hard, his mouth suddenly dry, his voice hoarse. "Angie. Angie Bennett. No, we were outside her close, watching for Billy, but we got a tug from the cops."

Maxie stared in disbelief at Franny and his mouth involuntarily dropped open. Then slowly, he lowered his head into his hands. Exhaling noisily, he shook his head and muttered, "This gets worse, by the minute. You got a pull from the police?"

"Well, it wasn't really a pull, just some fat cop and his pal asking our names," replied Franny, desperate to reassure Maxie the incident had no bearing on their presence in Govan.

But Maxie wasn't convinced. "Tell me you didn't give him your real names. Please! At least, tell me that!"

Franny, a soft sheen of sweat covering his bald head, stared at his feet then raised his head to look Maxie in the eye. Better get this over with, he thought. As soon as possible so I can get to fuck out of here. Hopefully with my balls where they should be.

"We gave him our real names Maxie, we'd no choice. The pig was no mug. He asked to see our bank cards."

Maxie groaned and, feeling suddenly deflated, sat back in the armchair. He could feel that control of this whole operation was slipping away from him. He had to get it back on track, but the death of that wee junkie was going to cause him some grief, some really bad grief. But the bags? The bags would have to wait, at least for the moment. He'd get them back, of that he was assuredly certain. But in the meantime he'd customers and commitments that wouldn't wait and promises to keep. No, he couldn't afford a fuck-up, not if he was to maintain his name and reputation and, with the vultures sitting in the wings, Maxie knew that any hiccup would have his rivals biting at the edges of his organisation. In his game, any sign of weakness was akin to admitting vulnerability and that, he knew from painful experience, would eventually lead to a direct challenge to his supremacy of the criminal underworld in the city. The hint of an idea slowly formed in his mind, something daring and exciting. Like the old times. Like the old Maxie McLean, hard man. Man of action. Maxie smiled to himself. But this budding idea, this venture would need to be tight, for now, just him and Franny. One-ball would be told in time, when it was too late to shout his mouth off and give the game away. He relaxed and sat back in the chair, the tension easing from his body. Plans would have to be made, timings worked out. Alibi's arranged, though that wouldn't be difficult, for how many people in this great city owed Maxie McLean a favour? Nodding to himself, his eyes darting back and forth, but seeing nothing, his mind raced. Yes! This would work. All it took was a little planning and a big set of balls and wasn't he the man for the job? Calm now, almost sociable, he turned and faced One-ball who still hovered nervously by the door, like a dog awaiting his master's pleasure. "One-ball, do me a favour son and nip out to the off-licence down the road. Box of cigars, eh? For your old pal," he asked, accompanying the request by

a smile and a friendly wink of his eye.
The sudden switch from murderous Maxie to sweetness and light confused Franny.
One-ball stared and, half suspecting this to be one of Maxie's tricks, nodded and backed into the hallway, leaving the door slightly ajar. So confused was he that he didn't notice Lena, standing in the shadow with tea tray in hand.
One-ball safely gone, Maxie turned to Franny and indicated he should have a seat. Then leaning forward and tapping the now bemused Franny on the knee, he whispered in a conspiratorial voice, "Right. Here's what we do."

Jean MacDonald answered the phone at the second ring, glancing at the clock and hoping the sound didn't rouse the children from their beds. The sound of falling rain in the background at first confused her, then the voice, choking with a heavy cold or, she wondered in surprise, emotion?
"Hello, Jean, is Archie there?"
"Oh, it's yourself Willie," she replied, unconsciously tidying her hair with her left hand,
"Hold on, Willie. Archie!" he heard her shout, "The phone."
As her husband reached for the receiver, his eyes registering curiosity, she mouthed the name, Willie MacKay.
Archie nodded in understanding. "Hello, Willie, what can I do you for?" the time honoured joke. He heard the sharp intake of breath and instinct told him that

something was definitely amiss, that Willie was gathering himself to speak. "Willie?" he asked again, "You still there, bud?" The silence was punctuated by the backdrop sound of the rain, then falteringly, his friend's voice, quiet and hesitant.
"Wee bit of a problem. You wouldn't be able to put me up for the night, by any chance? Just the one night, it's only that...."
"Look," Archie interrupted, shocked and suspecting that Willie was close to tears, "tell me when you get here. Do you want picked up?"
"No, no," firmer now, "you're all right, I'll jump a taxi. You're sure Jean won't mind, then?"
'You know she won't mind, just get yourself here, mate."
As Archie replaced the receiver, he turned to find Jean anxiously hovering at his back. "What'd you think?" he asked, his brow furrowed and eyes narrowed.
Jean sat down, her arm instinctively wrapping itself around her husbands neck as her fingers ruffled his hair, recognising the by now familiar tiredness of the early stages of her latest pregnancy. Her face hardened. She gently drew Archie's head to her bosom as she tersely replied in her soft Irish brogue, "I think that wife of his has finally driven him out. I'm telling you Archie MacDonald, she should be seeing a doctor. I'll bet we don't know the half of it. Remember the last time we visited them?"
Archie nodded his head, or as best he could with an earful of Jean thrust against it. He recalled the tension he and Jean experienced every time one of their boisterous toddlers slipped his grasp, a nervous Margaret MacKay ushering the child back to its parents, lest one of her precious ornaments be touched or, heaven forbid, broken.

Willie had tried to lighten the atmosphere, but it was evident Margaret neither wanted nor encouraged visitors. Not even a cup of tea offered. Archie could almost feel his pal's embarrassment. When they left, Margaret hadn't the courtesy to even see them to the door. Cold hearted bitch!   "Aye," he quietly replied, "I do remember. But what puzzled me was the house was immaculate, but she looked so slovenly, like she hadn't even bathed."

Jean MacDonald stroked her man's wispy hair. Pretty, with long dark locks and deep brown eyes, she was typical of many of the young women who had travelled over from their native Donegal to seek nursing training in one of the large, mainland hospitals. It was Jean's good fortune or misfortune, dependent on how she recalled those times, that she landed at the Glasgow Royal Infirmary where three years of enduring low wages, long hours and poor working conditions had qualified her in most aspects of human suffering. The social side of those formative years, of which some were evenings spent at the 'Savoy Club' dancing hall in Sauchiehall Street's, had introduced her to a then shy, young, probationary policeman. Nine years and three children later, Jean's once svelte like figure had rounded out a bit and though she'd lost her country-girl naivety, she still retained her natural Irish charm and hospitality. Proud of her husband and children and fiercely protective of all four, she was happy and content with her life. Admittedly, things could be tight financially, but they'd get by, for hadn't they always she reflected, her natural optimism as usual overcoming her husbands' Calvinistic background. This current pregnancy hadn't been planned, but her strict Catholic upbringing accepted that if it were God's wish, then the child would be loved, just as his or her brothers and sister already were.

Archie switched off the television and attempted some sort of semblance in the front room, tidying and stacking toys, while Jean went into the kitchen to prepare sandwiches, presuming that Willie might be hungry.

As she worked she thought about Margaret MacKay. There weren't many people that Jean had met whom she didn't take to, but she didn't like Margaret McKay from the outset and never had. She'd always felt there was something odd about Margaret, something Jean couldn't quite put her finger on. Certainly, Margaret had never offered friendship, nothing other than a coldly polite relationship founded on their husband's friendship and, Jean had to admit, she'd always been courteous, though formally so, in their initial brief meetings. On more than one occasion, Jean had suggested shopping trips, nights out, cinema trips, anything to progress their acquaintance, but all offers had been civilly rebuffed. Jean finally gave up and accepted what she had always suspected. Margaret didn't like her, though why, Jean didn't know, but Margaret MacKay clearly didn't envision herself socialising with the Irish wife of her husband's friend. It had briefly occurred to Jean that Margaret might have been prejudiced by Jean's overt Catholicism, but Archie had assured her that neither Willie nor Margaret were particularly religious. In the end, Jean simply gave up trying and accepted Margaret MacKay was not for forming friendship.

But the last disastrous visit to Willie and Margaret had been a real eye-opener for Jean, who found it difficult to associate the well-ordered, sterile house to the sad, dishevelled woman Margaret had become. A twelve

weeks secondment during her nursing training to a psychiatric ward did not qualify Jean as any kind of expert, yet she suspected Margaret to be in poor mental health and definitely in need of some form of counselling. Either that, she smiled to herself, or a good sound beating with a stout stick, such as was offered to Maureen O'Hara by John Wayne, in *'The Quiet Man'*. The rattling noise of an overworked diesel engine signalled the arrival of the hackney cab. Archie moved to open the door. Jean, catching his arm to restrain him, urgently whispered her advice. "Let him talk, don't badger him, okay?"
Archie stared at his wife, realising the wisdom of her advice and nodded his understanding of her logic. Turning, he smiled in greeting as Willie, head bowed and with his hands tucked into his pockets, walked up the narrow path.

Willie sat on the settee, a mug of tea in his hand; Archie in the armchair, Jean huddled on the armrest beside him, his hand on her knee, her arm flung about his shoulder. "Are you sure you want me here?" she asked again, hopeful that Willie would agree she could stay and not reveal his soul to just her husband, whose sympathy and counselling would likely involve the bottle of whisky under the kitchen sink and the poor man would be no better off. Willie smiled and, to her relief, nodded his consent. Wrapping both hands round the mug, he ignored the plate of sandwiches that lay untouched on the small table in front of him. Hesitantly at first, he apologised again for imposing himself at this late hour upon his friends, only to have him hushed quiet by Jean, who reminded him that was what friends were for. He nodded his grateful thanks, averting his eyes lest Jean see the tears of shame that lay there, threatening to overflow at her simple kindness. A silence descended upon the three. Willie, too choked to speak, Archie, hushed quiet by his wife's pinching fingers on his arm and Jean, who knew the distraught man needed time to gather his thoughts and would tell them what they needed to know, but only in his own, good time. Then Willie talked. He began shyly, almost apologetically and then as though warming to his story related his first meeting with Margaret Devlin, the young and pretty blonde shop assistant, recently returned to Glasgow from living several years in London. He, flushed with excitement at having just been appointed to the CID and seeking new shoes to go with his two new suits, eager to face the fresh challenge and keen to share his good fortune with someone else. Their first date, he recounted, a meal in a pizza restaurant in the city centre, where each discovered that neither had any family, he an orphan raised by a now deceased maiden aunt and living in the inherited, two bed-roomed lower cottage flat, while she laughingly described herself as a stray waif, having gone to London to seek fame and fortune, returning home to Glasgow after discovering that the influx of a large immigrant population prepared to work for low wages, had cornered the unskilled labour market and consequently driven the price of available flats beyond her reach. Two lonely people finding each other in a city of a million, he with some police friends and Margaret with a few friends from the shop. It was her idea to pool their resources she had called it and get married. "A whirlwind courtship", Margaret had laughingly called it. Following a brief ceremony at Martha Street registry

office, a wedding breakfast in the back lounge of a local pub and a lazy week in Lanzarotte, they settled in Willie's bachelor flat in Kings Park in the south side of Glasgow, agreeing it would serve their purpose till until such times they needed a larger place, the unspoken pact they would move when children began to arrive.
But children never did arrive. Within a few months, Willie continued, Margaret had given up her job, claiming the manager bullied her, but adamant that Willie wasn't to confront him on the issue. Willie argued, but gave in, as he would continue to do throughout their marriage. He and Margaret, she persuaded him, would live off Willie's wage while she took on the duties of housewife, in preparation for motherhood. But of course that didn't happen. The quarrels began a few months later. The slightest thing seemed to set Margaret off, her temper flaring at any perceived slight. On one occasion, when he raised the issue of having their own children, it provoked a fortnights silence and, through time, Willie learned to drop the subject altogether.
Realising that Willie was being as open and frank as he could be, Jean took the opportunity and softly asked the question that had niggled at her, for so long.
No, Willie frowned at Jean's interruption, as far as he knew there was no physical problem that prevented them having children though, he admitted with a wry smile, Margaret wasn't one to discuss her health, not even with him. Oddly enough, he added, neither of them, as far as he recalled, ever had any real need to visit their GP. Willie paused, placing his now empty mug on the small coffee table. With a sigh, he leaned forward and wringing his hands, continued his narrative. The shopping wouldn't be done unless Willie accompanied her. Any

time he left the house, he had to account for his time away from her, almost minute-by-minute. They had a car, certainly, but Margaret refused to learn to drive. The inducement of freedom simply didn't interest her. Margaret demonstrated an almost territorial attitude to her home and her jealous possessiveness became part of his life. And still he didn't quibble, hoping that one day things would improve. Margaret's behaviour grew ever more erratic and one by one, their few friends and acquaintances drifted away.

Embarrassed, Archie and Jean couldn't look at Willie, though he didn't seem to include them as having 'drifted away'.

Self-consciously, he told them of his tentative research in Margaret's magazines about the menopause and her reaction when he suggested that the change of life might be causing her mood swings.

Jean smiled, thinking that the less men know about women's bodies, the more they lump all their fear and anxieties into that one word - hormones.

Margaret, Willie continued, kept the house spick and span, nothing ever out of place. He was astute enough to know that her obsessive tidying of the house was more compulsion than good housekeeping, but didn't really see it as an issue worthy of psychiatric help, accepting it was just her way. "I sometimes felt," he supposed, 'that she was trying to prove something, something that she needed to show me ....' he never finished the sentence. Choking back a moan, Willie sat back, his eyes filling with tears. Jean lightly slapped her husbands shoulder and urged Archie from the chair.

"Archie, make Willie another cup of tea, there's a good fella. I'll just fetch some blankets and a pillow. And you," she addressed her guest in her best nursing, no-nonsense voice, 'are staying here as long as you want.' Then she smiled. 'And that, Willie McKay, is because you do have friends' and leaned across the top of him to lay a gentle kiss on his forehead.

Later that night, or more accurately during the early hours of the morning, lying awake on his back on the MacDonald's couch-bed in their front room, Willie couldn't believe that he, a grown man, had lost it in front of his friends like that. Bloody hell, I was crying like a bairn. Still, he frowned, he was sure that neither Archie nor Jean would ever bring his loss of composure to anyone. No, they just weren't the type. It didn't stop him being embarrassed, though. With a sigh he resolved that he'd go to work and after his shift, he would go home and settle the issue of his marriage for good. He loved Margaret, but he now accepted that she was destroying him. Weariness overtook him, but not before he made his decision. This time he was out forever.

Baljinder Patel or simply Bal to his workmates, liked the nightshift. Four straight nights left him three days off to work in the family corner shop and those three days wages he smiled, were all money in the bank towards a house for him and Leila. Their own place, something they'd longed for since their marriage two years previously. Then, his mind racing ahead to the future, perhaps start a family. The through the night bus service from George Square in the heart of Glasgow to the suburbs of Pollok was usually quiet at this time of the week, though at the weekend Bal knew the drunks could be a right handful. Fortunately, in response to a vigorous public safety campaign, the police had recently taken an interest in trouble on the buses. Thanks to a concerned company boss who looked after her employees, Bal in his protected cab wasn't at any real physical risk from the more aggressive bampots that travelled this route, though the screen didn't protect him from the racial insults that occasionally flew his way. Philosophically, he accepted that most of these slurs came from a real minority who'd have shouted abuse anyway, regardless of whether he was black, white, pink or a deep shade of purple, he thought, grinning to himself. As long as they couldn't break through the screen Bal could handle it and the shift allowance wasn't to be sneered at either. He glanced at the microphone, swinging from its curly cord above his head. The union had insisted that single manned buses be equipped with two-way radios, which was comforting to know that if there was a skirmish on his bus, Bal could sit happily in his cab and await the police to deal with the troublemakers. On more than one occasion, he had been only too pleased to have this vital lifeline.

Midnight gone and with the pubs closed, the night was quiet. Driving his bus westwards along Clyde Street towards the Jamaica Street Bridge, he hummed tunelessly to the latest Robbie Williams release. Bal liked the quiet of the city, staring at the patterns the moonlight made, bouncing off the darkened windows of the buildings on his right, while the lights shining from the buildings on the far side of the river reflected in the waters of the River Clyde that flowed between them. Glancing in his interior mirror, the few occupied seats included an old man, much the worse for drink, treating his fellow passengers to a Glasgow accented rendition of Frank Sinatra's '*My Way*'. Bal cruised slowly to a halt at a red traffic sign, then flicked the indicator switch that activated the yellow light to indicate he intended turning left and south over the bridge.

A young girl, short skirt, high boots and bleach blonde hair flowing behind her sprinted towards the bus, waving her arm. Bal smiled and pressed the button, causing the folding doors to gently hiss open. The breathless girl, face flushed from exertion and not more than eighteen he thought, flashed him a grateful smile and fumbled in her bag for change for the ticket machine. The light turned to green.

"Hold on hen," warned Bal, accelerating the bus slowly through the light and left onto the wide expanse of the bridge.

The girl reached for the metal rail to steady herself and dropped her bag and stooped to recover it.

At that point Bal saw the figure halfway along the bridge, on the other side of the road. Bal suddenly stood on his brakes, causing a muffled scream from the crouching girl, who tumbled cursing to the floor amid shouts of panic from his rear passengers. Hand trembling, he reached for the radio mike, hanging above his head. When asked later, though he couldn't explain why, all he could state was he instinctively knew there was something wrong. According to Bal`s subsequent report to the police, the figure with hair billowing in the breeze and calf length coat flapping open, climbed the parapet of the bridge and simply clambered over the wall, then fell from his sight.

Constable Charlie Ferguson's first nightshift week as a probationary police officer had showed little promise, so far. A few amiable drunks moved on and three cars with windows broken and items stolen had been his total experience to date. This, his third night out with Sergeant Jarvie had begun well, racing to a suspect break-in to a clothes shop in Argyle Street, only to discover the staff struggling with the metal shutters at the rear window, but now this. The call had been police coded, a bus driver requiring assistance. Charlie, dry mouth and sweaty palms, had psyched himself up for a bit of bother as the sergeant flipped the blue light on and sped to the scene. At their arrival, the sergeant had instructed Charlie to calm the noisy and cursing girl down while he took the bus driver off to one side. Now this wee slapper was giving Charlie grief so, keeping his cool, he promised he'd try to ensure she'd get home some time tonight. But only, he firmly told her, if she stopped using the 'F' word and shut up. He could see the uniformed bus driver, standing with sergeant Jarvie, was obviously upset and it didn't help any that this wee stop-out continued to moan the face off Charlie, pleading to get home before her dad found out she wasn't baby-sitting, the lie she'd obviously fed him. Quietly but steadily, he ushered the girl back into the warmth of the now stationary bus, the remaining passengers glued to the windows, desperate for some exciting story to relate to their family and friends later. Charlie thought someone was playing a radio, for he was almost certain he'd heard Frank Sinatra singing. Shrugging his shoulders, he turned towards the bridge. His supervisor, Sergeant Gordon Jarvie stood by the bridge parapet, trying to establish exactly what the bus driver Baljinder Patel had seen to cause him to have officers attend in such a hurry. Jarvie was in no doubt that Mr Patel, by now excitedly waving his arms about and breathlessly gasping out his story, had seen someone going over the edge and into the water. Zipping his fluorescent jacket up tight against the cold, Jarvie removed his cap and run his fingers through his shock of white hair. Experience had taught him that witnesses tended to relax better when dealing with a face, rather than an authoritive hat and uniform. Placing his hand on Mr Patel's shoulder, Jarvie smiled at him. "Now I know you've had a shock, Mr Patel, but I'd like to go over this just one more time," he encouraged, "Just for my benefit so that I haven't missed anything out." Five minutes later and now satisfied that he had obtained at least a summary of the incident, Jarvie guided Bal into the rear seat of the Panda, its blue light and yellow flashing indicators casting a ghostly hue as Charlie joined his supervisor at the bridge just as the fire service and another marked police vehicle arrived.

"What we got, Sarge?"

Glaring at his young colleague, Jarvie tightened his mouth and thought that his young protégé, barely returned from probationary training and already he thought he was an old sweat. Taking Charlie aside, Jarvie explained in simple terms, "Fetch the big torch from the car. Seems we might have a jumper, but it's to dark to see anything definite."

Charlie, excited now by the prospect of a real live incident, hurried to the car and returned with the torch. As he made to reach up and lean over the bridge, Jarvie took hold of the rear of his stab-proof vest and eased him back.

"Look at the surface, Charlie. When they built this bridge in days gone by, what kind of stone did they use?"
Charlie was puzzled, narrowing his eyes in concentration, not wishing to miss anything and look foolish. "Eh, shiny stone?"
Jarvie whistled air through his dentures and knew he'd a long way to go with this one. The lights were on, he decided, but there was nobody home. He tried again. "And what do we get off shiny surfaces?"
Charlie furrowed his brow and looked sheepish. "Will I try for the CID to do a fingerprints examination, Sarge?"
"Good idea, constable and while you're at it, fetch your waterproof coat to place over this spot, just in case the rain comes on. Oh, and Charlie," deciding a little constructive advice might not go amiss, "remember that a pause for thought is always worthwhile."
Charlie nodded his understanding and again hurried away.
Jarvie moved further down the parapet then leaned over, torch in hand. The driver had believed the person, a woman he was sure, had jumped or rather rolled over the parapet, right above the massive buttress supporting and almost in the centre of the bridge. Jarvie played the torch light down in a line directly below where Charlie had placed his coat, but stopped where the underside of the bridge met with the buttress. His wife was forever telling him that he needed glasses, that when he was reading his arms would only stretch so far, but he kept postponing the need, arguing it was just tiredness after a hard days work. He didn't want to admit that vanity was the real reason. However, he didn't need glasses, even in the poor light and at night, to show him that a dark pool of something, possibly blood, was adhering to the buttress

where it jutted out from under the bridge. If he'd guessed correctly and there had been a jumper, whoever it was seemed to have collided with the massive column on the way down and that didn't bode well for their chances of survival in the cold and menacing October water. When Charlie returned and reported the CID was en-route, Jarvie said with a sigh. "Better radio for the Inspector as well, son. I think it's going to be a long night."

The battered and bruised dark blue Vauxhall motorcar, once the pride of the CID police fleet, had seen better days. Colloquially known as a Heinz car, one owner, fifty-seven drivers, the vehicle was in its final year of service before going to the auction and now relegated for use by the divisional scenes of crime team. Tonight that team consisted of the driver, a young and pretty uniformed officer and her partner, Detective Constable Eddie 'ESSO' Jones, whose nickname originated from his predisposition towards increasing his monthly salary; Eat, Sleep, Shit, Overtime. In the twilight of his career, ESSO felt duty bound to screw the force for as much money as possible, logically reasoning that his retirement should be as comfortable and financially secure as possible. As his driver drew up at the scene on the bridge, ESSO was almost blinded by the large number of flashing emergency blue lights and halogen lights being set up by the support unit personnel. A bus lay stationary in the middle of the bridge and diversions were already in place, directing traffic away from the scene. Uniformed officers, some wearing brightly coloured orange jackets and with flickering torches in their hands, were moving down the embankment towards the riverside. For all that

ESSO realised there was little sound other than the hum of the diesel generators operating the halogen lights. ESSO pulled his bulky frame from the passenger seat and strolled towards Sergeant Gordon Jarvie, an old bar pal from days gone by. Stoutly built with thinning dark hair slicked back, his grey suit trousers shiny from too many overheated ironings and a black nylon anorak showing at least one cigarette burn on the left sleeve, ESSO greeted Jarvie with a smile, a cigarette dangling from his lips and ash flecks on his anorak collar. "Hello, Gordon, what we got here then?"

"Report of a jumper ESSO. I've had the boy," Jarvie indicated his probationer Charlie, "throw a coat over the bit where he or she, we're not sure which it is yet, apparently climbed on top of the parapet. It's a glazed marble effect stone and I was hoping you might get a print or something from it?"

ESSO screwed his face up and pinched the lit end of his cigarette between two nicotine stained fingers, then placed the half finished fag behind his right ear. Hunching his shoulders against the chilly night, he carefully lifted the coat from the bridge, then accepted Jarvie's torch from him and played the beam along the area that had been covered by the coat. Over his shoulder, he spoke to his driver and said, "Fetch the prints case, there's a doll."

Eyes blazing, the young uniformed officer was about to retort she wasn't anyone's fucking doll, but remembered her shift sergeant, Gordon Jarvie, was a drinking pal of this scruffy old fart, so thought it prudent to keep her mouth shut and finish her week secondment to scenes of crime with the minimum of fuss. Furious, she turned on her heel and stamped off, aware of but indifferent to the admiring glance of her fellow probationer, that prat Charlie Ferguson.

ESSO glanced upwards and guessed he'd be lucky if he had ten minutes before the next fall of rain. He fetched a small, but well used torch from his pocket. Slowly, he worked the narrow beam along the shiny surface of the stone. Shaking his head, he didn't hold out much hope but, he mused, better to try and fail than fail to try. With only months to serve till the conclusion of his career and though he didn't think it was likely he'd obtain any latent prints, he still prided himself on his continuing professional approach to the task in hand. His driver arrived, panting from lugging the heavy and powder stained metal case with her and trying to avoid the powder from staining her trousers, knowing that it was a nightmare to remove from the dark blue serge material. ESSO knew he'd wound the lassie up and took merciless pleasure in having her run after him. He thought her a snooty little bugger, having watched her turning her nose up at some of the less salubrious houses to which they'd been called. He believed himself to be an old fashioned copper, serving the public without fear or favour, a principle that had served him well for almost thirty years. The lassie had an attitude problem, thinking herself a class above many of those members of the public she was duty bound to serve. Times are changing and maybe, he admitted, it was the right time to go after all. Placing the heavy case on the parapet close to the spot he was about to examine, ESSO unlatched the lid and with a glance at the gathering clouds overhead, selected a small brush of fine horsehair. He then unscrewed a jar of grey coloured powder, grateful that no wind so far had disturbed the night air. Delicately, he dipped the brush into the powder and, with measured strokes, began to spread the powder on the stone using the torch in his left hand to direct his sweep. To his surprise, his trained eye soon identified the shape of not one but two handprints, faint but definitely there. Concentrating on these two outlines, he gently applied more powder and discerned a clearer pattern, seeing in his minds eye the angle of the hands, indicating the manner in which the body had used the steadying thrust of the hands to propel him or her over the side. From the case he collected two white coloured cards and a roll of clear, low adhesion tape. Tearing a piece of tape from the roll, he applied the tape over one of the areas highlighted by the powder and smoothed the tape down onto the cold stonework. Then very gently, he lifted a corner of the tape and peeled it from the stone, satisfied that the tape now brought with it the print he had powdered. Carefully, he placed the tape over one of the white cards, and then repeated the procedure with the second print. Finally, with a black, felt tipped pen, he recorded on the cards the time, date and a brief resume of the circumstances in which he'd found the handprints. Satisfied, he stood up.

Jarvie smiled at him, "Always a pleasure watching a professional at work, ESSO."

He nodded, pleased with the compliment and took a look over the bridge wall. He could see electric torches flickering at the rivers edge, indicating where the officers searched and who were now scouring the riverbank for evidence of a body.

Gordon Jarvie stood behind him.

Turning, he said, "I'll have these sent to the Fingerprint Department, first thing in the morning. So, anything else I can do for you while I'm here?"

Jarvie gloomily nodded his head and, beckoning ESSO to again look over the parapet, he shone his torch down onto the buttress below where they stood. "I'm not certain ESSO, but I think that's blood. What's the likelihood of you obtaining a sample, just in case this should prove to be criminal rather than suicide? Of course, it'll mean being lowered down in a harness." He smirked. "We've the Support Unit here with all their climbing equipment in that big van," he indicated with a backward thrust of his thumb at the vehicle behind them.
ESSO contemplated the fifteen-foot drop to the buttress. In the darkness, with the River Clyde, sinister and forbidding below, it was a daunting undertaking. Grinning, he turned to look at his young driver.
"No problem. I've got the very person."

Chapter 9

The harsh rattling of a diesel engine, straining to drive a passing bus, woke Willie at six am. The darkened room at first confused him till the ache in his back reminded him he lay upon the MacDonald's couch-bed. He swung his bare feet on to the carpeted floor, wincing slightly as a discarded plastic Lego brick dug its way into his left heel. Rubbing his stubbly chin with the palm of his hand, he run his tongue round the inside of a mouth that felt as furry as the two-day-old socks he pulled on. The pressure on his bladder decided that he'd have to risk the upstairs toilet. Still half dazed, he struggled into his trousers and, shoeless, sneaked into the hallway and quietly climbed the stairs, trying to avoid the squeak he knew to be somewhere halfway up the flight. A shadowy figure stood on the top landing, eerily illuminated by the child safe light plugged into the electric socket.

Jean MacDonald, coming out of her daughter's bedroom, pulled her dressing gown about her. With a finger to her puckered lips and a hand on her stomach, she whispered, "If you're coming to seduce me Willie McKay, you're too late again." They both giggled like kids as Jean continued softly, "I've put a disposable razor and a spare toothbrush in the bathroom and there's a bowl of cereal lying with coffee and the makings in the kitchen. If you're off early, then good luck," and leaned over to kiss him on the cheek.

Willie, surprised by her gesture, was touched and pleased at the simple thoughtfulness. As Jean turned to enter her bedroom, she smiled and waved goodbye. Willie nodded his farewell, suddenly too emotional to reply.

The harsh glare of the October sun streamed through the dirt-streaked windows of the third floor office that was located in the seedier part of Wellington Street, near to Glasgow city centre. The old-fashioned cast iron radiator that sat beneath the vast bay window discharged enough heat to enable the lone occupant of the office to cast off the tailored jacket that was carelessly thrown over the backrest of the swivel chair, itself occupied by its owner, Harry Cavanagh. Harry was at peace with the world. His large oak desk, situated just under the window, was littered with sheets of paper, each sheet in turn bearing handwritten columns and figures. None of the papers had identifying names, but the small man who pored over them knew to which of his large number of clients each paper referred. Occasionally, Harry made small addendums in his neat handwriting, to the papers. The computer monitor on the right hand side of the desk was switched on, its screen displaying the company screen saver, 'Cavanagh Investments', but its keyboard was locked and the password known only to the user. Importantly, all the business Harry conducted on the computer was daily downloaded by him to a memory stick and the stick taken home at night and locked securely within the small steel safe, hidden in the flat of the companies' sole accountant, investment broker and director, Harry Cavanagh. Harry was, if nothing else very, very security conscious. And he needed to be, for Harry's' clients were a select and publicity shy group and these clients included some of the more prominent members of the Glasgow criminal fraternity. Standing just five feet two inches in his stocking soles, Harry Cavanagh would never think of himself as a hard man and definitely not a gangster. Nearing sixty, thick lens spectacles sitting back on his forehead, his thinning hair a light brown shade, complemented weekly by a popular hair dye, Harry sat in his worn, but comfortable chair behind the desk. His tie undone and top shirt button loose, he sat with sleeves rolled up to the elbow and a well-chewed but unlit cigar between his podgy fingers, contemplating his latest transaction on behalf of his least favourite client, Maxie McLean. Harry, the master of dodgy business deals, again run the transaction through in his mind, wondering why Maxie had needed so much money in a hurry. An icy shiver run down his spine as he realised such curiosity might get him killed. Or worse, he grinned to himself, Maxie might go to another investment broker.   Harry's association and property dealing on behalf of Maxie was, he consistently persuaded himself, simply good business. That Harry wheeled and dealed, as he liked to term it, was his rationalisation for acting in his clients best interests, with of course very little of those interests being declared to Her Majesty's Inland Revenue. Besides, Harry smirked, "She doesn't need the money, she's got plenty of it herself," that was Harry's often-repeated little joke. He never considered himself to be crooked, simply a master at playing the financial game. His legitimate life, as he liked to call his previous experience in banking, included several years working at off shore accounting and investment and was a priceless skill when dealing with Maxie and his other clients, for Maxie wasn't Harry's only punter with a vested interest in keeping his earnings private.

The intercom on his desk beeped. The nasally voice of his teenage secretary Helen, proclaimed a visitor. Her voice grated on his nerves and her guttural Glasgow accent could strip paint from the walls.

"Hoy, Harry, there's that guy Maxie MacLean here to see you," she bawled through the speaker, "Can he come in?" Harry raised his eyes to heaven. Helen wasn't much of a secretary. Her typing was shite and she hadn't yet mastered the concept of the spell-check button. As for her clerical work, her filing system was absolute crap, but when she wore her habitual short, tight skirts with those longs legs and stooped and bent over the floor cabinet, Harry could feel the Viagra kicking in and that, he was happy to agree, was worth the pittance he paid her. He straightened his tie and donned his jacket as Maxie, immaculately groomed in a formal navy blue business suit, white shirt and red chequered tie with a briefcase in his left hand, came through the door. Right hand outstretched, Harry greeted Maxie like an old and valued friend, clasping his left hand on top of Maxie's firm grip. "How's it going, Maxie?"

Maxie, tight lipped, nodded in acknowledgement and though privately he didn't particularly like Harry Cavanagh, was astute enough to realise the small mans value for after all, hadn't their business dealings been successful for almost a decade? Besides, he also knew that Harry was frightened of him and that simple fact in Maxie's game of rules was better than any loyalty bonus card. "Not bad, Harry, not too bad and sorry to burst in like this without an appointment I mean. Wee problem I'd like to discuss with you. That thing switched off?" he indicated the intercom.

Harry raised a finger to his lips and walked past Maxie to his office door. "Helen, doll," he called out, "nip down the bakers and get me a couple of fruitcakes. Take the money out of the petty cash, there's a good girl." Harry grinned at Maxie and waited, rewarded a moment later with the sound of the slamming of the front door echoing through the building. "Okay, Maxie, what's on your mind?"

Maxie sat down, indicating Harry should do likewise. "The last deal you made for me, Harry. You'll recall I requested the conversion of certain commercial and residential properties in the Edinburgh area to be converted to cash, all bills to be Bank of England, in used notes and no denomination larger than fifty pond notes?" Harry swallowed, palms outstretched and immediately, concern showed on his face. "I did what you asked, Maxie. The deal with the Manchester Chinese guys went through as sweet as a...."

'Aye, I know that," replied Maxie, waving away Harry's

explanation. "What I want to know is when the... messenger," choosing his words carefully, "I arranged called here for the cash, what exactly did you say to him or you to him? Tell me everything that you can remember."

Harry was taken aback by the question, but recalling vividly the visit from the young lad, just three days ago. "Well, you did tell me that the," careful, thought Harry, "deal was on a time critical issue and I pushed the Chinks, the customers I mean, for a settlement. The usual arrangement, of course, with the agreed documented price for VAT purposes and the surplus, to avoid attention and evade the stamp duty, in cash. Plus my standard six per cent commission..."

"Aye, I know all that. Go on," Maxie waved his hand, impatiently. At six per cent, Harry was expensive, but worth it to keep the Inland Revenue off Maxie's trail.

"Anyway, a couple of days after the deal went through, I received a phone call from your man Franny McEwan, who told me that at a pre-arranged time a young guy called Billy Thomson would arrive at the office and it was to Thomson I was to hand over the cash. As I've done before, just as a precaution, you understand, I asked Franny for a description of this guy Thomson and the guy that arrived, fitted the description down to a tee. It was as straight forward as that. Franny stressed there was to be no fuss and under no circumstances was I to disclose to Thomson what he was carrying." A fine bead of sweat began to form on Harry's forehead, but he was reluctant to fetch his handkerchief from his pocket, lest Maxie think he had something to hide. "You know I wasn't to happy with..." he began, only to have Maxie, with a wave of his hand, cut him short.

"Aye, aye, I know," he impatiently replied. "The arrangement was our responsibility, that's not your problem. Was there anyone with this guy Thomson?" he asked Harry, his beady eyes locked into Harry's.

Harry's brow furrowed in concentration, safe in the knowledge that he was in the clear. If there had been a fuck-up, thank Christ it wasn't his. He shook his head. "I conducted the transfer here, in this office, so I didn't see anyone else. But I can ask my secretary Helen....."

"How was the money bundled?" Maxie interrupted.

"In two sports bags, black sports bags they were. Locked, as I was instructed, with them small padlock things, you know the type. Franny was quite specific about the two bags and the padlocks, but of course I won't be billing you for them. I gave the lad the padlock keys away with him. Two sets. One set per padlock."

Maxie closed his eyes in silent rage. Harry gave Thomson the keys to the fucking padlocks! How the fuck could he have been so stupid! Thomson wouldn't have needed to force the locks, he could have opened the bags, saw the contents and nobody would have been any the wiser. But, Maxie wondered, did he? Did young Thomson have the bottle to stiff Maxie McLean? He ground his teeth and decided, no. Junkie that he was, even if he did know the contents of the bag, Thomson would know his life was forfeit if he had even considered ripping off Maxie. No, the lad would have hidden the bags, but where? That was the problem now. Absent-mindedly, as if coming to a decision, he nodded his head and stared at Harry as a sudden thought flashed across his mind. No. Instinctively he knew Harry was telling the truth. He was literally shitting his pants, clearly too scared to cross Maxie and besides, this wasn't getting

Maxie any closer to the bags. Standing, Maxie lifted his briefcase and said "Thanks, Harry, if I need anything else, I'll get back to you. You might have a word with your tart, see if she can recall anything, but remember," tapping the side of his nose with a forefinger, "discretion at all times, eh?"

"No bother, big man," and next time will be too bloody soon, sighed a shaken and much relieved Harry.

Mickey 'The Greek' Metexas, his sallow complexion and dark curly hair indicative of his parent's Mediterranean origin, swung the wooden baseball bat slowly in his left hand, and then violently crashed it against the corrugated tin wall. The resounding echo bounced all down the length of the derelict warehouse. Nobody would hear the noise, he knew. Only wharf rats and the occasional teenage joyrider's, dumping their latest toy in the adjacent Mersey River, inhabited this part of the Liverpool dockland. He looked down and flicked an imaginary piece of fluff from the arm of his bright yellow shell suit.

When the bat struck the warehouse wall, Johnjo Donnegan might have jumped in panic-stricken surprise, but the black PVC tape that bound his arms and legs to the wooden chair held him tight, just as the same tape stretched tight against his mouth stopped him from crying out in fear. The tape didn't, however, prevent the tears from rolling down his cheeks.

Mickey's henchmen, Big Al O'Rourke and Sean Begley both cringed at the sound, knowing from experience that Mickey was working himself into a rage, all the better to set about the unfortunate Johnjo.

"So, lad," Mickey addressed the unfortunate Johnjo, his voice quiet but full of menace, "did I not tell you to torch the fucking car when you'd brought the stuff up from London?"

Eyes bulging with effort, the unfortunate Johnjo tried to reply, but of course the tape across his mouth didn't help any and a muffled grunt was all he could muster.

"Get that fucking tape off him, will ya!" ordered Mickey. Big Al, his professional wrestling days long gone but still light and fast on his feet, rushed to oblige and without preamble, tore away half of Johnjo's fledgling moustache as well.

"Sorry, Johnjo," muttered Big Al, trying to discard of the tape whose adhesive, with fine blond hairs attached, now stuck to his fingers.

"Don't fucking apologise to him!" screamed Mickey, again banging the bat off the wall.

Looking sheepish, Big Al backed off.

Sean, five foot six tall, thin build with a weasel face, sniggered nervously, pleased that Al was bearing the brunt of Mickey's wrath and not him.

Mickey sighed and glanced upwards at the asbestos roof, much of which now holed permitted the winter sun to shine through. He was surrounded by idiots. "As I was saying, Johnjo lad," he began again in an even voice, "what's your explanation for not torching the car?"

Mouth dry and lips chaffed from the tape, Johnjo croaked, "Me sister's Mickey. It was me sister's car. I had to give her it back, you see."

Mickey couldn't believe his ears. "I send you to London to fetch me back a bootful of gear and.... you use your fucking sister's motor to fetch it!" The baseball bat went clattering along the floor. Mickey run the couple of yards between him and the helpless Johnjo and started kicking him about the legs and body, but was restrained by Big Al and Sean, both of whom guessed that with the bat gone, Mickey no longer intended to murder or at least, severely damage Johnjo. Breathless from booting him, Mickey shrugged off his two lieutenants and circled the chair to recover his composure, then squatting in front of the now weeping Johnjo and as though speaking to a child, spoke softly to him. "Look, lad. The reason I told you to torch the frigging motor is that if any of the bags of gear that you had in the boot happened to burst or the powder spilt, if the rozzers had stopped you, I'd be out of a lot of paper and you'd be in a cell with some hairy arsed black guy and sleeping with your arse to the wall and your mouth tight shut! Don't you watch CSI on television, for fuck's sake? The cops can do all sorts of forensic tests these days and if they got you Johnjo lad and that might lead them back to me!" Johnjo vigorously nodded his head in understanding, happy to agree with anything Mickey said, just so long as it stopped him from becoming hysterically angry and kicking Johnjo again.

Calm now, Mickey stood and almost resignedly cuffed the hapless Johnjo lightly on the side of the head. Turning, he beckoned to Big Al. "Walk with me to my car."

Outside the warehouse, Mickey stopped and cautious as ever, looked about him before lighting a cigarette. He watched in fascination as the matchstick burned, holding it in a minor show of bravado as it extinguished on his fingertips. Tossing the burned end away, he blew on his fingers and asked, "What happened to the good old days, Al? I must be going soft. I'd have seen the time I'd have

put one in the back of Johnjo's head, for this kind of balls-up. Anyway, more to the point is the gear safe?"
"Yeah, Mickey, Johnjo might be a prat, but he's not that stupid."
Mickey stared at the big man, seriously doubting Big Al's assessment of Johnjo's intellectual ability. Drawing deeply on his cigarette, he thought about the danger that Johnjo's stupidity might had brought upon them. He knew the capability of the police surveillance units, but surmised the coppers would have nabbed Johnjo rather than risk losing such a massive load of smack. Whether he knew it or not, the fact that Johnjo had successfully delivered the gear to its current hiding place had saved the kids life. Mickey had a stack of money hidden away in a number of accounts, but the loss of such a lot of gear that he had already paid for would have not only meant severe financial hardship, but also repercussions from the law and with his previous convictions, Mickey could be certain he'd be drawing his pension in the nick. Grinding the remains of his cigarette under his heel, he instructed Big Al to take Sean and both accompany Johnjo to the safe house and confirm the drugs were stored in a dry room. "Well be moving the gear in the very near future. I've already lined up a customer, a guy up north that I've done a bit of business with before," he confided. Opening the door of his new Range Rover, he turned and grinned happily at the big man. "When this deal goes down, lad, we could all be very rich men."

Time no longer had meaning for Angie Bennett. Lying fully clothed, her body curled in a foetal position on top of the stained bedclothes. The morning sun filtering through the cheap, half closed curtains melted the slivers of ice that had formed on the metal-framed windows, creating a puddle of water that ran unchecked down the wall. Still in a half-slumber, she dragged herself awake from the nightmare that had been her sleep. The bleak, cold of the flat reflected in her body temperature that unknown to her, was just slightly above hypothermic. She moaned softly as her sea green eyes flickered open. Nothing, neither the cold nor hunger pangs could detract from her unrelenting need for a fix. Her head lay upon her numb right arm. Her eyes focused on the track marks on her forearm, some fresh, but mostly old and scarred; a testament to her first and true love, Heroin. Billy hadn't come back last night and Angie, her terror of the two men in the car overcoming her need for a fix, was too frightened to leave the flat to search for him. She shut her eyes tight, knowing from grim experience that any sudden movement would result in her body protesting with pain. She lay for a few minutes, mentally preparing her breathing to steady and prevent her hyperventilating. Two days without a fix meant ache and hurt. She went through the familiar exercise, her routine for rising. Slowly she wriggled her fingers and toes, continuing to breathe gradually, hoping to avoid the wave of nausea and bile that threatened to erupt from her mouth. Ten minutes passed and she felt sufficiently able to manoeuvre her body to a sitting position, then lowering her feet to the floor. Then slowly, very slowly, using her hands against the walls to steady herself, making her way along the narrow hallway to the dingy bathroom. The faecal smell of the grimy, stained toilet filled her nostrils. Stomach heaving, she fell to the floor on her knees, grasped the rim of the bowl and vomited a sickly, yellow coloured mucous. She continued to retch and as her body heaved, Angie knew that her bladder had been unable to resist the pressure and she'd wet herself. She was past caring about such things. Shaking with the exertion of throwing up, she dragged herself to a standing position facing the cracked and smudged mirror screwed to the wall above the sink. She didn't recognise the face that stared back, gaunt and lined, the face of a much older and ill-looking woman. A thin stream of saliva that dribbled from her mouth had run down her chin and soaked her dishevelled and tangled, shoulder length natural blonde hair. Angie cried and wept as she'd never wept before. Her thin frame shook as self-pity and shame combined to reduce her to a wailing, sobbing wreck. Her hands clasped to the wash hand basin, she sank to her knees, her forehead against the cool enamel of the sink. Her sobbing slowed to a moan and then, after a few minutes, stopped. She drew a deep breath. Wiping her eyes and nose with the sleeve of her cardigan, an idea slowly came to mind. She hauled herself to her feet, again staring at the stranger who faced her in the mirror. "Ina!" she muttered softly to herself. Ina, Billy's grandmother. She'd know were Billy was. She must get to Ina.

A new purpose to her life, one that might find her Billy and the fix she so desperately needed. An odour assailed her nostrils. With a sudden realisation and revulsion, she knew that she was the source of the smell, the product of several days' apathy in her grooming. Hurting or not, she'd need to bathe and do something with her face. A glimmer of hope seized her, a determination, based on he need to find Billy. Maybe Billy, her Billy, was with his Gran. Convinced now in her own mind that's where the fix was, her desperate plight further convinced herself that Billy meant for her to go there, to Ina Thomson's house.

As Mickey was swinging his bat, Harry Cavanagh's secretary Helen passed Maxie McLean making his way down the stairs. She pushed out her ample chest and brazenly smiled at Maxie, who apparently had other things on his mind and simply ignored her. Huffily, she stomped back to the office.
Harry, by now calmed down but still mopping his brow with a handkerchief, called her through to his office.
"The other day," he began, sitting behind his desk as he spoke, "that young guy that came and picked up the two bags. Do you remember him?"
Helen stared curiously at Harry. Something had upset the wee man and yes, she did remember. The weasel faced guy had looked like a junkie she'd thought, as he'd stood in her office with his nose running unabated, using his sleeve to wipe the snot away.
"Aye, what about him?" she asked Harry, her hands on her hips, long legs slightly apart, knowing her stance was provocative and probably exciting the old bugger.
Harry didn't seem to notice her flirtatious posture, his mind still racing at Maxie's unexpected visit. "Was he with anyone? Did you speak to him or anything?"
"Nope," she drawled, puzzled that Harry wasn't paying his usual attention to her, "he just came in, asked for you and I buzzed you to let you know he was here, nothing else. Is it important?"
"Nothing else, then, nothing you can recall? He just came and went?"
"Aye, came in, nervous like because he dropped his car

keys and ...."

"Car keys were they? He came in a car?"

"I don't *know* if he came in a car," Helen stressed, her interest now peaked, "but he had a bunch of keys in his hand. I thought they were car keys. I'm not sure," she shrugged her shoulders. But curiosity had pinched her nose. "What's this all about, Harry?"

"Nothing, hen," Harry replied, dismissively. "Look, put the kettle on and we'll have a cup of tea. Did you get the cakes?"

Chapter 10

The early rise having prompted him, Willie McKay had quietly departed the McDonald house, almost immediately caught a bus and arrived early for work, pleased to be at his desk even before his nemesis Ian Reid. It did occur to him to phone Margaret, thinking that she might be worried that he hadn't come home, but he thought the best thing was to give her some space, some time to come to terms with their argument. If she were worried, she would phone the office. Mind you, he reminded himself, she had never called headquarters before, but the number was in the phone book. Grimly satisfied that his out of character action might provoke some sort of response from his wife, he settled down to read the morning reports. At his desk, mug of tea in hand, he acknowledged the staff as they arrived.

The men, as men are, saw nothing different about Willie, but the women detectives and young Jackie Fulton shrewdly noted that he was wearing the same shirt and tie as the previous day and the slight nicks on his chin indicated he had shaved badly. The women detectives knowingly raised their eyebrows at each other and awaited the opportunity to meet in the Ladies loo to discuss the situation, while young Jackie could hardly contain herself for the chance to impart this juicy wee bit of gossip to Ian Reid.

As Willie McKay was settling down at his desk, Andy Dawson arrived for work in the basement room of headquarters that was affectionately known as the dungeon. He was boiling the kettle and spooning coffee into his stained mug when Mary Murdoch breezed in.
'Coffee?' he inquired.
Mary nodded and hung her jacket and bag on the hook set into the wall. She didn't dislike her neighbour, but was irritated by Andy's apparent lack of commitment to the job. Mary was ambitious and viewed the surveillance post as a stepping-stone in her quest for promotion and couldn't understand why an officer of Andy's undoubted talent and experience would content himself to rot away in this piss-hole of an office. Nor could she understand his liking surveillance duty. Lying about the rear of smelly vans or pursuing villains' cars at break-neck speed wasn't her idea of police work. Yes, she understood that not everyone was seeking to progress through the ranks and had even argued on her detective course during a debate, that the honourable rank of constable was a necessary function. But still, she believed that Andy had much more to offer the police than pissing his career away intelligence gathering, when he could have been out there projecting himself to the bosses.
Andy, for his part, couldn't give two tosses abut

promotion and was more interested in the tight, navy blue sweater that stretched across Mary's chest, silently promising himself that sometime today, when the time was right, he'd again try the old Glasgow patter. After all, he consoled himself, the worst that can happen is she can tell me to fuck off. He offered her the china mug she preferred. "I've a wee job on this morning, Mary. I want to nip upstairs and visit the Criminal Intelligence. There's nothing on the book that's immediate and the rest of the team are out on recce's for other jobs. You can either come with me or do you have something to do yourself?"

Mary furrowed her brow. An hour with Andy and she might be free then to nip out for some exercise then hunt down that blouse she was after. If she went on recce's she'd have no chance to get to the shops. "I don't mind. Will we go when we've had our coffee?"

Andy nodded, smiling inwardly, 'That's the first date she's agreed to. It can only get better.'

Jackie Fulton and Ian Reid stood close together, closeted in the small room that served as the Intelligence Department interview suite. Cupboard size with its small window looking out onto a brick wall ten feet away, the room had two wooden chairs facing each other across a scratched and scored, desk size table. A wall-mounted, wooden framed sign threatened dire consequences to any person who removed intelligence documents from the department without lawful permission. "I'm telling you Ian," she breathlessly repeated, "I don't think he's been home. That's the same shirt he's wearing that he had on yesterday," she tittered, holding her left hand up, the fingers covering her mouth, like an errant schoolgirl. Reid stroked his pencil thin moustache and assumed what he liked to believe was a look of concentration. He'd been nurturing the fine, blonde hair on his top lip in the vain hope that a moustache would add to his standing. Thinking himself to be feared but respected by his staff, Reid was ignorant that most of the detectives, aside from considering him an insufferable prick, also surmised his vanity was an indication of his naivety. But how, he pondered, could he turn Jackie's information to his advantage? To approach McKay was out of the question, for he'd no reason to quiz him on such a personal issue. The best he could think of.... a sharp knock on the door interrupted his thoughts.

With undue haste Jackie snatched open the door and, blushing guiltily, left the room, squeezing past the two plain-clothes officers that stood there and hurrying into the main corridor.

Reid, holding the door open, haughtily inspected the two officers, neither of whom was known to him. "Yes" he asked, inviting them into the room, "Can I help you?"

"DC's Dawson and Murdoch," Andy introduced them, "from the surveillance unit, can we speak to someone about the Maxie McLean operation?"

"What exactly do you want to know?"

"I have some information about one of McLean's associates. Is it you that's dealing with it?"

With an obvious impatience and annoyance that these two hadn't realised he was a supervisor, Reid instructed the two to remain in the room, curtly telling them he'd send someone to deal with their inquiry.

Andy, annoyed at their rude reception by Reid and almost wishing he hadn't bothered coming upstairs, turned to Mary. "Is it me or does he strike you as a real Richard Cranium?"

Mary screwed her face up and looked confused as Andy explained,

"Dick Head?"

She laughed loudly, nodding in understanding, but at the same time wondering why the wee lassie almost ran from the room. Her woman's intuition suspected something other than a professional relationship existed between the girl and the dickhead.

As the supervisor managing all Intelligence related operations, Reid knew the Maxie McLean operation was being overseen by Archie MacDonald and thought this the ideal opportunity to have a wee chat with him.

Approaching Willie's desk, he wrapped his knuckles down hard on the top of the computer monitor.

Willie had watched Reid approach, but feigned surprise and looked up.

"There's a couple of surveillance types in the interview room," Reid began, "asking about Maxie McLean. Attend to them, please and sort out their problem. And try not to be all day about it, eh?"

Willie was about to remind Reid that McLean's operation was the remit of Archie, but instead nodded in understanding and walked to the secure filing cabinet containing the relevant information.

Archie MacDonald heard Willie receive the instruction from Reid and wondered why he hadn't been dispatched, figuring that no doubt Reid had some ulterior motive. Watching Willie disappear through the door into the interview room, Reid sauntered over and sat on the edge of Archie's desk. He smiled down at him. "How's the family these days, Arch?"

Archie disliked being called 'Arch', no less than he disliked this snide prat. Acutely aware though his colleagues were seemingly engrossed in their paperwork or concentrating on their monitors, he knew that all ears in the office would be listening to this little scenario and having earlier seen both Reid and Jackie Fulton disappear into the interview room, he guessed why there was now this attempt at familiarity. Reid wanted information. But he wasn't getting it from Archie MacDonald. Archie sat back in his chair and clasped his hands behind his head. Smiling benignly, he looked up at his supervisor and nodded with a grin. "Fine, fine thanks Ian and yourself? Still shagging young Jackie, then?"

The office exploded into laughter as Reid almost fell off the desk.

Archie thought the sergeant was about to have an apoplectic fit. His mouth gaped open, but no sound came out. Reid, white faced and eyes blazing at the now grinning Archie, stormed back to his room, slamming the door behind him.

Hearing, but unaware of the cause for the loud laughter coming from the main office, Willie entered the interview room and closed the door behind him. He carried a thick, buff coloured folder under his am and introduced himself. With a glance, he inspected the officers warrant cards that hung around their necks on plastic beaded chain. Once satisfied as to their identity, Willie invited Andy and Mary to sit and placing the file between them, stood with his back against the wall and smiled. "So, you're here about Maxwell Graham McLean of this parish? How might I be of assistance?"

"It's actually Franny McEwan, I was hoping to discuss,"

replied Andy, "so from our observations I know that he's one of Maxie's right hand men, him and that lunatic One-ball Smith."
Opening the folder, Willie snapped the metal clips open and, extracting a photograph and passed it to Andy.
"We're talking about this guy, right?'
Andy nodded, "Aye, that's him," and related the sequence of circumstances surrounding the death of William Thomson, former resident of Govan, but latterly standing before the court of final judgement.
As Willie listened to Dawson's retelling of the incident that involved the police officer who was seemingly being blamed for Thomson's death, it occurred to him Dawson seemed to be a loyal friend, Willie thought and obviously upset that his mate Higgins was going through the mill over this allegation. With a sudden recollection of a newspaper article, he realised though he had been unaware of its significance at the time, he'd already known of William Thomson's demise. However, the tenuous connection between a dead junkie and Franny McLean, assuming it to be true, probably wouldn't advance their operation any, but if Andy was good enough to bring it to the attention of Criminal Intelligence, Willie felt obliged to demonstrate some enthusiasm. He was about to offer the pair a cup of tea, but was interrupted by Andy who produced a crumpled sheet of paper from his back pocket.
"I know the rubber heels mob will have primacy in the investigation and the notebook I mentioned will now have been delivered to them, but you know what that mob is like. The last thing on their mind will be intelligence. All they'll be looking for is a scapegoat to satisfy the media that the police hands are clean," Andy

moaned, subtly inferring that all Complaints and Discipline officers were fatherless thugs, a belief shared by many if not most of his police colleagues. "Anyway, I took the liberty of photocopying the page with Franny's phone number, if you wanted to add it to the file."
Willie examined the sheet of paper, bearing the two pages of handwritten script. "What's this strip of paper here?" he pointed at the sheet of paper.
Andy peered over Willie's shoulder. "Oh, a lassie operated the machine for me. When I handed her the notebook, she must have copied that receipt as well. The receipt was lodged in the book like a marker, between the two pages. Sorry, about that, I should have checked."
At his back, Mary sighed, thinking typical of Andy, things done at half measure.
Willie re-folded the sheet of paper and placed it on top of the file. Chewing his lower lip, he pondered the information brought to him by Andy and decided not to raise any hopes the detective might have, that this in any way could conceivably assist his pal, Higgins. Better to be straight with the big guy. "To be honest, other than association, I don't see it meaning anything. You will know as well as I do that Franny does the legwork for Maxie. He's the recruiter for the couriers and keeps them in line, usually with a good kicking. If they try to scam any of the money or drugs that they deal for Maxie's mob, well, I don't need to explain the consequences. The casualty departments in this city have seen enough of Maxie's victims to fill several wards. And as you quite rightly put it,' he grinned, "One-ball has his uses in that line of work as well."
Andy nodded in understanding. The police were well aware that statistics only reflected the reported crime in

the city. When the criminal fraternity had an internal discipline problem or beating to mete out, it was far more dangerous to report assaults to the police than accept the pain and hurt. Standing, Andy offered Willie his hand and said, "Thanks for your time. Sorry if I pulled you away from anything important."

"Not at all, I only wish I could be more helpful, but with targets like Maxie McLean it's a war of attrition. Operations conducted by you and Mary here assist in the identification and subsequent capture of the foot-soldiers, so to speak, but Maxie steers well clear of any hands on business and that's what makes the evidencing of a case against him difficult." He smiled, his favourite saying coming to mind. "A jigsaw is never complete unless we have all the pieces and who knows, one day this," he held up the sheet of paper, "might prove useful. But Maxie's time will come. He might be a boy from a council housing estate with a basic education, but we know he's completed a couple of night school courses so he has the proven ability to learn and assimilate information. His experience in the criminal world has earned him a fierce reputation that continues to thrive on fear and terror. As a young man, he'd been a real handful, violent and without conscience. But as he's got older, his strength now lies in his ability to terrorise those about him, make them fear the consequence of grassing him up to the police. He's not beyond threatening or even hurting the families of his own team, just to make them comply with some job that he's wanting done. Make no mistake, he's a thoroughly bad bastard and, in my opinion, capable of almost anything."

Mary, interrupting, asked, "What about his wife, Marlene McLean, what do you know about her?"

Willie smiled, suspecting any woman putting up with the likes of Maxie must have piqued the detective's natural female curiosity. He crossed his arms and leaned back against the wall, shaking his head slightly. "That's the curious side of his relationship. I'm not a physiologist and I have to admit I'd wondered about that myself." Frowning, he continued. "Marlene or Lena, as he calls her, was a tutor on one of his courses. We know from background profile checking that she arrived in Glasgow from village life up north and later graduated from Strathclyde University with a degree in accountancy. From there she landed a position teaching at one of the local council run colleges, tutoring mainly the mature unemployed and enforced redundancy students, you know, people trying to re-train themselves? Anyway, that's where she met Maxie and we can only presume that he turned Lena's head. A young woman living on a budget meets him with the flash car and cash in his pocket. You can guess the rest." He shrugged his shoulders. "Before she knew it, whipped up to Martha Street and married. Good-looking woman, if the photographs you guys take, do her any justice. And in answer to your question," he grimaced, "I would say that her fear of Maxie keeps her in place. We also know, from our friends at the Fraud Squad that Lena is the name on his business interests so in theory, she holds the reins so to speak, of his empire. But the true power, no question about that. That's Maxie, pure and simple."

Reaching into the file, he withdrew an A4 size colour photograph of Lena, hair tied back in a ponytail and dressed in her usual black top and black trousers, bent down to open the door of her Mercedes sports car, her head turning to face the unseen camera.

Andy recognised the photograph as one he had taken, some months previously.

"You'll see from the make of the car, she's not averse to spending Maxie's ill-gotten gains. Don't be fooled though," he added, "her fear of her husband will undoubtedly keep her in line, so it's likely that the fiscal side of their relationship will be controlled by Maxie."

"Bit of a honey," Willie remarked, glancing at the photograph.

Mary cast a side-glance at Andy. "Aye, it's been noticed by one or two," her sarcasm obvious to Willie.

He smiled. Clearly these two aren't an item, but did he detect a little hint of jealously in DC Murdoch's voice? He placed the two photographs and sheet of paper in the file and shuffled it closed. "Well, anything else I can do for you folks? Oh, you didn't get your tea."

"That's okay," replied Andy "if we dig anything else up, now that we've got a face and a name, we'll come calling," he beamed.

Willie saw the officers out and returned to the office. Of course he'd heard the laughter through the closed door, but hadn't given it any thought, however, the way his colleagues smiled at him, something had occurred when he'd been out of the room. Yes, he decided, there was definitely a funny atmosphere in the air. Returning to his desk and ignoring the grins about him, he laid down the file and opened the cover, removing the sheet of paper provided by Andy. He reached for a paper punch, but before filing it, he again glanced at the sheet and curiosity aroused, examined the image of the receipt that had been mistakenly copied with the notebook pages.

The copying machine had done a good job, but the writing was too small for him to clearly make out the writing upon the receipt. With a sigh, he knew that the days were numbered before he would have to contemplate reading glasses. Rummaging in his desk drawer, he smiled in satisfaction as he drew out an old fashioned magnifying glass, legacy of a CID prank-present at a Christmas night out some years previously and the butt of many jokes since. Examining the sheet through the glass, the receipt details leapt up at him. The shop name, 'Jackson's Auto Goods', with an address in the low numbers of the nearby Bath Street and a date that indicated a purchase had been made three days before. A set of numbers, seemingly representing the purchase, priced the item at nine pounds and ninety nine pence. The bottom of the sheet bore the name 'Mark'. Willie presumed that to be the name of the sales assistant. He sat back in his seat, puzzled. There was no definite evidence that Thomson had made the purchase, but the receipt had been found in his notebook and, if he did so, why would Billy Thomson, reputedly a penniless junkie, have spent almost ten quid in a car shop?

Making their way through the quiet corridors of police headquarters back to the dungeon, Andy and Mary walked in silence, each lost in their own thoughts. Mary couldn't understand why an evidently intelligent woman like Lena McLean could remain with a despicable man like Maxie McLean?
Andy, a half step behind her and with a sidelong glance, thought that if Mary wiggled her cute little bum any more, he was going to lose it and make a fool of himself.

"Seemed a decent guy, that 'Intel' man, McKay," Andy remarked.

"Certainly more sociable that his sergeant, anyway," she agreed.

"Lunch?" he hopefully inquired.

"Actually, I was considering going for a quick jog, but you're welcome to join me if you want," she replied, knowing fine well Andy wouldn't even consider breaking a sweat.

Even the thought of following Mary Murdoch's bum and perfectly rounded bouncing chest along St Vincent Street couldn't persuade Andy Dawson to pull on a tracksuit.

"See you when you come back," he sighed with disappointment.

Angie, now bathed and with her strawberry blonde hair washed and combed thoroughly, critically examined herself in the mirror. Amazing what war paint can do for a girl, she grinned self-consciously. But still hurting and with her stomach playing leapfrog, she at least looked if not felt better now that she'd tidied herself up. The cheap bottle green blouse, pale green skirt and black boots were just some of the items that remained from a once stylish wardrobe, most of her clothing having been sold to facilitate the purchase of drugs. Pulling on a cheap, thin, navy blue nylon hooded anorak, she walked to the bay window overlooking Rathlin Street and carefully pulled aside the torn netting curtain. From her first floor vantage point, Angie searched the street for any sign of the two men, the men who were hunting Billy. With a shudder, she remembered the day they came. The big fat bastard, the one called Franny; he'd been the scary one. The other one with the long hair, the one who'd slapped her, whose name she didn't know, brushing aside her flimsy defence without difficulty. At least he was predictable. The abusive and filthy names he'd called her were typical of that sort of man, mean and bullying, but Franny? His cold, pig like eyes and quiet, low voice had really frightened her. Having thought about it, what had scared her about Franny was his unpredictability. She hadn't been able to take her eyes from his, even when the other bastard was pulling at her, furtively groping at her breasts as he pretended to hold her. She hadn't known where Billy was, when they'd forced their way past her into the flat, pushing her aside as though she didn't exist. They'd believed her she guessed, but promised they would be back. She'd wept in shame and humiliation and lied and, swearing she would tell them when Billy returned. Fuck, she had been so frightened she would have told them anything to get them out of her flat, anything, except where Billy was. But she hadn't known even that. She looked around her at her possessions, pitiful though they were, it was all she had. The damage and destruction caused to the flat and her things by the longhaired one; that was just badness because they hadn't found Billy. Of course, she'd known Billy was due back to the flat, but balancing her fix against grassing him up to those two bastards? No dispute, was there? She'd needed the fix more than they wanted Billy. But Billy hadn't come back and now she had to find him... and fast. Carefully, she moved the sofa couch away from the front door, cringing as it scraped and squealed noisily on the unvarnished wooden floor. She listened with her ear pressed tight against the already damaged and flimsy door, but heard nothing. With bated breath, she undid the cheap lock and listened again, half expecting the two brutes to be standing outside on the landing. Still she heard nothing, no sound other than her drunken neighbour upstairs as usual berating his wife, her screeching abusive response resonating down the stairwell. A by now familiar sound and so common, it had become almost a background noise to Angie. Taking a deep breath, her hands shaking, she threw the door open and hurried through, pulling and locking it behind her, shoving the key into her jacket pocket. It briefly occurred to her that if she never returned to the flat, didn't go back, there was nothing there that mattered. Nothing that was personal or precious to her. No happy memories, even. With a start, she realised the horrible truth. She was nobody, a non-being. There was nobody to care for her, no-one except her Billy. I must find Billy.

Turning, she made towards the stairs. Nerves raw and shivering with anticipated fright, her stomach churning with the need for heroin, she tiptoed down the grey, stone stairs, pausing every few seconds for any unusual sound or any indication of a trap. Uncontrollably, she began to giggle, the thought striking her that anyone coming up the stairs would equally have a heart attack. It would be a close thing as to who would pass out first. Holding her breath till it hurt in her thin chest, she safely negotiated the stairs to the back courtyard door and, praying nobody was lurking there, skulked through the door and stumbled across the rear court, warily making her way across the moonscape ground, the bricks of the broken down perimeter wall threatening to trip her at every step. With a sigh of relief, Angie emerged into the busy Govan Road. Jacket hood up and head down, she made her way through the throng of pedestrians and headed for Ina Thomson's house.

As Angie was cautiously departing her flat, Franny McEwan was explaining to his partner One-ball, that Maxie's plan involved the use of a high-powered car, but of course one that was untraceable to the team in the unlikely event it attracted police attention.
One-ball was confused. "So," he pondered "we get ourselves a motor and somehow it has to be one that the cops can't trace back to us, eh? Aye, it's a puzzler right enough, Franny."
Franny raised his eyes to heaven. Surely this nut can't be *that* thick, he wondered? "One-ball, think about it. What kind of car can't the police associate with us?"
"Eh, naw, you've got me there, Franny."
"A stolen one, you idiot. We're going to blag a car from one of them high-rise car parks in the city centre. Now, do you have any ideas?" while thinking, if he does then that'll be a first.
Surprisingly, One-ball did have an idea and drove them in his vehicle to the large, concrete eight-storey car park located in the city centre at Cowcaddens, not far from the Caledonian University building. On arrival at the car park, they parked outside the massive edifice as One-ball explained his plan.
"We're looking for at least a two litre job, maybe a BMW or a fast Ford, about six, maybe seven years old that has one of them fancy electronic collision control awareness systems installed."
Franny was mystified, but let One-ball continue.

"I know the wee guy that works in the attendants booth, here," indicating with his hand the entrance to the car park. "He's behind in his debt to us, got a wee coke habit if you know what I mean?" sniggering at his own joke. "The only problem we have is the CCTV cameras monitoring the different levels. At this time of the day, most of the owners are working in the offices hereabouts, leaving their cars first thing and then picking them up at night when they finish work. They trust the place, because of the cameras. There's a lot of good quality motors in there too, because of the punters that work in or go to the university."

Franny interrupted him. "What's this thing about the computer what-you-call-it-system you spoke about, One-ball? We don't need anything too fancy, just a four door motor that can shift."

"Aye, I know that," One-ball replied patiently, realising that to Franny, who never took an interest in cars, this would go right over his head. He continued, "But the difficulty isn't in breaking into the motor, the difficulty is in breaking in without damaging the windows or doors. That's where the baseball bat, in the boot of this car, comes into play. Any obvious sign of damage to the car, when we're using it on the road, might get us a pull from the 'beasties', you know, traffic cops, understand?"

Franny didn't really understand, particularly in reference to the baseball bat. How the fuck can anyone be subtle with a baseball bat, he wondered and looked at One-ball in wonderment?

"Anyway," resumed One-ball, enjoying the novelty of explaining the situation to Franny. "Once I'm in the car it's an easy thing to get it running. Then, so as to gives us a decent start before the blagging is reported to the cops, we pay the parking fee for a ticket, which automatically raises the barrier and take off. But first I'd better have a word with my wee pal in the booth."

Leaving his car and entering the booth, One-ball went in to speak with his drug debtor.

Through the office window, Franny could see One-ball raising his hand and bringing it down sharply on the attendants' head, no doubt emphasising a point, he smirked.

Grinning, One-ball returned to the car and settled himself in the driver's seat. "There's going to be a power failure to the CCTV cameras, in twenty minutes," he told Franny, "so here's the plan."

Coffee at the city centre MacDonald's had sufficed for breakfast and Willie McKay had no interest in lunch, so decided to take a walk through the drizzling rain to Bath Street. As he strode through the lunchtime crowd, instinctively and deftly avoiding the umbrella assassins, he was troubled that he hadn't yet phoned home. He'd given the matter some thought and decided that it was better to face things head on and speak with Margaret tonight face to face, rather than endure a one sided conversation at the office, where even the most discreet of his colleagues might overhear and catch on to Willie's domestic problem. Of course Archie knew, but he was a friend and wouldn't reveal anything of a personal nature to the others. Still, he wondered at the curious, but not unsympathetic looks directed towards him this morning. No, he firmly decided, Archie wouldn't have said anything. The brisk walk seemed to clear his head. Pedestrians passed him by, irritated and annoyed that they had to raise their umbrellas to avoid striking the tall man who seemed to walk in a daze and be unaware of them. But Willie, ignorant of the scowls directed at him, had his mind on the receipt and couldn't fathom why it niggled at him. Probably nothing, he contemplated, but better to check it out anyway. No stone unturned, he grinned to himself. Striding onwards, he soon located the shop.

'Jackson's Auto Goods' was situated between a smart wine bar and a second hand bookshop. The large single window that needed cleaned was adorned by posters advertising cut price offers, a sure sign in Willie's mind that business wasn't too good in what was after all a predominantly restaurant area of the city centre. Pushing open the door activated a buzzer of the type used to alert staff to the presence of a customer. The interior, dimly lit, suggested an air of shabbiness.

"Can I help you?" growled a middle-aged man, dressed in a shabby, brown dustcoat and walking between narrow, ceiling high shelves, stacked to the brim with boxes and sale items. He peered at Willie through dirty, clouded bifocals.

Willie turned down his collar. Reaching into a coat pocket and producing his warrant card, he asked if Mark was on duty.

The man sighed, making obvious his disappointment that Willie was not a paying customer. Huffily, he declared himself to be Mr Jackson. He examined the warrant card and then curtly requested that Willie wait. Returning a moment later with a teenage boy in tow, Jackson flapped his hand at Willie and pointedly reminded the teenager Mark, that the shelves in the rear had still to be dusted. Willie grunted, pleased that he didn't have to suffer the

Jackson's of this world and their pettiness ,but then frowned as he suddenly remembered Ian Reid.

The lad approached Willie, cautiously and slightly overawed. "Can I help you, mister?"

Willie re-introduced himself to Mark, thinking that the teenager dressed in a green boiler suit with a mop of shaggy fair hair and wispy blonde beard reminded him of a cartoon character from the children's 'Scooby-Doo' show. He showed Mark the sheet of paper, folded to conceal the notebook pages. "Do you recognise this receipt, son?"

The boy nervously looked at the page. He read the script without any problem reminding Willie that indeed his eyesight needed to be checked. "It's a copy of a receipt from the shop, dated a few days ago. And it's got my name at the bottom, so I must have served the customer. Whoever operates the till," the boy explained, "uses their own staff number and it prints out the name at the bottom," he indicated with his forefinger. "Bit stupid really," he whispered, "because there's just the two of us now."

"Can you tell me, from the numbers there what it was you sold? You'll see I've written them at the bottom of the paper. My eyes aren't as young as yours", Willie joked, attempting to place the boy at ease.

Mark smiled, visibly relaxing now that he knew he wasn't the subject of Willie's inquiry. "Mr Jackson," he called to the back of the shop, "I'm just going into the till to check something for the detective." Conspiratorially, he whispered that Jackson usually hung about when Mark used the till, thinking everyone was a thief. The boy operated the till and punched in the numbers that Willie read to him from the sheet of paper. A digital readout displayed the item details on a small screen. Turning the screen to face Willie, Mark said, "Key-Hide. Shall I show you one?"

Leading Willie through the narrow passageway towards the rear of the shop, Mark fetched a small, dusty rectangular box from a high shelf and opening it, brought out a metal, rectangular tin with a magnet on one side. "It's for drivers who worry about losing their car key," he explained. "They put the spare one in the tin and the magnet sticks to the underside of the car or inside a bumper. They're not that popular," he whispered furtively, glancing over his shoulder, "We've got about four dozen in stock and I've been here nearly three months and I've only sold one, on the date on the receipt," pointing to the paper. Then, more positively, "I can remember the guy. Paid cash. I don't think I'd have been happy taking any kind of credit card from him."

Willie, sensing a strange anticipation, asked Mark to describe the buyer.

Mark's brow furrowed in concentration, trying to recall details of the customer and excited that he was speaking to a detective. He couldn't wait to impress his girlfriend about this, he thought. Maybe with a slight exaggeration perhaps, pretend the guy was a murderer. "Easy. I thought he looked like a junkie and was out to do a bit of shoplifting."

"You've no CCTV in here, then?"

The boy sniggered, coughing loudly to cover his laughter, lest his boss hear him. "No, old Jackson wouldn't pay for it. Too expensive, he says."

"So you think the purchaser was a junkie out doing a spot of shoplifting then?"

"Yes, it was the bags that made me suspicious."

"Bags?"

"Aye. Two sports bags he had with him. Brand new they were, dark coloured I think. Aye, definitely black," he nodded his head, "with little locks on them. Yeah, I'm sure about that. Two wee locks, like padlocks. I wondered at the time what was in them. Full of knocked-off stuff from other shops, I expect," he shrewdly guessed.

Chapter 11

The Fingerprint Department at Glasgow police headquarters is a bustling, busy office whose mainly civilian workforce is usually managed by police officers, but supervised at shop floor level by the more experienced civilian supervisor colleagues. The Department prides itself on its efficiency and boasts a high rate of convictions based on the evidence of fingerprints that are obtained or 'lifted' by scenes of crime personnel, at the locus and in a high number of cases uniquely identified as the culprit, by the Department specialists. The advent and introduction of computer technology to all aspects of police work now means that officers awaiting the outcome of a scenes of crime examination can often, courtesy of the Department, have their result within a day or two or if the crime is time critical, within hours, but subject at all times to rigorous and corroborative checking by at least one colleague.

Vinod Bhatia, known to his mates as Vinny, had been there for nearly two years. An affable and good looking young man in his mid twenties, Vinny was popular amongst his colleagues and completely unaware that many of the young, and some not so young, women that he worked with vied for his attention. Bright and articulate, Vinny still harboured a youthful shyness, but as he worked, little did he know that plans were afoot to draw young Vinny out from his shell. Still short a couple of years for the court recognised length of time required to competently give evidence in court as an 'expert witness', Vinny was nevertheless happy in his work; checking fingerprint 'lifts' against those held on record, and creating files for new 'lifts'. His methodical and meticulous detail to attention found him to be ideally suited to this type of work. He was, he was found of saying, one of the few people who enjoyed coming to work in this building. Plus daily seeing Julie Crossman, his lively red-haired colleague who worked two desks down, combined to make him a happy man. But that was something he was embarrassed to admit to anyone else. Vinny harboured aspirations of asking Julie out for a meal one night, but was acutely aware that his inherent shyness and fear of rejection might lead to awkwardness in the workplace.

For her part, the popular and vivacious Julie liked the quietly spoken Vinny and wondered why he hadn't made an approach, yet? She suspected, having caught him sneaking glances at her, that he liked her. Another week, she decided and she'd be doing the asking.

The duty supervisor saw the uniformed constable standing hesitantly at the door and rose from her desk, smiling at the young officer and inquired if she could help him? The constable explained he was delivering a fingerprint package from the city centre divisional enquiry department and repeated that his instruction was to stress it was urgent and was connected with a

suspected suicide the previous evening. Signing for the package, the supervisor read the accompany note. Approaching Vinny, she handed him the package.
"This has just been delivered, Vinny. It's a lift from the Jamaica Bridge, through the night. The local division think some poor soul took a tumble into the water and they're keen to identify. Can you see if you can do anything with it? Don't be under pressure, but yesterday will be fine," she laughed at her own humour as she patted his shoulder. The supervisor liked Vinny, not least because he was an incredibly fast, but conscientious worker. If anyone could get a result here, she privately thought, he would.

Julie, sneaking a glance over, watched Vinny accept the package and open it, removing the two cards from within. Brow furrowed, he read the details of the lift, smiling as he recognised the signature of ESSO Jones, anticipating the lifts would be as professional as night time conditions would allow. Most of the staff had their favourite scenes of crime officers, whether civvies' or cops, but ESSO was generally known throughout the Department for producing good work. That'll make it a bit easier, thought Vinny.

Julie, her curiosity peaked, rose from her desk and stood behind Vinny, watching over his shoulder as he used his desk-mounted magnifying glass to examine the cards. Skilled eyes hinted to Vinny that he was looking at two female handprints and likely a married woman. Of that he was almost certain, noting the narrow space where normally a wedding band split the third finger of the left hand from fully forming the lift. Unconsciously, he nodded his head and acting upon his own experience and intuition, made the definitive decision that indeed the victim was female. Reading the cards again, he assumed the reason for the almost perfect print was the owner had pressed down hard, probably as she was taking off over the edge to her fate he thought sadly, strangely affected that the prints he was examining belonged to a woman, now presumably dead. Unaware of her presence, Julie's hand on his shoulder startled him.

"Alright there, Vinny?"

"Aye," he sat back in his padded seat, taking a secret pleasure from her closeness, "just wondering what makes someone take his or her own life."

"It's the final selfishness," Julie replied, moving round his seat to lean against the edge of his desk and give him the best view of her long and slim legs. Aware now that she had his full and undivided attention, she continued. "Desperation, depression, guilt. There will be a number of reasons, I'm sure. But we're here and happy in our work, eh?" she smiled. Running her tongue round her lips, she took a deep breath and asked, "So how's about you and I going for a drink, some time, only if you want though?"

Vinny thought he'd died and gone to heaven. "Love to," he stammered, his eyes wide open in surprise, "maybe after work?"

"You're on. Now get back to work, you lazy bugger or I'll be reporting you," she joked, hips swinging in the charcoal grey pencil skirt as she returned to her desk. Vinny watched her go then turned to his magnifying glass, happy and relaxed. "Yah beauty," he thought, peering through the lens. "Now," his full attention concentrating on the two cards, "who are you, my love?"

Superintendent Iain Ross had earlier that day visited and spoken with Gerry Higgins and his wife and been shocked at the change in Higgins, in such a short time. It was obvious the man had taken the boy Thomson's death very badly; blaming himself for the outcome of what had began as a simple pursuit. And all for the sake of two hundred ruddy pounds, Ross had thought, the closest he permitted himself to an expletive. But now he replaced the telephone in its cradle and stared at his hand, the knuckles white with tension. He hadn't realised how tightly he had been gripping the receiver. Slowly, he let out a breath. The return call from his contact, an old and valued friend now serving with the Complaints and Discipline Department, had been quicker than even he expected. Ross knew that protocol regarding the outcome of the investigation into the death of William Thomson, required the Deputy Chief Constable to be the bearer of the news, however good or bad such news was. But when a mans career, family circumstances and, in this case, perhaps even Gerry Higgins mental health was involved, Ross believed that news should be expedited as soon as possible. Well, the matter has been settled now. Pushing himself upright to his feet, he walked to the large grey coloured, metal board that covered much of the wall beside his desk. The board had insets into which were tucked small white personnel cards, each card bearing the personal details of the individual officers who made up the division and included their home address and contact telephone number. Of course, many a secretary had tried to introduce Ross to the complexities of the desktop PC, but stubbornly, he had resisted all attempts to bring him into the 21st century and personally updated his old contact board. Higgins, he noted, was high on the board,

indicating his seniority in his shift. Reaching up and removing the card, Ross returned to his desk and stared at the card, gathering his thoughts as he prepared himself to make the call. As though suddenly coming to a decision, he grasped the receiver and dialled the home phone number that was typed upon the card. Patiently, he licked his lips, his mouth suddenly dry. At the third ring, the phone was answered.
"Mrs Higgins? It's Superintendent Iain Ross. I have good news," he smiled, "some very good news indeed."

After ensuring there was no one lurking about on the fourth floor of the high-rise car park at Cowcaddens, Franny McEwan sat pensively in the driver's seat of One-ball Smith's Audi saloon and watched him approach a BMW, baseball bat in his right hand. The recce around the car park had been nerve-wracking for Franny, inspecting what vehicles were available until finally both had agreed the aging but gleaming black coloured BMW car was ideally suited for their purpose. One-ball, grinning like a Cheshire cat and obviously relishing the opportunity to revert to his youthful pastime, purchased two exit tickets in preparation for leaving the car park – one for his own car and one for their soon to be new acquisition. One-ball again glanced around him, saw no one around then, clasping the baseball bat in both hands, struck the front bumper of the BMW with a powerful blow. Franny was tense and alert to every sound, but even with the Audi's engine ticking over, he clearly heard the clicking sound as the BMW's on-board computer, fooled into believing the vehicle had been in a collision, popped the door locks open in anticipation of the cars occupants fleeing to safety. One-ball snatched opened the driver's door and threw the bat into the rear seat, then returned to the Audi from where he collected a short, metal bar with a stout, metal sleeve and a threaded point. Climbing into the BMW driver's seat, he placed the threaded end of the tool against the ignition barrel then slid the heavy metal sleeve on the bar downwards with a powerful thump. The threaded end of the bar, forced downwards, bit into the metal and locked itself into the ignition barrel. One-ball took a deep breath then with a mighty tug, heaved the metal bar upwards and tore the ignition barrel from its casing. Casting the bar and now useless barrel into the rear seat, he hunkered down to obtain a better view of the revealed mass of wiring. Expertly, he pulled off the small, plastic insulation sheaths, exposing the bare copper wires. Selecting two wires, he twisted them together and obtained an electrical spark. The engine suddenly roared into life. Grinning, he sat up and pulled the door closed then buckled on the seat belt. Turning, he gave Franny the thumbs up and gently eased the BMW out from its parking bay.

Watching the scene and shaking his head in wonder, Franny later reckoned the whole operation took less than sixty seconds. "One-ball, my son," he muttered to himself, "You fucking amaze me." The Audi and the BMW exited the car park in convoy. Franny wasn't surprised to see the attendant wasn't in the booth. Continuing in convoy, the vehicles drove to a large, sprawling council estate in the Maryhill area of Glasgow where One-ball reversed the BMW into an old, rundown lock-up and left the vehicle to await its fate. After securing the roller shutter door with a heavy padlock, his final act was to give the thumbs up to the old, grey haired woman leaning out of the window of the second floor flat that overlooked the lock-up, a cigarette clasped between the fingers of her right hand. "My auntie Mary," he explained to Franny, as he got back into his Audi. "Any nosey polis activity round about the lock-up and we'll get a phone call.'

Maxie McLean drove to a transport café on the south side of Glasgow, a favourite haunt of motor bikers and early deliverymen, but usually quiet in the afternoon. Driving past the café, he continuously checked his rear view mirror, suspicious of any vehicle he saw or thought he saw more than twice within a short distance. Three times he deliberately circled a roundabout, all the time watching for a tail, ignoring the shaking head of a driving instructor, who assumed him to be lost or drunk. Taking a route familiar to him, Maxie returned to the café where after parking on the waste ground at the front of the rundown building that served as a car park, he sat within his vehicle watching the traffic pass him by. Satisfied, or as best he could be, that he hadn't been followed he left his vehicle and entered the café. The place was empty of customers. The dozen or so tables of differing size and shape were each protected with a fading red checked PVC cloth, each table sporting condiments of varying description with most of the ketchup bottles showing congealed sauce round the rims. A notice greeting customers offered an all day breakfast for two pounds ninety-nine pence, while warning that credit would not be given. Greeting the proprietor, an old acquaintance from back when they ran together in the same teenage gang, Maxie ordered a mug of tea and bacon roll, then graciously tried to pay, knowing that his offer would be refused.

"Maxie McLean's money is no good in here," refused his former comrade, proud that someone of Maxie's reputation would frequent his place.

After the customary reminiscences, Maxie chose a table in a corner, sitting with his back to the wall and watching the door. The seat also provided him with a good, unobstructed view of his car, through the plate glass window. Nobody could get close to either Maxie or his car without his being aware. The food arrived, but lay untouched. Maxie wasn't hungry, but needed an excuse to be there. Sipping the strong tea, he optimistically hoped that maybe the police were having a day off and there was no surveillance. But you could never be sure, with those fuckers. Like it or not, he had to admit the devious bastards were good at what they did. Caution and anti-surveillance with Maxie had become as habit-forming as putting on an old coat. The public phone attached to the wall by his table was one of the old style kiosks, its rounded Perspex hood, once transparent, now scratched and scored by numerous cigarette burns and hanging limply by only three securing screws. The wall beside the phone, with its handwritten messages, read like a pervert's telephone directory, promising everything from straight to kinky sex. Some, Maxie saw, intimated canine pets were welcome, while another enterprising individual was happy to accept American Express. Maxie glanced at his wristwatch, stood and leaned into the phone hood. He laid a handful of coins on the top of the grey, metal coin box and dialled a number. The phone

rang but once, then a familiar voice answered, "Hello?" to which Maxie responded, "It's me."
"Hello, lad, how are you?" acknowledged Mickey the Greek.

For more hours than she could recall, Angie Bennett had huddled in the dark corner of a building across the road from Ina Thomson's close. She'd walked round Ina's tenement twice now, watching and waiting for Billy, sure that the Franny and his mate were close by. Every figure or car that entered the street filled her with dread. Her body ached and shivered with the craving for a fix. She knew it wouldn't be long before her need overcame her caution and her terror of the two men. Paranoia, the constant companion of junkies, she inwardly thought as she rocked back and forwards on her heels and drew her thin anorak about her shoulders. She continued watching and waiting and shivering, but not just with the cold.

Archie MacDonald watched as Willie McKay returned to the office and hung his wet overcoat on the coat rail, wondering how his mate was holding up. He was uncertain if he should approach Willie, worried that his friend might see Archie's concern as meddling. Better to let him make the move first, Archie thought. However, there was one thing. He opened up with a greeting.
"Hello, Willie. Enjoy the walk? Never figured you for a fresh air fiend."
"Needed a bit of time Archie, you know, think things over, like."

"Oh, I understand. Look, did Pampas ask you to speak to two of the target people earlier on today, about the Maxie McLean file?"

Willie nodded his head, "Aye, but it didn't add much to what we already know."

Archie produced an intelligence report form and handed it to Willie. "This hit my desk this morning, thought it might be related," he began, explaining the content as Willie idly scanned the report. "A constable Simpson at Govan sent it in. I realise it's not about Maxie McLean, but it mentions Franny McEwan and One-ball Smith, his bullyboys. The cop seems to think there might be a connection with two local junkies, an Angela Bennett and her boyfriend, a William Thomson that got himself killed, the other day. Nothing concrete, more a brick wall," he quipped, "but the cop thought it worthy of firing in to us, anyway. What do you think?"

Willie was dumbstruck. That was the second time he'd heard William Thomson mentioned today. As Archie droned on, apologising that Willie had the inquiry dumped on him, he quickly read the text and was in no doubt that the cop, Dougie Simpson, had got it right. "Can you leave it with me, Archie? I've got the file here anyway and I'll update it, if you like?"

Archie was surprised, but happy to pass the report on. Hadn't he enough of his own paperwork to deal with? "Sure," he agreed. Then, in a low voice "Look, about last night. Jean said to tell you you're very welcome, anytime. You know that don't you? And if..."

"I'm grateful Archie, but I'm off home tonight. This has to be settled one way or the other."

Archie nodded his head and smiled encouragingly, clapping Willie on the shoulder, and then moving off to his own desk.

Willie sat down heavily at his own desk, unsure why he hadn't told Archie, probably his closest friend, about his visit to Jackson's? He wasn't being deliberately evasive or trying to be secretive, it wasn't in his nature. But then why hadn't he discussed it, picked Archie's brains? Willie settled back and re-read the report in front of him. Opening his drawer, he drew out a large, blank writing pad and laid it in front of him. As an intelligence officer with considerable experience, Willie knew that his aptitude lay in the assessment of intelligence. No matter how that intelligence was acquired, he had the rare ability to collate often-unconnected information products and produce a clear and defined picture that could be acted upon. "So let's put together what we have, eh?" he mumbled to himself.

Making copious notes and drawing connecting lines, Willie industriously spent the next couple of minutes assessing his information. With his pencil, he wrote on his pad: Willie Thomson and his girlfriend Angela Bennett, both drug abusers, then he drew a line to his next names. Franny McEwan and David One-ball Smith, henchmen and enforcers and then he drew a line to Maxwell 'Maxie' McLean. He stared at what he had written and continued, adding question marks to his next set of names. *Thomson sought by McEwan and Smith - on Maxie's behalf? Thomson carries two locked sports bags and purchases a 'Key-Hide' - to secrete a key? What key*, he continued writing. *The key to the padlocked bags? Thomson dead,* he wrote and added - *a tragic accident, according to Andy Dawson. McEwan and Smith go after the girlfriend, but are they thwarted by the cop Dougie Simpson?*

The bags, Willie contemplated and believed his assessment to be correct. It's all to do with the bags. And Maxie and his boys think the girlfriend knows where the bags are. Sitting back in his chair, he put down his pencil, closed his eyes and rubbed his face. Tearing the sheet from the pad, Willie folded it and put it into a trouser pocket. For the time being, what little he knew or guessed could wait. He glanced at the clock above the door, pensively dreading it reach 5pm. At that time, his shift would be over and Willie's heart thumping in his chest reminded him he had a far more pressing matter to deal with.

Chapter 12

As the late afternoon sun settled across the city, Vinny Bhatia sat miserably at his desk in the Fingerprints Department and scowled at no one in particular. The identity of the owner of the set of palm prints continued to elude him. He had lost count of the number of comparison checks he had made and his frustration was evident to see. Glumly, he contemplated stamping the enquiry form 'Not known to this Department', an admittance that the subject had either never been recorded as having been fingerprinted or that Vinny had failed to identify the subject. With a sudden thought and more in desperation than hope, Vinny decided one final check was worthwhile and approached the corner and little used cabinet containing the Department's archived material. He was conscious of Julie Crossman looking pointedly at the large wall clock, reminding him their tryst was set for this evening, a date he had hoped and dreamed about and he sure as hell wasn't about to blow now. Searching through the cabinet, Vinny retrieved a number of filed items relating to unknown or missing females and returned to his desk to begin his inspection. Halfway through the pile, Vinny stopped. Holding his breath, he blinked rapidly and re-examined the prints. Almost in disbelief but daring to hope, he cross-matched the now outdated fingerprint form with those that had been submitted by ESSO Jones. Shaking his head, he exhaled, drew a deep breath and examined the new and archived sets of prints, a third time. No mistake. Sitting back in his seat, he smiled and silently punched the air with his fist.

Julie, watching and realising Vinny had discovered something, approached his desk.

"Look at these, Julie, and tell me what you see?" he grinned at her.

Julie bent over the magnifying glass and examined the prints. "Match," she declared, returning his grin, "no doubt about it. Is that the probable suicide?"

Vinny nodded, too excited to speak and waved his arm to attract the attention of his supervisor.

Julie picked up the archived prints, noting that the writing on the yellowing card was now faded and slightly blurred. Her brow furrowed, as realisation dawned, then her eyes widened. "But Vinny, this person, Margaret Thomson. She's been missing for over twenty years!"

Mickey 'The Greek' Metexas, relaxed in his favourite armchair in his large and comfortable lounge, the wide screen television tuned to a horse racing channel and blaring out an excited commentary. A tray with a half drunk can of lager sat upon a table at his elbow. The lounge was a visible homage to his first love, Liverpool FC, with red bunting and pictures of his favourite players adorning the walls. A heavy set and hirsute man, Mickey wore a heavy gold medallion on his hairy chest and, casually dressed in jeans and red football top, parodied 'Yosser Hughes', the fictional Liverpudlian character from the popular television drama of the nineteen eighties television series, *'Boys from the Black Stuff'*. However, while the character 'Yosser' suffered mental illness that led to desperate and uncontrollable acts of violence, Mickey cultivated his reputation for the same violence, but in his case without the mental illness. His lengthy criminal record attested to his progressively violent acts and he was acutely conscious of his solicitors' latest admonition; one more solid conviction and its goodbye Mickey. On a leather sofa opposite sat Mickey's trusted lieutenants, Big Al O'Rourke and Sean Begley, both of whom were similarly dressed in jeans and casual sweat tops, each with an opened lager can in their hands.

O'Rourke, seemingly at ease but not quite, as he didn't completely trust his boss, was reporting the examination of the gear brought up from London by their courier, Johnjo Donnegan. "Johnjo did a good job, stashing the gear, Mickey. His sister moved into a bought house in a private estate, a couple of months ago. Her old man dumped her, a few weeks ago and fucked off with a tart from Birkenhead, so the sister's short of a few bob for the mortgage. So as long as she's kept sweet with an 'earner', she'll be happy. Maybe a hundred and fifty quid a week," he suggested, "for housing the gear for us?"

Mickey nodded his agreement, his attention half taken with the closing stages of the horse race. He'd five hundred pounds riding on the result of this race, so one hundred and fifty quid was loose change to him.

"She's been having some work done on the house," Al continued, "an extension like, to the rear, so there have been plenty of comings and goings and the neighbours are keeping themselves to themselves. Anyway, during the extension work, Johnjo built a trap door in the floor and it's as dry as a bricklayer's throat after a weeks graft, so it won't be affected by dampness. No problem there. The gear can lie in that hole till kingdom come."

"What about the sister? Can she be trusted?" Mickey wheezed as he sipped from his can. His horse had come in a close second, but that was life, he sighed.

Big Al placed his can down on the side table and thoughtfully stroked his chin. "She's my only concern, is Johnjo's sister. Since her old man took off, she's started shoving coke up her nose and she's doing more lines in a day than British Telecom. As well as that, she's having punters back to her gaff doing the... the business, with her."

For a big man, Mickey thought, Al could be an old woman when it came to sex talk. Must be his Catholic upbringing, he sniffed.

Sean coughed and swallowed hard, hoping the other two didn't notice the slight tremble of his hand as he tightened the grip on his can. Word about Johnjo's sister and her recent easy attitude to casual sex had got round, but he didn't want Mickey and Big Al to find out what he'd been up to.

Big Al was shaking his head, disapproval evident in his voice, as he continued, "And she's got kids in the house.

If any of the punters shagging her should suspect the gears there," he thumped one of his massive fists down on his knee, "we might have a problem, like."

"Does she know what would happen to her if she was the case of the gear being rumbled?" Mickey asked, one eyebrow raised with concern.

"She knows," was Al's response.

Satisfied that the drugs were at least for the moment safe, Mickey finished his lager and thought about Johnjo, contemplating the trip that he was arranging for him.

"Can we trust the little git?" he asked.

Big Al took a breath and ventured his opinion. "When we had him down the warehouse Mickey, you scared the shite out of him. To be honest, you scared the shite out of me."

All three laughed as Mickey stood up and moved to turn down the sound on the television. Standing with his back to the impressive sized stone fireplace, the portrait of Bill Shankly proudly mounted above it, Mickey disclosed the details of the telephone conversation he had with Maxie McLean. Then, with his hands clasped behind his back he faced the two Scousers and decided to discuss the plan with them. "Now, you both know I don't really trust these Scotch wankers, but that's where the money is at the minute. McLean has been going a long time, up there in Jockland and he's got the distribution network in place, awaiting our foreign friend."

Sean Begley looked puzzled. "Foreign friend?" he asked. Mickey sighed. Sean was a capable guy, when told exactly what was wanted of him, but sometimes....

"China White, Sean, the purest of the smack. And the stuff the Jamaicans in London got for us is about eighty to eighty-five per cent. Any idea how many times the Jock's can cut that?"

They both shook their head, their attention fully focused on their boss.

"But that's their problem," Mickey continued, "where their profit lies. So, like I was saying, I've agreed with our man that we'll get the gear up to him. I'm not giving him credit or time to pay for *that* amount of gear, so payment will be at the time of delivery. And that," he said smiling "is where Johnjo comes back into the fold." He stepped away from the fireplace and called through to the kitchen, shouting for his wife to bring more lager. That done, he sat down in his armchair. "I've agreed with McLean that the handover will take place at a busy service station, that way its unlikely two cars will attract any attention than if it were done at a quiet place, like a park. We'll travel in one car, with Johnjo travelling behind us, with the gear, in another car. That way," he smirked, "in the unlikely event he gets a pull from the rozzers, we're clear."

"What about protection?" asked a clearly anxious Sean. Mickey paused and stared at Sean, who panicked and thought maybe he shouldn't have interrupted his boss. Then slowly, Mickey nodded his head. "I've thought about that," he admitted, pleased that Sean was now thinking like a team player, "but it's a straight up and down run and McLean knows that any rip-off will mean his balls on my wall. But you're right, lad. Given the amount of money involved in this it would be stupid not to take some simple precautions." Turning slightly to face O'Rourke, he said, "Al, can you arrange for a couple of Black and Decker's, the nine millimetre ones, for the night of the run? A limited hire should do."

Big Al scratched his chin, his brow furrowed and thoughtful. "Could be costly, Mickey. The armourer usually likes the full price up front, and pays the deposit back when the guns are returned, less the cost of the hire of course. Just in case the guns go walkabout, know what I mean?" inferring the threat of a possible police seizure. "Besides that, there's an additional cost if the things fired, because we're talking ballistics and that means a new barrel."

Mickey considered Al's answer then clapped and rubbed his hands together, his decision made. "Do it. The money we're going to make on this deal far outweighs any expenses. And I don't expect to be shooting the things off."

His wife, collar length bleached blonde hair, tight sweater showing off her surgically enhanced tits and skin tight jogging pants, entered the lounge carrying a tray upon which stood three cans of lager. As she provocatively bent over the low table, Sean respectfully looked away, frightened Mickey might catch him ogling his wife's arse.

Mickey reached for a can. "Now, me lovely lads, how's about a few beers?" he wickedly grinned.

The sergeant at the enquiry desk at Govan police office put the phone down. Slowly, he raised his right hand and scratched his scalp through his thinning hair. Pushing aside the sealed plastic bag with the label attached that lay on his desk, he reached for his notepad, reading the scribbled note he had just written. The call from the Fingerprints Department supervisor had been a real blast from the past. Margaret Thomson? The name meant nothing to him and the incident reference number had been issued long before he arrived in the division. Glancing at the clock, he sighed and reckoned he'd have a quick look for the report, a perfunctory check to enable him, with hand on heart, to truthfully say he'd tried to find a file even after this length of time. Extremely unlikely, he figured, particularly since this steel and glass monstrosity around him had replaced the original Victorian station down in Orkney Street that received the report. The old building now lay boarded up, empty and derelict and probably with some of the older farts still inside, he grinned to himself. Looking again at the case file number he'd written on his notepad, he thought about phoning she who must be obeyed and warning her he might be late yet again, but decided that was an ear bashing he didn't really need just now. Wearily he pushed himself up from his desk and headed down to the filing room, his footsteps echoing as he walked through the new and drab deserted corridors to the basement, where the documents from past times were stored and now collecting dust. The cage containing old files was unlocked. And why, he reasoned, for who'd want to steal all this crap? His heart sank as he surveyed the endless boxed files on the shelving. Again checking the case number on his notepad, he started searching for the file pertaining to that year and quickly realised whoever had stored these files had likely presumed there wouldn't be anyone looking for anything in a hurry, for the years were out of sequence and the whole set-up was in his opinion, a complete fucking shambles.

Breathing slowly to avoid inhaling the musty dust mites that danced in the fluorescent light, the sergeant decided to take one, quick shufti at a row of files. He glanced at his watch and decided to give it a solid ten minutes, knowing that if he incurred unnecessary overtime, there would be hell to pay from his Inspector. To his utter amazement, the third file he inspected had the year he sought marked upon its dust cover. The label read 'Missing Persons' in faint but legible copper plate writing. Drawing the file from its cardboard sleeve, he quickly ran his finger over the brown, alphabetical index that was lying at the front and secured through the metal clips. Turning to the page marked 'T', he stopped at the case number he wanted and obtained the indexed number. The old report consisted of several pages, fastened together by a rusted staple. Smiling at his unbelievable luck, he saw that the pages were typed with handwritten notes attached and a visible ring stain where a cup or mug had been placed down on top of the report. A photograph, curled at the edges, was paper clipped onto the front page and displayed the posed head and shoulder shot of a young, pretty girl wearing a cheese cloth top, dark auburn hair with a bright red bow tied on top of her head. The girl smiled self-consciously at the camera. Nodding his head, the sergeant grinned in delight. Sometimes, Jimmy my boy, Lady Luck is on your side. Glancing through the file, the sergeant stopped smiling, a sudden chill sweeping through him. Placing the report back on top of the file, he put both hands on the frame and slowly leaned forward, eyes closed, his head sagging against the cool metal shelving. The last known address of Margaret Thomson, missing person, was immediately familiar to him. He'd been there recently, to the home of Ina Thomson. Dear God, he thought, swallowing hard, Margaret was her daughter.

As darkness overcame the October day, shadows merged and a chill seized the night air. Angie Bennett was hurting, the cold adding to her discomfort and pain, the thin jacket offering little protection against the biting wind that billowed and blew against the corner of the building where she had sought refuge. Her legs threatened to give way any second and send her weakened body crashing to the ground. She knew if she didn't move soon, she would succumb to her condition. She was also hallucinating. Terror stalked her. Every shadow took form and became Franny and his vicious sidekick. Countless times she had walked past the close where the Thomson family home was situated. She not been inside the house, hadn't even previously met Billy's Gran. Several times she had nearly entered, but each time her fear overcame her need. Not this time, though. Desperation had set in. Barely conscious of her appearance and the attention it attracted from wary passers-by, Angie knew she had no choice. She had to find Billy and now.   Standing at the close entrance, she pushed against the stiff, outer door and stumbled into the ill-light foyer of the close. She groped her way along the wall towards the Thomson house, the scraping sound of the heels of her cheap boots echoing off the stone floor. The old fashioned, but brightly polished brass nameplate screwed onto the wooden door was above a round security peephole of the type that enabled the occupant to see who was outside, before opening the door. Rapping the door with her knuckles, Angie stood back and tried to stand erect, unconsciously pulling straight the cheap nylon jacket while patting her hair into place. She saw a pinprick of light appear at the peephole and realised someone was on the other side of the door.

The light faded and an elderly female voice called, "Who are you? What do you want?"

"I'm looking for Billy, Mrs Thomson. I'm Angie, Angela Bennett." She licked her dry and cracked lips, "his girlfriend," she added. Oh God, please, please, let Billy be there, she silently prayed, Please, please! Angie thought she heard a sob, then the sound of the lock being turned and the door opened, but just a crack, just wide enough for her to make out the shadowy figure of a pale faced woman, grey hair and wearing an old fashioned wrap-around apron over a navy blue cardigan.

Don't you know lass?

Angie was confused. Know what? "I need to see Billy, Mrs Thomson. Is he here?" The door opened further. Mrs Thomson, Angie could see, had been crying, a handkerchief crunched up in her hand.

"You had better come away in, lass. Please, come in," invited Ina, standing back to allow Angie to squeeze past her in the narrow hallway, her hand directing the younger woman towards the sitting room at the rear of the ground floor flat.

Angie stepped from the cold hallway into a sitting room, a throwback to the nineteen-fifties with solid, functional furniture and a two bar electric fire, flowered wallpaper and plain, heavy dark curtains, closed to keep out the chill which penetrated the single glazed, wooden framed windows.

"Please sit down," Ina Thomson offered, stiffly formal and indicating with her hand the chair sitting next to the

fire and clearly recently occupied by herself.
Angie sat down, suddenly tired and sleepy in the warmth of the room. "Is he not here, then, Mrs Thomson? Billy?"
Ina Thomson stared down at the young woman. Of course, Billy had spoken about her in one brief moment of embarrassed admittance and even declared he loved her. But he never brought her round to visit. Because, Ina had guessed, just like her Billy, the young woman Angie Bennett was a drug addict, she sighed. Ina wrung her hands together, the news that she was about to impart hanging about her shoulders like some great and awful weight. "Angela, love, there was an accident," she began, now tearing at the handkerchief in her hands. "Billy was running, running away from the police. He fell..."
Angie sat still, suddenly chilled again despite the warmth of the room, too afraid to hear the rest,
"....and hit his head. I'm sorry, Angela, I don't know how to tell you this," Ina said, sobbing now, "but Billy died."
Angie, numb now. No Billy. No fix. Billy dead?
Darkness enveloped her.

Parking his car in the driveway, Maxie pressed the remote control button that closed the electric gates, then stood watching them thud together, safely secure in his own little kingdom. He was pleased with the outcome of the telephone call, happy that the deal was going ahead as he and Mickey had planned. "Or," he smirked, "as Mickey the Greek thinks he has planned."

Lena McLean hated her husband and despised herself for fearing him. Standing at the front door, holding it open, she watched as Maxie locked the vehicle and strode up the path towards her. She forced a smile of greeting, knowing any hint of mood or indifference would create an atmosphere or attract a torrent of abuse. Lena McLean, she thought wryly, the Stepford Wife. She could never know that among others, DC Mary Murdoch also wondered why a strikingly attractive woman like Lena had become involved with a man like Maxie. Had she the opportunity to answer that question, she would have undoubtedly explained that any girl whose formative years were spent in a small rural village, would have been attracted to big city life. A man like Maxie, seemingly sophisticated, evidently rich and undoubtedly capable of charm and who commanded the attention and respect throughout the city's restaurateurs and club owner's, was like a film star to the excited, young, and naive Lena. Combined with his flattering and expensive gifts, he had seemed the perfect choice for an overwhelmed Lena. Had I known then, what I know now.... she reflected ruefully. Soon to learn the true origins of his fortune, Lena was perceptive enough to realise that Maxie not only married a young and extremely bright wife, he gained a fully qualified accountant, one that he could and frequently did brutalise, whose name he insisted fronted the various dealings he made and in his mind legitimised the properties he owned. While having little doubt that she was being used in professional terms, Lena was astutely aware that any investigation into Maxie's empire and subsequent legal enquiry would all be traced back to her. It would be seen as her responsibility, her downfall, her disgrace and her eventual custodial sentence.

Maxie brushed his lips against her cheek and walked past her, calling over his shoulder a demand to know when dinner would be ready.

As previous pain reminded her, Lena had the meal prepared, fearful that any tardiness with his food would result in uncontrollable rage, the consequence being chastisement in the only way he knew. With his fists. Tonight though, Maxie was in good humour, suggesting they eat then visit the local cinema. Probably his usual bombs and bullets type of movie, but something, she wondered, has pleased him today. Her curiosity roused, Lena fetched him a freshly squeezed, chilled orange juice and brought it to him in the lounge. Maxie sat in his favourite chair, TV remote in hand and idly flicking through the news channels. Handing him the glass, she stood behind him and massaged his brow with her fingertips, a trick she'd learned that pleased him, though inwardly it repulsed her to run her delicate fingers through his greying and flaky scalp. "How's your day been?" she murmured.

"Good, good," he replied absently, in his mind recounting the phone call with Mickey, satisfied the bastard hadn't picked up anything other than good vibes from Maxie. "I fixed a wee deal, sweet as honey."

She knew any deal involving Maxie had to mean drugs. Though she had never used nor had any experience of drugs, she thought the whole idea vile and it sickened her that she was living on the profits of such an industry. Ignorance in Lena's case was not bliss. Seizing her chance, she light-heartedly asked, "And will this *big* deal mean you having to go anywhere?"

His eyes closed, Lena's fingers running soothingly across

his head, Maxie was feeling really relaxed and, he had to admit, pleased with himself. The thought of stitching up that Scouse sod caused him to grin. "No, it's a local job. I'm going to do a number on a guy that thinks he's dealing with yokels," he boasted. He sighed contentedly as Lena's fingers worked their magic. "The Scouse prick won't know what's hit him, by the time I'm through with him." His forehead creased as his brow furrowed and his eyes flashed open, his suspicion evident. He reached up and grabbed Lena by the wrist, forcing her to bend down and around to face him, twisting her body sideways to stop the pain. "But you'll be forgetting what I've said, my sweetness and light," he sneered, as he released her with a jerk, ignoring her cry of pain as she fell to the carpeted floor. "After all, I'm doing all this for you."

Chapter 13

Willie McKay alighted from the train at Kings Park railway station, deep in thought and oblivious to the crush of passengers around him that raced to the narrow stairs leading up the main road. Hands in pockets, he didn't notice the fine drizzle that soaked his hair as he slowly and reluctantly walked the road to his house. In truth he was fearful that his arrival home would provoke an immediate argument before he had the opportunity to speak plainly and calmly. In his mind, he went over and over his speech, preparing himself for confrontation. However, no matter the outcome, whether Margaret pleaded or cursed, he'd made up his mind. Willie was leaving her, of that he was certain. At last, he arrived at the house. Curious, he wondered at the dark front windows and the absence of any light from the rear kitchen window, usually seen casting its glow across the back lawn. His Ford Mondeo sat in the driveway; a silent sentry indicating to potential thieves there might be life at home. He pushed open the gate, the squeak reminding him for the thousandth time the hinge needed oiling and slowly proceeded along the path, the stone chips crunching beneath his feet. As he made to insert his key, the unlocked door swung open at the slight pressure he exerted. Surprised, he took a step backwards then realised he was being foolish, that Margaret would never stand behind the door with a rolling pin. That only happened in cartoons. Taking a deep breath, he shoved the door fully open and stepped into the dark hallway, his fingers searching for the switch and called out. "Margaret? It's me, love. I'm home." His stomach knotting, Willie switched on the hall light. The sudden brightness caused him to blink as his eyes adjusted. The hallway felt unnaturally cold and he run his hand along the wall radiator, only to discover the central heating must be switched off. Again he called out Margaret's name, but heard no answering reply, but then again, it wasn't unusual for her to ignore his return home. Moving through the house, flicking light switches on, Willie repeatedly called his wife's name, but to no avail. He was puzzled for it seemed not only wasn't Margaret McKay at home, but she'd gone out and left the house unlocked.

Angie Bennett opened her eyes and slowly came to, surprised at first to find herself lying on her back then wondering where she was. The whiteness above she saw was a ceiling. She felt hot, very hot. A hand holding a damp cloth caressed her forehead. For an instance she thought it was her mother and reached to stroke the hand, then reality set in. She wasn't at home and probably never would be again. But where was she? A concerned face appeared above her, lips tight together, eyes red-rimmed. Angie tried to raise her head, now realising she was lying on Ina Thomson's front room floor.

Ina's hand braced her neck as with her other hand, she gently placed a cup against Angie's lips. "You'll be okay now, love, here, take a wee drink of water."

"What happened?"

"You fell, fainted really. It was the shock. I didn't mean to tell you like that, about Billy, but I don't know how else I cold have broken the news. I'm so sorry. You were too heavy for an old body like me to lift. I just had to let you lie there, till you woke up. Are you alright now, can you sit up?" Ina helped Angie rise and manoeuvred her into a chair. "Is there anyone I can call? I don't have a phone, but the woman upstairs would let me use her phone, for emergency's, like. It gives her the chance to listen in, the old gossip that she is."

"No there's nobody. Just me and," remembering now, the tears stinging her eyes. "No there's just me."

Ina recognised the signs and knew the girl was hurting, for hadn't her Billy been like that countless times? Throughout her years, Ina Thomson had lived a good life. Maybe not on her knees praying at every opportunity, to let people see how pious she was, like some of they old hypocrites she saw down at the shops with their holier than thou attitude, but God fearing nevertheless and Christian enough to know when another human being needed support and a helping hand. All her life she'd cared for someone else. All her life she'd served others, never once thinking of her own needs. In a heartbeat, she was uncommonly angry now, remembering her Bert, who in his bigotry never heeded *her* views on religion, believing it *his* marital right to determine how they lived their lives according to *his* philosophy. Then as quickly as the heartbeat passed, her anger abated, picturing in her minds eye her Margaret, their lovely wee Rita, whom Bert, she angrily recalled drove from their home because of *his* bigotry.

But when Margaret left her parting gift was Billy, whom Ina cared for throughout his young life, bestowing her unconditional motherly love on her grandson. Rearing him as best she knew how, sharing moments of joy, then enduring the pain caused by his drug abuse, especially during the terrible bouts of withdrawal. She stared down at Angie. Just like this wee girl is suffering now. Stroking Angie's fevered brow, Ina drew a deep breath and took a decision, a stance against the injustices suffered by her throughout her life. "Well, my dear," she softly whispered to the young woman, "I'm a bit like you. I've nobody now, either, so why don't you and I just get to know each other for now and we'll see how things go, eh? But for now," reaching her hand to the back of the armchair and pulling herself upright, "I might have something that will help."

Willie was mystified. Where the hell was she? From the coldness throughout the house, it seemed to him that Margaret had been gone for some time. A thought occurred to him and he walked to the closet in the hallway where he pulled open the door. He rummaged at

the coats hanging there, but his first sight had been correct. Her raincoat was missing. The front room lay as he remembered it from the day before. Oddly enough, the only thing out of place being the evening newspaper he'd brought home, pages torn and scattered about the floor as though tossed aside by an angry child. Automatically, Willie began lifting the crumpled newspaper and placed it on the couch He realised he was still wearing his damp overcoat and shrugged it off, laying it over the back of the couch as his mind tried to work out where Margaret could be. She'd no friends. Well, not any that he knew of and no family. So where would she go? He'd better check and see if her clothes were still in the drawers in the small bedroom, but first things first, he decided. Better get some heating into the house. He walked into the kitchen and adjusted the central heating thermostat clock, hearing the system purr into life. As an afterthought, he reached for the back door. Locked. Turning, he went through the door into the front room,
"Hello, Willie."
"*BLOODY HELL!*" he cried out, staggering back in fright.
Adele Cairns, his elderly upstairs neighbour, stood in his front room, beige coloured raincoat thrown over her ankle length nightdress and belted at the waist, a clear, plastic rain cover over her neat and tidy permed hair and a stout wooden walking stick clasped firmly in her two hands and raised high above her head. "The front door was lying open and I thought you might be a burglar, Willie, so I came down to give you a good hiding. How are you?"
"I'm having a bloody heart attack, Adele is how I am. Jesus Christ! You scared the sh....life out of me!"

Adele lowered the walking stick and placed it on the floor. With a sigh, she sat down on Willie's couch. "My Jack used to use this stick, when he was alive. Thought it might come in handy again, one day. By the way, Margaret's not here, Willie. I think she's left you," she smiled at him. "Are you just about to have a cup of tea, then?"

Willie, his breathing and pulse slowly returning to normal, agreed it would be a good idea to put the kettle on. "You're right, Adele. Why don't we have a cup of tea, then you can tell me what you know."

The enquiry department sergeant informed his Inspector of the development in the Missing Person file relating to Margaret Thomson. Both concurred there seemed little doubt that the Fingerprint Department's information must be correct and would have to be followed up straight away. That of course meant informing the next of kin, as soon as possible. "Tonight, preferably," said the Inspector, in the full knowledge he was going home to his dinner.

"Very good, Sir," agreed the unhappy sergeant, in the full knowledge he wasn't going home to his dinner.

Vinny Bhatia and Julie Crossman used the identification of ESSO Jones handprints as an excuse to celebrate with a pizza and a few drinks at a well-known and popular city centre hostelry, close to police headquarters. Several drinks later, a relaxed, happy and slightly tipsy Vinny, his arm about the shoulder of his red haired beauty, thought he was the luckiest guy alive.

An equally tipsy Julie decided that tonight, if Vinny played his cards right, he would be the luckiest guy alive.

Robert 'Bingo' Chalmers and his newly acquired girlfriend, Avril Metcalfe wandered hand in hand through the waste ground at the rear of the old brickwork in the Partick area of Glasgow. Both fourth year students at the local high school, they had been going out together for almost a week, a new record as far as Bingo was concerned. He didn't particularly fancy Avril, as she apparently did him, but he'd heard rumours and stories that she was an easy lay and that was sufficient indication for him to give her a line of patter, his eventual goal to lose his virginity with her. Had Bingo but known, his quest was not unique, having been embarked upon by generations of pimply youths since time immemorial. Avril, admittedly, wasn't the nicest looking bird he'd gone out with; truth be told she was overweight and known locally as 'Anvil' Metcalfe, testament to the fact her face appeared to have been subjected to several beatings with a big hammer. The angry looking pimple that seemed to glare at him from the right side of her nose was a bit off-putting, but as he reminded himself, he wasn't looking for a long-term relationship. Not at fifteen years of age, anyway. Nevertheless, Bingo fancied his chances with Avril and in preparation for the great event, had pinched five condoms from his older brother's wallet, while silently thanking the Glasgow District Council for introducing sex education to his school. Bingo had three condoms remaining, the other two having been used for fitting practise on the forefinger of his left hand.

For her part Avril was in love. Bingo Chalmers was gorgeous, she decided, though obviously not as good looking as the guy in fifth year with the Justin Timberlake hair style and the cool tattoo tiger on his forearm, but there were certain advantages to going out with Bingo, the main one being that cow Mandy Carson not having a boyfriend, while Avril now did. She guessed why Bingo was leading her down towards the River Clyde. Scattered and derelict buildings were all over the area, refuges for the wino's that haunted the wasteland. Sometimes Avril's older sister came down here with her pals and Avril had heard her boasting about smoking a joint down this way, with her boyfriend. She figured that's where Bingo intended leading her, to one of the derelict buildings for a grope at her. She tried to recall what her sister had told her. "He'll probably start with the chat-up line, all 'lovey-dovey' then fondle your tits through your blouse and try to get your bra off." Her sister had agreed a quick feel through her blouse was in order, "but let him in at your bare tits" she'd warned "and he'll have a hand down your knickers quicker than our Da' throwing back a pint."

Bingo was by now getting quite excited. He knew exactly where he was leading Avril. His mate Ronnie had told him about an old, dry mattress located in the shed next to the water, where they used to keep small rowing boats. Ronnie boasted he'd had plenty of birds on that old mattress, but Bingo didn't believe him. It was known locally that if Ronnie told you it was Friday, you had to check the calendar to make sure.

The two teenagers, each with their own agenda, tripped

and stumbled across the uneven ground, Bingo hurriedly pulling at Avril's sweaty hand, while she pretended reluctance and practised being shy and coy. The moonlight shone brightly, its glow reflecting off the nearby river and highlighting a route through the debris of a once busy industrial area. The sharp outline of a large, three sided wooden shed beckoned them to their eventual destination. Cautiously, with heart pounding and not just from passion, Bingo pushed open one of the two doors that creaked as the unused hinges toiled against the rust. Eager to appear bold in front of Avril, he entered the dark and forbidding hut and stopped to listen, but the only sound he could hear was the gentle slap of water against the concrete slipway sloping down to the open side of the shed, that faced onto the dark and foreboding river. Slivers of moonlight streaked down from the pitted corrugated tin roof.

"I'm scared, Bingo, let's not go in there," pleaded Avril, hoping her voice sounded husky and like the film star in the movie last week, but desperate for her hero to drag her through the door and do all the things her sister warned her against.

"Eh, it'll be alright, I'm here," replied Bingo in the deepest voice he could muster, with his mouth dry and swallowing hard, terrified that some mad, wino-junkie would leap out and try to cut his throat, in which case he secretly planned to run like fuck and as for Avril? Well, if that happened he'd already decided, she was on her own!

Adele Cairns cupped her china mug in her two hands and sat forward on the couch, her face full of concern.
"I'm truly sorry I startled you, Willie. Are you alright now?"
Willie theatrically placed his hand on his chest, pretended to mop his brow and grinned. "Fine, Adele, but I pity the bad guys in this city if you take up crime fighting."
Adele chuckled, pleased that Willie wasn't annoyed with her for threatening him with the stick.
"Now," he sat down opposite, pulling his armchair close to her, "what can you tell me about Margaret, I mean, when did you see her last?"
"Last night, Willie, about an hour after you left."
Willie didn't ask how Adele knew what time he had departed, guessing it was pretty obvious that Margaret's shouting and bawling that followed Willie out of the door must have been heard by the whole street.
Unaccountably, he baulked at the memory. "Did you see her leave?"
"Well, you know me Willie McKay," Adele blushed, "if it's happening in the street then I usually see it. Not that I'm nosey by nature," she defended, "just that people lead such interesting lives, compared to mine." She sighed wistfully. "My day used to be so busy, taken up with work then when I retired, looking after my Jack during his illness." She stopped speaking, a fleeting memory causing her to smile. "And you were so good to him, Willie, helping with the wheelchair and tending his garden when he no longer could. Fetching his paper and changing his library books. I haven't forgotten that, nor ever will. I've said it before, you're a good man, Willie McKay and if only Margaret...." Adele stopped, thinking perhaps she had said too much, for after all was said and

done, Margaret was Willie's wife, for better or worse. Willie, unconsciously drawing on his listening skills, decided to allow Adele to blether on at her own pace. He didn't want her flustered. Besides, he thought, time was on his side.

"But, enough of that. Margaret. Right, where was I? Oh, yes. Well, after you... left, she continued to shout and swear and the language! Willie, I was shocked, I was. You know what it's like, these old houses have paper-thin walls. It was the war, you know, after the war every kind of material was in such short supply, the builders cut down where they could."

Willie sat patiently, his mug now cold and empty.

"I digress again," Adele tittered. "Margaret. Well, she was wailing and carrying on. At one point I thought I'd better come downstairs, see if she was alright? But I didn't. To be honest, Willie," she reached out and touched his knee, her skin almost bleached white, the knuckle joint enlarged by the onset of arthritis, "I was a bit frightened. I know that you and Margaret have had your problems."

Adele hesitated then seemingly decided to be totally honest. "Lord knows, I think the whole street's aware how difficult it's been for you both," but thinking to herself not both, for you, Willie.

Great, growled Willie to himself, I'm the talk of the neighbourhood. Willie McKay, failed husband and all-round plonker. He sat back in his seat as Adele continued.

"Then there was quiet. I mean, I didn't hear anything for a while, just silence. Not, you understand, that I had my ear pressed to the floorboards, but after all the carry-on it was a blessed relief to know things had settled down. I think it might have been about an hour, after you'd gone. I heard a scream. It fairly shook me, I can tell you, and I rushed to the front window. The streetlight was shining down the path and the next thing I saw was your Margaret, with her coat on, running down the driveway, past your car. Well, it was so odd that I thought perhaps she had been drinking, for she sort of bounced off the hedge. When she got to the gate she flung it open and Willie," Adele leaned forward to stress her point, "I mean flung it as though she was trying to tear if from its hinges! Then the strangest thing, she simply ran down the street."

Adele sat back, happy that she had recounted the whole story, just like a real police witness.

Willie sat still, his eyes wide and mouth agape, astounded at Adele's graphic account of Margaret's flight from their home. After what seemed like moments, he spoke, his voice quivering with emotion.

"Down the street, you say. In which direction?"

"She turned right out of the gate, but that's all I can say, Willie. The only other thing that was odd," Adele was almost apologetic, "I know this will sound silly."

"Go on," urged Willie.

"But she was pulling at her hair, with both hands. Now, isn't that strange?"

The marked police vehicle stopped outside the tenement and the sergeant switched off the engine. He sat for a moment, gathering his thoughts, dreading the moment he'd have to get out of the car. The young probationary police officer, sitting in the passenger seat, only knew that she'd to accompany the sergeant to this house where he was to break the news of a possible death. Her presence was required simply because she was female. The constable resented being here, resented the fact that in this so-called enlightened day and age that because she was a woman it was assumed she'd be able to provide solace and comfort, better than her male colleagues. Today's police service, she knew, prided itself on its equal opportunity programme and much of the initial police training was channelled towards this popular and politically correct issue. But old habits die hard and still the bosses insisted that where possible, a woman had to accompany a man when delivering death messages or, in this case, a 'possible' death message. How can someone be 'possibly' dead, she wondered?

Sitting in the driver's seat, the sergeant was conscious of the tight-lipped constable's resentment, but he didn't care, oblivious to her feelings on the matter. He was hungry, tired and upset at being landed with this awful duty. Turning round, he reached into the back seat and lifted his cap and the plastic bag with the label attached, then opened his door.

"Right, Megan," he said, "put away your petted lip and we'll get this done."

Chapter 14

Satisfied that no bogeymen were within the derelict shed waiting to ambush and murder him, Bingo Chalmers had wrestled a reluctant, or so he believed, Avril Metcalfe against the wooden wall. Looking at Avril in the moonlight that filtered through the cracks in the wall and the holes in the roof, Bingo knew nothing could ever convince him that she was a long time commitment. However, he persuaded himself yet again, needs must. "Easy, Bingo," Avril complained, though not unduly strongly, "take your time. I'm not going anywhere," while sticking her tongue down his throat and causing him to gag slightly. To his surprise, Bingo found himself expertly spun round and pushed back against the wall. She's stronger than she looks, he realised, worrying slightly that maybe the seduction wasn't totally his initiative. Avril, her face flushed and the pimple on her nose glowing like a beacon, frantically reached down for his zipper, her passion overcoming her sister's good advice.

Brilliant, grinned Bingo, the blood rushing from his head to other parts of his anatomy. Sliding one hand towards Avril's soft, ample breasts and attempting to pull her blouse material free from the tight waistband of her jeans with the other, Bingo was already mentally concocting a story for the benefit of his schoolmates, of the sexual conquest of Avril Metcalfe. The grin faded quickly when, looking over her shoulder, he glimpsed a face that seemingly floated on the water and stared back at him. Bingo screamed as Avril pulled at his zipper.

"Sorry," she moaned in what she assumed to be a husky voice, "did I catch your willie in the zip?"

Bingo, unable to break eye contact with the ghostly apparition, tried to point with both hands to the face in the water, but raising his arms caused him to encircled her large, body and this was perceived by Avril as an opportunity to once more thrust herself at Bingo, literally smothering him with the enormous expanse of her breasts.

"*NO,*" he screamed, pushing her away, "*THERE!*"

Avril, facing Bingo, stepped back from him, blazing mad at the sudden change in her youthful Romeo.

"What the fuck are you on about?" she demanded, hands on her hips.

Throat suddenly dry and tongue-tied, Bingo could only point.

Turning slowly, a sense of dread seizing her, Avril Metcalfe followed Bingo's finger to where he pointed and that, Bingo gleefully later related to his pals, was when Avril Metcalfe really went ballistic.

Tommy Morrison and Alex Morgan were looking forward to their refreshment break. Travelling in their police Transit van towards Partick police office, the uniformed constables were dumbfounded by their last call, a man who'd reported his flat broken into. Not that the officers were particularly callous or unsympathetic to the man's predicament, but he was, they both suspected, a closet racist. Returning home from his work to discover his flat had been turned over, the outraged complainer had been further upset when he found the culprits left behind a calling card, having defecated on his lounge carpet.

Morrison steered the vehicle round the corner into Castlebank Street as Morgan, swaying with the movement of the van, pulled his seat belt forward to slacken it and allow him to bend down. The plastic bag between his feet contained their fish suppers and was in danger of tipping over. Retrieving a can of soft drink from the bag, he tugged the ring-pull and held the can towards Morrison.

Shaking his head at the offer, his partner chuckled as he recalled the red faced flat owner ranting and raving and persisting that it was his downstairs Asian neighbours who must have broken in. When he insisted the officer's sweep the faeces into a cardboard box and take it with them, for the purpose of having it forensically tested, Morrison had nearly lost it and went into a choking fit. Thankfully, his partner had kept his head and persuaded the guy there was nothing of forensic evidence in the faeces.

"I'm telling you," the man had literally screamed at them, "there will be curry powder in that shite!"

Door to door inquiries had revealed the Asian neighbours to be a decent, hard working young couple who themselves provided an excellent description of a teenage and Persil white suspect fitting the profile of a local thief, well known to both officers.

As he raised the can to his lips, Morgan opened his mouth to swallow. Unfortunately for him, that's when a hysterical Bingo Chalmers, frantically waving his arms, ran from the darkness of the adjacent waste ground into the road in front of the van, forcing Morrison to slam his foot down and brake hard. As Bingo banged on the van bonnet, Morrison didn't know whether to get out and arrest this crazy, wee lunatic or provide mouth-to-mouth resuscitation to his now choking partner.

The problem was solved for him when Bingo wrenched open the driver's door and breathlessly gasped, "Body in the water!"

Ina Thomson had witnessed the decline of her community through the years. Unemployment, alcohol and drugs; all had contributed to the apathetic state of the area in which she resided. The people had changed too, she reflected. Neighbour no longer trusted neighbour, doors had to be triple locked and thieving had become an accepted way of life. '*An Isolated Community*', a newspaper had headlined an article when describing her district and she as much as anyone was to blame, for she believed if the community had held together, it wouldn't be in this dilemma now. She wrapped a shawl round Angela's thin shoulders and left her sitting by the warmth of the fire. The girl, her eyes dull and lifeless and streaks of cheap mascara staining her cheeks, had whispered her thanks and then lowered her head to stare at the two bright electric rods that gave off such a dry heat.

Ina gently caressed the girls' head then went into her bedroom. In all the times the police had called here for Billy, the officers had never once searched Ina's bedroom. Whether impressed by her quiet dignity or simply discounting any notion that Mrs Thomson be capable of deceiving them in the concealment of drugs, she didn't know. And that was fortunate, for Ina had a secret.

She'd lived with Billy long enough to know his habits and hiding places and once in a vain, but simplistic attempt to wean him off the horrid stuff, had many months previously stole into his room and taken the small zipped, clear plastic bag containing his drug equipment and the little bag of powder that lay with it.

Billy of course had been mad with fury and even resorted to calling her awful names, a thing he had never done before. She remembered her shame and disappointment in him. Then his almost childish attempts to persuade her, his tears and ranting that she didn't understand, his plea to be forgiven and to have his kit, as he called it, returned to him. He had called her hard hearted and worse, she shuddered at the memory, much worse. But she had stood firm, pretending the items had been taken by her to the council dump and destroyed. It hadn't made any difference, of course. Billy had left the house and, within a short time, obtained new needles and more heroin. Now, Ina wearily sighed, the secret would be shared with Angela.

Stiffly, her back aching, she put her hands on a small bedside cabinet to support herself as she slowly and awkwardly bent over and lowered herself to her knees. That done, she half pushed, half lifted the cabinet, shoving it till it moved, squealing and protesting on the linoleum, to a few feet from where it sat. With her stiff, aged fingers, she drew back a corner of the worn lino, and then prised open a floorboard, revealing a small space beneath from which she removed a clear, plastic bag.

Replacing the floorboard and carpet, she stood and returned to the front room. Angela now dozed in the chair, her breathing laboured and body trembling. Shaking her gently, Ina watched as her eyes opened, focusing on the plastic bag Ina held in her trembling hand.

"Angela, pet, I know this is wrong, but I can't watch you suffer like this. I've lost my Billy and you are all that I have to remember him by," the sob caught in her throat. Dear God, she prayed, what am I doing? But she had made her decision. She *must* be strong.

"I don't know how else to help you. These are some

things I took..." crying now, tears coursing their way down her cheeks "...from his room, to try and stop him from taking drugs, you understand? If you need to take it, I'll understand, but I won't be able to help after this. If you want, I can be here for you, but I can only help you if you'll let me. But not to get you more drugs, okay? Do you understand, dear? There will be no more."

Angie choked back her response, her mind befuddled by the gesture that this woman, Billy's Grandmother, was taking such a chance for her? She pushed herself to her feet and stood unsteadily, then threw her arms about Ina and both wept into each other's shoulder.

Ina gently prised Angie away, unable to look her in the face, a sudden realisation of the dreadful thing she had done.

"The bathrooms in the hallway and we'll speak...when you're done."

Nodding, Angie took the plastic bag and stumbled towards the bathroom.

The sergeant, accompanied by his constable, stood before Ina Thomson's door and taking a deep breath, rattled the letterbox.

Ina Thomson, her face chalk white, opened the door and almost collapsed with fright when she saw the officers. The sergeant mistook her alarm for a reaction to his visit and thinking her about to faint, reached out to take her arm and helped Ina inside the house to a chair by her fireside.

"Fetch a glass of water," he called over his shoulder.

The constable entered the small kitchen and returned

with the water. "Here, drink this Mrs Thomson," she offered.

Ina sipped at the water, alarmed and confused as to why the police were again visiting her. Then she remembered Angie was in the bathroom and what Angie was doing. But how could they know, she wondered?

The sergeant removed his hat and sat on the edge of the chair opposite, the constable standing between them. Rubbing his head, he said "Mrs Thomson, there's no easy way to break further bad news."

Ina clutched at her throat. Further bad news?

"Do you recall when I broke the news about Billy? You mentioned to me that his mother, Margaret, had left when he was a small child?"

"Aye, that's right," replied Ina, her voice faltering, "but we've never heard from Rita since then. Have you found her, do you know where she is?"

A faint spark of hope passed through Ina's heart, that her Rita, after all these years was found. Could it be possible?

The sergeant looked down at his feet. Gritting his teeth he wondered why, of all the fucking sergeants and Inspectors in the station, why did it have to be him doing this. He raised his head and looked Ina in the eye, deciding this woman deserved the honest truth, hurtful though it might be.

"It's not as straight forward as that, Mrs Thomson." He tried to breathe evenly, as he continued. "We had a report of a person, a woman it was thought at the time, falling from the Jamaica Bridge into the River Clyde. Evidence, which was obtained at the time, subsequently causes us to believe that person might...no," he decided the truth should be told, "it was Margaret Thomson."

To Ina, it seemed a sudden chill had descended on the room. She couldn't believe what the sergeant was telling her. It was just too much to take in. She hardly recognised her own voice when at last she spoke.
"Did someone see Rita.... Margaret," she corrected herself, "falling over the bridge? How do you know for sure it was her?"
The sergeant knew she was grasping at straws, hoping beyond hope that the awful news he had brought wasn't true.
"Fingerprints, Mrs Thomson. Your daughters' fingerprints match the ones that we got on the bridge, the fingerprints that you allowed us to take from her room, all they years ago, when you first reported your daughter missing."
Ina was stunned. "After all these years, you kept her fingerprints?"
Aye, the sergeant thought to himself and if I hadn't been so fucking conscientious finding that file I wouldn't be breaking this news now and upsetting this poor soul. "It's procedure," he explained, the standard response to a thousand such questions. "We never give up on a missing person."
"But if she fell in, mightn't she have swum to safety? Margaret was a good swimmer, you know. She won a medal with the Girl Guides."
The sergeant shook his head. "I'm sorry, no. It's very likely, according to the officers that attended the scene, that she banged her head on one of the stone pillars that support the bridge. Nor did it help that it was during the night, which might have hindered any rescue attempt."
The noise of a flushing toilet echoed from the hallway through to the front room. All three instinctively turned

and looked to the door as Angie entered, her face flushed, eyes glazed.

Startled at the sight of uniformed police, her speech slurred, she asked "Is everything okay, Mrs Thomson?" Ina, her heart pounding, introduced Angie. "This is Angela, she's," correcting herself, "was my Billy's girlfriend. Love, could you wait in Billy's room, just now? I won't be long."

Confused and frightened by the presence of the officers, Angie turned and panicked. What room was Billy's? Taking a chance, she pushed open a door and was rewarded by the sight of Kylie Minogue, leering at her from a poster. With a sigh of relief, Angie entered and closed the door behind her.

The sergeant wasn't fooled. He didn't know the girl, but if he couldn't spot a junkie with his service, he'd as well throw the towel in. Turning to Ina, he said, "The thing is, there's been no reports of any body being found. I'm going to be brutally honest with you, Mrs Thomson. In my opinion, it is only a question of time. You understand? Till your daughter is found I mean."

Megan, the young constable, stood listening to her supervisor and to her surprise she now understood why the sergeant had brought her. No amount of training could prepare her for this part of the job, breaking someone's heart. Strangely moved by the composure of this old woman, her shoulders slumped slightly and resisted with strong will the almost overwhelming temptation to reach out and console this poor soul. A lump formed in her throat and she realised she couldn't do what the sergeant was doing, not with her short service. Ever the realist, Megan silently accepted she still had much to learn.

Ina dabbed a handkerchief at her eyes. So much happening in such a short time. Rita. How could she have been living in Glasgow and not come to visit her mother? What had Ina done that as was so terrible to deserve that? The sergeant had brought a plastic bag with him that now sat on the floor by his chair.

"I've some other news, Mrs Thomson. The inquiry into Billy's death has concluded that it was an accident. It seems that when he was running away, he's stumbled on a glass bottle, causing him to lose his footing. It had been raining that morning and the place was pretty wet. It wasn't anyone's fault. An accident. It just happened," he finished lamely.

Lifting the bag from the floor, he continued. "The investigating officer at police headquarters has instructed me to return Billy's personal effects," but not, he had noticed, the notebook. No doubt the drug squad would be poring over the names in the notebook, trying to piece together a picture of Billy's drug dealing activities.

The sergeant placed the bag on the floor beside him, a conciliatory gesture, lost to the now gently weeping Ina. Technically, he knew he should have obtained her signature for the bag, but rightly guessed now wasn't the time for such formality. With a lump in his own throat, he scraped his chair across the worn carpet to be near her. Reaching out, he took her hand in his and continued in a soft voice, "You'll be aware that Billy has been removed to the city mortuary at the Candleriggs? I can arrange for you to have a private viewing, if you'd like to visit? If you needed transport...."

She smiled through her tears, acknowledging the comfort this stranger was trying to provide her.

"Yes, I'd like that, but I'll manage to get there myself,

thank you sergeant. Would it be alright if I was to go tomorrow, perhaps in the morning?"

The sergeant nodded his head, "Of course Mrs Thomson. Any time that suits you. The only thing that remains for me to tell you is that if we have any news about your daughter, I'll have someone inform you right away.'

Still holding her hand, he squeezed it gently, 'I'm truly sorry this has happened, Mrs Thomson. I wish there was more that I could do. Oh, there's just one other thing."

Reaching into the breast pocket of his tunic, he withdrew his notebook. Opening the book he said "I found this photograph in the file that we had on Margaret. I thought you might like to have it," and handed her the picture of the smiling girl.

Surprised, Ina took the photo and stared at it, the memory of that day when it was taken by her Bert coming almost immediately to her mind.

Now standing, the sergeant made to leave then asked in an apologetic voice, "I'm sorry to be a nuisance, would you mind if I used your loo?" and smiled at her. "One cup of tea, four visits," he softly quipped.

Still staring at the photograph, Ina nodded, hardly hearing the request.

The sergeant closed and locked the bathroom door behind him and immediately bent down to examine the waste bin.

"Thought so," he said, producing the empty plastic bag. A smaller bag with the residue of a powdery substance adhering to it was stuffed inside the larger bag. Closing the toilet lid, he sat down and looked at both bags. That wee junkie bitch had obviously shot up in the toilet, while he was giving that poor old soul the bad news. As if she hadn't enough on her plate. Well, he wasn't about to cause her any more grief. Angrily he crushed both bags together and then shoved them savagely into his trouser pocket. They would go in the outside bin at the office, he thought. No reason for anyone to know. Flushing the toilet, he went back to the front room and took his leave of Mrs Thomson.

Chapter 15

Constable Tommy Morrison drove the police van across the rutted ground, angry that his fish supper was growing cold and inedible in its wrapper at Alex Morgan's feet. The headlights picked out most of the potholes and bumpy ground, but still it was a struggle keeping the van moving. Over his shoulder an excited Bingo, crouching between the two front seats, pointed out the route to the hut. Holding on to the headrests, he could hardly contain himself as he glimpsed the shed in the moonlight.
"Over there mister," he pointed, "behind that big pile of rocks."
Drawing the vehicle to a stop, Morrison applied the handbrake and turned to his passengers.
"Right, this is about as far as we can take the van or I'll lose an axle. It's foot from hereon in."
Alex Morgan, his black coloured police issue blouson soaked through with sugary juice, wasn't a happy man.
"This had better be the real thing, wee man," he turned and scowled at Bingo, "because if it's a windup, you are dead, get me?"
"Don't forget the price of two fish suppers as well," muttered Morrison.
Donning their bulky, fluorescent jackets against the cold, the officers grabbed their powerful torches from the rear

of the van and followed Bingo, tripping and swearing over the uneven ground as they made their way to the wooden shed.

"I thought you said you were with a girl?" Morgan asked the teenager, deftly avoiding a pothole filled with dank water.

"I was, but she took one look at the stiff and legged it. I tried to tell her that I'd protect her, but you know what birds are like," he boasted, bravado oozing from him now that he had the protection of two large police officers to take on all baddies. He grinned to himself. What a story he had for his mates.

Morgan and Morison looked at each other, both silently agreeing that this wee shite who thought he was John Wayne, needed a reality toe up the arse. Stumbling the last few yards, they soon reached the hut.

"Now, where's this body then?" asked Morison, playing his torch onto the water.

"It was about there," Bingo indicated with his finger, then innocently asked, "will I get a reward or something?"

Morgan raised his eyes to heaven. What do they teach these kids at school, these days, he wondered.

"There," cried an excited Bingo, grasping Morison's arm, "over there. There it is."

Morrison shone his torch in the direction pointed out by Bingo. The corpse floated gently on the river swell, face upwards and head towards the bank. Morrison exhaled. "Poor sod," he thought, shaking his head, "poor bloody sod."

Harry Cavanagh didn't particularly relish phoning Maxie McLean at home, but something as important as this, even out of office hours, couldn't wait. "Hello Maxie, Harry here. I tried to get you earlier, but Lena said you were out on business."

"Things to do, Harry. Do you have something for me?"

"That matter we discussed today in my office. My secretary informs me the subject was carrying keys. Car keys she thought. I don't know if that will help?" he said, holding his breath.

A short pause followed then Maxie replied, "Maybe, either way Harry, I'm grateful for the call. Speak to you soon, bye."

Dismissing Harry, Maxie replaced the phone and drew on his cigar, inhaling the smoke deep into his lungs. Car keys, he wondered. Must be the motor Franny had gotten Billy for the collection of the gear and he wouldn't want Billy wandering about the city with the bags, just in case he got a pull from some nosey bastard copper. Maxie was a little disappointed, for Harry's information didn't take him any further forward. Still, he had to concede the car was smart thinking on Franny's part. Billy's instruction had been to collect the bags then deliver them directly to Franny for safekeeping, in the meantime. Billy was a patsy, a courier, nothing more. When he hadn't shown at the appointed time, that's when Maxie had set the dogs on him. Maxie sat down. Inhaling the smoke, he blew out slowly and rolled the thick cigar between the tips of his fingers, watching the lighted end flicker, as he thought. Could it be that Franny was ripping him off? No. He discounted that immediately. Though Maxie didn't trust anyone, Franny was the nearest thing he had to a confidante. Besides, he reasoned, Franny not only had his own pile, the money they would both make from this deal would set them up for life. One-ball? Sniggering, he discounted him as a player, mainly due to his stupidity. But wee Billy Thomson, the joker in the pack?

Hired by Franny, Wee Billy didn't know what was in the bags or did he? Could he have guessed? Probably. Even Billy wouldn't be that thick, collecting two locked bags from a financial dealer's office. Maxie continue to roll the cigar between his fingers, watching the smoke spiral upwards to the ceiling. But would he have the balls to rip off Maxie McLean? He'd have known it would cost him his life and that of his grandmother if he'd even entertained the thought.

Possibly, Maxie finally admitted to himself, well aware of the lure of the coin, just possibly. On the other hand, maybe Billy thought he was being watched by the police. Maybe he'd hidden the bags. But where? His house? No, too obvious. Would he have told anyone? His bird or his grandmother maybe?

Maxie finished his cigar and ground the butt in the ashtray, absent-mindedly waving the smoke from him. The bags! Where are the bags? Nodding his head, he came to a decision.

The junkie bird, he decided. If Billy's told anyone, it will be his bird.

Chapter 16

The all night supermarket was busy as usual and the queues didn't seem to be getting any smaller. The incessant 1980's pop music that droned on in the background couldn't allay the shoppers' impatience, as three flustered members of staff struggled to cope with a checkout system designed for eight operators. Her two-year-old toddler, sitting in the kiddie seat of the trolley and idly kicking at her thighs, didn't improve Katie Docherty's temper. Impatiently, she glanced at her wristwatch and realised that her guests would be due in just over an hour and her husband, useless prat that he was in the kitchen, would be panic-stricken by the time she got home.

Her mobile phone rang. She scrambled in her shoulder bag amongst every conceivable item that women can't leave home without and, in her case, included spare dummy teats and a clean disposable nappy for her daughter. Eventually she grasped the phone, its insistent ring attracting attention from every bugger within ten yards. It didn't occur to her that her good looks and flaming red hair was already a beacon to every hot-blooded male within staring distance.

"Yes!" she snapped, preparing herself for the whine of her husband.

"Hello, boss," the deep voice inquired, "got you at a bad time?"

Detective Inspector Alan Byrne had never said a truer word. Taking a deep breath and knowing it could only be bad news, she greeted him.

"Hello, Alan, what's up?"

"Got a live one," he replied, "well, figuratively speaking. Body washed up at an old jetty on our side of the river, down behind Castlebank Street."

Katie sighed. As the duty Detective Chief Inspector on call, she should have known better than go through with tonight's dinner arrangements. Already she could predict her husband's fury.

"No chance a gentle shove over to the Govan side of the

river could be arranged?" she queried, moving forward in the queue.

"Tried that but the tide's against us," Byrne laughed, hearing the sounds of a busy store and an irate toddler through the phone.

"I assume that everything is in place," her tone as discreet as the bystanders sudden interest would allow. Byrne had cottoned on to her predicament and proceeded with a one sided conversation, informing Katie that the police casualty surgeon had been called to formally pronounce life extinct, the technical support boys had cordoned off and tented the scene and the uniformed support unit boys were examining the shore line for anything of evidential value.

At last, within striking distance of the till, Katie began stacking shopping onto the conveyor belt and with her phone jammed under her chin, acknowledged the call, trusting her deputy would have everything in hand. Her main problem now, she grimaced, was to teach and then persuade her useless husband to tackle a microwave oven.

After seeing Adele back upstairs, Willie McKay sat and contemplated his next move then he came to a decision. Clearly, Margaret's actions were not normal, irrationally running from the house in the manner described by his elderly neighbour. Added to that, he knew of no relatives nor friends she would or could turn to and the time she had been away added to his concern for her safety.

Her safety, now why had he thought that, he wondered? Did he really believe his wife capable of harming herself? Pragmatically, he came to accept that Margaret in her recent state of mind, was more than capable of injuring herself. A sudden fear enveloped him and his stomach lurched. Shaking his head as though to clear it he reached for the phone and dialled the number of his local police office.

In a dark corner that escaped the floodlights of the nearby building in the Annfield area of Liverpool, Big Al O'Rourke sat in his car and watched the kids of the local swimming club exit the building and get into their parent's vehicles. He switched on the radio that he had previously tuned to a local station that played his favourite Country & Western music and listened as Marty Robbins again gunned down the bad guy in the town of El Paso. He grinned to himself, thinking it was appropriate music to accompany his meeting with the man he knew as the Armourer.

An old style dark green Ford Escort van drove into the car park, its headlights dancing against the vehicles departing and the side of the building where Al sat in his car. Slowly, the van did a full circuit of the car park, checking for a covert police presence Al assumed, before coming to rest beside his car, the driver's door against his own door. The space between the vehicles was less than a foot, lessening the opportunity for anyone who might be watching to witness a handover between the drivers.

The van window was wound down.

"Alright, lad?" enquired the Armourer, his oil skin jacket zipped almost to his chin and cloth cap pulled low over his eyes.

Al grinned. He and the Armourer went back a long way. In a low voice, Al greeted him and added, "You got my message, then. Two shooters, each with two full mags and payment tonight and that includes the deposit. Return within three days. Agreed?"

The Armourer nodded and turned to reach over the back of his seat. With a final look about him, he handed over a gent's blue coloured shoebox, bound by a piece of cord. Al noticed the Armourer was wearing transparent surgical gloves. He took the box and returned a bulky, brown envelope. Indicating the gloves, Al commented, "Take no chances, eh?"

"That's why I continue to be in business," the Armourer curtly replied, "nice dealing with you."

At that, the window was wound up and the van drove off. With a furtive look about him, Al undid the knotted cord and removed the lid of the box. It wasn't that he didn't trust the Armourer, he thought to convince himself, but in this business it pays to be careful. A faint smell of oil emanated from the box. Inside, wrapped in a two day old local newspaper, lay two military style Browning nine millimetre semi-automatic handguns, the black painted metal highly polished, with some silver showing through where the paint had chipped. Turning one of the guns over in his huge hands, Al recognised the arrow of the Ministry of Defence, stamped into the metal on the barrel. Packed in with the guns lay four magazines each, Al later discovered, containing twelve rounds of copper headed NATO issue ammunition. Resisting the urge to load the gun with a magazine, Al replaced the lid and, lifting his mobile phone from the passenger seat, punched in a preset number.

"Hello, Mickey? We're on, lad. The Black and Decker's have arrived."

While Big Al O'Rourke was completing his arrangement with the Armourer, Maxie McLean was holding a counsel of war with his two lieutenants. A nagging doubt lingered in Maxie's mind. Lena had been acting strangely the past few months and on one occasion, had answered him back. In Maxie's book that was unacceptable behaviour and she'd been rewarded with a slap across her smart mouth. She hadn't answered back since, he thought grimly. In his own way, he regretted hitting her, but bought her a nice pair of diamond earrings as an apology and that reminded him. He hadn't seen her wearing the earrings since he gave them to her.

He had thought long and hard about what troubled him and decided that his doubt existed because Lena knew too much about his business, far too much. Secretive by nature, Maxie was shrewd enough to realise his business was always vulnerable to the actions of the law and he had never been a man who left doors open. No, he decided, Lena had become a source of niggling irritation and he knew in his heart that the day would come when he would have to face dealing with her. But that decision was a long way off yet. That she feared him was obvious. That she hated him was plain to see every time he went near her and their sexual union was not so much passion as her discharging her wifely duty. So then, he wondered, why the loving attention yesterday when he had returned home?

His thoughts were disturbed by Franny.

"Sorry, what did you say Franny?"

"I was asking if you had completed the arrangements with our friend down south?"

"What arrangements?" interrupted One-ball.

Maxie and Franny smiled.

"I had a little arrangement with an associate of mine from down south, who is going to supply us with some gear," disclosed Maxie, grinning broadly, "a lot of gear. The deal is that one of his boys, I don't know who yet, will travel in the early afternoon, arriving about late evening at the service station near to Hamilton, off the M74, you know the one?"

One-ball nodded, remembering the service station where on two nerve-wracking occasions he'd collected commodity that had been driven at speed from down south. One-ball didn't like being outside the city, believing that people who lived anywhere outside Glasgow city limits were all sheep-shaggers.

"His guy," Maxie continued, "the courier, will have a bootful of China White, almost pure, and that means we can cut it as many times as we want."

Franny and One-ball understood what Maxie meant. They'd dealt in the China White before and considered it one of the most potent heroin batches they had ever had the good fortune to obtain. The stuff, properly cut and distributed, could earn them a small fortune. Usually, as they had done before, the heroin was blended with a variety of mixing agents. One such mixer was Manitol, a pharmaceutical product. Yet their yield could be stretched even further when they used mixers such as household flour or even talcum powder or on occasion, worst. Using this form of dilution, the strength diminished but the profit could be increased by as much as five hundred percent, dependent on the level of adulteration. As a result the delivered heroin was spread further, thereby the greater the profit. Maxie's organisation, tried and tested, already had the industrial type coffee blenders and mixing agents in place in houses and premises throughout the city while their owners patiently awaited delivery of the promised heroin, waiting to mix the ingredients.

The greater risk, of course, lay with the dealer, whose possession and local distribution of the heroin involved an ever increasing number of workers and customers, not all of whom could be trusted. The intensive vigilance of the authorities, who consistently demanded harsher penalties and had recently introduced the reward system for information leading to conviction and further increased the likelihood of detection by the police. The police themselves, all three men knew, did not slouch in tracking down drug dealers and their much-publicised successes in the forfeiture of wealth acquired by drug dealing had driven some of Maxie's rivals to abandon the risky, yet lucrative venture.

He lit a cigar and continued, "The courier will be driving an old style dark blue Vauxhall Cavalier, the saloon type. Ring any bells?" One-ball shook his head.

Patiently, Maxie encouraged at him.

"Think, One-ball, who was recently given an old blue Cavalier, by Franny?"

One-ball furrowed his brow, his eyes half-closed in concentration, fearful of making a mistake and again being thought the fool by Maxie.

"Billy Thomson?" he hesitantly replied.

"Correct," enthused a suddenly buoyant Maxie. "Billy Thomson. And that's who will be collecting the gear, on our behalf."

One-ball looked at the now sniggering Maxie and Franny and thought they must be mad.

"But, he's dead, boss, Billy's dead," he exclaimed.

"Aye, but Mickey the Greek doesn't know that," guffawed Maxie loudly.

Franny was now almost bent double, tears of laughter rolling down his florid cheeks, but One-ball still didn't fully understand. "So, we're going to pretend that we're Billy Thomson?"

Still laughing, Maxie then filled One-ball in with the rest of the plan.

"When the courier arrives at the service station," Maxie began, "he will expect to be met by Billy Thomson whom he's met with on previous deliveries and who will also driving a dark blue Cavalier. The courier will park at a pre-agreed spot on a road running behind the service station motel, exchange car keys with Billy then each will drive the other's vehicle away. Billy will have the Cavalier containing the gear and the courier will drive home the Cavalier with the payment in the boot. That way all the two have to do is change cars, no handing over bags or anything like that, Understand?"

One-ball slowly nodded his head. He wasn't a total fucking idiot, he thought to himself, that part was easy enough to get a handle on, but what was this about Billy Thomson?

"Only the courier won't be met by Billy," Maxie continued, "but by us in our new toy, the BMW you blagged the other day."

One-ball looked confused. "But we don't have the payment because Billy got killed before he delivered it to Franny."

Patiently, Maxie agreed. "That's an issue we'll deal with in time, but we're on a schedule for the gear, so the deal with Mickey takes priority because the gear is where the greatest profit lies. If I was to tell Mickey the Greek that we didn't have the money, he would sell the China elsewhere and we would be out a lot of profit. Don't worry, One-ball," he reassured his man, "I haven't forgotten about the two bags. Let's just say the bags will be," he paused, then said, "additional profit," and smirked as he added, "I feel sure either Billy's granny or his bird will be able to help us find them, especially with you persuading them to remember."

One-ball, nodded his head in understanding. He liked that idea. Hurting people, he had to admit, was what he did best and he would enjoy some time with Billy's bird, the wee blonde junkie lassie.

"As for pretending to be Billy," Maxie laughed "that'll only happen if the courier thinks Billy Thomson is two guys with balaclavas and big fucking baseball bats!"

All three burst into uncontrollable laughter, though for his part, One-ball still hadn't fully grasped what he was laughing about.

In the kitchen next door, Lena McLean listened to the three men loudly laughing and very slowly slid her bottom off the polished worktop and onto the cold tiles. She slipped her bare feet into the strapless sandals then gently placed the glass tumbler down on top of the worktop and removed the piece of cotton wool from her left ear. The partition wall, a wooden stud and plasterboard construction, was designed to insulate but was not, as Lena had previously discovered, totally soundproof. As she eavesdropped, she knew that she hadn't heard the full discussion between the three men, but enough to enable her to jot down a few notes on the piece of paper she now folded and slipped into the pocket of her slacks.

Franny McEwan drove away from Maxie's palatial home in his own car and run the meeting through in his mind. He was worried and hadn't been fooled by Maxie's seemingly indifferent attitude to the two bags. Arranging for that wee shite Billy Thomson to collect the bags had been Franny's idea and Maxie wasn't the type of guy that would let something like that go. No, Franny had too many vivid memories of punters that had crossed Maxie or, in his twisted view he perceived that had let him down, and the hurt that had been inflicted on them. So why wasn't he ranting and raving at Franny? Sure, he'd boast about how confident he was of getting the bags back and, right enough, that clown One-ball would enjoy the opportunity to hurt the old woman and Thomson's junkie girlfriend. No, he decided, Maxie wouldn't be letting Franny's failure go. Failure? He shivered. For that's what it was, a failure. By employing Thomson, Franny had unwittingly let Maxie down. Convincing himself that Maxie's retribution might be any time, he muttered to himself, "What can I do to get off the hook?"

DCI Katie Docherty arrived at the riverside still smarting from her argument with her husband. Accusing her of dumping her shopping and her daughter, he'd protested her abandonment of him, as he phrased it, and stormed off into his study in another one of his too frequent sullen moods. She sighed. Her position as a Detective Chief Inspector had been hard won, but her husband still found difficulty coming to terms with the odd hours she worked. She silently vowed she'd make it up to him, in one way or another.

The police officer manning the entrance to the cordoned off area of waste ground, by the rivers edge, recognised Katie and flashed her a smile as he raised the blue and white tape high enough for her car to pass under. Parking her car beside those already arrived, her first impression of the locus was of a hive of activity, with uniformed officers and white, boiler-suited scenes of crime personnel moving back and fro. She sat on the tailboard of her Volvo estate and pulled on a pair of mud splattered, Wellington boots. Her thoughts were interrupted by the approach of her deputy.

A large man, almost six three in height, stocky build with a full head of dark brown hair and a neatly trimmed RAF style moustache, Alan Byrne liked and respected his boss. Though slightly younger than Byrne, he believed Katie Docherty to be an extremely competent and tenacious detective, wise beyond her years and privately predicted she was smart and sharp enough to reach the top of the tree. For her part, Katie relied heavily on her deputy's vast CID experience and wasn't beyond seeking his advice in matters where she might otherwise flounder. Together, she reckoned, they made a damn fine team and had already achieved some impressive convictions.

"Hello, Katie, find us okay then?"

"Couldn't really miss you Alan, what with the large

white tent and halogen lights everywhere. Did I see the press, back there?" she indicated towards the roadway with her head.

"Local rag. Told them to contact the media office at HQ, but they insist on hanging around, flashing their fivers at the wooden tops."

Alan, she knew from weary experience, didn't have a high regard for his uniformed colleagues. "Okay, that's me ready," stamping her feet in the boots. "What's the score, then?"

Byrne led the way to the floodlit tent then drawing back the flap, he ushered Katie inside where for a second the bright lights dazzled her. In the centre of the ground covered by the tent she saw a blue nylon sheet, pegged into the ground at the corners and upon which lay the spread eagled body of a woman, the hair plastered across her face, fawn coloured, coat unbelted and lying open to reveal a sodden nightdress underneath.

A young cop standing just inside the tent, wrote her name and timed arrival with trembling hands in his notebook as she entered, then respectfully stood aside. He can't be more than twenty-one, Katie surmised as she nodded to him, seeing his pallid face and his eyes turned upwards in an attempt not to stare at the sight of the dead woman. The young officer was swallowing hard. Quietly and with some compassion to preserve his pride, she asked if he might wish to wait outside while she examined the body. Byrne was nearly knocked over as the cop fled the tent, then seconds later both heard the sound of him discharging his stomach contents into the river. Poker-faced, Katie glanced at her colleague. They both knew that being a police officer didn't immune one to the sight of death.

Turning her attention to the woman on the sheet Katie donned skin-tight plastic surgical gloves as she stood for a moment and visually examined the corpse. She saw that the nightdress had ridden up to the woman's waist and exposed her practical cami-knickers, her legs like her face, a pallid and ghostly white from submergence in the cold water of the River Clyde.

"No dignity in death," she murmured to herself.

"Scenes of crime have photographed and examined the body," reported Byrne.

Likewise wearing surgical gloves, he bent over the body and gently stroked the hair from the woman's forehead, revealing an ugly, open wound to her right temple, now washed clean by the river. Katie knew that many bodies pulled from the river often had wounds inflicted post mortem, usually the result of a collision with sailing craft, their engines or simply, like so much flotsam, from being banged against solid objects by the current.

"She's taken a real belt on the head here," he said, pointing to the wound,

"wedding ring, no watch or other jewellery. I haven't been through the pockets yet, thought I'd leave that till we move her to the mortuary, if that's okay with you?"

"I agree. There's more opportunity there to inspect the body properly. Poor soul. If you accompany the body, Alan, I'll have the back shift check missing person reports, but at the moment I'm not happy with the wound so until it's proven otherwise, I'm marking this down as a suspicious death. I'll get back to the office and prepare an information bulletin for all stations and a media script. I'll also give the ACC (Crime) a bell and let him know the score for the Chief's daily report in the morning."

"Do you want me to contact the duty Deputy Procurator

Fiscal?"

Katie considered, aware that the PF's department had primacy for all bodies found outdoor, in suspicious circumstances or in any situation, which might result in court proceedings.

"No, time enough for that. If you're satisfied with the scenes of crime and photographs that have been taken then there's nothing for the duty Deputy PF to see here. Let's wait for the post mortem in the morning."

The two officers responding to Willie McKay's phone call arrived in an unmarked police car. As they sat on his couch, Willie recounted his wife's personal details; age, height, description and clothes last seen dressed in. The photograph he handed over was a couple of years old and even then, he saw with a regretful sigh, Margaret had been scowling. The officers duly noted the particulars in their notebooks and slowly he recounted the circumstances of their last encounter, finishing with him walking through the door. Willie knew the officers would be knocking on neighbour's doors and thought it prudent to include the verbal abuse he had endured, for he was certain his neighbour's accounts wouldn't leave anything out. The senior constable, in her late thirties, was brisk and officious and clearly not impressed by Willie's profession as a colleague. Curtly, she requested she be shown round the house. Her bullish request was courteously polite, but Willie knew she wasn't about to take no for an answer. He wanted to tell her there were no bodies lying under the bed and was astounded when she dropped to her knees and searched there. The younger officer, visibly embarrassed by his companion's action, stated he was going upstairs to speak with Mrs Cairns and left the house.

"No," said Willie "my wife has no friends that I know of."

"No family that I know of."

"No hobbies."

"She is a full time housewife."

"No, she didn't drive."

And finally,

"No, I didn't hurt my wife and I don't know where she is."

Satisfied there was no more to learn and with Willie's and Adele Cairns statements duly noted, the female cop snapped closed her notebook and informed Willie they'd be in touch, then both officers left.

Seeing them to the front door and a little shaken, Willie was grateful for the concealed look of sympathy the younger constable gave him, clearly trying to convey his apology for the undue harshness of his partners questioning.

He closed the front door and leaned against it with his forehead touching the cool glass panel. Christ, he suddenly thought, I've just described a woman who didn't go out, knew nobody and hated me. Just who the fuck have I been living with, all these years?

Straightening up, he returned to the front room, fetched a little used bottle of whisky and a glass from a cupboard, poured a generous measure and sat down. Taking a deep gulp of the fiery liquid, he reached for the phone to speak with the only person in whom he could confide, Archie MacDonald.

Ina Thomson, her hands tightly stuffed in her apron pockets to prevent them from shaking, sighed with relief when at last the police officers left. Hearing them close the front door behind them, she stood and went to Billy's room. Pushing the door open, the light from the hallway spilled into the darkened room and shone on Angie, lying asleep on the top of Billy's bed.

Ina stood looking at the pale, thin girl; so young she thought and so helpless in sleep. As softly as she dare, she pulled the counterpane over Angie and then stroked a wisp of hair from her closed eyes. Quietly, she tiptoed from the room, pulling the door tightly closed, behind her.

In the kitchen Ina pondered the news the sergeant had brought. She had always known in her heart, she would not see her Rita again or at least, not in this life. As she'd grown older, Ina had unconsciously returned to praying, not every day but sometimes when the loneliness of age pressed her, she found herself whispering her thoughts to Him. Not church prayers, she admitted, but enough to let Him know she had not forgotten Him, that one day she would stand before Him and confess her sin, her greatest sin, the sin of weakness for allowing her husband to drive her Rita from her mother and baby son.

The kettle boiled and whistled its tune but she ignored it, her thoughts turning to the strange circumstance which denied her in her twilight years, the grandson she had reared, but provided her with the opportunity to care again. Care for Angie.

This time, she promised herself, clenching her fists

tightly, no matter how hard it will be, this time I will not fail.

Chapter 17

Glasgow city mortuary is located just over 100 yards to the north of the River Clyde and is sandwiched between the old and the new High Courts. Its solid, oak doors face east towards Glasgow Green, the huge area of parkland where in days long past, miscreants, having committed such wanton crime ranging from murder to simple theft, measured their length after being hung by the neck from the Gallows. In more recent time the Green has hosted public concerts and fairs, but always the shadow of the Courts and mortuary loom over that green and pleasant place.
The mortuary has seen a goodly number of the Glasgow's citizens laid out in its cold, austere rooms and from here, its patrons have travelled to every corner of the city and beyond, seeking final peace in the many cemeteries and crematoriums around Glasgow. Stories, myths and legends surround the mortuary and evidence, often revealed by the post mortem examination of its clientele, have resulted in and been produced as evidence in many a criminal trial at the adjacent High Court.

To this place Detective Inspector Alan Byrne travelled in an unmarked police car driven by one of the divisional late shift detective constables, unconsciously pleased that for decorum, a female officer would also be present at the examination of the woman's body.
His task was simple. First, deposit at the mortuary the body that was now travelling with the contracted

undertakers in their plain and unmarked dark coloured Transit van in front of him; secondly, witness the search and removal of attire from the body. The corpse being a woman, Byrne's natural good manners didn't like to think of it as stripping the body; thirdly, to indicate to the scenes of crime officer anything Byrne considered worthy of photographing, such as bruises and finally and most importantly, note anything that might identity the unfortunate woman.

The nightshift staff of the mortuary had already been alerted to the pending arrival of the body and had the back doors unlocked and ready to open, awaiting the police to supervise its introduction into the building. Like a well-oiled machine, the process went smoothly and efficiently. The barest gesture of greeting was exchanged, all parties anxious and eager to complete their task; the staff to return to their video in the restroom, the undertakers to their office and the police to their beds.

An overwhelming smell of formaldehyde assailed Byrne, reminding him of past visits and too many suspicious deaths. He cracked a joke to his driver, gallows humour being the coppers response to sights and tasks from which the ordinary citizen might shirk and simultaneously reached into his coat pocket for the small phial that contained the scented hand-cream he would later use to dab under his nose, to negate the awful smell that resulted from post-mortem examination.

Within a few minutes, the body of the woman, recently recovered from the River Clyde at Partick in the City of Glasgow, lay on her back upon a stainless steel table. Indented gullies and holes that perforated the table identified its true purpose, to better facilitate the drainage of blood during the surgical examination of a human body. In silence and with dignity, the body, its whiteness reflected by the harsh overhead lighting, had been carefully stripped and was now devoid of the clothing that lay upon an adjacent table. Byrne could see no visible marks, save the river washed wound upon the forehead. The photographer used the brighter light to his advantage and snapped several pictures. Once completed, a crisply starched, white linen shroud was produced by the mortuary staff and snapped open, then placed over the body to restore a modicum of modesty.

As procedure dictated the scenes of crime officer carefully and as Byrne watched, with some degree of gentleness, obtained the fingerprints of the woman.

No one spoke.

The female detective, wearing thin plastic gloves, turned to search the clothing, beginning with the coat.

"Here, boss," she called to Byrne.

Turning, he saw that she held in her hand what appeared to be a folded piece of newspaper, now soggy and with some of the ink run.

"Chances are," continued the detective "if I get it back to the office in one piece, I might be able to lay it flat on a radiator and try to dry it out. What do you think?"

Nodding his head, Byrne agreed.

"Might be worth the effort, so see what you can do, anyway." As his colleague carefully placed the paper into a paper bag, Byrne lifted the coat. From a side pocket he retrieved what he presumed to be house keys. The same pocket revealed a small rectangle of paper, a receipt.

With a satisfied grunt, Alan showed the paper to his colleague. The paper was not wholly spoiled by the water and quite legible.

"This is a bank printout that's issued by ATM's, cash

machines," he added unnecessarily.

His colleague grinned.

"I don't get them anymore," she chuckled. "The machine just bursts into hysterical laughter when I put my card in."

Alan smiled at her, pleased at her tension-breaking joke and hopeful that this slip of paper might provide the clue to the identity of this unfortunate woman.

No need, he decided looking at his watch, phoning Katie Docherty at this time. Glancing at the body he reflected that for once, time was on his side.

Archie MacDonald lay awake, Jean softly snoring beside him. He thought about the phone call from Willie and wished there was something he could do for him. Slowly, so as not to disturb his wife, he slid from between the sheets and tip-toed from the small room, carefully avoiding stepping on the creaky *I'll get round to it* floorboard. Quietly he made his way downstairs. Safely in the kitchen he switched on both the light and the electric kettle, spooning coffee into a mug as it boiled.

"I'll take one of those."

Jean stood leaning on the doorframe, smiling at her husband.

"Can't sleep, big boy?"

Archie grinned. With that flimsy nightie and her breasts heavy with pregnancy, he still thought his wife as sexy as the day they had met. Jean walked towards him and put her arms around his ample waist.

"I was thinking about Willie. I'd like to help him, but I can't think of anything," he admitted, while holding her close and stroking her hair

Jean sighed, turned and sat down at the small breakfast table. Her Archie was a good man and a hard worker she knew but still, sometimes he needed a good shove.

"If you want my advice, Archie MacDonald, I'd say the best thing you can do is be supportive to your pal. That and maybe you can have a quiet wee word with Roddy Munroe."

Archie was aghast.

"But I can't go running to a boss," he complained, "that'd be gossiping about Willie's private life. I can't do that."

"Male pride and pigheadedness," she scoffed, her Irish lilt becoming more pronounced the angrier she got. "You know as well as I do that Willie's life with that harridan wife of his needs sorting out. He won't ask for time off after that trouble you told me about, with that sergeant Reid. So, who can give him time off? Can you give him time off to do that or will it be Roddy Munroe?" she persisted.

Then, more softly "I know it will be hard and likely Willie will be angry, if he finds out. But sometimes being a friend is more that just listening. You're not a selfish man, Archie MacDonald and you're worried that you'll lose Willie if you do this. But he needs you to look out for him, even if he doesn't realise it at the moment. He's not a daft man, is Willie and yes, he might be angry, but in time he'll come to understand that you care about him, because he is your friend."

She stopped then, knowing that to go on would only labour the point she was making.

His shoulders drooped in defeat. Archie knew she was right.

"We'd better get to bed, then," he suggested, then dashed any hope she might have had for a passionate clinch when he added, "Because I'll need to be into work early, to grass up my mate."

Chapter 18

Janice Leckie enjoyed her job. The last twelve months had been hard going, with all the telephone and computer technology to learn, the procedures and really, just getting used to being back to full time working again. Yes, she smiled to herself, life was on the up and the extra income her salary brought into the house would mean that she and her husband might yet be able to make that visit to New Zealand and see her son and his wife, not to mention their children. Her grandchildren. Her throat tightened at the thought. This job might just make that happen.

Janice settled back into her padded, swivel chair and adjusted her headset. She decided she liked the shifts, though the early shift at police headquarters was a killer, rising at five thirty each morning for the six-thirty am start. She took consolation in the ease of the early morning parking and the first couple of hours in the control room, when the place was quiet that allowed her to catch up with her knitting. The police officers that worked alongside her would rib and tease her, but she knew they liked her and would voluntarily cover for her at the telephone consul, allowing her to slip away for a quick and highly prohibited cigarette in the back room. Of course, the home baking she brought in for their tea breaks helped.

"Bless them," she thought.

A green light on the panel in front of Janice activated. She pushed the button and lifted her pencil. "Good morning, Police Headquarters how...."
"Listen," interrupted the voice, "I know my call is being taped, but I also want you to write this down."
As Janice listened, her eyes widened. Frantically she scribbled on her pad. But Janice didn't write down the caller's information, for as the caller said, that was being recorded and could be played back. No, Janice had her own idea about the call.

Mickey 'the Greek' Metexas stretched and yawned, scratched his backside and belched.
"You're a pig," his wife good-naturedly complained.
Mickey laughed. He leered at his wife, wearing the gold lame trousers, long slim legs and, even after bearing the kids, still tight in the arse.
"Just get me breakfast on, woman or you'll really see me being a pig."
His wife opened the fridge and selected eggs and meat.
"Fry-up?" she asked.
"Usual, doll," replied Mickey, concentrating on the sports page of his favourite daily rag.
The wall phone rang in the kitchen. Mickey's young son, school blazer and grey shorts hanging down at his knees grabbed the receiver.
"Who?" the boy asked, his face screwed up in concentration.
"Give us here, tiger," said Mickey, taking the phone and gently ruffling the boy's mop of unruly hair.
"Who's that?" he briskly asked.

Mickey's face changed and his jaw dropped as the caller told him to shut up and listen.

For the next few minutes, Mickey's wife saw her husband's facial expression transform from surprise through to shock, then deep rage. Holding the phone away from him, he looked at it incredulously and then with savage fury, repeatedly smashed the receiver against the cradle.

His wife, anxious and frightened now timidly asked, "Mickey, what's wrong? What's happened?"

"*Shut the fuck up!*" he screamed at her, "*Let me think!*"

For the second time within a few short hours, Angie Bennett woke in Ina Thomson's home and again could not recall where she was. The posters on the wall at first confused her, but then she remembered she was in Billy's room. With a start, she also remembered Billy was dead. Her throat hurt and the cramps in her legs, stomach and arms were there, but not as painful as the previous day. It came back to her slowly, as a dim light grows brighter. Billy's granny giving her Billy's works and....

Oh my God, recalling her fright. The police were here. Her panic overcame her usual morning preparation for getting out of bed and quickly, she threw back the cover and swung her legs off the bed then stopped. Who had placed the cover over her? The sudden movement had made her dizzy and nauseous. A knock on the door startled her and then it gently swung open.

"Thought you might like a wee cup of tea, hen."

A smiling Ina Thomson glided into the room, setting the cup and saucer down on a stained and chipped wooden

bedside table. Angie shook her head in an effort to clear it then stared up at the older woman. Her throat still hurt, but she manage to stammer a question.
"What time is it, Mrs Thomson?"
"Still early, Angie," Ina soothed, "there's no need for you to rush. Do you think you would you be able to eat some breakfast?"
"I don't know," she shyly replied, "my stomach's not been too good recently, if you know what I mean," then eager to please, "but maybe I could try something?"
Ina continued to smile.
"Look, you'll want to freshen up a bit. You know where the bathroom is. I put a clean towel and a new toothbrush out for you. Just come through to the front room, when you're ready," and turned to go.
"Mrs Thomson....." Angie replied, her eyes suddenly moist.
"No need to say anything, Angie. Let's eat first then we'll have a wee chat, eh?"
Left alone, Angie felt the tears well up in her eyes. The simple thoughtfulness of this woman had touched her far more than she realised. Her body trembling, she carefully stood upright and experienced an emotion long forgotten. Kindness.

His wife, he reluctantly now accepted, was right. Archie MacDonald was at his desk, nursing a mug of tea almost an hour before any of his colleagues. The morning traffic was lighter than usual and for once he had experienced a traffic free journey to work. That, he conceded, gave him time to mull over his approach to the

Detective Chief Inspector. Archie had served under Munroe for eighteen months and considered him a good boss. But that didn't make him feel any less of a Judas, revealing details of his friend's private life. Yet he had to admit, Willie McKay would roll on, never complaining and getting on with things, never considering that his personal life was as much a concern to his friends as was his professional life to the police.

The door banged open and Roddy Munroe entered the office. It had always been a point of principle with him that Munroe liked to be first in to the office, before his staff and was therefore surprised to see Archie.

Munroe greeted him and jokingly inquired, "Wife throw you out, young man or have you an ulterior motive for sneaking into work at this ungodly hour?"

Archie knew Munroe was jesting, but taking a deep breath he stood as he replied, "Might I have a quiet word boss? In confidence, you understand?"

Brow furrowed, Munroe finished hanging up his coat, looked at Archie then nodded and invitation for Archie to follow him into the cloistered privacy of his room.

Mickey slammed the kitchen door behind him, and then paced up and down his lengthy driveway, drawing deeply on a cigarette and trying to clear his head. Confused and angry, he tried to make sense of the phone call. Slowly, he calmed down, but only after taking his frustration out on the plastic wheelie bin that now lay on its side and bore the footmarks of his fury. He came to a decision and unclipped his mobile phone from his belt.

"Sean, it's me! Fetch big Al and get your arse round here

pronto. I'm at the house! No, no. I'll tell you when you get here. Yeah, I'm mad. I'm fucking mad. Oh, and those Black and Decker's? That, me lad, was one of your better ideas!"

Katie Docherty, an oversize, white plastic apron encompassing her bottle green coloured trouser suit, stood by the metal examination table. Representing the Procurator Fiscals Department, a young bespectacled Depute Fiscal, neat dark blue tie, white shirt and what she guessed was the obligatory pin striped navy blue suit, stood slightly to one side, trying to appear nonchalant, but failing dismally, his face pale, rapid breathing and averted eyes an indication of his imminent faint. A detective sergeant stood by him, smiling slightly and awaiting his collapse to the floor. The detective didn't like lawyers, no matter whose side they claimed to represent and was considering letting the little shit drop straight down to the hard, tiled floor. A trainee detective constable, attending his first post mortem and responsible for any items that might later be used in evidence, stood behind them, patiently waiting to convey any samples his boss or the Pathologist deemed necessary for further examination to the Glasgow University Forensic Medical Department in the west end of the city. The duty pathologist, a cheerful and shapely blonde haired woman about Katie's age, pretty with a slash of vivid red lipstick and brilliant white, even teeth, donned a green gown and drew on slightly thicker than normal surgical gloves. She smiled and asked after Katie's daughter. Katie liked the pathologist, aware she had just emerged from an acrimonious divorce and rid herself of a philandering husband. Some might call that good luck she wryly thought, recalling her husbands curt and off hand manner at their breakfast table. The meal, he had delighted in informing her, had been a disaster and of course it was all her fault. With an effort, she forced herself to concentrate on the matter at hand. The naked body of the mystery woman lay upon the table before them.

Katie, a wisp of perfumed hand-cream lightly dabbed under her nose to counter the smell that permeated the building, hated this part of her job. The sight of blood and bone wasn't the problem. What she found disturbing was the absence of dignity, the manner in which a once vibrant and living being is surgically torn asunder and condensed to two or three pages of medical jargon. She watched intently as the procedure commenced. The pathologist slowly and expertly examined the body, deftly running her fingers inch by inch, ever so lightly along, under and over every part of the form that was before her, searching for anything that was twisted, broken or foreign to the body. At the head, she turned and probed the skull, subtly checking for bone crunch, continually feeling and probing the scalp. Raising the lids, she shone a small but bright light into the eyes. Throughout, she commented into the microphone that was suspended by its electric flex, above the table and recording all her examination.

Satisfied with her preliminary examination, she closely scrutinised the wound on the forehead, using a powerful magnifying glass to peer at the broken skin. Still not a word or comment to the observers. Shaking her head and chewing her lower lip, she finally turned to Katie. "Of course without a full autopsy I can't be certain, but I'm

not convinced we're looking at murder."
Footsteps on the tiled floor caused the group to turn round. Alan Byrne had arrived and was carrying a package under his arm.
"Hello boss, might I have a word?"
Katie, raising her eyebrows, indicated the pathologist. Alan nodded, agreeing the doctor should be present.
All three made their way to the nearby family room that was usually set aside for identification purposes, permitting grieving relatives to view their loved ones through a curtained window. A bunch of freshly picked and highly scented flowers within a vase stood upon the polished surface of a coffee table. Wooden backed chairs were placed against the wall beneath a double glazed window, through which the sun beamed into the room and also served to reduce the noise of passing traffic to a quiet hum.
Byrne indicated they should sit down.
"Bit of a puzzler, here," began Byrne, "but first things first," he said, turning to address the pathologist. "I have a report that a subject, likely a woman, was seen falling from the Jamaica Bridge into the River Clyde, the other night. Definitely no other person involved. The witness, a bus driver, is quite categorical in his statement that the person was alone," he stressed again, "and climbed over the side of the bridge of her own accord. To all intent and purpose, it seemed to be a suicide. The officers that attended the scene were quick off the mark and had the scenes of crime car," then turned to Katie, "ESSO Jones, Boss?"
Katie smiled. Who didn't know ESSO Jones?
The pathologist looked puzzled. "ESSO Jones?"
"I'll explain later," said Katie, "Go on, Alan."

"Where was I? Oh, aye. ESSO manage to obtain two lifts, two very good handprints by all accounts, where the subject pushed over the wall. Unfortunately, the subject seemingly struck a bridge support falling down into the water because ESSO also obtained fresh, heavy blood staining from the bridge support. The sample has been lodged at our Forensic Department and is awaiting corroborating analysis."

Katie could guess where this was leading.

"Last night, the duty scenes of crime fingerprinted our mystery woman. Fortunately Gordon Jarvie, a sergeant in the city centre Division, read the report of our body being fished from the water and offered his suicide subject as a possible match and hey presto."

"Our suicide subject?" Katie ventured.

"Correct," agreed Byrne with a smile. "Fingerprints have verified and identified our body and the suicide subject as one and the same, a Margaret Thomson. I'm certain," again he addressed the pathologist, "that if you provide us with a blood sample, we'll have a positive match with the sample obtained from the bridge support."

"In that case," said the pathologist, "In light of the evidence brought to us by Alan," nodding to Byrne "I would concur that the head wound is compatible with having been struck with or having struck against a heavy object and that," she continued, peeling off her gloves, "would seem to be my involvement concluded for the moment. I'm sure you will agree the case is no longer a priority and I'll see that she's attended to in due course. I suspect it will be tomorrow morning before I attend to her autopsy, which might provide you the time you need to track down some next of kin. In the meantime, I have more pressing matters at hand, so I'll just get cleared up and the paperwork should be available to you, probably tomorrow afternoon," smiling again, "unless you find someone else floating in the River Clyde before then. Good morning, Katie and good work, Alan," she flashed a huge smile at him.

Katie was pleased. Alan Byrne was, in her book, a real star and if she was any judge of feminine wiles, impressing the pathologist with more than his detective work. "Well done Alan, now we can turn it over to the reporting division which, if my memory serves me right," Katie said with a grin, "is the city centre guys. Their baby now, I believe."

Alan stood, shaking his head and with a frown on his face.

"You're going to tell me there's a problem?" Katie asked.

"That's not the end of it. Aye, it's no longer a suspect death, but according to what I've learned from the Govan division, Margaret Thomson has been missing for over twenty years. The local boys are on their way now to inform her mother and ask her to attend here to formally identify our body."

Katie stared at Alan, slowly shaking her head.

"Alan, tell me that's the lot? There's not more, there can't be."

Alan took a deep breath. "I ran a check through the Fraud Squad on the bank details I took from a printout slip I found in Thomson's pocket. I had them phone me with the result, just five minutes before I got here." Fishing in his pocket he produced a scrap of paper. Reading from the paper, he continued. "The details refer to a joint current account in the name of Mr William McKay and Mrs Margaret McKay. The address is over in the Kings

Park area. Unless I'm way off course, it seems likely that Margaret Thomson, our missing person is, or was also known as Margaret McKay."

Roddy Munroe stood at the main door of police headquarters, ostensibly out for a morning stroll and a smoke at his pipe, quietly chatting to the uniformed commissionaire.
Willie McKay, walking to the front door saw Munroe as he turned the corner. He slowed as he approached Munroe.
"Morning, boss. Catching the fresh air?" he grinned, nodding at Munroe's pipe.
"Morning, Willie. Aye and no. The fresh air is of no use to an old pipe man like me, so no, I'm just here polluting the atmosphere and waiting for you."
"Me?"
"Walk with me," he asked, pointing with his pipe to the corner Willie had just turned from. The two men strolled leisurely along the front of the red-bricked building.
"Willie, I'll not beat about the bush. I'd rather speak to you here, man to man, than in the office and have the jungle telegraph catch on to our conversation. You know what it is like, in there," Munroe used his pipe to point back at the building. "Fart and the wind speed is up on the board before the smell has drifted away."
Willie nodded, conscious that his boss was slowly leading him up the street, away from the front door. They stopped at the corner.
'"The thing is you are one of my best men," he continued in a voice heavy with the northern brogue, "I'll not deny

that, but it is obvious not just to me, but also to others that you are currently under some, how can I put this without offending you, domestic pressure? I know that you won't wish to discuss your private life with an old sod like me, but as of now," Munroe stopped to empty his pipe of ash and, tapping it against the stonework of the building, repeated "as of now, you are on leave. No questions or argument, okay?"

Willie made to protest, quickly realising that only Archie could have spoken with Munroe.

As if reading his thoughts, Munroe was quick to add, "And don't go on a witch-hunt, looking for my source. We both know I'm talking about Archie. There are more than just him in that office that like you and some of us," he gruffly coughed, "are determined to look out for you. Willie," he clapped his hand on the younger detectives shoulder. "You have more friends than you realise. And that's why I'm suggesting.... no," he looked Willie in the eye, "that's why I'm ordering you to take time to sort yourself out."

Aware he was in a no-win situation, Willie accepted the inevitable and nodded.

"Okay, boss. Just so you know, there hasn't been any update on Margaret. I phoned the desk sergeant at my local station, before I came to work, but he couldn't tell me anything. I'm gutted. The hardest thing is the not knowing to where she's gone.'

Munroe could see Willie was having a hard time of it and knew he'd made the right decision. Willie McKay wasn't fit for work. Willie wasn't fit for anything in this state. Munroe, still clasping Willie's shoulder, squeezed tightly in a rare show of companionship.

"Go home now, there's a good lad and get some rest. I'll

make a few calls and see if I can learn anything. Just stay in touch."
Willie nodded and turned. Without a backward glance he went home.
Home to wait.
Wait and wonder.

Chapter 19

Finishing her toiletry, Angie found Ina Thomson had set the small wooden trestle table in the front room with a worn, but clean tablecloth and laid two settings. The floral patterns of the matching china cups and plates was faded and though the cutlery was old, it burnished brightly in the sunlight that streamed through the spotless window. The room was warm, heat emanating from the small electric fire that burned in the hearth.
Ina couldn't recall the last time she had formally set the small table with her prized china and cutlery, gifts at her wedding so long ago. Slightly embarrassed, she beckoned Angie to sit and ushered her to the chair nearest the fire.
"Come away in, dear. If you're anything like Billy, you probably won't feel like eating much in the morning, but try a little something. I guarantee you will feel better with something inside you."
Despite herself and the morning nausea she normally experienced, Angie found her mouth watering at the smell of the bacon, sizzling in the pan.
"Maybe, just a little," she conceded, surprised that her appetite took over her usual reluctance to eat.
Later, as they sat facing each other and comfortable in their silence, Angie felt the need to explain, a desire to unburden to this gentle woman. Ina let the dirty plates lie

on the table, unwilling to interrupt the moment as Angie began slowly, describing her life before the drugs, then related the downward spiral that seemed relentless. She spoke of her introduction to Billy, of his unexpected and over whelming need to protect her and their first flickering flame of affection, fuelled by their mutual dependency.

She revealed Billy's desire to escape their addiction and move south to London where they planned a new life and how his plan had included Ina.

Ina's mouth flickered into a smile. Typical Billy, she thought, always the daydreamer.

Angie continued, unconscious of her actions as she slowly but steadily rocked back and forward in her chair, her hands clasped tightly in her lap. Describing Billy as her saviour and her protector against the men who would hurt her.

Ina's brow creased in recollection.

"Were these men large and cruel?"

Angie nodded, Ina's brief but sure description encompassing all the physical attributes of Franny and his pal. Both realised they each spoke of the men who had sought Billy; curtly polite to Ina, yet violent and hurtful to Angie.

Ina was angry that two, large bullying men, could harm this wee girl. Well, she firmly decided, *not* while she's in my house. It didn't occur to her that she couldn't physically protect Angie.

"But why did they want Billy?" she asked, her curiosity aroused.

Angie shrugged her thin shoulders and shook her head. "All that Billy would tell me was they needed him for a job, but he had screwed...." Angie blushed, and searching for the word, then said "...outwitted them. I think they wanted their car back."

"Their car?" Ina's eyes betrayed her confusion.

"They told me they had loaned Billy a car, a dark blue one. I'm not sure what kind. And they wanted to know where he was and where the car was."

"Now why would my Billy need a car?" Ina wondered, knowing he wasn't a qualified driver, or rather didn't have a licence. She decided there were things that Billy had obviously kept from her and was hurt and disappointed at these secrets.

The door knocked, startling them both.

Ina saw the panic in Angie's face. She reached over and patted Angie's hand.

"Stay where you are, love. I'll get that," but fearing it might be the same two men, cautiously whispered, "Just don't make a noise. I won't be letting anyone in."

But it wasn't the two men Ina saw through the peephole, it was the navy blue colour of a police uniform. A voice called to her from outside the door.

"Mrs Thomson, I don't know if you recall, I'm constable Megan Davidson. I was here with the sergeant?"

Ina had thought the young woman looked familiar. She wrestled with the heavy duty bolt and finally unlocked the door.

"Come in. Do you have any news?" she gasped.

And on this, their third visit to her home in as many days, the police again tore the heart from Ina Thomson.

With Katie Docherty driving at her usual break-neck speed, Alan Byrne took the opportunity to phone their station and inform the team of the intention to follow up the address for Margaret Thomson or McKay or whoever she was, he thought. The female detective acknowledged Alan's call and reminded him of the soggy piece of paper discovered in Thomson's pocket. Alan recalled the detective had intended drying it out.

"I did manage to get it dried out," she confirmed, "though probably not as good as the lab might have done, but most of it is readable."

"Anything interesting?" he inquired.

"It was the local evening paper, a couple of days old, now. I called the news desk and had them e-mail me over the relevant page."

Clever girl, thought Alan, mentally noting her resourcefulness, something he wouldn't forget.

"One side was an advert for the new superstore in Clydebank," she continued, "but the other side had some local news items. One, I figured might be of interest. It was a report about a death in Govan, a young guy called William Thomson, the same surname, boss. Any use to you?"

As Katie weaved in and out of the traffic, Alan fumbled in his pocket for a pen and scrap of paper, while glancing at the roadway ahead and doing his Fred Astaire impression, foot tapping at an imaginary brake on his side of the floor.

"Not sure yet, but read me the details anyway," he instructed.

Willie McKay arrived home to find three people standing talking, at his front door. Adele Cairns stood between the tall, well built man and the business suited woman who turned at his approach.

He recognised Alan Byrne and that could only mean the good looking red head was Byrne's boss, DCI Katie Docherty.

As Adele hurried towards him, her arms outstretched, he could see the tears in her eyes.

The two detectives looked uncomfortable and his throat went suddenly dry, for Willie McKay knew then why they had come.

Mickey the Greek was not a happy man. In fact, right at this minute he was an extremely outraged and furious psychopath, beyond reasonable control and capable of any violent deed.

Big Al O'Rourke and Sean Begley understood and shared Mickey's rage. His recount of the telephone call had placed them all in jeopardy and they were angry enough to want the lying jock bastards to get what they deserved and, by Christ, that's what the jock bastards were going to get.

"So they'll rip us off, eh," Mickey growled, punching his right fist into his left hand and shrewdly including Big Al and Sean in his assessment of the jock bastard's intentions. "Well, they haven't reckoned on us, eh lads?"

Big Al was inwardly seething and livid, but outwardly calm. His boss could lose it and without thought, take off immediately for Scotland to exact a bloody revenge.

But Al knew that a response to this information called for a plan, not hot-headed action. And so, quietly and with composure, he suggested an alternative arrangement for the delivery of their China White to the jock bastard, Maxie McLean.

Johnjo Donnegan received the telephone summons to attend at Mickey's house right away. Ever keen and willing to help and wisely believing he'd better be getting his arse in gear, Johnjo arrived at Mickey's house within twenty minutes of the call. With dry mouth and shaky hands, he knocked upon the large, wooden double doors, conscious of the CCTV camera situated high on the wall that monitored his presence. The doors were thrown open and Mickey stood there, resplendent in Liverpool team shirt and with two cans of lager, still in their plastic noose and dangling from his left hand.
"Come in lad, come in," he jovially invited Johnjo. "You'll have a beer, eh?"
Johnjo was nervous. In all the time he'd run gear for Mickey, he'd never been invited to his home and now here was Mickey offering him a beer? This didn't bode well, thought Johnjo suspiciously. Something is definitely not right.
Leading the smaller man through to the massive lounge, Mickey invited him to sit down.
"I've been thinking, Johnjo. I've got me lads Big Al and Sean, but I'm going to be needing a Third Man," he laughed, "like Harry Lime, you know?"
Johnjo didn't know, but laughed with Mickey anyway, too frightened to admit he'd no interest in football and ignorant of the names of all the Liverpool football team.
"I know we've had out little differences in the past, but," continued Mickey, "it was on me mind that as we've

been working together all these years you might want to think about a step up in the organisation, a promotion so to speak. How does that sound?"
Johnjo was flabbergasted. Working together with Mickey? This was too fucking weird.
"Yeah, Mickey," he stuttered "that sounds great."
"Excellent," beamed Mickey, handing Johnjo a can of lager and slapping him on the back "so, as you are now a trusted man, good lad, there's a little thing I want you to do for me."

Willie McKay sat on his couch, resting his head in his hands. Adele Cairns, quietly weeping but assuring Katie Docherty that she would be fine, had returned to her own house. Alan Byrne was in the kitchen making coffee and marvelling at the neat and tidy orderliness of the units, comparing it to his own divorced chaos.
Katie Docherty sat helpless in the front room, silently cursing Byrne for body swerving her and leaving her to sit awkwardly, facing Willie and not knowing how to comfort him. She stared at the bowed head. She had heard of him, of course and when working on previous major inquiries, received some excellent information that he had knitted together, but never actually met him. Certainly, Alan Byrne had nothing but praise for the man, but now this. What a fucking introduction, she thought miserably.
"I suppose there's no doubt?" Willie raised his head and asked her.
Katie rummaged in her handbag and removed a small plastic exhibit bag, which she handed to him. Inside the

bag Willie saw a set of keys.
"We found these in the pocket of her coat. Just before you arrived and getting no response at the door, we tried the keys and they fitted the locks," she explained, half apologetically. "I'm so very sorry, Willie."
Willie didn't weep. He supposed that would come later, but for now he wanted facts, knowing that the sooner he learned what happened, the easier he'd accept it, come to term or what ever politically correct term that was popular for grief these days.
"Willie," Katie hesitantly began, "we've a bit of a mystery about your wife, Margaret. What was her maiden name?"
Surprised by the question, Willie stared at her.
"Devlin, she said she was Margaret Devlin when I met her."
Katie looked at Byrne, accepting a mug from him and placing it on the carpet at her feet.
"There's no easy way to break this to you. We have information that her real name was Thomson, Margaret Thomson, who was reported missing by her parents over twenty years ago."
Willie was stunned. He shook his head.
"No, there must be a mistake. Margaret was an orphan, no family."
Then suddenly there was confusion in his eyes. "What information?"
Byrne sat down. He looked at Willie, wondering at the pressure and strain this must be adding to his grief. He said, "We had fingerprints confirm her identity and we've traced her mother who lives in Govan. As we speak, an officer has been dispatched to break the news. There's no doubt, Willie. What we don't know is why

your wife changed her name?"
He glanced at the written note he produced from his pocket. "It might be significant that we found a newspaper cutting in her coat pocket and one item was about the recent death in Govan of a William Thomson. Does the name mean anything to you?"
Willie felt as if he was going through an information overload. He swallowed hard, wondering why he felt so hot yet a sudden chill was tingling at his spine. William Thomson. That name kept cropping up. For a reason that he didn't at that time understand, he didn't acknowledge the name. Shaking his head, he sipped from the mug cupped in his hands.
"No, it doesn't ring any immediate bells."
Katie stood and with a slight nod to Alan Byrne, asked Willie, "Is there anyone we can call, for you? Anything we can do at all?" she offered.
"Where is she, where's Margaret now?"
"The city mortuary, Willie," answered Byrne, "Can we take you there? You might want to see her."
'No, I'm grateful for the offer, but if you don't mind I'll take some time to get myself together. You know how it is. I've got my car outside. I'll call up there, later. Perhaps you could arrange for me to...."
"Yes, of course, that's no problem," said Katie hastily, adding "there's also the question of identification, Willie. I understand her....Margaret's mother... will be invited to attend. Will that be alright with you?"
Willie looked at her, the light of comprehension dawning. Margaret's mother. How odd to hear that term. "I'm sorry, it's just that after all these years, it sounds so strange. Yes, of course. She has every right. I have no problem with that."

As the two detectives made their way to their car, Katie turned to glance back at the house then turned to Byrne and spoke.
"Well, aside from formal identification and the paperwork, that seems to have wrapped that up. I don't see that any crime has been committed."
Byrne shook his head, aware of the movement of curtains at nearby windows and indicated with a nod they should get in. Turning, he caught hold of his seat belt, which was always a wise move when Katie drove. Glancing at his boss, her red locks billowing behind her as the blast from her open window caught her hair, he thought hell; this is like the Ride of the Valkrye. He considered her question and, finally snapping home his belt, replied, "What we have, in my opinion, is a woman who decided to take off from the paternal home twenty odd years ago, then for some unaccountable reason changed her name, married one of our own, topped herself and left a number of broken hearts. I appreciate that is a very simplistic way to put it, but aside from the morality of her actions, I agree. I don't see that either she or anyone else has committed any crime. Certainly, nothing that should involve CID. From what we've learned, the report to the PF will make interesting reading, but that," he smirked, "will be the reporting officer's problem and there doesn't seem to be anything that suggests a follow-up enquiry is required. How does that sound?"
Katie nodded her assent, her full concentration deployed to beating the lumbering bus to the changing traffic lights.
"I agree. And you know what they say, Detective

Inspector Byrne," grinning now, "rank has its privileges. So, my dear friend, the report is yours. And try not to use too many big words. You know how easily confused the PF's department get."

Conference Room number two at police headquarters was far too large for just the five people who sat about the table, their coffee cups placed on plastic coasters to avoid leaving ring marks on the gleaming, polished surface. Coloured prints of police officers in action roles adorned the walls, the subjects engaged in a variety of public-spirited scenes. Bright daylight flooded the fifth floor room and the blinds remained open, for no other building overlooked the room.
The five occupants of the room sat at the table. Cardboard files with light brown covers lay closed on the table in front of four of those seated. Detective Chief Superintendent Tom Morrison, Departmental Head of Intelligence, had deemed his own room too small for this meeting. He wanted space to spread the files and photographs and the sizeable table was ideally suited. Besides, he liked the idea of using the large room, believing it added prestige to his rank.
Not yet forty years of age and with a degree in psychology from Glasgow University, Morrison was one of the new breed of senior police officers that had fast tracked through the police ranks. Some of his critics maliciously whispered his lack of street policing experience was a shortcoming and that he not only lacked both leadership and management skills, but was far too conscious of his public image to deal with the real job of

arresting criminals. But Morrison was oblivious to these barbs and had his own agenda. He had learned the position of Assistant Chief Constable (Crime) would soon be vacant and with a few high profile successes under his belt, believed himself to be the front-runner for the job.

Roddy Munroe, present to represent the sharp edge of intelligence, didn't totally disagree with this general opinion, but though he believed him to be ambitious, thought Morrison would not shirk his responsibility when it came to the so-called crunch. A rare commodity in today's police service, he sighed, idly glancing over to where his Detective sergeant, Ian Reid was setting up a small tape recorder on the table. Munroe was equally aware that a successful operation, based on today's meeting, would certainly enhance Morrison's media reputation. This, he knew, was particularly relevant if the rumour were true that the ACC (Crime) was due to retire in the foreseeable future.

Morrison's deputy, Superintendent Alison McRae sat with pencil and pad, prepared to take notes. The fifth member present was Inspector Jimmy 'Dusty' Miller of the Communications Department that was located on the top floor of the building.

"Right, folks, thank you for attending today so," began Morrison, opening the meeting "let's start with the tape," while nodding at Ian Reid.

They listened as the tape recorder whirled round to the starting point and heard the voice of the police operator, Janice Leckie, greet the caller. The voice began by instructing that Leckie to take notes. The tape ran on and their interest grew. Unconsciously, the group held their breath, intently listening to the sound of the voice.

Alison McRae furiously scribbled notes on her pad. "Stop, go back a bit," she instructed Reid. The voice repeated the names.

A clicking noise signalled the end of the recording. McRae looked at Morrison, a quiet smile playing about her lips.

"You thinking what I'm thinking?" she asked.

Morrison took a deep breath and nodded his head.

"Dusty," Morrison said to the Inspector, "you've something to add?"

Miller had many years of service under his belt, but had only recognised some of the names mentioned in the recoding. He knew that this meeting was of significant importance and didn't want to fuck up in front of these people. He took a deep breath. "Yes sir, it was a Mrs Janice Leckie, one of our civilian telephonists, who received the call. Contrary to the instruction made by the caller, Janice made her own notes and," he continued, lifting a sheet of paper from the table, "she's written as follows."

"The caller was trying to avoid a local accent, though as you heard, certainly a Scottish accent. Janice suggests either imitating or originating from the East coast. However, while conscious of the confidential details of the message, we obtained permission," and at this juncture nodded to Munroe, "had the technical support boys make a background analysis of the noise. It wasn't overly helpful, but indicated the call was made from a public telephone in a supermarket, the loudspeaker system you heard in the tape was advertising cut-price soup," he smiled.

He leaned forward, resting his forearms on the table and continued.

"Janice was of the opinion the caller was reading from a prepared note or similar text. No hesitation or use of colloquialisms in the statement during the call and, according to Janice, the caller's authoritive voice caused Janice to guess either a practised speech or someone used to speaking in public, maybe a confident speaker. As for the caller's age, Janice admits she's guessing, but places the caller between late twenties or early forties."

Miller put down the sheet of paper and sat back.

Morrison smiled. "Can I presume Dusty, there are no other copies of this tape?"

Miller shook his head in agreement.

"Correct. That's the only one, sir and I can assure you the information the tape contains will not be discussed further within my department."

"Thanks Dusty, that'll be all for now. Please be sure to thank Mrs Leckie for her contribution."

Miller stood and took his leave of the group.

Morrison glanced at the closed files. Turning to Munroe, he asked, "Does recent intelligence bear out any of this information, Roddy?"

Munroe, as usual dry smoking his pipe, drew his hand over his silvery grey hair and turned to his notes lying before him.

"Please open the files in front of you," he requested, as Reid passed them to Morrison and McRae.

"Maxie McLean needs no introduction," began Munroe. "We've tried to put the squeeze on him for several years, but he's tied up his organisation in runners and middlemen. He's the proverbial spider, sitting in the centre of the web. His two close associates, Francis 'Franny' McEwan and David 'One-ball' Smith," indicating their photographs with his pipe, "are less well known publicly, but extensively recorded by us. Maxie's not beyond violence of course, but he usually has these two nutter's bang heads for him these days. Smith, in particular, is a real sadistic fucker."

Munroe flinched, red faced, "Excuse me Alison."

McRae grinned and acknowledged the apology, "Always the gentleman, Roddy."

"As I was saying, recent surveillance reports suggest regular meeting between all three, usually at McLean's house. However, we recently evidenced him departing his abode and driving north into the city. He conducted serious anti-surveillance techniques so professionally that the target squad pulled off him, rather than compromise their presence."

"Lack of bottle from the cowboys," interrupted Reid with a snigger, keen to impress on Morrison his own opinion of the intelligence gathering surveillance teams.

No one spoke and a sudden chill ran down Reid's spine. He swallowed hard and immediately realised he had badly misjudged his audience. His snipe at his colleagues did not go down well.

Munroe turned to him and smiled without humour.

"Ian, do you think you might fetch a fresh pot of coffee, there's a good lad."

Scraping his chair back, his face scarlet with embarrassment, Reid lifted the now cold container and left the room.

"I'm sorry about that," apologised Munroe.

There was no need to say more. Morrison and McRae, well versed in the politics of management, recognised the death-knell of a career in criminal intelligence when it beat loudly in their face.

Munroe again turned to his open file. "Now, as I was

saying. The caller has, in my humble opinion," which drew a smile from Morrison, "delivered to us information that seems to indicate either the caller is a member of his organisation or part of the team delivering the drugs. The information, if indeed it is true, is too precise to be guesswork. We have to ask ourselves, what does the caller gain from the arrest of Maxie McLean? A financial reward? None has been offered, so that can be discounted. Some sort of revenge? Maxie has hurt a lot of people, in his time so that can't be ruled out."

Munroe carefully laid his pipe on the saucer of his cup. "One other alternative is that the caller is either or perhaps acting on behalf of, a rival dealer, whose distribution opportunities and consumer list would soar dramatically if Mr McLean were removed from the scene."

Alison McRae's brow furrowed. Leaning forward, she drummed her pencil against the tape recorder casing. "The bottom line here, what's your assessment of the information, Roddy? After all, this is your bread and butter," she probed.

Munroe absentmindedly lifted his pipe and tapped it against the table, a ruse that afforded him a precious few seconds to formulate his response. Alison McRae might be in the twilight years of her career, he thought, but she still had a razor sharp mind as well as the best pair of legs that he had seen for a long time. He looked directly at her.

"If the caller is correct, I am surprised that McLean intends to personally participate in the rip-off. Nevertheless, having listened to the tape, it is my opinion the information is believed by the caller to be genuine." He leaned forward to add emphasis to his words.

"You'll note I said 'believed by the caller'. How much the caller has learned, been told or surmised, we can only guess. I must add that at this time, we have nothing to corroborate the callers' information, nothing other than surveillance logs that seem to indicate an increase in regularity of the meetings between the three suspects. These meetings, I must stress, might not have anything to do with what we have heard on the tape."

He sat back and having tapped out his pipe, placed it on the table and again leaned forward on his elbows, rubbing his hands together.

"However, if genuine, I believe that this information presents us with the opportunity to catch red-handed, not only one of the leading distributors in the local drug scene and his henchmen, but also the courier of a major supplier from down south. A success such as this might reinforce our request for more funding from the Scottish Justice Department, not to mention," he sat back in his seat and folded his arms, "the excellent media coverage that could parallel the current anti-drugs campaign being conducted by the Force."

Tall, slim and attractive, her once natural blonde hair now highlighted by expensive lotions, but still the object of attention from many of her colleagues, Alison McRae had a reputation as a shrewd and astute woman. Knowing Munroe of old, she quickly understood he had deliberately baited his argument with the inference of media coverage in the belief Morrison could not resist an opportunity to promote his department. Aside from that, she'd earlier caught the bugger looking at her legs. Life in the old dog yet, she'd wryly thought.

McRae and Munroe remained silent, allowing Morrison, who was deep in thought, time to study the photograph of

Maxie McLean and consider Munroe's reply.

"As I see it," responded Morrison eventually, "and presuming the information to be true, there are two options we may consider. One is to simply deter McLean by overtly surveying him, instruct the team to 'show out' and thereby forcing him to cancel his plans. The negative side to such an option is that he might merely cancel his current arrangements and, in due course, reinstate the plan later. Should this happen, we have no way of knowing if the caller will again obtain information or indeed even call us. The positive side to this option is by preventing this alleged rip-off, we might save some poor bugger, drug dealer or not from, at best, serious injury. Regretfully," he smiled at his subordinates, "I have no need to remind you that we have a duty of care, even to drug dealing scum such as these."

Morrison leaned on the desk and stroked his chin.

"The second option is, again accepting the informant is telling the truth, to conduct a pro-active operation. The negative position is that the financial cost of mounting such an operation, particularly with the resources it will require, will undoubtedly dent our overstretched budget, given that we're talking overtime for almost all the personnel we'd need to deploy. However, if we *do* mount an operation and it proves to be successful, the result is, of course, self-evident; a noteworthy arrest and seizure."

Sitting back, he turned to McRae.

"What's your considered opinion Alison?"

McRae tapped her pencil against her gleaming white teeth, shining in the slash of deep red lipstick.

"It's a question of balance. We're presently conducting a war of attrition with the major players, picking off their runners and couriers, but seldom gathering sufficient evidence to nail the main men. Taking out someone like Maxie McLean would leave a large hole in the local drug scene and the resulting power struggle between the rest of the main players is likely to create a turf war and get a bit bloody, but we could benefit in the long run. Particularly," she continued, "in the field of intelligence. Maxie's fall is sure to divide loyalties or rather, dependencies. I'm veering towards going with the information. I know the cost might seem prohibitive right now, but I believe the advantages far outweigh the disadvantages. If nothing else a tactical operation such as this will test our coordination efficiency between the different departments. Now that," she grinned "would make it worthwhile. Might I also add that we've been getting some bad press recently and the mounting death toll through overdosing has placed a tremendous strain on our public opinion to deal with the drug crisis." She sat back and peered beneath long eyelashes at Munroe, the unspoken agreement between them that said - *Got him*.

Munroe silently applauded McRae's tactic. Like him, she knew Morrison would not be able to resist a media coup. Morrison nodded his head in understanding and turned to face Munroe.

"Roddy?"

Munroe instinctively knew Morrison had already made his mind up, however, but was thinking himself cunning by allowing Munroe to believe he was included in the decision.

Munroe looked directly at his Head of Department.

"I have no need to stress that we are time critical, for this information is hot and current and I believe it would be remiss of us to ignore this information. Unsolicited though it may be, the caller *did* intimate special knowledge of the targets and because of that, I further believe it is worthy of considering an operation." Slapping both hands down on the table, Morrison seemingly came to a sudden decision.

"Okay, we're agreed then. We go with the information. Roddy," he instructed "arrange briefing packs for all concerned. Alison, I'm appointing you operational commander and I'll leave you to liaise with your counterpart at Operations. Right," he said looking at his watch, "Lunch?"

Chapter 20

The electrics of his Ford Mondeo now liberally sprayed with WD40 oil, Willie McKay drove through the midday traffic to the city mortuary. His wipers squeaked noisily as they laboured to clear the windscreen of the light rain that was falling.

Freshly showered, but having shaved badly, and wearing a dark suit, white shirt and black tie, Willie parked in a bay across the street from the old High Court. He sat with his hands on the driving wheel. Reluctantly, he prepared himself to leave the warmth of the car, but knowing the answer to the first of his many questions lay inside the red tiled and sandstone building. Steeling himself, he turned up his jacket collar, locked the car and skipped between the heavy traffic, earning a two-fingered salute from an irate taxi driver who braked sharply to avoid colliding with him. Pushing through the heavy oak doors, he was greeted by a grey haired, solemn faced porter, dressed in an immaculate white dustcoat, black trousers and white shirt with a City of Glasgow motif on the plain, bottle green tie, the porter smiled softly, his eyebrows raised in question.

Willie turned down his collar and wiped his damp face with a clean, white handkerchief.

"My names William McKay," he said , "I've come to see....come to view the body of my wife, Margaret McKay."

The porter again smiled politely and asked him to take a seat in an adjoining waiting room.

Willie entered the small, but neat and tidy room and took a seat on the padded bench that was placed beneath the high window. A plain wooden coffee table was laid out with the daily newspapers and brochures advertising local funeral services. As he waited, he reminded himself that while serving as a divisional CID detective, he had often visited the mortuary during enquiries, but never as a private citizen.

The porter returned, concern etched on his face and his hands clasped in front of him.

"I'm so sorry, but we don't have a Margaret McKay with us. Might I ask who informed you of her presence with us?" he asked in a practised and solicitous manner.

Willie rubbed his forehead. Of course, he had forgotten that she might not be here as Margaret McKay.

"Perhaps you have her under the name Margaret Thomson?"

Realisation dawned. The porter smiled softly and nodded his head. "Of course, Mister McKay and again, I do apologise, I should have known. Would you care to join the other family members?"

Willie swallowed hard. Other family members? He has to be referring to Margaret's mother, the woman whom Margaret had lied was dead. He stood and turned towards the window, fearful he might lose his composure. Taking a deep breath, he asked, "Perhaps I might have a private moment with my wife? I'd rather not meet anyone else just at this moment."

Turning to the porter, he took a deep breath "However," he continued, "if you could oblige me by asking Mrs Thomson to wait for ten minutes, I'd be keen to speak with her."

The porter nodded, presuming a family row. In his experience, bereavement tended to overshadow any previous quarrel.

"That's no problem, Mister McKay. I'll pass on your request. Now, sir," one arm raised indicating the way through the corridor, "would you care to accompany me to the viewing room?"

Johnjo Donnegan was in high spirits. His conversation with Mickey had gone better than even Johnjo could have imagined. Valued member of the team, Mickey had called him. Third man in the organisation, Mickey had said. And a car as well. Yes, Johnjo thought, life can only get sweeter now.

Arriving at his sister's house in the old Vauxhall Cavalier, Johnjo locked the driver's door and stood back to admire his new acquisition. Admittedly, not that much to look at, but it was only the beginning, as Mickey had promised.

He swaggered up the weed-ridden path. The next-door neighbour, a fireman his sister had told him, was in his garden raking cut grass into a pile and watching Johnjo approach the sister's back door.

"What you staring at?" challenged Johnjo, his new status with Mickey fuelling his bravado.
The fireman walked to the wooden, dividing fence that Johnjo now saw was awfully low and easily mountable. "You'd better be a visitor to that house, lad or you are getting this rake up your arse sideways," threatened the enraged fireman, lifting the rake to demonstrate that his wasn't an idle threat.
"Yeah, it's me sisters gaff, mate," Johnjo hurriedly replied, his new found courage deserting him, desperately knocking on the back door and hurrying inside the new kitchen as his sister opened it.
The door safely closed, he leaned with his back against it and sighed with relief. His sister, her eyes glazed over, curiously asked "What was that all about?"
"Nothing, just some guy next door getting heavy, but I told him where I'd stick his rake if he wasn't careful," bragged Johnjo, while cautiously peeping though the window to be certain the bastard wasn't going to come crashing through the door after him.
His sister, Johnjo guessed, had apparently been running another line. Her mouth hung open, her eyes listless and faint traces of an off-white coloured powder were stuck to the snot on her nose. Her children sat silent, heads bowed and morose at the kitchen table, a plate of potato crisps with a chunk of cheese and a can of cola in front of both. Dirty and stained crockery and dishes littered the worktops and the sink was overflowing with pots. Johnjo felt sorry of the children, but knew that anything he said would be taken as criticism and only rile his sister. Better not get her started, not now that he was so close to making it big. Glancing again at his niece and nephew, his conscious got the better of him and decided a word of

caution wouldn't go amiss. He stared at his sister.
Her dark brown hair lying loose and untidily about her shoulders, pale face pinched and devoid of make-up, Johnjo was shocked to discover that in such a short time, she was rapidly falling to pieces. Previously a smart and stylish dresser, but now she was wearing a stained red halter top, tight faded blue denims and scruffy black shoes that apparently hadn't seen a cleaning cloth in weeks. A yellowing bruise under her left eye should have attracted comment he knew, but again realised this wasn't the time for an argument.
"You better watch out, girl. The amount of that shite you're shoving up your nose is going to be the death of you," he warned.
"Never, Johnjo lad, I can handle it. It's the only pleasure I get," she giggled.
Not if what I hear down the local boozer about you is true, Johnjo sighed to himself.
"I've come for me stuff," he told her, "so if you can keep the kids in the front room for maybe ten minutes?"
His sister ushered the unresisting children from the kitchen, making vague promises of late night television if they didn't stamp their crisps into her living room carpet, then closed the door behind her.
Once alone, Johnjo fetched a table knife from a kitchen drawer and, dropping to his knees, prised open the hiding place and stared at the packages. A heavy whiff of perfumed toilet cake hit his nostrils, strong enough to mask any smell that might have oozed from the packages. Quickly counting the packages to satisfy himself that none had been removed, he reckoned it would take at least four trips to get them all from the house to the car. However, that wasn't his main concern

right now. His problem was getting the gear into the boot of the car without that nosey bastard next door guessing what was in the bags. He stood up and dusted off his hands.
"Hey sis," he shouted through the closed door, "can I borrow the kids schoolbags?"

Ina Thomson looked up at the tall man in the dark suit that stood in the doorway. Angie, sitting beside her, gripped Ina's hand tighter and hesitantly asked, "Are you Mister McKay?"
Willie nodded, his eyes on the frail looking woman sitting before him, while wondering who the young lassie was.
"Mrs Thomson?" he softly inquired, staring at Ina.
She nodded, her face ashen, not trusting herself to speak. Angie, feeling like and intruder, realised this was a private moment.
"I'll see if there's anywhere I can get us a wee cup of tea," she said lamely and then to Ina "Will you be okay?"
Again, Ina nodded, lips tightly closed and still afraid to speak for she knew her voice would break and the unshed tears would flow.
As Angie made to leave she turned, bent and kissed Ina gently on the top of her grey head then left, quietly closing the door behind her. The noise of her footsteps echoed on the highly polished, wooden floorboards in the corridor outside.
Willie sat down in a chair across the room from Ina, aware that his presence must be as upsetting for this woman as hers was to him. They sat in awkward silence

for a moment, and then he raised his head and looking at her, gently spoke.

"From what I've been told, Mrs Thomson, it seems we both have a lot to discuss. I'm very sorry. I understand from my colleagues that not only have you lost a daughter, but your grandson too."

Her lips trembling at the kind words, Ina looked down at the floor then, as if a great weight hung from her neck, slowly raised her head to look at Willie.

"Perhaps," he began, "we should leave and go some place where we might be more comfortable?"

She sighed heavily.

"Rita," she told him, "we called her Rita. She was christened Margaret, but we shortened it. It was her father's idea, a family tradition he said, because that was how her granny was known. Rita."

Willie stared, a half smile played about his mouth.

"Funny, she never mentioned that. But to be honest Mrs Thomson, there was a lot of things Margaret....Rita," the name seemed odd to say out loud, "never mentioned."

A smile broke through Ina's cloud of depression. She took a deep breath.

"Maybe we could go to my house and have a wee chat there, if you like?"

"Seems like a good idea to me. The young girl, is she a relative?" he asked.

Her brow furrowed, unsure how much she should tell this man for, after all was said and done, he was still a policeman.

"You could say that, but before we go, would you mind if I just say goodbye to my grandson Billy?"

Willie nodded, wondering if he should fetch the lassie to accompany her.

She made to stand, using the arm of the chair to assist her. Instinctively he rose quickly to help her, taking her arm as she drew herself upright.
"Angie," she told him. 'Her name's Angie. Angie Bennett."
She walked slowly to the door and he called after her.
"I have a car outside. Why I don't I wait there and you can take your time. Take as long as you need. I won't be going anywhere without you," he promised.

Sean Begley sat in the driver's seat of the newly washed Range Rover with Mickey the Greek lounging in the front passenger seat, a pair of designer framed sunglasses perched on his nose. Big Al O'Rourke's massive frame sprawled across the rear seat. All three men were dressed in shirts and ties and wearing lounge suits, albeit the jackets were off and folded across the back parcel shelf. The two handguns were wrapped in cloth and hidden in a toolbox in the boot. Mickey knew that to all intent and purposes, they would appear to any patrolling police as businessmen travelling north and pass at the very least, a cursory examination.
"I know we're not expecting a tug on the road up," Mickey had explained, "but if by the odd chance some traffic fucker wants a better look at us...."
The gang understood the fickle fate of fortune and the simple but effective clothing ruse had worked in the past. The police, they knew from experience, suffered from unconscious stereotyping, believing that most bad guys dressed in rough or casual clothing. After all, Mickey had grinned, wasn't Strangeways nick full of those who

hadn't taken simple precautions?

Patiently, the three men sat in a side road near to a service station off the M58 motorway, watching for the old style, dark blue Cavalier.

"You're sure Johnjo knows exactly what he is to do?" asked Big Al, for the third time in as many minutes.

"Calm down, you old fucking woman," chastised Mickey, half turning to grin at Al as he chewed at a chocolate bar. He glanced at his wristwatch.

"Right, once again. In about ten minutes, Johnjo is to drive past us at fifty-five miles an hour and flash his lights twice when he passes the service station here. We simply tail onto the back of him and follow him up the road. No communication till we get to Abington services. He pulls in and refuels whether he needs to or not. We drive past the Abington services, stop at a convenient spot, get the guns from the boot, push the peddle to the floor and on to the Hamilton services before Johnjo arrives. That way we're waiting on him, alright?"

Sean nodded his head in agreement, but Al, ever the pessimist, leaned across between the head rests and persisted. "But why are we taking the China with us if we're not handing it over?"

"Because," Mickey slowly explained, "Johnjo would think there was something wrong if we told him to travel up with it, wouldn't he now? Besides, when we've settled with these Jock bastards, all we'll do is take the gear back down the road with us and no harm done, eh?"

"But he doesn't know what's going down, does he?" Mickey shook his head then said with an exaggerated sigh.

"Of course not, do you think I'm an idiot? As far as Johnjo is concerned, he's going to meet this guy Billy

Thomson that he knows, at Hamilton, exchange car keys, jump into Thomson's car then drive back to Abington where he thinks we'll be waiting to collect the cash." Laughing, Mickey continued, "Johnjo, or the *Third Man* as he now thinks he is, doesn't have the bottle for this. Christ, you both know the little bugger as well as I do. He'd shit his pants if he thought there was any problem." The flashing of headlights from a passing Cavalier alerted them to Johnjo.
"He's early, the prick. Right, lads," said an excited Mickey, urging Sean ton manoeuvre the Range Rover onto the motorway, "let's get this done.'

Andy Dawson drove the surveillance vehicle into the police training school that is located in the suburbs of the town of East Kilbride and steered the car expertly into a narrow parking bay.
Mary Murdoch, in the passenger seat, flashed a warrant card at the approaching uniformed attendant, who nodded in greeting and pointed to the main building.
"If you're here for the meeting, miss," he said, "I've been instructed to tell you it's due to start anytime. There's a sign in the corridor placed to direct you to the cinema. You enter by the front door," he added, pointing to the ornate entrance.
"Some place," commented Andy, looking over at the new complex. "Must have cost a packet and now I know where all my overtime's gone in the last couple of years." Privately, he thought it was likely to be the only time he'd ever get to take Mary to any film theatre.
Mary slid herself from the passenger seat and went to the

rear of the vehicle.

"Get your act together Dawson and help me with these radios," she grumbled, staring at the cardboard boxes in the boot crammed with handsets and receivers and then bending into the boot to retrieve those boxes that had slid out of reach.

Andy paused, taking a brief few seconds to sigh with delight at the sight of his colleagues shapely, denim clad buttocks.

Together, they carried the equipment between them and followed the sign posted directions to an upstairs cinema that also doubled as a conference room. A hubbub of noise confronted Andy and Mary as they pulled open the heavy double doors.

Already present were about forty officers in an assortment of uniforms and plain clothes.

Amongst those seated Andy saw drug squad and surveillance colleagues, tactical firearms officers, a couple of dog handlers and the white-topped caps of the traffic police, sitting slightly apart and aloof from the rest because, he thought, nobody really likes those bastards anyway.

Standing on the raised stage and apparently in deep conversation, Andy saw Detective Chief Superintendent Tom Morrison, his deputy Detective Superintendent Alison McRae, Detective Chief Inspector Roddy Munroe and two other officers, one in plain clothes whom Andy knew as his own Detective Inspector; the uniformed officer in the black jumpsuit, he guessed, would be in charge of the firearms team.

"Are you two the last?" called Alison McRae.

He nodded, then shouted back, "Just fetching the radio's, boss."

"Sit down then and we'll begin."
The drone of voices dropped to a whisper, and then there was silence. A screen behind her lit up as McRae introduced herself, while the other four on stage sat on chairs on the stage, to one side and slightly behind her.
"Thank you for all coming," she effortlessly began, "particularly as it means you all having to incur overtime," her jovial sarcasm greeted by an appreciative laugh.
"There are three objectives to this operation. The primary objective is the arrest and seizure of at least three major figures in the Glasgow drug scene."
Using a handheld remote control, McRae operated the hi-tech computer equipment secreted beneath a nearby table and the oversized image of Maxie McLean flashed onto the screen.
"Tango one, Maxwell Graham McLean. A Godfather figure whom if you've any police service at all or," a huge smile on her face, "at least read the Sunday tabloids, will need no introduction. Mister McLean has been around as long as I've been serving," here she smiled again, "no comments, please."
Andy didn't care how old McRae was or how long she had been serving. Like most of the male officers in the room, he had already decided she was an extremely foxy lady.

As he had been instructed, Johnjo stuck to the inside lane of the M6 motorway while continuously watching for the Range Rover in his mirror. He was excited and drummed his fingers on the steering wheel, keeping time with the

beat blasting out 'rap' music from the in-car stereo and singing tunelessly to the music. It had not occurred to him that the drugs he carried in the boot of the vehicle could conceivably cost him many years of freedom. Mickey the Greek had organised the deal and that, as far as he was concerned, made Johnjo fireproof. After all, he reasoned Mickey never, ever got caught simply because he was too smart for the rozzers. Johnjo was lucky to be part of Mickey's organisation. Yes, he thought, my quid's in and things can only get better. In his rear view mirror he saw a police car approach at speed, its blue light reflecting off the wet road surface. With dry mouth and sweaty palms, he stared ahead then watched the vehicle go past him and disappear into the distance, the officer in the passenger seat having given Johnjo no more than a passing glance. Relieved, Johnjo burst into laughter then realised he was holding the steering wheel so tightly his knuckles were white.
Get a grip, he inwardly berated himself, Mickey's depending on you, lad.

Hands on shapely hips, McRae continued her briefing. Turning to the screen, she pointed her remote and pressed a button. The screen changed to display the heavy jowls and shaven head of a man resembling a Sumo wrestler, who stared wide-eyed at the camera, a leer on his face.
"Tango two, Francis McEwan. Don't let the cheerful grin and fat face fool you. This is a dangerous individual, well used to violence, who had accrued an incredible list of violent convictions until he teamed up with McLean. That's when he got smart, stopped getting caught and is

now acknowledged as the second in charge of their little band."

"Tango three," another image flashed up.

"David Smith. His nickname is 'One-ball' and," she said, looking inquiringly at the dog-handler's, "you guys might consider finishing the job tonight, eh?"

The room erupted in laughter. The incident in which One-ball had acquired his nickname and deformity had long since passed into police legend. "Relax people, please," she requested.

Once more, silence settled across the room.

"The operation is three-fold," she reiterated, scanning her audience who were now hanging on her every word, their mood suddenly sombre as the full realisation of the importance of the operation became clear.

Behind her, Roddy Munroe smiled, pleased to discover that Alison McRae certainly knew how to present a briefing.

"Firstly," she continued, "the safety of all concerned and that, ladies and gentlemen, means yours first. It is unlikely that any civilians will become involved, but don't discount their nosiness, so remain alert to the possibility. Secondly, the arrest of Tango's one, two and three and any associates who might become involved. Thirdly, the seizure of what is assessed to be a major consignment of illegal substance. If Maxie runs true to form, ladies and gentlemen, I think we're looking at heroin."

Turning once again to change the screen behind her, McRae presented a succession of colour photographs of the target venue and disclosed that two Covert Rural Observation Personnel were already in position. This announcement drew further laughter when, eyebrows raised she remarked the weather office predicted no further rain. Most of those present appreciated the hardship that CROP officers endured in pursuit of their chosen discipline, knowing that inclement weather could mean extreme discomfort to anyone lying in a ditch or beneath a bush. Not only physical discomfort, but rain also presented tactical problems and the falling water tended to distort images viewed through optical sights, particularly at night.

McRae continued her address, issuing call signs to the various units and their deployment positions at the locus. Satisfied that all relevant points had been covered, she then invited questions.

Hesitantly, a hand went up from a young drugs squad officer, embarrassed to be the first to speak.

"Are you able to tell us, Ma'am, where the information originated from?"

"The provenance of the intelligence," responded McRae, "remains with Mister Munroe's department. However, I can assure you that the information has been thoroughly discussed between myself, Mister Morrison and Mister Munroe and we are satisfied it is genuine," or as satisfied as we can be, she thought dryly.

A second hand went up.

"You've suggested the opposition will likely be carrying pick helves or baseball bats, but I see tactical firearms here tonight. Why is that?"

"If I might interrupt, Superintendent," said Morrison, standing and pulling straight his jacket as he moved to the front of the dais, "that was my decision. I have reviewed the previous convictions of the suspects and, based on their recorded propensity for violence, I decided that in the interests of safety, we'd utilise our tactical colleagues."

"Do we have any information on the courier?" queried a third voice.

"Nothing," replied McRae, glancing over her shoulder at Munroe who was shaking his head, "other than the drugs will be arriving from England via the M74 motorway." She looked round the room.

"Any further questions, no? Then, ladies and gentlemen, can I request you break off into your teams and check over your equipment. Thank you."

The arterial highway that connects Scotland's major western city with its English neighbour was and is a continuing source of political controversy. At some stretches the road narrows to a two-lane motorway, at other stretches becoming the A74 dual carriageway. Its upgrade has been slow and, to the frustrating annoyance of its habitual users, the volume of traffic using the road adds to the regular congestion.

As Mickey and his crew travelled its length, they unanimously agreed the only good thing about the road was its return lane to England.

With the October sun slowly settling like a fiery ball and disappearing over the Border hills, they watched as Johnjo slowed on the A74, the Cavaliers brakes lights come on and he indicated his intention to pull into the busy service station at Abington. Sean drove past the now stationary Cavalier and the men saw Johnjo climbing out of the driver's seat and approach a petrol pump.

Driving a further quarter of a mile, Sean turned into a

minor side road that soon became a dirt track.
A homemade signpost pointed up the gradually narrowing track towards a sheep farm. Turning the vehicle at a break in the hedgerow beside the track, he drove back down the inclined and rutted trail, breathing a sigh of relief that he hadn't bogged the vehicle in the clinging mud. He stopped the Range Rover 20 metres from the junction with the A74 and switched off the engine and lights. The three men alighted from the vehicle and stepped out into the track to stretch their legs. Big Al moved to the rear of the vehicle, pulled open the back door and leaned into the boot space. Retrieving a dark coloured, plastic carrier bag, he withdrew from it three navy blue coloured, hooded sweat tops, all large size, which the three men then quickly donned, loosening the top button of their shirts, but keeping their neckties on. Mickey had already planned that the dark sweat tops would conceal and keep clean their light coloured shirts for their return journey.
Reaching again for the toolbox and with a sideways glance about him, Al covered it with his massive frame and deftly removed the shoebox containing the two handguns. Wrapping the shoebox in the empty plastic bag, he returned to the rear seat.
"Right," said Mickey with a grin, "let's be on our way lads. We've an appointment to keep with some smart Jock bastards."

Chapter 21

Willie McKay stopped the car outside Ina Thomson's close. Angie, first out from the back seat of the Mondeo, opened Ina's door and helped her from the car and into the house, glancing timidly behind her to ensure Willie intended following.

Willie locked his car and looking about him, saw the neglected state of the area. When Margaret was growing up here, he thought to himself, the place would have been so much different. He lightly patted the roof of the Mondeo and smiled to himself. If the state of the area was anything to go by, he might be saying goodbye to his car and inwardly smiled, thinking, that might not be such a bad thing.

Angie had left the front door ajar. Knocking on the wooden door, he self-consciously called out, "Just me," then wiped his shoes on the well-used horsehair doormat and stepped into a dark, but warm hallway. The house was, he saw, old fashioned, but neat and tidy. Ina stood nervously by the fireplace holding her hands clasped in front of her and bid him sit down. He could hear Angie behind the flowery curtain that led to the small kitchen, the sound of running water indicating she was filling the kettle for tea.

The atmosphere was strangely formal. With a start, Willie realised that Ina Thomson, regardless of anything else, was and had been for some years, his mother-in-law and he smiled at the thought. Ina again bade him sit in the large, soft chair by the fireplace. Willie suspected this was the chair normally favoured by Ina, but courtesy required she would offer the chair to guests. He nodded in appreciation and sat down. She sat opposite him in a plain backed, dining chair, her hands again folded demurely in her lap.

Hesitantly at first, they began to speak. First pleasantries then Willie learned of Margaret's childhood, her life as a rebellious teenager, her desire to improve herself and her overwhelming need for security. He asked no questions, simply let Ina relate Margaret's young life, at her own pace.

Angie folded back the kitchen curtain and entered the sitting room carrying an old fashioned, wooden handled tray. She set the tray down on a stool and poured tea into two china cups that lay upon matching saucers. Willie assumed this would be Ina's best China, usually the pride of the Glasgow housewife. He watched Angie pour milk into his cup and saw that her hand shook slightly. That done, she sat in a second dining chair, near the kitchen. Willie had already guessed Angie's problem, but wouldn't comment unless either Ina or Angie referred to it.

"How did you meet my Rita?"' he heard Ina ask. He sat back with his tea and took his time, recounting the straightforward tale of her daughter meeting a young policeman, both falling in love and marrying.

On the way to the house, Willie had thought that this woman deserved to know about Margaret, the good as well as the bad. Then, realising that truth at this late stage would benefit no one, he decided there was little point in adding to Ina Thomson's burden and his brief account of his life with Margaret would not include the melancholic moods, depression and guilt that apparently contributed to her death and had decided to describe their marriage, if not happy and affectionate, then comfortable and secure. Nevertheless, Willie was inwardly angry and blazing mad that the woman who had vowed never to have children with him, had abandoned her only son. But, he knew, it wasn't this elderly woman's fault and his natural compassion took hold of the turmoil that was his emotions.

He asked Ina about Billy and learned of the grief the boys' death brought to his grandmother, of Billy's girlfriend Angie and finally in the end, of his mother, Margaret Thomson or McKay.

Briefly, he reflected on the times the name William 'Billy' Thomson had intruded in his life. One time junkie, son of his wife Margaret Thomson or Devlin or McKay or whatever the fuck she wanted to call herself, he thought bitterly.

A thought occurred and raced through his mind.

"The name Devlin she used as her maiden name," Willie asked. "Where did Margaret get that from?" he wondered.

Ina stared at him and clasped her hand to her throat.

"My God, that's a name I haven't heard in a long time," she gasped. "Devlin, Martin Devlin. He was the father of Margaret's child, Billy's father. But he never knew, Margaret didn't tell him."

Stunned, Willie shook his head. So many secrets she'd kept from him. Their whole life had been a lie.

Angie, sitting quietly in the corner slipped out of the room and into the kitchen. She was starting to hurt again, needing another fix. The crazy thing, she realised with a start, was an overwhelming desire that intruded in her own pain, the knowledge that Ina Thomson needed her more. With a sigh, she put the kettle on again, thinking to herself that those two in there could be quite a while yet.

As the Liverpool team and their unwitting patsy resumed their journey north, Franny McEwan and One-ball Smith collected the stolen BMW motorcar from its lock-up in the Maryhill housing estate. As a precaution, they drove round the council estate in One-balls Audi, satisfying themselves there was no police surveillance waiting to spring a trap and lastly phoned One-balls auntie, who hung out of her tenement window and grinned at her favourite nephew with her thumb up, indicating that all was clear. Collecting the car, the two men left One-ball's Audi at a council-parking bay, before driving out of Glasgow eastwards in the stolen BMW and onto the busy M8 motorway. Nervously, Franny glanced at his watch, anxious that the heavy volume of traffic wouldn't delay them.

"Relax," One-ball told him, "the traffic starts to smooth out once we're beyond the Stirling by-pass. We'll have plenty of time."

Franny took a deep breath. He had enough on his mind, worrying about Maxie and the possibility of repercussions with the Billy Thomson fuck-up. But that, he hoped, would be sorted out; if not by him then by One-ball.

"Do you think we should have changed the plates?" he asked One-ball, surprised at the calmness of the normally up-tight bugger.

One-ball screwed his face in deliberation.

"Naw," he decided, "the cops have enough on their plate at this time of night, with the punters all racing to get home for their dinner. Most of they bastards are doing traffic point duty, at this time of the evening and the last thing on their mind will be a blagged motor, knocked off a couple of days ago. And look about you, Franny. Do you see how many black BMW's there are on the road?"

Franny turned his head and sure enough, there were at least two other black BMW's, albeit slightly different

models, travelling the same road a short space apart.
"Popular car this," One-ball continued, "any wanker can get one," and laughed at his own joke.
They continued onto the A8 dual carriageway and again satisfied there was no surveillance trailing them, pulled off into a side road that led to a large industrial estate. Now mostly empty and deserted, warning signs threatened legal action against trespassers, but the factory units were partially derelict and not worthy of the attention of a security guard. Driving slowly around the dilapidated units, One-ball satisfied himself there was nobody hanging about to witness their presence and stopped the car beside an abandoned non-descript, grey coloured van, its tyres flat and bodywork rusted. With a metallic screech, he hauled opened the protesting rear door and nodded in satisfaction. The navy blue boiler suits and two baseball bats, hidden under a pile of old tyres, were exactly where he had left them this morning.
"Suit the colour of your eyes, Franny," he joked as he threw an oversize boiler suit to the big man.
Wearing their boiler suits and sitting on the rear floor of the van, their legs dangling over the back, Franny lit them both a cigar as both men awaited the arrival of Maxie.

The empty clear, plastic bag sitting on the floor beside Willie had a police label attached to it. The contents, he presumed, were the bits and pieces spread out on the sideboard next to his elbow.
"Billy's things the police brought back," Ina had explained, then apologised; she had to "pop out with

Angie for half an hour, a pre-arranged doctor's appointment," she confided. "No thanks, there's no need for a lift, it's just round the road," she had told him. Begging him to stay a little longer, she added "We've more things to discuss," then pulling on an old, beige coloured raincoat and headscarf, ushered the now anxious girl out the front door.

Patiently, Willie sat back in the soft chair, the warmth of fire in the small room and the previous restless night conspiring to spread the shroud of sleep. Slowly, he closed his eyes and as weariness took over, the pounding in his head eased slightly.

As Franny and One-ball collected the stolen BMW, Maxie McLean was preparing himself to leave the house to meet them at their agreed rendeavous. Dressing himself in black denim jeans, black woollen sweater and carefully removing all his jewellery, he looked at himself in the full length bedroom mirror and saw a gaunt, middle-aged man with a slight paunch round his waist, greying hair and pock marked face.

"What the fuck am I all about?" he asked himself, then smiled, for Maxie knew that he missed this part of his profession, the cracking of heads and the thieving, the rush of adrenaline produced by the excitement of the 'turn'.

Lena, a bathrobe draped about her and with her hair newly washed, entered the room then hesitated as she saw Maxie.

"I'm sorry," she stammered "I didn't mean to disturb you."

"That's all right doll, I was just off out anyway. Wee meeting with the guys tonight, so don't wait up, eh?" The scent of her perfume wafted across the room and then to his surprise, pleased to discover he was becoming stimulated by the sight of Lena and the thought of the evening's work ahead.

"Okay love?" he asked, his voice slightly husky as he reached for her and drew her to him. He placed his right hand inside the bathrobe to stroke her left breast in a rare display of affection.

Her body tensed and she neither looked at him nor protested the caress. Her indifference angered him and a sudden rage overtook his sexual need. With his left hand, he seized her by the hair and pulled her downwards. His affectionate caress had become a vicelike clench, then violently he twisted her nipple, causing her to cry out in pain and fall sobbing to the floor, one hand on her bruised and painful breast, the other across her face in expectation of the blows that she knew would rain down on her.

But he drew back and stepped away from her, his face distorted by disgust, his body shaking with fury. This wasn't the time for a beating. With a grunt he left, pausing only to call her a "Frigid cold bitch," then deliberately slam the bedroom door.

Outside the house and walking to his car, Maxie lit a cigarette to calm his nerves and then spent his customary few minutes looking either way down his street for police surveillance vehicles. Had his mind not been on his confrontation with Lena, he might have paid more attention to the old Citroen saloon, empty and parked 150 metres down the road from the house. The fixed remote controlled camera, concealed in the driver's side

headlamp, relayed his movements via a mobile phone uplink to the technical control centre at the police training school, located in East Kilbride.
The technical operator sitting in front of the screen adjusted the zoom on the remote controlled camera, then satisfied with his observation, turned to Alison McRae and said, "Tango one just quit his house now, ma'am."

Willie guessed where Ina and the lassie Angie were going. The girl was beginning to sweat and stagger. He knew that in Govan there was a local health clinic that would likely give her something to tide her over. Shook his head at the battle Ina faced, if she was to help Billy's girlfriend. Bloody hell, a sudden thought struck him. Does that mean Billy Thomson was my stepson? So, Billy's girlfriend, how then, did that relate to Willie, he wondered? Things were moving too quickly for him to take all of this in, he realised with a shudder.
Shrugging his shoulders he turned to place his empty cup on the sideboard and saw again the contents of the bag. Idly curious, he lifted a cheap penknife. Opening the blade he saw it to be scored and dirty and in his opinion, a genuine health hazard. He guessed the blade had been used for more than cutting string as he carefully closed it and thought he had better mention to Ina that he should dispose of it, out of harms way and preferably in the River Clyde. He stopped and shivered at what he had been thinking. The River Clyde, beloved waterway of the Glasgow folk and the subject of many local traditional songs. The river would never mean the same to Willie or Ina again. Not after this. A plastic trouser belt for a

twenty-eight inch waist he saw, smiling self-consciously at the thought he would never see that size again. Mingled together were some loose change and two or three used and crumpled tickets. Typical of the police, he smiled, log everything in and return everything back, even bus tickets. His interest aroused, he examined the tickets. Two were, as he suspected, bus tickets and both dated the same day, oddly, the day Billy died. A single journey from Glasgow Airport to Paisley and a similar ticket from Paisley to Govan and the third ticket he saw was a receipt for the 24hour car park at the airport, again dated the day he died.
Now, he wondered, why would Billy Thomson be in a car park at Glasgow Airport?

Detective Superintendent Alison McRae smiled at the controller and gave him the thumbs up.
"Control to all stations," the controller announced, "Tango one is on the move."
Tom Morrison, standing nearby with Roddy Munroe, gave McRae a slight nod with his head, a summons she couldn't ignore as she followed him into the corridor. Satisfied they couldn't be overhead, he quizzed her.
"You decided not to have him followed?"
McRae shook her head, prepared for the question and a little surprised he hadn't broached the subject earlier. A suspicion gnawed at her that Morrison might not be as astute as he presented himself.
"The reports that I've read indicate that McLean has been demonstrating some excellent anti-surveillance moves, in the recent past."

She crossed her arms across her breasts. At five foot ten, McRae could look many of her colleagues in the eye and Morrison, just an inch taller, was no exception. Nor, it was widely known, was she a shrinking violet. She continued. "We've ploughed a lot of resources into this operation and we already know where his final destination is to be. I'd rather cover the location that McLean intends meeting with the courier, than gamble a risk of losing the whole operation should one of the surveillance team becoming compromised. Right now," her hand moved to her throat, her fingers twirling the thin gold chain about her neck, "my guess is that McLean and his boys will be hyped up and their heads will spinning on their shoulders faster than a Blythswood Square tart looking for a punter."

Morrison visibly recoiled. The vulgarity of his colleagues was something that he had never quite come to terms with. He turned and stepped towards the control room then stopped and faced her again.

"I can't", then swallowed hard as he quickly corrected himself, "we can't afford any mistakes, Alison. I hope you're right about this." Morrison spun on his heel and walked back through the swing doors and re-entered the control room.

My God, she thought, surprised. He's not just worried he's shitting his pants that this might reflect badly on him. The nagging doubt that for some time had played at the back of her mind was fast becoming reality.

She half smiled, understanding now that if anything does go wrong, then Alison, old girl, you are most definitely going to be on your own.

The town of Hamilton geographically lies to the south east of Glasgow and is separated from its local rival, the town of Motherwell by the M74 motorway, the main arterial link between Scotland and England. A bustling and thriving area, both Hamilton and Motherwell boast wide, spacious parkland adjacent to the motorway that during the day are visited by families, nature lovers and pet owners. But by night, the same parks become the haunt of teenagers, fearful members of the gay community and clandestine meeting places for errant husbands and wives, though usually someone else's. The motorway service station that lies on the northbound route to Glasgow is a busy thoroughfare, providing restaurant, fuel, overnight parking facilities for truckers and motel accommodation for the weary traveller. The roads and car parks to the front of the service station are in the main, well lit and open. To the rear of the service station are situated the roads providing access for the vehicles that supply and stock the service station. These roads are not so well lit and seldom used by the public, particularly during the hours of darkness.

Alison McRae, in collusion with the surveillance team leader, had deployed her resources well.

The two CROP surveillance officers, both attired head-to-toe in waterproof, camouflaged Gortex suits, netted veils and liberally plastered with odourless camouflage creams upon their faces, shivered in the October evening as they hid among the abundant and dense foliage at the rear of the service station. The pair took it in turn to operate their night image intensifiers, more popularly known as night-sights, as they constantly monitored the target area, breaking their overall field of vision down into readily identifiable aspects. In a short time, they had agreed code names for the sectioned off area so that any movement within that area would not need discussion nor reference points. Using this method, communication via their throat mikes would be kept to a minimum and their sweep with the night-sight would follow a determined pattern, ensuring that nothing should or would be missed. Patiently, they shivered and silently awaited the arrival of the suspects, their sole function to identify and report the suspect's movement and behaviour, but to take absolutely no action in the event of an arrest situation.

Conventional surveillance and drug squad officers, deployed as arrest teams, sat or lay back in their vehicles amongst the many cars and trucks parked in the service station. Some snoozed while others listened to the local radio station's live report of an evening football match. The close proximity of the service station's cafeteria enabled these officers in turn, to obtain a constant supply of tea, coffee and toilet facilities that meant, unlike their CROP colleagues, the officers were relatively comfortable.
The two dog handlers rested in their van, less than a minute's fast drive away from the rendeavous area, a deck of cards and pile of matchsticks between them. Their dogs dozed in the cages behind the seats, ears pricking up each time the van radio cackled into life at the regular "No change" updates from the two CROP officers, keen to apprise their waiting colleagues of the situation and frequently tested their radios, anxious that the radios continued to function normally in the damp conditions.

The Firearms Tactical Team squatted in the rear of their hired box van, chewing gum to keep their mouths salivated and constantly checking their weaponry, loading and re-loading. Just in case. Their team leader used a pencil thin torch to read and re-read his briefing pack. In the unlikely event they might be called for, he wanted to be fully cognisant of his instructions. The team familiarly knew this period as the 'dry mouth, sweaty palm' time.

The four traffic officers waited in the double-manned vehicles, each vehicle positioned to pursue any getaway car that made off either north or south on the motorway. Bored, they whined about the attitude of their colleagues, wives, girlfriends or anyone who didn't have the good fortune to be a member of the Traffic Department.

Now attired in their one-piece boiler suits, woollen balaclava masks on their laps and baseball bats lying out of sight on the floor, One-ball drove the stolen BMW car at a speed just within the designated limit for the road leading to the Bellshill bypass. The vehicle negotiated the busy Wraith Interchange and passed underneath the M74 motorway. Conscious that he would be driving in twilight conditions; One-ball had ensured all the vehicle's lights were in working order, to prevent any pull from the beasties, and practised driving the road that would eventually lead to the rear of the Hamilton motorway service station.

Behind the wheel, One-ball was in his element and desperate to impress Maxie with his driving skills. However, he could only do that if they were being

pursued and according to Maxie's plan, that was not likely to happen. Maybe next time, he hoped.
Sitting in the back of the car with Franny, Maxie's constant glancing back through the rear window was beginning to grate on his nerves.
"For fucks sake, Maxie, you're giving me the heebie-jeebies, watching all the time," he moaned.
Maxie grinned at him.
"Calm down, you big Jessie," he teased the large man, "it doesn't do any harm to keep an open eye out for the coppers. You know as well as I do, the bastards are getting better all the time. They're a big mob and can change their cars and teams faster than you or I can burn them."
Franny reluctantly agreed, knowing that Maxie's actions were right, that the police had the resources to put a dozen cars and as many men out following Maxie and the rest of them, round the clock. Hadn't he himself burned a couple in a Renault, only last week?

As they approached their destination, Maxie run through their plan yet again.
"Now," he began, "I'm confident that our meeting is unlikely to be seen by any passers-by and that means anything that goes down won't be reported to the police. Anyway," he added, "the whole thing shouldn't take more than a few minutes, tops. So, once again children the meeting's been arranged between Mickey's courier and our deceased friend, the late Billy Thomson."
At that comment, One-ball sniggered from the front of the car, as Maxie continued.

"Our Billy was known to their courier and as far as we are concerned, he was the only one outside we three who had knowledge of the meeting tonight and was trusted and sent by us to get the business done, get it?"
Franny and One-ball both nodded their heads in agreement that they understood, so far.
"So, when Mickey learns that *his* courier has been turned over and *his* gear stolen he'll get on the blower to scream at *me*. And what I'll tell him is that Thomson has not only turned over Mickey's courier, but fucked off with *my* money as well. Then I'll offer to *help* the English twat hunt down the rats who had turned over *his* courier and stole *my* money,' he grinned as he emphasised his words, using his enthusiasm to encourage the other two to believe in his plan.
Franny wasn't stupid and could see a huge hole in the scheme, and said so.
"Maxie, what if Mickey doesn't believe you? I mean, it's a bit iffy, isn't it? No Billy Thomson and three strange guys with bats and masks come out of the dark and fucking off with his gear?"
Maxie shook his head.
"The simple plans are the best, Franny and if Mickey doesn't believe our account, then so what? The fat English bastard can do his worst and we all know he isn't going to find Thomson, who'll be buried soon enough, anyway. Besides, he tries to send anyone up here for a bit of bother and he's got our mob to deal with," scoffing at the very idea that Mickey the Greek would dare to even consider taking on Maxie McLean. Calm now, he patted Franny's knee.
"Don't overestimate the bastard. He's just another junkie dealer and don't forget, I've been around a lot longer

than he has. And anyway, he'll only have the word of his courier against mine."

Maxie sat back, content that he'd won them over with his argument and considered his secret, his plan that he'd not revealed, not even to Franny. His strategy to take the proceeds from the sale of Mickey's gear, recover the lost bags from Thomson's bird, have Harry Cavanagh convert all his properties to cash. Then take his fortune and fuck off to some place warm, anywhere that had no extradition and where the women were dusky. Somewhere nice and safe and more importantly, on his own.

In the brightly lit, but small control room at the police training centre in East Kilbride, Detective Chief Superintendent Tom Morrison paced up and down behind the staff seated at their consoles, occasionally tapping a shoulder to request a situation report, or sitrep for short, from the surveillance officers at the locus, all of whom reported, "No change." His impatience finally annoyed Alison McRae, who caught the staff casting sideways glances at each other, their meaningful looks indicating their frustration at the boss's worry at the lack of action. And right now, she thought, I need them on their toes, not worried that their boss has no confidence in the troops on the ground.

"Why don't we go to the canteen for a coffee?" she suggested, her arm on Morison's arm and indicating the door, "If there's any movement, I'm sure Roddy will have someone fetch us," she hinted, looking directly at Munroe.

"Indeed," agreed Munroe, "and perhaps you might fetch

me back a cup of coffee?" he asked.
Morrison, acutely suspicious that he was being steered out of the control room, reluctantly agreed and walked with McRae down the stairs to the canteen on the ground floor.
Seated at table in the almost empty lounge, he asked, "Honestly, Alison, your considered opinion. What are the chances of this going belly-up?"
"We've covered every angle that I can think of, Tom. Don't get your knickers in a twist," she said, squeezing his arm. "It's out of our hands now, anyway. The outcome of the operation, strangely enough, now lies with Maxie McLean. His actions determine what will happen next."

Returning to her ground floor flat in Govan, Ina Thomson apologised repeatedly for leaving Willie alone and insisted he stay for another cup of tea. Angie he saw seemed much better and he assumed the health clinic had given her something to ease her pain, probably an initial treatment prior to beginning long and difficult process of the withdrawal programme.
Hearing the sound of water gushing into the aluminium kettle, Willie beckoned for the young girl to sit in the chair, opposite him.
"You have a drug problem, love?" he bluntly asked, suspecting the methadone prescription was working its magic and offering the girl some relief.
Angie turned her glazed eyes towards him.
"I have now, but I'll get better, Mister McKay, that I can promise you. You know, people look at me and see a

junkie, a wee idiot that got herself hooked on drugs. Well, they're absolutely right. I am a junkie, a drug addict. For now. But I can get better. It's an illness, admittedly, self-inflicted. But I've been low and seen the devil. I know I can't get any lower. I lost my family and friends and my best friend, my wee sister, and my Billy...." she broke off as a sob caught in her throat. "My wee sister," she continued, "who looked up to me and trusted me. And how did I reward that trust? I'll tell you, Mr McKay. I stole from her, betrayed her," the tears now flowing unchecked down her cheeks, "but I'll get better," she said again, "I promise you. I will."

Willie was taken aback by her eloquence and, he later admitted to himself, impressed by the gritty determination in the girl's eyes.

Ina, standing unobserved and listening from the kitchen doorway, came behind her and held her close.

"You'll have help, love," she smiled, pressing her lips tight together to prevent her from crying. "You're my special project, now. Right," she urged Angie to rise from the chair and steered by the shoulders, "away with you and lie down for a wee rest while I have another word with Mister McKay."

They both watched as the girl left, turning shyly to wave to Willie then closing the front room door behind her. Ina moved to sit down.

"Please, Willie," he smilingly suggested to her.

She returned Willie's smile, pleased at the informality. "Well, in that case call me Ina."

Angie stood in the hallway and listened. She liked Mr McKay and even though he was a policeman, didn't believe he meant any harm to Ina. And for the first time in the recent past, she went to bed feeling safe, knowing

that Ina was close by.
Hearing the squeak of the bedroom door closing, Ina seemed to visibly relax.
"You know, Willie, life has a funny way of working out. I've lost a grandson that I loved and cared for, but gained a young girl who needs my help. I thought I might have found my daughter, but lost her and instead, found you, a son-in-law I didn't even know I had," she shook her head and added, "and all in such a short time. I don't think I'll get over Rita's... do you mind me calling her Rita?"
Willie shook his head. "Of course not," he smiled.
"Losing Rita," she continued, "but truth be told, I lost her over twenty years ago." Both sat as an awkward silence fell over them. Ina looked at him, deciding she liked what she saw. Perhaps not a strikingly handsome man, but a strong face and good build. A man whom people would instinctively trust, she decided.
"Tell me about yourself, Willie."

The camouflaged surveillance man suddenly came alert. Slowly, so as not to disturb the overhanging bushes, he gently shook his dozing neighbour. The second man tensed, but lay still. Softly, he whispered into his throat microphone.
"Bravo one to base. We have movement, dark coloured four by four vehicle, registration number yankee-yankee-golf-three-eight-eight; three occupants, two in the front, one in the rear. Now stopped at rear road with all lights out, over."
"Quick as you can please, get me a check on that number," instructed McRae, leaning over the operator.

DC Andy Dawson turned and, with a wry smile and sneaky look at her pert breasts, gently shook DC Mary Murdoch awake.

She turned and looked at him, rubbing the sleep from her eyes, annoyed at being snapped out of her dream.

"Playtime," he grinned at her.

Johnjo hummed tunelessly to himself. Checking the clock on the dashboard in front of him, he saw he was slightly behind time and pressed down on the accelerator.

"Vehicle last registered to a finance company in Birkenhead, no current keeper, Ma'am."

McRae wrote in her notepad: *Courier?*

Turning to a Detective sergeant, she snapped at her, "Contact the local Merseyside station that serves the Birkenhead area and see if they have any criminal intelligence on the user of that vehicle," then added with a polite smile, "if you please."

Roddy Munroe smiled at McRae's thoughtful courtesy. If only we had more bosses like her, he mused.

McRae leaned over the radio controller.

"Tell all stations we have a suspect vehicle on the plot, now dubbed Victor One and to standby. No action meantime."

One-ball drove along the darkened road and eased the BMW over a concrete speed ramp. In the distance he could see the Duke of Hamilton Mausoleum, the world famous domed shaped building that dominated the skyline and was situated near to the motorway but, more importantly to One-ball, a visible indication that he was approaching the road at the rear of the service station. "Nearly there," he announced to his passengers with relief.

The two officers in the rear of the unmarked transit van were suspicious of the car that slowly passed them by. Three up, they saw. "Bravo six to base, that's a bravo mike whisky saloon vehicle, registration number papa-zulu-whisky-one six-two-one just passed us, three occupants and now towards the locus. One driving and two in the rear, over."

"Check please, soon as you can," McRae ordered crisp and clearly, aware her instruction was unnecessary but really just wanting to show Morrison that she was in charge.

Mickey licked his lips, suddenly aware he was very thirsty. His breathing, shallow and rapid betrayed his anxiety.
Sean Begley in the driver's seat looked at his boss in the darkness and wondered. Was the mad bastard worried or,

he hesitated to even consider it, frightened?
Mickey, a handgun clenched in his upright fist, turned to face Al O'Rourke.
"Remember, lad," he spat, "if there's any hint of these bastards trying to take the gear....", the gun waving in Al's face, the vehemence evident in Mickey's eyes.

"Ma'am?" the operator turned to McRae, trying to control the excitement in his voice, "the BMW registration number PZW 1621 reported stolen from a high rise car park at Cowcaddens in Glasgow."
McRae smiled grimly and turned to Morrison and Munroe.
"The game's afoot, to coin a phrase," hopeful that she sounded more confident that she was. She crossed her arms over her chest and held herself tight, aware that the knuckles of her hands were white with tension.
The operator broadcast the arrival of the stolen vehicle, now designated Victor Two.

The camouflaged surveillance officer swallowed hard and held the bulky night sight as tightly as he could, but still thought he was seeing things. The fluorescent green images seemed to merge together. But no, he was certain, or as certain as anyone could be looking at a green lighted image through a night-sight.
"Bravo one to base, urgent!"
"Go ahead bravo one."
"Shooters in the four by four vehicle, at least one," the officer hissed, agitation evident in his voice.

McRae, suddenly alert, shook her head and snatched the microphone handset from the controller and depressed the switch.

"Calmly please, bravo one. Repeat. Confirm who has a firearm?" "Bravo one," the officer repeated his call-sign, breathing heavily now, the adrenaline kicking in as he fumbled with frozen fingers at the night sight and tried to focus on the subject with the handgun.

"Front seat passenger, Victor One. Looked like a handgun. I'm repeating, looked like a handgun!"

Morrison reached for McRae's arm and firmly drew her aside.

"Shouldn't you consider moving the firearms team up?" he hissed at her, his eyes wide and his face close enough for her to see a little ball of spittle at the side of his mouth.

She stared at him, a sudden revelation that he was not all he seemed to be, knowing that the staff in the control room were listening, if not watching, and hoping she sounded calmer than she felt, she replied in an even and soft voice, "Not yet, they're not surveillance trained and their sudden presence would undoubtedly compromise the operation. At the moment and *at best*," she stressed, her eyes locked into his, "all we have is a stolen car and a possible, and I must emphasise, a *possible* firearms offence."

She shrugged out of his grasp and from the corner of her eye, saw that Roddy Munroe had subtly moved closer. "It's dark out there," she hissed, "and those men have been lying in the cold for several hours now. We can't be sure.... Christ, *he* can't be sure of what he saw. I'm not prepared to strike prematurely on the little information I have."

"Now sir," she stared back at Morrison and conscious of the tension in the room, "if I might be permitted to get back to the radio?"

Roddy Munroe watched the exchange between them, knowing that Morrison's nerves were on edge, yet fiercely pleased that McRae had the bottle to remind the stupid twat who was running the show. Just the same, he thought, I'm glad it's not me having to make the decision.

Ina followed Willie to the door then, drawing a cardigan about her shoulders against the damp and cold, walked with him to the close entry.

Glancing at the dark sky he turned his jacket collar up against the slight fall of rain and smiled at her.

"You'd better get indoors, Ina before you catch your death with this weather."

"I'm a tough old bird, Willie." She raised her chin, a belated defiance to the world. "I've seen off my husband and now my daughter and grandson. It'll take more than the rain to do me any harm. Besides," she reminded him, "I've a new challenge now. That wee girl needs someone."

She lifted her hand and warmly rubbed his arm.

"I suppose we all do, don't we?"

Willie smiled again, pleased at the gesture and amazed at the resilience of this good woman.

To her surprise and delight, he placed his hands on her

shoulders then bent down and tenderly kissed her cheek. Instinctively, she threw her arms about his neck and drew him to her. They embraced for a few seconds, then both stood apart, shyly embarrassed by their show of affection.

"You'll keep in touch?" she called as he walked to his car.

He opened the door and nodded. "Soon," he promised then, almost as an afterthought, "After all, you're family, aren't you?"

The man wearing a bright coloured fluorescent jacket, baseball cap and carrying a rucksack over his shoulder, walked along the path adjacent to the road, apparently on his way home after a shift at the service station. Even at this distance, Maxie could hear the strains of a well-known Irish republican song as the man, whistling off-tune, disappeared into the darkness. "Fenian prick," Franny sneered while Maxie and One-ball both laughed. DC Andy Dawson stopped whistling and pressed the button of the small, covert microphone clipped onto his collar.

"Confirming Tango one in front passenger seat, Tango two in rear seat and Tango three, driver's seat, over."

His earpiece crackled.

"Acknowledged."

Johnjo passed the large, blue motorway sign that warned him the Larkhall turn-off was approaching and licked his lips in anticipation, suddenly aware of a dry throat. He knew from previous deliveries that he was almost there, that a few more minutes at this speed would bring him to the service station.

He thought of Mickey and the others, waiting at the Abington services for Johnjo to return with the money. Relying on him, knowing they could trust him with such an important job. He had no memory of anyone ever having faith in him. Always the runner, he thought bitterly, always on the edge of the gang, never asked for his opinion. Well, that was changing. No, had changed. Mickey trusted him, wanted him 'in'. One of the boys now, the third man. Yes, he decided, life was definitely on the up.

Again, McRae looked at her watch. According to their information, the rendeavous time was so very close. Should she have taken Morrison's advice, she again asked herself? Indecision would only cloud her judgement, she knew. No, hers was the right decision. Of that she was sure. The radio cackled again, the disembodied voice calling out across the speaker "Bravo one to base. Rear passenger victor one out of vehicle. Standby! No, wait. Cancel standby, he's taking a piss." Then after a minute's pause, "He's returned to the vehicle. No change."

"Hoped you've washed your hands," sniggered Mickey. Big Al grinned. He hated to admit it, even to himself, but the tension was getting to him. He'd just had a run-out and now here he was again, needing another piss. Better hold it, he thought, pride overcoming any long term damage to his kidneys.

One-ball was drumming his fingers on the steering wheel.
"For fucks sake, One-ball, quit it," snapped Maxie.
"Right, let's go over it again."
Franny put back his head and sighed.
Maxie turned, scowling. "Practise makes perfect, right? *Right*" "Okay, Maxie, keep the head," soothed Franny.
Leaning forward between the headrests in front, Franny went through the agreed plan.
"The Cavalier with the Scouser shows up, over there," pointing through the darkness in the general area of the agreed meeting spot. "One-ball here stays with the motor, engine off. You and I with the bats," pointing to the baseball bats on the floor, "approach the Cavalier from the rear. I put the guy's windscreen in with my bat and you grab him out of the motor. Take him to the boot, grab the stuff and run like fuck. *Owzatt!*" he caricatured a cricketer, hands held apart.
Maxie smiled, relieved by Franny's display of calm.
A sudden thought struck One-ball. "What if he chases you or fights back?"
"Then," Maxie said with a grim smirk, "he gets introduced to Mr Snoopy," reaching down and stroking the baseball bat lying on the floor.

Roddy Munroe tapped down his pipe. God, what I'd give for a smoke, he thought.

The tension in the operations room was electric. Morrison was on his mobile phone, updating the Assistant Chief Constable of Crime, his low voice a mumble but likely, Munroe guessed, preparing the way for a Pontius Pilate act if the operation went sour.

He watched McRae as she paced back and forth behind the radio operator, desperate for information, but reluctant to call any of the teams on the plot for fear of provoking a rash show-out, panic or worse.

Johnjo saw the tall overhead lights of the service station and then the sign requesting traffic slow down in preparation for taking the nearside lane into the service station car park. He slowed the Cavalier and turned into the nearside lane, his stomach turning cartwheels.

Mickey the Greek checked his watch and swallowed hard. Anytime now.

Franny thought about the house in Spain with the photograph and details he'd found on the Internet. Staring at the back of Maxie and One-ball's heads, he thought, one final turn with these two jokers and he'd be off and rid of the pair of them.

Tom Morrison reflected on the conversation he'd had with the ACC (Crime). A little encouragement would have been nice, he mused, rather than the threat of dire consequence if he fucked up. But then again, he considered, sneaking a glance at McRae's back, isn't that why we have deputies?

McRae, without consulting Morrison, made her decision. Leaning over the operator, she took hold of the microphone.
"Base to Bravo five. You have authorisation for an armed arrest. Repeat, I am authorising an armed arrest. Stand by meantime, but be prepared to move up to the locus on my command. All stations acknowledge that Tactical Firearms have primacy in the event of an arrest scenario, over."
One by one and in numerical order, the surveillance teams, firearms team, dog handlers and traffic cars acknowledged the order.
The operator updated his written log with the details of McRae's call and noted the team's responses.

A surprised Andy Dawson tapped at his covert earpiece, as if not believing what he'd just heard, then muttered to himself, "Christ, she's not fucking about, is she?"

Slowly driving past the parked vehicles in front of the restaurant, Johnjo looked for the entrance to the side road that he knew would lead him to the rear of the service station. Unhurriedly, he drove past the courting couple, passionately embraced and seemingly oblivious to his leering stare.

Disengaging herself from her neighbour and shoving away the hand he was sneakily trying to slip under her blouse, the drug squad officer spoke quietly into her microphone.

"Bravo three to base, dark coloured Cavalier, driver only, now towards the rear road and the locus, over," then to her neighbour, "and you, you bastard, try that again and I'll fucking murder you!" she hissed.

At a nod from McRae, the senior operator spoke into his microphone.

"All stations standby, standby! Suspect vehicle, dark coloured Vauxhall Cavalier, designation victor three, now approaching the locus."

The plain-clothes Traffic department driver of the navy blue Transit van with the logo of a well-known local delivery company on the side of the van was more used to attending traffic accidents than getting involved in this kind of caper. The van, now carrying the tactical firearms team designated Bravo Five, was unwieldy and clumsy, nothing like his usual vehicles. He started the engine and licked his lips. His response to a 'go' would determine how fast he could put his team into play and he didn't want any mishaps. The firearms team leader leaned over from the back and patted his shoulder encouragingly.

"No sweat, Jimmy, get us there then get your head down, okay?"
Jimmy the driver nodded, his mouth too dry to speak.

Andy Dawson, back in the car with Mary Murdoch, watched the Cavalier creep down the road towards the meeting point. He was aware that his partner beside him was breathing heavily.
Wish that I could get her pulse racing like that, he thought.

"Get your masks on," instructed Maxie, watching as the lights of the Cavalier approached.

"Bravo one to base," whispered the camouflaged officer, wiping the lens of the night sight at his eyes, "Occupants of victor one about to de-bus from vehicle."

Mickey, from the darkness of his Range Rover, couldn't see any vehicle other than the approaching Cavalier, but knew in his heart the two-timing bastards were hereabouts. The caller had warned him that McLean was tricky, that he could expect trouble when he tackled him and his team. But Mickey, a lifetime of violent experience behind him, secretly relished the thought of

giving it to the Scotch bastard.
"Right, lads, here we go then."

"Bravo one to base, front and rear passengers now out of victor one, driver remains with vehicle, over...wait, wait! Urgent, both males have handguns, repeating, both have handguns," then more loudly, seconds before he released the microphone switch, "*SHIT!*"

Johnjo coasted the car to a halt and switching off the engine, extinguished the main beam but kept the sidelights on. He didn't think he'd have to remain here too long. Billy the Jock guy was usually sharp, if not already waiting. He switched on the interior light, stretched his arms and yawned as the sudden fatigue of several hours of concentrated driving overcame him. Reaching across to the passenger seat, he picked up the bottle of juice.

"Bravo six to base," a smooth voice reported in, "Tango's two and three, both masked and carrying long items, possibly pick handles or similar. Now out of vehicle and approaching, no, bent over and creeping towards the Vauxhall, I mean victor three," then unnecessarily adding, 'the Cavalier, over."

McRae stood bolt upright, her body tensing. She suddenly understood and, glancing at Munroe, saw he did to. It was a rip-off by Maxie, sure enough, but the team in the four by four were there to prevent it. And with guns! They'd all been set-up by the caller, the scheming bastard!

Pushing the operator out of her way she grabbed at the microphone, all pretence of calm now gone. She shouted into it, '*Bravo five*! STRIKE! STRIKE! STRIKE! And use extreme caution, it's a set-up! The guns are to be used on the Tango Targets. *Get in there now*!"

Catching her breath, she forced herself to be calm and continued, "All stations, beware! This is a set-up! Attention, non-armed personnel! *Do not, I repeat do not engage any of the targets at this time*!'

The controller scribbled furiously on his pad, anxious to get McRae's instructions down on paper. Just in case.

Mickey crouched down, Big Al beside him, both pointing their guns towards the Cavalier where they could just make out Johnjo, bottle of juice in one hand and picking at a bogey in his nose with the other. Al nervously sniggered, secretly relieved that the darkness hid the slight shaking of the weapon he held in his hand.

Mickey used his left hand to tug at Al's sleeve and indicated with a nod to beyond the Cavalier. At the rear of the vehicle, two figures could be seen bent low to the ground and approaching the car.

"It's them! They've got axe handles or something," grunted Al.

Jimmy the Traffic Department driver gunned his engine and took off, wheels screaming in protest. The smell of burnt rubber hit the eight members of the firearms team, dressed in black jumpsuits, body armour, Kevlar helmets and goggles, with short barrelled carbines slung on harnesses on their chests. They braced themselves using the ropes they'd hooked into the roof struts for support. The two officers at the back of the van held tightly onto the straps they'd contrived that would allow them to quickly open the roller shutter door and exit the van, within seconds.

Maxie nodded to Franny and they both stood up, baseball bats above raised their heads. Without a sound they ran the remaining few yards to the Cavalier. Heart pounding, Franny made his way round the passenger side of the vehicle and saw the driver sitting relaxed, probably blinded by the interior car light and apparently unaware of their presence. He raised his bat to strike the windscreen then waited the few seconds as he watched Maxie get into position. Maxie run to the driver's door and, yanking it open, grabbed the driver by the hair and pulled him screaming, out of his seat. Franny grinned and drew the bat back, to strike the windscreen.

As Johnjo was being pulled from his seat, Mickey raced to the Cavalier, covering the last few yards then stopped, breathing hard and holding his gun in both hands, just like he'd seen Clint Eastwood do a thousand times on video, "*McLean you bastard*!' he screamed, pointing the weapon at Maxie.

Big Al, his breathing laboured, stopped beside Mickey and pointed his gun at Franny, who stood frozen, his bat still held above his head, his jaw hanging slack. "Don't move! And lower the stick, fatso," shouted Al.

Oh, shit, thought Franny. How the fuck do I lower the bat if I've not to move?

Maxie was equally dumbstruck! How the *fuck* did Metexas know he'd be there, he wondered?

"Thought you'd rip *me* off, did you?" Mickey gasped, his palms suddenly sweaty and breath laboured, gripping the gun tighter to prevent it slipping from his grasp.

One-ball, watching from the BMW and recognising Mickey even from this distance in the dark, slowly slid down in his seat. If that nutter comes this way, he decided, I'm away!

Jimmy the Traffic cop drove the Transit van at speed, ignoring the plaintive cries and curses from the team in the rear as they bounced all over the van each time he crashed over a speed bump.

Mickey walked the few yards that lay between him and Maxie, his breathing becoming more rapid and working himself into a rage, as he got closer. Al, one eye on Mickey while keeping Franny covered with his gun, kept step with his boss, hoping Franny wouldn't realise that

Al's hands were shaking and the sweat of his hands was making it difficult to keep a hold of this fucking thing.

Johnjo, hair still entangled in Maxie's fingers lay half in, half out of the driver's seat. His face almost touching the ground, he looked under the car door and was astonished to see Mickey the Greek holding a gun! Too afraid to move he wondered what the fuck was going on! Not the least of his worries was the knowledge that he should have used the men's room at Abington, recognising the warm trickle that now run down his leg and was settling in the crutch of his trousers.

"Mickey," greeted Maxie affably, a half smile playing on his lips, wondering how the fuck he was going to explain this away, yet strangely fascinated by the sight of the gun in Metexas's hand, that now pointed at his face.
"Nice to see you, too, Maxie."

McRae, every sinew of her body crying out with tension, paced the control room, anxiously awaiting an update from the resources on the ground. She glanced at the large clock above the operator and was astounded to discover that just one minute had elapsed since she'd ordered the strike. No one spoke.

Further pleasantries between Mickey and Maxie were curtailed by the high-pitched scream of a protesting engine as Jimmy the driver raced the Transit van into the vicinity. Skidding to a halt twenty metres from the Cavalier, the vans headlights now on full beam and illuminating the scene, the sight of two suspects holding guns was enough for Jimmy, who hurriedly threw himself to the floor of the cab, cursing in his panic as his seatbelt held him fast. A smack at the release button dropped him free and on top of the knob of the gear stick that caught him with a thud, in the groin.
'GO! GO! GO!' screamed the team leader from the rear, unnecessarily as it happened for the roller shutter doors had already been flung upwards, crashing into their casing. The team spilled out from the van into the darkness, dispersing as they'd trained and covering each other as they each sought a position from which to aim their weapons at the suspects.

Johnjo and the others, momentarily blinded by the headlights of the Transit, looked in stunned silence at the sudden arrival of the van, now disgorging armed police officers from its rear and all of whom seemed to be shouting, *"ARMED POLICE! DROP YOUR WEAPONS! STAND STILL!"*
Maxie was the first to react, releasing his hold on Johnjo's hair and dropping his baseball bat, he turned to run back to the BMW, desperately hoping the enveloping darkness would screen him from the arriving coppers.
As Mickey spun round, he caught sight of Maxie trying to get away and instinctively pulled the trigger, firing one

bullet.

Simply put, the discharge of a low velocity, nine-millimetre bullet from a Browning semi-automatic handgun occurs when the trigger is pulled, causing the firing pin to strike the base of the round. A small explosion takes place inside the chamber of the gun and the bullet part of the round is fired through the barrel, the empty casing of the round almost immediately being ejected outwards by the working parts of the gun that are pushed backwards by the force of the explosion. These working parts, having ejected the empty casing, push back against a powerful spring and are then propelled forward to bring forth another bullet from the weapon's magazine that is situated in the handgrip. The weapon is therefore re-cocked and ready to fire again.

The round consists of two parts. The shell casing encompasses the bullet and also contains the propellant that when ignited, produces the explosion and provides the momentum to drive the bullet from the barrel. The bullet, comprising an inner core made of lead, usually has a copper and nickel outer casing to give it more punch and to keep the lead, being a softer metal, in shape as it is hurtled from the barrel and towards its intended target. As the bullet is shot through the barrel of the handgun it is spun like a top in a corkscrew pattern by the grooves inside the barrel. The hot gases, resulting from the explosion and which follow the bullet through the barrel, meet the colder air and in consequence, a loud bang occurs.

All within less time it takes a heart to beat.

The laws of chance affect us all. Had Maxie stood still as commanded by the arriving police officers, he would certainly have been arrested. However, the shot fired by Mickey struck the Cavalier door and ricocheted off the door lock at an almost impossible right angle. Slowed slightly by the impact with the door, the bullet nevertheless still carried enough power to drive into the back of the fleeing Maxie's skull where it met some resistance from his upper jaw. The collision with his jaw caused the bullet to again veer and exit with a sizeable chunk of his brain through his left eye before finally winging its way to embed itself in the wall of the service station, some 150 metres away, where it was discovered two days later by searching forensic officers. Maxie, dead before he hit the ground, regretfully didn't have time for a final thought.

The two camouflaged officers of the Bravo one team, all thought of covert surveillance abandoned, were now vying for a better look at the unfolding scene before them, while the radioman hoarsely screamed into his throat mike, *"SHOTS FIRED! SHOTS FIRED!"*

The echo of the shot fired by Mickey had hardly died when he turned to face the armed police. Shocked and slightly dazzled by the flash and the report of the weapon going off in his hand, he was on the verge of explaining he really didn't mean to fire the fucking thing. Unfortunately for him, in the confusion his explanation was lost on the officers who only saw a suspect pointing a gun at them and who had, a second before, had shot and possibly killed a fellow suspect.

In their view, that was sufficient cause for the officers to return fire. The report of their weapons being discharged, almost simultaneously, was immediately followed by a deafening silence.

Mickey was confused by the glare of the muzzle flashes, then lifted off his feet and flung down onto his back as seven of the eight bullets fired by the police struck him in various parts of his body. Unlike Maxie, he had just time to smile in the knowledge he had done for that two-timing Scotch bastard, Maxie McLean.

"DROP THAT FUCKING GUN!" the team leader screamed at Big Al, all protocol now exhausted, as eight determined and advancing black clad demons approached him, their guns all seemingly pointed at his head. Shaking with fear, Al threw the gun down and away from him. In anticipation of the next command, he slowly sunk to his knees then wisely spread-eagled himself on the ground.

Franny, meantime still standing beside the Cavalier, quickly realised the police wouldn't shoot an unarmed fleeing man. At least not in Scotland, he hoped. Taking advantage of the confusion and seizing his opportunity, he took off into the darkness and ran faster than he thought a man his size was capable of. Legs pumping, heart pounding, he stumbled across the uneven field next to the road, ignoring the band of pain that stretched across his ample girth and the cries that pursued him into the night. Banking on the heavily armed coppers being more interested in dealing with their armed adversary, he presumed that a cordon would be thrown around the area and gambled on reaching the town centre of Hamilton before the police could catch him. His mistake, he later came to realise, was looking behind him. Had he considered what was in front he might have seen the large metal baton being wielded by the wee police bird, who whacked it across his knee cap. Crashing heavily to the ground, holding his knee and screaming in pain, he didn't see detective Mary Murdoch standing over him as she politely inquired, "Going somewhere, fat boy?"

Back at the operations room, the cry of "Shots fired" startled Alison McRae. Turning, she realised Morrison was no longer in the room. Roddy Munroe, standing behind her, gripped her arm at the elbow and urgently whispered, "Don't lose it Alison. Get a grip. Let them sort it out, on the ground. Wait for a result and then take charge!"
Roddy stepped back and away, sure than no one else had seen him speak to her. Everyone, he noticed, had eyes only for the radio transmitter, all willing the set to spurt out further information.
The seconds dragged by.
"BRAVO ONE TO BASE!" screamed the transmitter.
"MORE SHOTS FIRED, JESUS CHRIST! IT WAS OUR GUYS. BAD GUY DOWN!"
then silence.
Taking a deep breath, Alison reached for the microphone

then stopped. With a half glance at Munroe, she placed a reassuring hand on the operators shoulder and instructed him, "Please have Bravo one report more slowly and keep the questions 'yes and no', understand?"
The radio operator looked at her, nodded his head and pressed the button.
"Base to Bravo one, situation report please, over."

Willie McKay arrived home. From the outside and in the darkness, the house looked cold and forbidding, the windows with curtains open staring back at his like sightless eyes. Locking his car, he glanced into the night air, watching the movement of the clouds, the moon partially hidden and a fine drizzle of rain falling, causing his eyes to blink. He leaned back against the old car and stood for a few moments, letting the water wash over his face, then the tension eased from his body and softly, he wept.

At the conclusion of the incident, following the arrest of the five surviving gang members and their removal to police cells, the area sealed and secured.
A tight lipped Alison McRae accompanied Tom Morrison and Roddy Munroe to the scene. Morrison was aware of McRae's tension and disappointment in him. For her part, McRae was furious and surly responded to his questions, aware her curt answers sounded churlish yet unable to refrain from displaying the anger she felt towards him.
Munroe remained silent, watching and noting everything

that was said should he be required, he wryly thought, to recall any of their conversation at a later date.

The Inspector in charge of the surveillance teams greeted Morrison. The bodies, they saw, lying were they had fallen. Already the technical support teams had moved in. Harsh halogen lighting on telescopic stands illuminated the area, with scenes of crime officers photographing and tagging items in preparation for removal to their laboratories. Ducking back under the blue and white plastic tape that abounded the area, Morrison said, "There's nothing for us to do here at the minute, Alison." She kicked at a loose piece of turf with her toe then raised her head to look him in the eye.

"If you don't mind, sir I'll stay for a while. I want to get the feel of the area. After all," she turned and looked about her, "there's every likelihood this might go to a criminal trial and as the officer in charge, I want to know every facet of my case."

Without a backward glance, she wrapped her heavy coat about her and made her way towards the senior scenes of crime officer.

With a curt nod, Morrison walked to the car then turned to Munroe.

"I think I'll stay as well, sir," called Munroe, pre-empting the offer of a lift, his pipe firmly jammed between his teeth.

Morrison didn't acknowledge, but turned and climbed into his car, indicating to the driver to move off.

Munroe joined McRae as she inspected the heroin that had been found in the boot of the Cavalier.

"You stupid old bugger," she smiled at him, "he'll take that as an indication of your disapproval at his sloping shoulders back at the operations room and assume that you'll side with me if this goes to an enquiry in front of the Chief."

Munroe, removed his pipe from his teeth, held it up and looked at it against the dark sky.

"Aye, maybe. We both know he bottled out as soon as the firearms issue arose, but you didn't. That's why I'm here and besides, he's not got your fabulous legs," he said with a wide grin.

Chapter 22

The following morning, the newspapers, radio and national television news reported what one popular tabloid headlined 'Gunfight at the Hamilton Corral!' In age old tradition, the police, represented by the Assistant Chief Constable of Crime, released a statement providing a sketchy account of the circumstances that had resulted in the death of two men, later identified by the predictably anonymous police source that is common to all such stories, as 'leading figures in the underworld of crime.'

"No", insisted the Assistant Chief Constable of Crime, "names will not be disclosed until relatives have been informed."

However, the two slain 'drug lords' were later publicly identified when their respective photographs, purchased at no little expense from disenchanted family members, appeared on the evening news.

"Yes," the ACC grimly continued, "an independent inquiry to be conducted by an outside Force will determine if the police acted correctly."

Anxious reporters, eager for quotable comments, sought the views of the respective pro- and anti-gun lobbies.

Other reporters, never allowing the truth to interfere with a good story, submitted stories that bordered on the outrageous.

An elderly and bedraggled service station cleaner appeared twice on consecutive news bulletins, recounting to the young and pretty reporter in graphic detail his observations as he watched the two desperate criminals battle it out with armed Special Air Service troops, until it was discovered that at the time of the incident, the star witness had in fact been off duty and attending an alcoholics anonymous meeting in Glasgow. The hugely embarrassed reporter, it was later learned, allowed the cleaner to retain his ex gratis payment.

The inquiry continued. Every inch of the scene of the encounter was scoured for anything of evidential value with the surviving members of the gangs taken to three separate police stations in an effort to thwart any attempt at collusion between them or interference by the media. Following a unit debrief, the firearms team were separately counselled and their thoughts and feelings noted for future discussion and training issues. One, it was cruelly rumoured, confessed to experiencing a sexual excitement as he watched the hapless Mickey Metexas fall to the ground, in the privately held belief it might assist him later in a lawsuit against the police, for emotional distress.

Archie McDonald hadn't seen Willie since he'd stayed overnight at the McDonald house. Carrying a dozen morning rolls, a packet of bacon, the local tabloids and a burden of guilt, he took a deep breath and with some trepidation, pressed the doorbell. Willie came to the door, unshaven and in his dressing gown.

"Paper delivery and I've brought rolls in case you wanted to feed me," beamed Archie, holding his groceries in the air, but prepared to step back in case his pal took a swing at him.

"If it isn't Archie the grass," scowled Willie, his eyebrows narrowed before nodding to beckon Archie in and turning to walk back into the house.

At least he hasn't slammed the door, thought Archie as he followed Willie into the kitchen.

"Breakfast?" asked Willie, switching on the cooker.

"So you've forgiven me, then?"

Willie bent over the gas cooker and reached into the oven for a frying pan.

"No, nothing to forgive, Archie' he answered over his shoulder. "You did what you thought was best for me. Besides, I suspect that you, who haven't had an original thought in your life, were sent to speak to Munroe, by Jean, the real brains of the family, eh?"

Archie sighed with relief, took off his jacket and sat down at the kitchen table.

"Aye, you're right. You know what she's like. She thought you needed a bit of time, to yourself."

"Well, tell her she was correct." With a sigh, he turned to his friend and continued, "You know about Margaret?"

Archie nodded, unsure what to say. Should he offer condolence or what? Wishing Jean had come with him, he decided to just come right out with it.

"The DCI in the inquiry, Katie Docherty, she called in to see Roddy Munroe after she'd been here apparently.

Munroe knows I'm your pal and called me into his office and I got the full story, same time he did. He wanted to come with me today, but felt that you'd probably want to belt my jaw and probably wouldn't like any witnesses." Bent over the cooker, Willie smiled, pleased Archie was trying to cheer him, but knowing that Munroe had been right. He couldn't face too many visitors. Not today, so soon after.....

"So," Archie grinned, "have you heard the news this morning?"

Willie shook his head and, while he boiled a kettle of water and prepared Archie's breakfast rolls, he heard in full and colourful detail the story of the Gunfight at the Hamilton Corral.

Interviews with the suspects, conducted by members of the Serious Crime Squad, had little difficulty persuading the three Englishmen to confess their complicity in the attempt to bring such a massive quantity of heroin into Scotland.

Big Al O'Rourke and Sean Begley blamed each other for the possession of the handguns and then mutually agreed that Mickey, the real culprit, had threatened them into assisting him to scare Maxie McLean and his boys.

"Intention to shoot McLean?" gasped an outraged Big Al, "No sir, never. I swear it, on my child's life!"

Franny McEwan, limping into the interview room on his new aluminium NHS crutches, tried to hoodwink his interrogators with threats of legal action against the dirty wee bitch that had surely crippled him for life, alleging he had simply been a victim of circumstance. The stony faced officers listened as Franny graphically recounted stopping at the service station for a cup of tea, gone into the darkness for a pee, heard the shots and taken off in fear of his life. Unable to explain the absence of his car, hence his reason for being at the service station, he presumed it had been stolen and wished now to report its theft. As one of the officers placed a baseball bat wrapped in a cellophane bag on the desk in front of Franny, the other officer explained the value of fingerprints, particularly on varnished wood. Franny, ever the realist, crumpled and asked for a deal.

The lawyer acting for his associate One-ball Smith quickly made a vociferous complaint that her client had been strongly coerced into signing a confession. The outraged lawyer complained that the police had tortured her client, contending while One-ball had been holding the unlocked cell door with one hand and protecting his remaining testicle with the other, two police Alsatian dogs had patrolled the passage outside the cell, barking and scratching at the terrified One-ball's door. The claim was, of course, strenuously denied by the police, who assured the lawyer that police dogs were fed a strict, high protein diet and had no interest in her clients one, remaining and at the time, shrivelling testicle.

Then of course, there was Johnjo Donnegan. Having watched several cinema films of IRA terrorists being interviewed, he decided to emulate these hardened terrorist suspects by staring into a corner of the interview room and say nothing, regardless of what torture the police might inflict upon him. Johnjo lasted for almost five minutes, before agreeing to tell all in exchange for a McDonald's Happy Meal and a clean, dry pair of trousers.

The common thread that run through all the interviews was the realisation that they were caught and what information could they offer towards a reduced sentence?

At police headquarters, the Chief Constable read and re-read Detective Superintendent Alison McRae's summarised operational report concerning the previous night's incident at the Hamilton service station. The addendum by her boss Tom Morrison was, he thought, bland and impartial, neither supportive nor critical of McRae's management of the incident. The Chief sat back in his leather-padded chair. In response to an ongoing public health initiative, he'd given up smoking some years previously, but still had the occasional craving for the comfort of a cigarette between his fingers. The Chief thought of McRae and her service record. He'd known Alison a long time, and he wryly recalled; wasn't he the man who'd appointed her to her current position?
A good officer and, smiling to himself, a man's copper. As for young Tom Morrison, the Chief wasn't blind to Morison's aspirations, but he'd a long way to go before he was ready to assume the Chief's role. Certainly ambitious and very competent, if a touch insecure. Something he'd suspected but not been sure of. At least, he stared again at the report in front of him, not till he'd read these comments.
The Chief thought of his quiet and discreet telephone conversation with that old rogue Munroe. One thing he knew for certain, if Munroe hadn't thought it worth mentioning, it wouldn't have reached the Chief's ears. He had been considering Morrison as a replacement for

the ACC (Crime), who was due to retire in eighteen months. With a sigh he reached again for the report and knew that Morrison wasn't quite ready for that kind of promotion or at least, not yet. As to the outcome of the incident, well, according to the Superintendent in charge of Media Affairs, the public and media response, with the usual critics to be sure, was overwhelming in support for his officer's actions. The evening papers had vilified McLean and this fellow Metexas and portrayed them as public enemies, bringing their drugs into Scotland to poison the sons and daughters of the working class man. There was little doubt the subsequent inquiry would vindicate the firearms team and the arrested accomplices had already rolled over with their confessions. All in all, he thought, a good nights work.

With a flourish, the Chief initialled the report and, in thoughtful mood, added the comment, Good work.

Chapter 23

The name 'Glasgow International Airport' has been described as a bit of a misnomer, for the actual area which provides the one main international runway and numerous surrounding terminal buildings is situated in the County of Renfrewshire, whose main town Paisley sits to the south of the airport and within easier reach of the airport, than the city itself.

The airport services most of the world's popular airlines as well as a number of private companies and attracts almost eight million travellers each year, considerably more than the population of Scotland. Most of the travellers arrive at the airport by taxi or public transport. However, to accommodate the day-trippers and distant visitors, short and long-stay car parks are available. Providing, of course, the appropriate fee has been paid and woe betide any owner who overstays his paid term.

The morning dawned bright and clear as he stepped from the bus. To the casual observer, he looked no different to any other traveller bound for Glasgow airport, that morning. Slightly taller than average height, of medium build and wearing a dark coloured anorak with dark trousers, plain dark shoes and a navy blue coloured baseball cap pulled low over his eyes, he easily carried the rucksack that was slung over his shoulder, which of course wasn't difficult, for in its zipped interior the rucksack carried nothing more than a large, folded, bottle green coloured, nylon kitbag. The sunglasses he wore may have been seemed unusual for the time of year, but was not particularly out place at the airport where all manner of dress is worn.

Moving among the early rush of commuters, hurrying to catch the predominantly business flights to their UK and foreign-based destinations, he orientated himself and saw where he had to go. With a glance at the large, plate glass windows, he saw nothing behind him that seemed familiar, then crossed over between the parked taxis and made for featureless concrete structure that served as the multi-storey, twenty-four hour car park. Once through the pedestrian swing door, he walked a few yards then paused in the dimly lit corridor and stooped to tie his shoelace, glancing over his shoulder as he bent down. Again satisfied that nobody had followed him, he began his walk, starting on the ground floor and taking his time, casually glancing at the vehicles parked neatly in their bays. The sound of squealing tyres alerted him to an approaching vehicle coming down the ramp towards the sign-posted exit. Stepping between two parked cars, his head down, he fumbled in a jacket pocket as if searching for keys and, from beneath the skip of his hat, watched as a pretty, blonde uniformed air stewardess slowly drove her small Renault Clio past him and down the slope to the exit, her eyes wide and brow furrowed, concentrating on the narrow lane that ran between the parked cars. Grimly smiling almost with relief, he watched the car pass by and saw the brake lights flickering on and off and rightly guessed the girl to be an inexperienced driver, too intent on her manoeuvring to have seen him.

Stepping back out in front of the cars he continued his walk, searching for the vehicle he knew must be here. He glanced about him, saw that he was alone and looked for the CCTV cameras' he knew must be located in the ceiling area of the car park. His experience of such equipment was limited, but he knew that to be cost effective the cameras had to be regularly maintained and his limited knowledge of the airport was that the car park was several years old. He reasoned that the equipment, if still in working order, would have been installed at the time of construction and probably be first generation with black and white film and likely using now outdated video recorders. Likely, he thought, the same videotapes being used over and over, their value being decreased as each tape was wound on continuously. In addition, he guessed that the car park owners would place more faith in the strong, metal exit barrier and the occasional patrolling security officer, to deter theft of their charges, rather than worry about the possibility of theft from the vehicles. Continuing his stroll, he arrived at the second floor and saw a Vauxhall Cavalier, dark blue in colour and seemingly abandoned, having been festooned daily with non-payment parking stickers, placed to alert the owner that the twenty-four hour parking period was now over and threatening court action if additional charges were not paid immediately. His breath quickened as he walked past the vehicle, feeling the tension in his hands as he gripped his rucksack tighter. He had no doubt, this was the one. Walking the length of the ramp, he turned and again satisfied that he was alone, stepped between the Cavalier and the adjoining vehicle and donned a pair of clear, plastic gloves that he took from the front pocket of his rucksack. Stooping low beside the driver's door he run his hand around the front wheel arch of the Cavalier. Finding nothing, he squatted and continued along the drivers side of the car, probing with his fingers until, at last, he reached the rear wheel arch where his fingers encountered the short, metallic rectangular box he sought. With a sigh of relief, he tugged and released the magnet holding the box to the underside metal of the arch. Crouched beside the car, his fingers shaking, he prised open the metal box and discovered the car key within. Raising himself slightly, he looked about him and seeing no one, slowly got to his feet and moved to the rear of the car. With the key he unlocked and raised the squeaky lid of the boot, unconsciously thinking the hinges could use a drop of oil. Under an old blanket lay two, new black coloured sports bags. With a sharp intake of breath, he opened his backpack and retrieved the nylon kitbag, into which he shoved the two sports bags and his own rucksack. With all three stuffed into the kitbag, the man gently closed the boot of the car and, finally, removed his gloves which he placed in his jacket pocket with the key and rectangular box. With a last look about

him, he slung the kitbag over his shoulder and made his way to the stairs leading to the ground floor.
Leaving the car park and striding into the bright sunlight, he unhurriedly made his way across the road to the airport terminal building where he again made use of the plate glass windows of the terminal building to look behind him. Satisfying himself again that he was not being followed, he headed for the crowded bus terminus. On his way to the Paisley bound bus, he discreetly dropped his plastic gloves with the key and metallic box into a large, waste disposal container that was already half filled with the remnants of the morning travellers coffee cups and sandwich boxes.

Chapter 24

A few days after the dramatic incident at Hamilton service station, a small knot of people stood silently at a cemetery in the south side of Glasgow.
In the brightness of the October day, the assembled group watched as Margaret McKay, nee Thomson and her son, William Thomson were laid to rest together, united at last.
The bereaved included Margaret's husband William McKay, who stood between her mother Ina Thomson and William Thomson's girlfriend, Angela Bennett, an arm around the two women's shoulders, drawing them close. Those who watched saw the younger woman shaking slightly and sympathised, thinking the cold chill and heartache must surely be taking its toll.
Mourners included detective colleagues of Mr McKay, some with their wives and a close neighbour, Adele Cairns. The small wake was held in a local hotel.

"Will you take some time off and get yourself together, Willie?" inquired Roddy Munroe.
Willie peered into the glass of whisky he held and shook his head.
"I'm not sure that I'll be coming back, Roddy. I'm considering a complete break, a change of climate. I'm approaching retirement time anyway and I fancy that with no ties here, getting away might be beneficial. If I go now, I realise I might not get the full pension, but what I do get, with my savings and all, I should be able to get by." He took a sip of his whisky and licked his lips. "Somewhere warm, I think. Spain maybe, or one of the Balearic islands. To be frank, I haven't had a holiday in a long time."
Munroe jabbed at Willie with the end of his pipe. "I'd be sorry to lose you. You've been an asset to the department, but to tell the truth, I envy you the opportunity. My family are grown and married now with their own children. But the wife won't leave the grandkids."
"Can I steal this man away for a wee minute?"
Adele Cairns stood smiling, her hand on Willie's arm.
"They've done you very well, Willie," she said, pointing to the buffet table laid out in the hotel reception room as she drew him to one side. "I've been talking to Margaret's mother Ina, A very nice lady. I think we will be good friends."
Willie nodded and looked to where Ina and Angie stood talking to Archie and Jean McDonald, or more correctly, Ina spoke while Angie stood close by her side.
"She's not had many breaks," he agreed. "I was telling

Roddy Munroe, my boss, that I'm considering leaving the police and going abroad, Adele. Do you think Ina would consider house minding for me? While I'm away, I mean?"
Adele looked thoughtful.
"I'd be very sorry to lose you Willie McKay. You know what you mean to me, however," she sighed, "if you've made up you mind then I'm sure if you ask her, she'd think about it. From what she was telling me she'd be delighted to get that wee girl," pointing to Angie, "away from the Govan area. And of course it will be company for me."
"Well now, Adele Cairns," he replied, with a twinkle in his eye, "you wouldn't be losing me at all, merely transferring your attentions to someone else, someone like Ina whom I'm sure would appreciate the help you can give, sorting out young Angie."
Both Willie and Munroe turned to look at Angie, whose hand lay protectively on Ina Thomson's arm. Willie was pleased to see that the girl, still pale and gaunt, wearing the newly purchased black coloured skirted suit he'd bought for her, stood erect with a recent confidence about her, something she'd likely not experienced in a long time. His eyes rested on Ina and he made a promise to himself. He still believed he had failed Margaret and nothing anyone could say would change that feeling, but he would not fail this honourable woman.
On that issue, he was determined.

Chapter 25

The trial of those who survived the police ambush at Hamilton service station attracted much publicity, mostly due to the use of firearms by the police that resulted in the death of two men and the high criminal profiles of the deceased. The story headlined for two days and might have continued, but was ousted from the front page by the shocking and titillating revelations of a Government Minister's wife who, abandoned by her husband for a young male gigolo, revealed in graphic detail her own previous life as a male bus driver in Bradford.

By quiet and mutual agreement between the Crown and representing Defence Counsel, Francis 'Franny' McEwan and David 'One-ball' Smith pled guilty to a number of charges relating only to their participation in the receiving of illegal substances, namely heroin, at the Hamilton service station. Other than this issue, both refused to make any further comment about their association or previous criminal history with Maxie McLean.
Similarly, Algernon 'Big Al' O'Rourke, Sean Begley and Jonathon 'Johnjo' Donnegan pled guilty to the conveyance of the said heroin to Hamilton service station, with a private agreement regarding Mr O'Rourke's alleged possession of a firearm at that place. Mr O'Rourke, it was unkindly hinted, provided specific information relative to the supplier of such weapons in exchange for certain privileges, namely, incarceration in a Scottish prison where the said supplier, a 'Mr Armourer', couldn't exact revenge on the now super-grass O'Rourke.
All five men professed their deepest apologies for their involvement in the crime.
His Lordship recognised young Mr Donnegan for the stooge he was and he was duly treated with leniency, but

not the other four who received heavy custodial sentences.

As Alison McRae had rightly predicted, a parochial war broke out amongst the Glasgow criminal fraternity, all eager to attain control of the late Maxie McLean's sizeable empire. Local dealers found new and willing customers, when the massive seizure at the Hamilton service station resulted in a deficit of heroin. Consequently, street crime rose as junkies stole and robbed to pay the higher prices. The police, and by circumstance the public, it seemed, had become a victim of their own success.

Lena McLean became the target of much media scrutiny. Described by one local tabloid as 'The Gangster's Moll', photographs of her entering or departing her house pictured her as a waif like creature, dressed entirely in black, wearing a headscarf, large sunglasses and with head bowed.
However, a meeting held in the less than salubrious office of Maxie's accountant, Harry Cavanagh, some days after Maxie's demise, found Lena in high spirits. Harry, struck by Lena's undoubted good looks, turned on the charm, only to find himself pinned between a rock and a hard place as the now formidable Mrs McLean instructed Harry to immediately convert all Maxie's holdings to cash, the proceeds to be wired to a foreign bank account whose details Lena provided him with. A dumbstruck Harry attempted to stall Lena, who pertly

reminded him that she had kept written records of Maxie's deals, all of which named Harry as the middleman. With visions of the VAT man knocking at his door, Harry had no option but to comply. Lena, of course, courteously agreed to his usual fee. She did express some curiosity as to the whereabouts of certain unaccountable funds, payment for properties in Edinburgh that had been recently sold, but eventually accepted Harry's explanation that the money, all Bank of England notes and no denomination larger than fifty pounds, had been delivered to one of Maxie's couriers and that Maxie had been making his own enquiries re the money. Knowing Harry's fear of Maxie, Lena had little option but to believe the overweight and perspiring man. Eager to be off before the taxman took an interest in Maxie's financial empire, Lena decided that pursuing the one point two million pounds would detain her in the country longer than she intended. Coming to a decision, she determined that searching for the money might only cause her unnecessary delay and problems. Anyway, she reasoned, Maxie had been a very, very wealthy man. The lost money didn't figure in her plans.

Shortly after having Maxie cremated, Lena left instructions for the sale of her house and was soon heading for sunnier climates. Prior to boarding her flight, one of her final acts was to destroy all the records on Maxie's instruction that she had kept secreted in the house. Smiling, she made sure that amongst the documents put on the blazing bonfire in the large brick-built barbeque, was the scrap of paper she had kept hidden that bore the home telephone number of the recently deceased Mickey Metexas.

At his boss's insistence, Willie McKay initially took bereavement leave from the police then almost immediately retired, citing his reason as personal. Nobody was fooled. Willie obviously hadn't gotten over his wife's suicide, it was whispered in the office, but with a certain degree of sympathy for the popular officer. A small farewell reception at a local pub close to headquarters, was attended by far more people than he anticipated, all of whom had kind things to say about DC McKay. When presented with his departure gifts and asked to make a speech, Willie seemed to be overcome and, blurting out his thanks, quietly made to slip out of the pub for home. As he went through the side door, his name was called from behind.
"Going without a cheerio to your old pal, then?"
"Sorry, Archie. I thought it best to just leave quietly."
Archie, tie undone and smelling of beer, stepped forward and placed his hand on Willie's shoulder.
"What's the plan then, something else lined up?"
"No," replied Willie with a sigh. "Nothing work wise, anyway. You know I've been thinking about a clean break, maybe moving away. Costa Del Sol," he smiled "sun and sangria, so I'm told."
"If I thought our pension would stretch that far," Archie laughed "I'd have gone long ago. But seriously, you'd leave all this?" he asked, pointing to the dirty alleyway and overcast, cloudy night. "Besides," he added, "what about your house?"
"I've a couple of house-sitters in mind for looking after it," replied Willie, grinning. "So, if I do find myself somewhere away in the sun, you'd visit?"

Archie bowed his head. Willie McKay, whether he realised it or not, was Archie's best pal and no way was Archie letting this guy get out of touch. Raising his head he looked Willie straight in the eye, dreading this moment of farewell.

"Think you can put up with Jean, me and three, no, almost four screaming kids?"

"There will always be room in my house for you, Archie. Here," he said, holding out his hand, the old Gaelic phrase coming to mind, "here's my hand and here's my heart." With a choked cry, both men embraced.

"Anybody see's us, they'll think we're a couple of shirt lifters," Archie said laughing, his eyes misty and his heart heavy. But not that he'd ever admit to it.

With a nod, Willie turned and walked into the dark.

Two weeks later, Willie welcomed a nervous Ina and wide-eyed Angie to their new home. Adele Cairns, having unashamedly adopted them both, had already prepared tea and cake and stood excitedly in Willie's front room, hopping from foot to foot and eager to help her new friends unpack. While Willie supervised the unloading of the few items of furniture Ina had brought with her, she fetched him a much needed cup of tea.

"Are you sure about this, Willie?" Ina asked for the umpteenth time, marvelling at the lovely area, the tidy garden and newly decorated house, the tears in her eyes threatening to overwhelm her.

"It's what Margaret would have wanted. Besides, who could I trust to keep an eye on Adele here while I'm off and living the life of Reilly?" he replied, smiling happily

as he placed his arm about his elderly neighbour.
He didn't add that without Ina's knowledge, he had arranged with his bank to open an account for her and for a small deposit to be made monthly to supplement her pension. Shyly,
Angie reached forward and took Willie's hand. "Thanks, Mr McKay. You know we'll be fine, don't you?"
Willie squeezed her hand. "Of that I've no doubt, but I'll be in touch regularly, keeping my eye on you, so to speak," he said smiling, "and I'll be expecting regular visits....from the three of you," he smiled.

Willie's final act, prior to departing for the airport, was to loads his old car with half a dozen cardboard boxes of junk and visited the local council dump where he threw the boxes, including two new sports bags with broken zips, into a half full rubbish skip.

Needless to say, this story is a work of fiction.
If you have enjoyed the story, you may wish to visit the author's website at:
www.glasgowcrimefiction.co.uk

The author also welcomes feedback and can be contacted at:
george.donald.books@hotmail.co.uk

Printed in Great Britain
by Amazon